Europa

Book III of The Last Stop Trilogy

Europa

Book III of The Last Stop Trilogy

Michael H. Burnam

LODESTONE
BOOKS

Winchester, UK
Washington, USA

JOHN HUNT PUBLISHING

First published by Lodestone Books, 2019
Lodestone Books is an imprint of John Hunt Publishing Ltd., No. 3 East Street,
Alresford, Hampshire SO24 9EE, UK
office@jhpbooks.net
www.johnhuntpublishing.com

For distributor details and how to order please visit the 'Ordering' section on our website.

ISBN: 978 1 78904 204 7
978 1 78904 205 4 (ebook)
Library of Congress Control Number: 2018950700

A CIP catalogue record for this book is available from the British Library.

Design: Stuart Davies

UK: Printed and bound by CPI Group (UK) Ltd, Croydon, CR0 4YY
US: Printed and bound by Thomson-Shore, 7300 West Joy Road, Dexter, MI 48130

To my sons Joshua and Bradley who are everything I hoped I'd be one day, and so much more. Enjoy the journey!

Dad

Prologue

Europa – 200,000 Earth-years before

Metzi felt the ice shudder beneath her feet, followed by an ominous crack. "What's happening?" she exclaimed.

"The gravitational effects of the comet are tearing our world apart." Tona glanced towards the airlock. "Get on that disc before it's too late!"

"I won't leave you!"

The ice convulsed again, so violently they struggled to stay on their feet. Metzi's father shouted to them as he ran across the hangar floor. "We have to leave now!" Behind him, two silver discs pulsated with bands of brilliant blue light. One glowed brighter and had a smooth and featureless exterior. The second disc had an open door with a silver ramp extending from it.

Metzi took Tona's hand and faced her father. "I won't leave without Tona."

Her father's face creased with anguish. "We can't take him with us."

"Then I'm staying."

"You'll be killed!"

Metzi's lips trembled as she spoke. "Tell my mother and sister I love them … and tell them that abandoning Tona's people goes against everything we've been taught."

With a loud clang, the airlock closed behind the brighter disc and the hanger's space doors opened to a starry night dominated by the multi-colored face of the planet Jupiter. Two heartbeats later, the disc floated out and accelerated past Jupiter, becoming another star, until it disappeared.

A crewman from the remaining disc ran towards them. Behind him, the band of energy around the disc grew in brightness. "Come now or we'll have to leave without you," he called.

"Go with your father," Tona pleaded.

She averted her eyes. "No."

After a glance at Metzi's father, the crewman ran back to the disc.

Metzi's father reached out his hand. "Please ...." She turned her back on him. The klaxon sounded again signaling the cycling of the second airlock. After a last glance at his daughter, Metzi's father ran to the second disc and up the ramp.

The doorway in the disc disappeared and the disc's band of energy erupted with blinding light. Tona pulled Metzi into his arms and looked away as the airlock closed with a loud clang. They moved hand in hand to the airlock's viewing window and watched the space doors open. Metzi sobbed in Tona's arms as the disc with her family accelerated away.

Two elderly men stepped out of the elevator connecting the hanger to the domed city ten thousand meters below, under Europa's ocean. They moved past Metzi and Tona to the airlock window and looked out. Ahotei, the younger and more tempestuous of the two, pounded the thick glass with his fist. "We've come too far to have it end like this!"

Tocho, the taller and older of the two, looked over his shoulder at Metzi and Tona. "There's another choice, but we must hurry.

Earth, present day

Mickey rolled away from Vickie and tiptoed to the window. After looking back to make sure she was still asleep, he pushed aside the curtain letting in the moonlight. The sleeve of his nightshirt fell back revealing a streak of silver, alien tissue that began at his palm and extended to his elbow. It reflected the moonlight, glowing like quicksilver. Mickey stared at it and his blood boiled with anger. He clawed at the alien tissue with his normal hand, using his nails to separate the inorganic flesh from his human tissues, leaving a ragged wound oozing blood. The lesion healed within seconds, without a trace, and his blood, where it had dripped onto the carpet, ignited with a flash of light and disappeared in a puff of smoke.

Vickie swung her legs over the side of the bed, calling, "Can't sleep?"

Mickey lowered his sleeve and dropped his arm. "Too much pepperoni on the pizza."

Vickie joined him at the window. "What's going on?"

"Nothing."

Vickie forced him to look at her. "That's bullshit and you know it."

He turned away. "Nothing's wrong. Leave me alone."

Tears welled up in Vickie's eyes. "Are you getting cold feet about the wedding?"

"No!"

"Then tell me what's wrong."

Mickey pulled back his sleeve exposing the streak of alien tissue.

Vickie stared at his arm. "What ...?"

"A gift from our silver friends," he replied angrily. He covered his arm again.

"I don't understand," Vickie said.

Mickey went to the closet and started getting dressed. "Take care of your palm disc."

"What the hell does that mean?" she exclaimed.

Mickey finished tying his shoes. "It started happening that day at the White House – when I used a knife to short-circuit mine."

Vickie's heart pounded in her chest. "You're not making sense!"

"My nannites are turning me into a Europan!" Mickey shouted. "Is that plain enough for you?" He grabbed a few items of clothing and stuffed them into a duffle bag.

"That's not possible."

Mickey pulled the strap of his duffle bag over his shoulder and left the bedroom. "Don't follow me."

"Where are you going?"

He called to her from their apartment's front door. "I'm putting an end to this Europan bullshit, once and for all."

Vickie ran into the living room. "We'll fix this together, just like we always do!"

Mickey was gone.

Book I

Chapter One

Europa, two hundred thousand Earth-years before

Ahotei watched from the shadows as two men in black robes walked past on the opposite side of the street. When they were out of sight, he sprinted to the doorway of one of the small shops lining the street and rapped three times on the door. The sign above the door read 'Apothecary'. An old woman wearing an apron opened it, letting light spill onto the street and Ahotei ducked inside. Quickly closing it behind him, she brought her finger to her lips signaling silence. Seconds passed and they kept their eyes fixed on the door. After several minutes without any sign of discovery, she nodded and Ahotei loosened his coat.

The apothecary shop had floor to ceiling shelves crowded with bottles of various sizes filled with murky liquids and dark shapes. Without speaking, because her tongue had been cut out years before for the crime of heresy, the woman moved to one of the shelves and pushed a bottle filled with sea snails half a hand's width from its original position. The wall moved aside revealing a hidden room and Ahotei passed through. When the woman moved the bottle back to its original position, the wall slid back and she picked up her broom and resumed sweeping.

A long rectangular table made from the spirals of dried mollusk shells took up most of the room. The top of the table was crowded with a collection of glass beakers and long-necked flasks containing colored liquids. Tangles of clear tubing connected some of the flasks. Others had been capped and labeled with a dark marker. A flask in the center of the table held a brackish liquid boiling over a coal-fed brazier. Brown vapor rising from it became trapped in an inverted funnel positioned above and then drifted into a coiled glass tube connected to another glass flask cooling on ice in a bowl a meter away. In the chilled flask, the vapor re-condensed becoming brown sludge with the consistency of tar.

Tocho stood behind the sludge-filled flask sporting a self-satisfied grin. He stood half a head taller than Ahotei, and was thinner and less muscled—the prototypical academician. He repositioned his thick glasses back over the bridge of his nose, and then realized that he couldn't see because the lenses had become opaque from accumulated vapor. Frowning, he rubbed the glasses on his sleeve and put them on again.

"Can you see now?" Ahotei smirked. He leaned over the boiling brown liquid, sniffed the steam rising from it, and pulled back grimacing. "I hope that's not dinner."

"Tonight I've cooked up a feast for the mind, not our bellies," Tocho replied. "Do you want to hear what it is?"

Ahotei moved to the wall and studied an array of skeletons. Tocho had mounted the bleached bones and shells of sea creatures vertically in the order of their complexity, beginning with the shell of a small mollusk on the lower left and finishing on the upper right with a much larger skeleton with a backbone and hinged, toothy jaws. Ahotei touched the jaws and feigned being bitten. "No, but I know you're going to tell me anyway. So get on with it and make it brief. My stomach is rumbling with dumb hunger."

"You can survive starvation long enough to learn something."

Ahotei sighed. "Get it over with."

Tocho cleared his throat. "I've performed an experiment tonight that will shape science for generations to come."

"Last I heard, science is still heresy," Ahotei muttered. "Now, can we eat?"

Tocho ignored him. "I've mixed ground shells as a source of carbon, added nitrogen from my excrement treated with a strong acid to break it down ..."

Ahotei held up his hand. "Wait! You didn't use your own ..."

"I did," Tocho said matter-of-factly.

"That's disgusting."

"It's called being resourceful," Tocho replied. "Do you know what happens when I boil those elementary compounds together?"

Ahotei wrinkled his nose. "They smell very bad."

Tocho pointed at the flask with the tarry substance. "They combine to form something truly remarkable. "

"Foul smelling brown sludge is remarkable?"

Tocho beamed with excitement. "Foul smelling sludge with organic compounds. Do you know why that's important?"

"Who cares?" Ahotei growled.

"Those compounds are found in every living thing, mollusks, fish, and a sample of my hair."

Ahotei raised his arms in frustration. "So what?"

"It means all living things are made from the same basic compounds." Tocho held up a flask filled with water. "This is seawater. Do you see anything swimming in it?"

Ahotei glanced at the flask. "Nothing big enough to eat."

Tocho spilled some of the water on a glass dish and held it high over the light from a flame. He pointed at a magnifying lens on the table. "Use that to look at the water and tell me what you see."

Ahotei did as instructed. "I see dots moving around, dust or something."

"Those dots are alive."

Ahotei frowned. "Don't be ridiculous. There's nothing alive that small."

"They are alive! Those dots are tiny animals made from the same organic compounds as you and me. We're all chemically related, from the smallest swimming dots to big burly blacksmiths like you."

Ahotei put the dish down. "So our great God Asani made all kinds of animals, even tiny ones, using the same raw materials. So what?"

Tocho took off his glasses. "Ask yourself this, why would a god bother making microscopic animals?"

"How should I know what gods think?"

"What if all life started out as tiny animals?" Tocho pointed at the line of skeletons on the wall. "What if little animals evolved into bigger, more complicated ones over time, and the process repeated over and over until you and I were formed?"

"A snail can't turn into a fish," Ahotei scoffed.

Tocho leaned against the lab bench. "But if it's true, think of the implications. Life is a spontaneous process that doesn't require a god."

Ahotei held up his hand. "Hold on. If you're saying life evolved from those dots swimming in the water, how did the dots get here?"

Tocho held up the flask with tar. "From this."

Ahotei smirked. "Maybe you're descended from a boiling turd, but not me."

"You're missing the point! Water, heat, and simple organic compounds mixed together form more complex organic compounds found in all living things. What if those compounds combined over time to form swimming dots, and over even more time those dots evolved into us?"

Ahotei rubbed his chin. "There's still quite a leap of faith in your hypothesis, professor."

Tocho put his glasses back on. "I'm listening."

"How do dumb compounds know how to combine to form those little animals?" Ahotei leaned closer. "Or how about this? How does your foul smelling brown sludge know how to become alive?"

Tocho paced around the table. "I haven't figured that part out yet."

Ahotei sighed. "Very interesting. Can we eat now?"

Tocho stopped pacing. "Remember that hydrothermal vent we saw on the ocean bottom?"

Ahotei slumped down on a stool. "I remember we almost died getting there."

"Do you recall that the life forms we saw swimming around that vent looked far more primitive than anything we see swimming near the city?"

Ahotei paused to remember. "Weird worms and pale fish without eyes."

"All the components of living things occur around those vents—water, heat, and minerals spewing from beneath the ocean floor. What if that's where life began? What if life happens on its own without a god?"

Ahotei grimaced. "The priests killed my father for saying things like that."

"Help me prove I'm right and we'll put a stop to it."

"How?"

Tocho placed his hands on the table and leaned forward. "By going down again, to that vent, so I can take more samples."

Ahotei shook his head. "Are you crazy? We were lucky to make it back alive the first time. Now you want to go down again, and this time open the fish trap door to collect your precious samples? We'll drown, Mr. Smart Guy."

Tocho smiled. "No we won't. I have that part figured out."

"I was afraid you'd say that."

Tocho reached under the table and held up a transparent disc with a hole in the center of it the diameter of his finger. "This is the new cover I made for the fish trap."

Ahotei leaned forward. "You poked a hole in it?" He chuckled. "That should keep the water out."

"The hole is for our air hose." Tocho reached under the table and pulled out a coil of flexible transparent tubing attached to a bellows. "Ramu will pump the bellows to send us fresh air through the tubing so we can stay down longer."

Ahotei raised an eyebrow. "You'd trust that worthless trap handler with our lives a second time?"

"He was fine the first time."

Ahotei shook his head again. "This gets worse every minute." He thought for a moment. "We still have to open the trap to grab your samples."

Tocho reached underneath the table and held up a bucket with a hinged lid. "We hook this bucket to the bottom of the trap. When the trap lands on the bottom, the lid pushes inside the bucket letting in sea water and hopefully some of the animals swimming around. When we lift off the bottom, a spring pushes the lid closed, trapping what's inside... Pretty clever, isn't it?"

"I'll go down again on one condition." Ahotei rested his arms on the table and leaned forward toward Tocho. "We stop our ascent halfway up."

Tocho raised both his eyebrows. "Why would we do that?"

"To see if the great God Asani is really down there holding up the city with one of her godly hands."

"I don't believe that any more than you do," Tocho scoffed. "Besides, we'll get caught in the current. What if the cable breaks?"

"I need the cable to swing so we can get close enough to see underneath the city."

Tocho threw up his hands. "You'd risk our lives for that?"

"To prove the Sect is lying to us, yes," Aheotei exclaimed. "It's the same thing you're trying to do."

"No it isn't. I'm a scientist searching for the truth."

Ahotei's nostrils flared. "I'm avenging my father's death."

Tocho studied his friend's face. "You were planning on going down again even before I brought it up, weren't you?"

Ahotei relaxed. "True, but I'm not happy about betting our lives on that sloth Ramu again."

"We can't go down without someone manning the cable. And we can't stay down long enough without someone pumping the bellows to send us fresh air. We need Ramu, and we can't risk involving anyone else."

Ahotei got to his feet. "What happens if he stops pumping the bellows and takes off?"

"We pay him half before we go down, and the rest after he pulls us up," Tocho replied.

Ahotei took a glittering bar of platinum from his pocket and put it on the table. "Here's my half. Put up yours."

Tocho emptied his pockets. "I'm just a poor apothecary."

Ahotei frowned and took out another bar. "Same lame excuse you used last time."

Chapter Two

They mounted the deck holding the fish traps, carrying duffle bags and dressed in warm clothes. The four traps, hollow metal spheres twice the height of a man with a hinged door at their apex, sat in cradles at the four corners of the deck. The baited traps suspended by thick metal cables were pushed through an opening in the city's force field known as the portal and lowered to the ocean floor by men known as trap handlers. After several hours on the bottom, the trap handlers winched up the traps and removed the sea creatures collected inside.

One of the trap handlers, a man named Ramu, walked over to them. He stood a hand taller than Ahoeti, with arms twice as thick. After looking around to make sure they hadn't been seen, he pointed at Tocho's bucket. "What's that?"

"A trap to catch more of the snails we like in our stew," Tocho replied.

Ramu looked closer. "How do you plan on lowering it down?"

"It goes down with the trap, attached to the bottom of it by the tentacles of sea animals with large suckers."

Ramu sneered. "You know no one is allowed to tamper with the traps. The penalty is death."

Tocho winked. "No one will know. Watch." He pressed the bucket against the side of the trap and the suckers held it in place. It pulled free with a popping sound. "See? Not a scratch."

Ramu wiped the sweat from his brow and glanced around. "Too dangerous."

Ahotei waved two platinum bars in front of Ramu's nose. "Who's going to know?"

Ramu looked at the bars and licked his lips. "If the priests find out, we'll all be put to death."

Ahotei waved the two bars again. Ramu reached for them, but Ahotei pulled them back. "One now, and one more when you pull us up." He extended one of the bars.

Ramu grabbed the bar of platinum and stuffed it in his pocket. "Get in and be quick about it."

"One more thing." Tocho opened his satchel and took out the new transparent top for the trap connected to the bellows and tubing. "You pump the bellows while we're down. It forces air through the tubing that attaches to this new transparent top so we can stay down longer."

Ramu looked around again. "I can't pump the bellows while I'm handling the cable."

"You don't pump until we're on the bottom, a count of three hundred, and then you pull us up," Tocho said.

"And a count of fifty more when we stop halfway up," Ahotei added.

Ramu's mouth fell open. "You can't stop. You'll get caught in the current. What if the cable breaks? The penalty for losing the trap is death!"

Tocho reached into Ahotei's pocket and pulled out two more platinum bars. "Four bars. One more now, and two more when we return to the surface."

Ahotei glared at Tocho, and then spoke to Ramu. "Think of all the drinks you can buy your friends with four bars."

Ramu grabbed the second bar. "Attach your bucket and get in before anyone sees!"

Tocho mounted the bucket to the side of the trap, ascended the ladder, and dropped down inside. Ahotei followed and Tocho fixed the transparent disc in place, sealing them in.

The trap shuddered as Ramu pushed it through the portal. It swung on the cable, buffeted by the current that circulated around the city.

Tochu braced himself by extending his arms and legs. "Get ready!"

Ahotei did the same and looked up. "You sure your new disc isn't going to leak?"

"No."

Ramu released the cable and the trap dropped. Its descent was smooth until it bounced on the ocean bottom, throwing both of them to what was now the trap's floor. The trap was constructed with extra weight on one side causing it to land with its opening horizontal to the ocean floor allowing not only fish but mollusks and snails living close to the ocean bottom to come inside, attracted by the bait. Tocho's transparent disc covered the door keeping the trap sealed and allowing them to look out.

Tocho knelt, placing his cheek near the hole connected to their air hose. "I feel air coming in. Ramu's pumping the bellows."

Ahotei pushed next to him and peered out of the disc. "There's some kind of glow out there."

Tocho smiled. "I brought lights."

"How'd you do that?"

"I stuffed dried leaves from plants that glow in contact with water into transparent tubes with holes wound around the bucket. When water seeps in, the leaves glow."

Ahotei peered into the murk. "Smart." A fish with tiny eyes and no pigment swam next to the disc, poked it with its beak, and swam away.

Tocho pointed. "There's a volcanic vent." He took a roll of parchment made from dried sea fronds and a writing implement from his satchel and sketched a picture of it.

"The bottom, around the vent, is carpeted with strange looking tube worms," Ahotei said. "Never saw any of those guys before."

Tocho started another sketch. "Let's hope I trapped one of them in the bucket."

A pile of sketches later, the cable pulled taut jerking the metal sphere upright. They struggled to reposition themselves as they started their ascent.

Ahotei gripped Tocho's shoulder and shouted. "Brace yourself in case Ramu stops halfway up like he's supposed to!"

Their ascent went smoothly until the trap stopped halfway up. It began to swing in the current. "Hang on!" Ahotei shouted. He started counting backward from fifty as he strained to look out through the transparent disc. "50, 49, 48!" he called out. With each count, the motion of the trap became more violent.

"This is what you wanted," Tocho shouted as he tried to hang on. "Can you see anything under the city?"

"We're spinning too fast for me to see anything!" Ahotei shouted back. "I'm getting dizzy."

Tocho belched. "I think I'm going to throw up."

The trap accelerated sharply to the side, and with a popping sound, the air hose pulled free. Freezing water sprayed through the opening and the trap plunged for the bottom.

Tocho tried to shield his eyes from the jet of water with his arm. "The cable broke! What do we do?"

"Pray!" Ahotei shouted.

After several seconds of free fall, during which the trap rotated throwing them from side to side, they could feel the trap slowing.

"We're slowing down! Maybe the cable didn't break," Ahotei yelled. He braved the jet of water hitting his face and peered out. "I still can't see anything!"

"Try to ... " Tocho began. His sentence ended when the trap came to a sudden stop slamming both of them into its thick, metal wall.

* * *

Ahotei opened his eyes. "Tocho?"

Tocho grunted. "Get off me so I can breathe."

Ahotei rolled off Tocho and wiped his hand across his forehead. "Looks like you can bleed after you're dead."

Tocho got to his knees and blinked to focus. "We're not dead, but the disc's gone and we didn't drown. The question is, why?"

He crawled to the top of the trap and looked out.

"Do you see anything?" Ahotei asked.

Tocho gasped. "Yes, but I'm not sure what …"

Chapter Three

Ahotei scrambled on his hands and knees next to Tocho. "Do you see Asani?"

"We're in a strange room with lights," Tocho replied. "It's huge." He climbed out.

Ahotei crawled out and stood next to him. They looked around. "Where are we?" Ahotei whispered.

The trap lay on its side in a puddle of seawater inside a featureless rectangular space of considerable size, without doors or windows. Tocho blew out his breath. "The walls, floor and ceiling are constructed from a silver material with an unblemished matte surface glowing with soft light."

"Great. Where are we?" Ahotei whispered.

"I have no idea." Tocho pointed at the far wall. "Look over there. Something's happening."

They watched a circular area of the far wall darken and melt away forming a rectangular opening twice the height of a man. Tocho started toward it.

"Is that a good idea?" Ahotei called to him. "Maybe we should stay here."

"And do what? Starve to death?" Tocho replied.

Ahotei followed. "I have a bad feeling about this."

Halfway to the rectangular opening, Tocho stopped and bounced on the balls of his feet. "The floor has a strange feel to it. Kind of spongy." He poked it with his foot. The silver material dimpled, then liquefied and flowed into the depression, refilling it. "It's solid, but a liquid, too. How bizarre."

They continued to the opening and peered through into a corridor five times the width of a man's shoulders. It had the same silver floor and walls, stretching a great distance in a straight line, without another doorway in sight. The walls inside glowed a pale blue.

"Maybe this is where Asani lives," Ahotei whispered.

Tocho strained to see down the corridor, but he could see no end in sight. "The current flows under the city. Logically, that's where we are." He stepped through, and as soon as both his feet were on the floor, started moving down the corridor. Startled, he almost lost his balance but regained his footing and looked down. The floor appeared stationary, yet he continued moving forward. "I'm moving, but I don't know why. Follow me, before we get separated!"

Ahotei stepped through the opening and the floor carried him after Tocho at the same constant speed. "Not sure I like this," he shouted.

They moved steadily down the corridor at constant speed without any apparent destination. After several minutes, a wall of silver appeared in the distance blocking their path.

"There's a wall up there, and we don't seem to be slowing," Ahotei called out.

"I see it!" Tocho shouted back.

"Should we jump off?" Ahotei yelled.

Tocho glanced over his shoulder. "To where?"

"We could run backward!"

A meter from the wall, another opening formed and they passed through into a smaller, circular room. Their forward motion stopped in front of six pillars of the same silver material that appeared to be extensions of the floor. The pillars surrounded a round platform made from the same substance. Above it, a glowing sphere ten times the volume of a man's head spun in mid-air projecting random patterns of colored light that danced around the walls.

"Is that Asani?" Ahotei whispered.

"More likely some kind of advanced machine," Tocho said in a normal tone of voice.

The globe stopped spinning and radiated a uniform golden glow.

Ahotei looked back towards the portal. It was no longer there. "Leaving is no longer an option."

Tocho reached out with his hand to touch the closest pillar. As his fingers moved closer to it, the pillar quivered and leaned towards him. He pulled back his hand and the pillar resumed its original form. "Interesting."

"Is that thing alive?" Ahotei asked.

The golden globe projected a beam of light that moved down Tocho's body from head to toe. When it reached his toes, it winked out. Tocho flexed his hand. "Wasn't painful, but I definitely felt something."

The beam winked on again and scanned Ahotei in the same manner. When it reached his toes, the chamber reverberated with a strange-sounding voice speaking in their native language. "Organic beings, approach the pillars for a full diagnostic."

Neither moved.

"There is nothing to fear."

"Yeah, right," Ahotei muttered. He whispered to Tocho. "Are you sure that's not Asani?"

"Who are you?" Tocho called out.

"If it calms your primitive brain's excitatory centers to label what you see, you may refer to this facility as the Nexus."

"Are we beneath the city?" Tocho asked.

"Approach the pillars and be healed."

"I'm not sick," Ahotei said.

"You have a tear in the integument above your ocular sensor, as well as other defects."

Ahotei glanced at Tocho. "What does that mean?"

Tocho pointed at his eye. "You have a cut over your eye."

"Approach the pillars," the voice repeated.

Tocho took a step closer to the nearest pillar of silver and reached out with his hand. As before, the pillar quivered and leaned toward him. Tocho hesitated.

"Don't do it," Ahotei said under his breath.

"If the Nexus wanted to kill us, we'd already be dead." Tocho touched the pillar and its silver substance flowed up his arm and around his body, covering all of him up to his chin.

"Tocho!" Ahotei shouted.

Tocho held up his hand coated with silver. "It's okay. Don't ask me why, but I feel really good." The substance under his chin swelled forming a transparent collar that flowed over his head forming a clear bubble. Tocho spoke again, but the quality of his voice had changed. "It's weird, but I feel relaxed ... even happy. Go ahead, touch one of them."

"No sure about this," Ahotei muttered. He touched the pillar closest to him and within seconds he, too, was cocooned in silver with a clear bubble over his head. He smiled. "You're right. I feel so relaxed. This is better than sex."

Tocho yawned and his eyes fluttered closed. Within seconds, both men were asleep.

* * *

Tocho's eyes popped open. Still cocooned, he was seated on the pillar facing the globe. He could turn his head and saw Ahotei awake and similarly positioned. "How do you feel?" Tocho asked.

"Great," Ahotei replied. "How long were we out?"

"Five of your cycles," the Nexus replied, not out loud, but in their heads.

"I heard the voice in my head," Ahotei said.

Both men involuntarily raised their right arms with their palms turned inward and the silver material flowed away stopping at their elbows. Ahotei flexed his hand. "What's on our palms?" Each had a disc of silver centered on his palm.

The Nexus spoke to them. "Your palm disc is a neuro-transceiver connected to the Nexus."

"That's how we can hear you in our heads?" Tocho asked.

"Correct."

"What else did you do to us?"

"You no longer require corrective ocular lenses, your blood pressure has been lowered, and your kidney function has been augmented."

"What about me?" Ahotei asked.

"You have received similar corrective measures. Your lifespans have been increased."

Tocho glanced at Ahotei. "How long?"

"The calculation contains variables with unknown values."

"Such as?" Tocho asked.

"How you maintain your bodies."

"Where are we?" Tocho asked.

The Nexus changed to a globe with multi-colored bands and they saw a smaller globe traveling around it. The smaller globe increased in size becoming a white ball with random grey and black streaks. "You are here," the Nexus replied.

"I don't understand," Tocho said.

It appeared as if they were moving towards the smaller globe at high speed. Just before they had the illusion of crashing into the white globe's surface, it changed to a hollow sphere of water with a point of light beneath its surface. The point of light continued growing, becoming something recognizable."

"That's our city," Tocho said with astonishment.

The image of the city grew and they could see more detail. Then the perspective changed and they could see underneath.

"What's that?" Ahotei asked.

"Your current location, a stone construct in the geometric shape of a pyramid," the Nexus replied.

"What's it doing there?" Tocho asked.

The image of the pyramid grew and they could see several chambers within it. One of the chambers glowed with light.

"That's the chamber we're in and the Nexus," Ahotei said.

"If that's underneath the city, everything we've been taught is a lie. Unless …" Tocho spoke to the Nexus. "Are you a god?"

"Choose an answer that fits your reality," the Nexus replied. "The result is the same."

Ahotei scratched at his palm disc with his fingernail. The disc remained unblemished. "When can we leave?"

The bubbles over their heads evaporated and the silver cocoons flowed down their bodies and disappeared into the floor. As they stood flexing their arms and legs, a smaller glowing orb the size of a man's fist rose from the substance of the platform.

"A baby Nexus?" Ahotei asked.

The Nexus spoke to them. "The sphere is a repository of information. Take it and return to the city."

Tocho picked up the sphere and looked at it. The small transparent orb swirled with fluffy, glowing clouds of yellow and gold. "It's beautiful."

The floor moved them towards a portal forming in the wall. Tocho looked back at the Nexus. "What kind of information does the sphere contain?"

The Nexus didn't answer.

They were almost to the portal. "What if somebody tries to steal it from us?" Ahotei asked.

"Impossible." The Nexus started spinning again, descended, and merged with the substance of the platform. Then the platform began to spin becoming a silent tornado of quicksilver that flowed to the floor and disappeared.

The two men moved single file through the portal and down the corridor at the same constant speed as before. Tocho put the sphere in his pocket and concentrated on keeping his balance.

"Looks like we're going home," Ahotei called to him. "Or somewhere."

Tocho glanced back. "We have to agree on what to say when we get there."

"We'll show them the sphere and these silver gizmos on our palms."

"What will we say the sphere is, and where did we get it?" Tocho asked. "If the priests find out, they'll take it from us and lock us up." He took the sphere from his pocket and held it up. The orb glowed brighter than before and swirled with a kaleidoscope of multicolored lights that played across Tocho's face. "It looks different. Wonder what that means?"

"The Nexus told us that the sphere can't be taken from us," Ahotei called to him.

Tocho put the sphere back in his pocket. "But not why. We don't even know what it is."

"The Nexus said it contains information."

Tocho frowned. "What kind of information? The recipe for fish stew?"

The floor carried them ever higher in a graceful spiral. "Do you feel any different?" Ahotei asked.

Tocho looked down, and then he pulled back and closed his eyes. "No."

Ahotei flexed his bicep. "I do."

The moving floor leveled off and entered a corridor that led to a wall of fitted grey stones with a pyramidal entrance in the center of it. As they moved closer, they could see faded ancient writing inscribed on smaller stones framing the entrance. The floor carried them through and stopped at the edge of stone steps that led up into the dark.

Tocho left the walkway and mounted one of the stone steps. "We must be in the pyramid under the city." He ran his hand along a row of carved symbols and started up the stone stairs with Ahotei following.

They stepped through another framed opening at the top of the stairs into a much larger pyramidal chamber with the height of ten men. As they entered, a soft blue light illuminated the chamber.

Ahotei looked around. "Ever notice that there aren't any pyramids in the city or anything shaped like a pyramid, not even a mailbox?"

Tocho stopped and thought for a moment. "Now that you mention it, no."

Ahotei pointed to the far wall. "Look over there, more symbols in the shape of a portal without an opening."

They went to the far wall and Tocho ran his hand along the face of the stones. "These stones weren't cut any time recently." He pulled back his hand. "Something's happening."

The stone inside the border of glyphs shimmered and transformed into a transparent window. They looked through into a richly decorated room with stone walls and saw two priests in green robes engaged in conversation. The taller man wore a mitered hat with ancient symbols embroidered in silver around the brim, and a gold necklace with a jeweled pendant around his neck. He appeared to be speaking with the unmistakable air of authority to the shorter man who also wore fancy robes and a less impressive hat.

"That's the High Priest and his Chamberlain," Ahotei whispered. "We're in the Temple, and this must be the way out." He extended his hand.

"Wait!" Tocho cautioned, but not before Ahotei's arm passed through the transparent window. Ahotei yanked it back, but not before the High Priest saw it and froze. The taller man wearing the mitered hat moved closer to the portal and appeared to be looking through. After a moment, still facing the portal, he stepped back and motioned to the Chamberlain to join him. The Chamberlain moved to his side and appeared to look through at Tocho and Ahotei, but shook his head indicating that he hadn't seen anything. He listened to something the High Priest said, nodded, and moved away out of sight.

"He saw your arm, but I don't think he can see us if we stay behind the portal," Tocho whispered. "I've had a run-in with the Chamberlain before. Nasty fellow."

The Chamberlain returned a moment later with two black-robed priests brandishing long, curved and serrated knives.

Ahotei frowned. "Your old friend brought two of his goons with blades. If that's the way out of here, any ideas what we do next?"

Tocho frowned. "Not a lot of options. I'll go first." Before Ahotei could protest, Tocho stepped through the portal. As soon as he appeared on the other side, the two black-robed priests grabbed him and pinned his arms to his side.

Stroking his chin, the High Priest walked around Tocho. "Who are you, and how did you enter the Sacred Portal?"

Tocho glared back at him. "Let me go and I'll tell you."

"I know that one," the Chamberlain said. "He's an apothecary who dabbles in the dark arts."

"That's nonsense," Tocho said. "I'm a scientist."

Ahotei barreled through the portal and collided with the priest holding Tocho. The knife flew from the priest's hand and he skidded across the floor into the wall. The second priest threw Tocho to the ground and raised his knife shoulder high, point first. He snarled at Ahotei. "Prepare to bleed, pagan garbage."

Smiling, Ahotei crossed his arms and stood his ground. "Whenever you're ready, priestly scum."

"Ahotei!" Tocho exclaimed. "What are you doing?"

"Don't worry, I got this," Ahotei replied.

The priest lunged forward sweeping his wicked blade in a downward arc. As the knife flashed toward Ahotei's chest, he grabbed it and bent the metal blade in half. Grinning, Ahotei held up the now useless weapon so everyone could see it and then tossed it clattering to the floor in front of the High Priest. "Anybody else wants to try me?" He helped Tocho to his feet.

The High Priest swept his eyes from Ahotei to Tocho. "Who are you?"

"I'm Tocho, an apothecary." Tocho pointed at Ahotei. "He's Ahotei, a blacksmith."

The High Priest nodded at the Chamberlain and he hurried

out of the chamber. "No one has passed through the Sacred Portal in recorded time," the High Priest said. He circled Tocho and Ahotei. "Except for you two quite ordinary men." He smoothed his robes. "I demand to know why."

Ahotei smirked. "Maybe we're not as ordinary as you think."

The Chamberlain returned with four black-robed priests, two of them holding Ramu who was trembling with fear. Ramu kept his eyes away from Tocho and Ahotei. The Chamberlain pointed at Ramu. "Say what you know."

Ramu swallowed hard. "They went down in the fish trap."

"That isn't possible," the High Priest scoffed.

"It's true," Tocho said. "We've done it before."

The High Priest took a step closer to Tocho and narrowed his eyes. "Why?"

"To see what's down there," Tocho replied.

"By the way," Ahotei chimed in, "there's no god holding up the city in her mighty hand."

The High Priest glared at Ahotei, but the Chamberlain spoke first. "Your fool stunt cost us one of the traps. You've compromised the food supply for the entire city!" His face reddened with anger. "You and your friend should be put to death, the worthless trap handler too."

Ramu slumped in the arms of the two priests, moaning. "No."

Ahotei leered at the Chamberlain. "That might be tougher than you think."

Tocho took the sphere from his pocket and held it high. The orb burst into light, filling the chamber with multi-colored beams that played across the stone walls. Shielding his eyes, the Chamberlain stepped back, as did the priests. Two of them fled.

The High Priest remained where he was, stony-faced in the sphere's glare. "What is that?"

Tocho brought his arm down and the sphere dimmed to its usual, more mellow appearance. "The proof that what we've said is true. We encountered a glowing ball many times this size below the city that spoke to us and called itself the Nexus. It gave us this glowing orb and told us that it contains information."

"Who is the Nexus?" the High Priest asked.

"It's not a who. It's a machine," Tocho replied.

The High Priest's eyes narrowed. "Truly, you were below the city?" Tocho nodded and held up the sphere again reigniting its stunning visual display. The High Priest smoothed his robes. "What other proof can you offer?"

"That isn't enough?" Ahotei asked.

"A remarkable parlor trick, nothing more," the High Priest replied.

Tocho dropped his arm and the sphere dimmed. "We passed through the Sacred Portal. You saw for yourselves. Why did you keep it a secret?"

The High Priest didn't reply.

Tocho tossed the sphere on the stone floor. It rolled toward the High Priest and came to rest near his foot. "Pick it up and see if it's a parlor trick," Tocho said.

"Is that a good idea?" Ahotei whispered near Tocho's ear.

"Testing a theory," Tocho replied.

The High Priest made no move to pick up the sphere and instead, gestured to the Chamberlain. Sweating, the Chamberlain hesitated, then came forward and stood close to the sphere looking down at it. The orb lay at his feet glowing with soft blue and gold clouds. After a glance at the High Priest, with a trembling hand, he picked up the sphere keeping it as far from his face as his arm would permit. The sphere brightened again, this time with soft swirling clouds of multi-colored light. The Chamberlain murmured, "It's beautiful," and brought it closer to his face.

The clouds inside the sphere changed from white to yellow, then to orange with streaks of fiery red. Screaming in pain, the Chamberlain dropped the sphere and stared at his hand, now covered with angry blisters. Pale and sweating, he clutched his hand to his chest and ran from the chamber.

Tocho picked up the sphere and it filled again with soft, white and yellow clouds. He tossed it from hand to hand like a juggler, caught it with one hand, and extended it toward the High Priest. Once again the sphere burst with angry red light. The High Priest backed away.

Tocho put the sphere in his pocket. "I suggest we work together to understand what knowledge this glowing sphere contains."

The High Priest's eyes turned cold and menacing. "This entire episode must be kept a secret."

"I disagree," Tocho said. "Everyone has the right to know."

The High Priest's face reddened and he pointed at Tocho. "I won't allow you to poison our people's minds."

Ahotei stepped between them. "Who gave you the right to decide what we can know?"

The High Priest studied Ahotei's face. "I remember you, and your blasphemous father," he sneered. "He was given the chance to recant and refused. Don't make the same fatal mistake."

Ahotei's face tightened with rage. "My father was a good man. You executed him for the crime of thinking for himself!" Tocho held Ahotei back.

"You fool," the High Priest said. "Without Asani's laws, none of us would survive."

"You lied to us! There's no god beneath the city," Ahotei shouted back.

"What difference does it make?" the High Priest scoffed. "Our religion is an ancient set of laws meant to ensure our people's survival."

Tocho released Ahotei. "Your laws are enforced by the myth of an all-powerful god."

The High Priest removed his hat and sat on one of the room's stone benches. "Our ancestors were savages who killed for sport. Their evil could not be overcome by logic; it required the threat of punishment administered by a higher power."

"Isn't it better to base our lives on truth?" Tocho asked.

The High Priest smiled. "Tell me, apothecary, what is truth?"

Tocho thought for a moment. "That which is right and honest."

The High Priest stood and replaced his hat. "The truth is what we call the things we choose to believe in, nothing more."

The Chamberlain returned with his hand wrapped in gauze. A dozen priests followed him and took up positions around the room.

Tocho glanced at the priests and took out the sphere. "How will you explain this or the silver discs on the palms of our hands?" Tocho held up his palm, so did Ahotei.

"I don't intend to," the High Priest replied. "Put down the glowing orb and I'll seal the room."

Tocho's expression hardened. "No."

"Very well." The High Priest nodded at the Chamberlain.

"Seize them!" the Chamberlain shouted. The priests pulled long knives from their robes and encircled Ahotei and Tocho.

Ahotei turned his back on Tocho and spoke to him over his shoulder, "There's too many of them."

Tocho felt the sphere vibrating in his pocket. He took it out and held it up. The sphere's light became blinding.

The priests froze in place, shielding their eyes, uncertain what to do.

"It's a trick!" the Chamberlain shouted. "Take them!"

Before the priests could advance, the chamber plunged into a darkness so profound it became difficult to breathe.

Chapter Four

A shimmering globe, four meters in diameter, roiling with clouds of white light blossomed in the darkness above their heads and slowly spun.

"It's Asani!" one of the priests shouted from somewhere in the dark.

Tocho heard the sound of metal clattering to the floor and the rustle of robes. He gripped Ahotei's shoulder holding him in place. "It's the Nexus."

"What's it doing here?" Ahotei asked.

The Nexus broke up into a string of eight colored balls orbiting a larger globe burning with fiery yellow light. The largest colored ball, the sixth counting outward from the burning orb, grew in size giving the illusion that they were moving toward it. More and more of its features became visible, bands of color–red, purple, and shades of brown. As the image zoomed in closer, they could see smaller dots orbiting around it. One dot grew in size as if they were moving towards it. It appeared white in color, covered with black and grey linear streaks in a random pattern. A much smaller ball of light with a luminescent tail appeared a short distance away moving toward it.

"We've seen some of this before," Tocho called out. "The smaller globe is filled with water with our city inside."

In a silent explosion of color, the image of Europa ballooned outward, increasing ten times in size, rushing toward them. Screams and shouts of fear erupted in the dark of the chamber.

"It's an illusion," Tocho shouted. "The Nexus is trying to tell us something. It's using pictures instead of words."

The air around them scintillated with light, becoming a fiery cloud with no substance. Tocho waved his arm above his head and felt nothing. He could see their city before him inside a glowing sphere of light within Europa's ocean. "That's our city," he shouted.

The High Priest's voice filled with wonder came to them through the dark. "I see it!" Other voices in the darkened chamber added more exclamations creating a din of sound.

Tocho shouted to be heard, his words echoing off the stone walls. "Our city and our ocean are inside a white sphere of ice, like an egg. The surface of the ice has cracks and fissures."

The image of the city grew larger, and they could see features on the sea bottom. A fish swam in front of Ahotei. He reached out to touch it, but his hand passed through and the fish swam by unperturbed. The perspective changed again and the globe of the city grew larger. When the image stabilized, they were standing on a familiar street. "That's my house!" one of the priests exclaimed. He ran through the image of his door and collided with the chamber's cold stone wall. Moaning, he fell to the ground trembling with fear.

The Nexus created the illusion that they were moving down the street to a vacant area outside the city close to the perimeter force field. The image stopped and they watched a large rectangular building grow before their eyes. They moved inside the building and saw a door that opened to a metal box large enough for four men. The door to the box closed and the box began carrying them upward at a dizzying speed. "Make it stop!" someone shouted. After several seconds, the door reopened to the inside of another building, larger than the first. The structure had multiple levels ringing a cavernous central space. It appeared as though they were moving toward a metal railing on one of the higher levels. When they reached it, the image looked down.

They could see three, smooth, ovoid silver discs, each the size of a house and six times as tall as a man, squatting on short, tripod legs in the building's central space. A ring of electric blue light encircled one of the discs. As the seconds passed, the ring of light grew in intensity, becoming blinding, and the disc rose into the air. Doors opened on the outside of the building and the disc passed through. The image rushed forward and stopped outside the building. They could see an expanse of grey-white ice and a sky of black dappled with twinkling lights. The image swung around and they saw a giant orb in the sky circled with bands of color. Moments later, they were inside the building again looking at the other two discs. Similar rings of light appeared on first one, and then the other. The two discs floated in the air and moved outside the building, and they, too, became lost in the black sky.

"What are those things?" Ahotei whispered to Tocho.

"My guess is they're flying machines," Tocho replied.

"Flying to where?"

The perspective changed, creating the illusion that they were traveling at high speed away from the city and then away from Europa itself. They were out in the black sky the discs had flown into, between the large orb with bands of color and the smaller sphere representing their world. The smaller orb, near their world, trialing an iridescent tail, reappeared. It grew larger as it approached.

The voice of the Nexus resonated off the chamber's walls. "Behold, the end of the beginning." The image of the smaller orb, which they would later understand to be a comet, collided with their world shattering its shell of ice sending a massive plume of water into the black void. The titanic collision of the comet and their world produced a curtain of vapor that burst from the ragged rent in the ice and completely obscured their world. When gravity pulled the water back, their world had changed. Its ocean churned with silent cyclones of water. Volcanic activity erupted from its core sending more plumes of water to the surface fracturing the ice, sending geysers of steam into the void only to fall back again. This continued for several seconds until the watery chaos waned and they could see the ocean bottom again. Nothing looked the same.

"What happened to our city?" Ahotei asked.

"It's gone," Tocho replied softly.

Screams and shouts erupted as the others in the chamber struggled to comprehend what they'd seen. The image of their world disappeared and they were in total darkness again, pierced by the voice of the Nexus. "Your city will be destroyed in twenty-one thousand cycles. Behold. I will provide you with the means to leave." A beam of light the thickness of a man's finger projected from the Nexus and danced around the chamber so rapidly it appeared as a blur. The stone briefly glowed everywhere it struck the wall. After darting about most of the chamber's walls, the light in the chamber returned and the Nexus was gone.

"What just happened?" Ahotei asked Tocho.

"You heard the Nexus. In twenty thousand cycles, the city will be destroyed by something coming from outside our world," Tocho said, visibly shaken. He walked to the nearest wall, followed by the High Priest. All the chamber's walls were covered by pictures and symbols burned into the rock. Tocho ran his fingers along one of them. "The rock's still warm." He continued moving along the wall and stopped at a pictographic image of the comet striking Europa. "These are representations of what the Nexus showed us." He moved several strides further and pointed to another section of images showing the figure of a man holding up a circle with rays projecting from it. At the end of the rays were the symbols 1 + 1 = 2. "Basic mathematics," Tocho muttered. "Why show us something we already know?"

The High Priest straightened his posture and his robes. "The great God Asani has spoken. We must obey."

Tocho turned to him. "The Nexus is not a god. It's an advanced machine."

"You're sure of that?" the High Priest asked. "You've seen a god before and you're sure that what we just witnessed isn't one of them?" He turned to the Chamberlain and pointed at Tocho and Ahotei. "These two men are the emissaries of Asani. They bear Her mark on the palms of their hands and are the keepers of Her glowing orb. They will not be harmed."

"Yes, Excellency," the Chamberlain said with his head bowed.

Ahotei strolled around the chamber holding up his palm with the silver disc showing, studying the faces of the priests. Several paled as he approached and averted their eyes. Even the Chamberlain's bravado was replaced by a look of fear.

Tocho frowned at the High Priest. "What shall we say happened here when the people ask? A glowing orb showed us incomprehensible pictures telling us our world will end and left us images burned into the temple walls?"

"No one here will speak of it under pain of death," the High Priest replied. He pointed at the Chamberlain. "Leave us."

The Chamberlain bowed his head. "Yes, Excellency." He and all the priests filed out.

"You saw their faces. You won't be able to keep this a secret," Ahotei said.

The High Priest glanced at him but didn't reply.

"You heard the Nexus," Tocho said. "We have to decipher these symbols. Our fate depends on it."

The High Priest smoothed his robes. "Leave that to me."

"Wait," Tocho said. "You called us Asani's emissaries. We should have access."

"You have done our people a great service," the High Priest replied evenly. "We are grateful, but your job is done."

"You have no right," Ahotei growled.

The High Priest glared at him. "Don't test me, blacksmith."

Tocho squeezed Ahotei's arm, stopping his reply and spoke to the High Priest. "There may be more information inside the Sphere which only we can access. I suggest we return here in ten cycles to continue our *private* discussion."

The High Priest stroked his chin. "I agree under one condition, that you speak about this with no one."

"We agree," Tocho said. Ahotei clenched both his fists and turned away.

* * *

Tocho and Ahotei started down the Temple steps passing several priests who gaped at them, but said nothing. Tocho had the sphere in his pocket. "If we keep our mouths shut about all this, we're no better than that murderer," Ahotei said under his breath.

Tocho whispered back. "We don't have a choice, at least for now."

Chapter Five

Later that night they faced each other across the lab table with the Sphere between them. "It looks different again," Tocho said.

Ahotei leaned closer. "Wish it would say something." The Sphere swirled with grey and black clouds backlit by unseen lightning. Flashes of it played across Ahotei's face. "The Nexus told us it has information inside. All I see are clouds ready to pour rain."

Tocho stared at the Sphere. "Why didn't the Nexus tell us how to speak to it?"

Ahotei looked around Tocho's laboratory. "Have any scrap metal lying around?"

Tocho pointed to the far corner. "Over there. Why?"

Ahotei retrieved a metal bar, hefted it, and slapped it in the palm of his hand. "This should work."

Tocho looked up. "What are you doing?"

"Performing an experiment of my own." Ahotei held up the bar and with little apparent effort, pushed the ends of it together. "Thought so," he said smiling. He dropped the bar on the lab table where it landed with a loud clang.

Tocho picked up the bent metal bar. "That was impressive."

"Let's continue the experiment by finding a few priests and see what we can do to them."

Tocho frowned. "A pleasant thought, but impractical. There's too many of them." He picked up the Sphere. "Damn you, speak to me!" The Sphere's appearance remained the same. "The High Priest was right. It's a worthless parlor trick." He put the Sphere down and swept it off the table. The orb bounced on the stone floor, rolled to the wall, and illuminated with dazzling white light.

"Looks like you made it mad," Ahotei said. He shielded his eyes from the glare.

The Sphere rolled back toward the table and hopped back on top, landing on a pile of dried vegetable sheets that Tocho used to record his observations. Its luminosity changed to a softer multicolored light, and it began to blink. The two men moved closer to watch.

Blinking faster as it moved, the Sphere rolled across the blank page in a straight line, leaving behind a string of diagrams burned into the cloth. It repeated this until the entire page was filled with lines of symbols and diagrams reminiscent of what they'd seen the Nexus do in the temple. When Tocho pulled the sheet from under the Sphere and studied it, the orb began to inscribe the blank sheet underneath with more symbols and diagrams. This process continued for three more sheets, then the Sphere dimmed and returned to its usual state.

Tocho held up the first sheet. "Amazing!" he exclaimed.

Ahotei picked up the second sheet and studied it. "I see pictures of a campfire, boiling pots of water, and gears. Do you know what any of this means?"

Tocho placed the five sheets in a line on the lab table. "Not yet." He thought for a moment. "Let's start with what we know. The Nexus told us that we need to leave the city before it's destroyed in twenty thousand cycles. It intends to help us, but we don't know how. We also know that the means of our escape somehow involves the equation 1 + 1 = 2."

"If the Nexus is trying to help us, why give us an impossible riddle?" Ahotei asked.

Tocho slumped on a stool. "I don't know, and I have ten days to solve it."

* * *

They left for the Temple on the morning of the tenth cycle following their return from beneath the city. Tocho had the Sphere in his pocket.

"Do you have a plan for what we do next?" Ahotei asked under his breath. "Or are you going to fake it?"

"I wouldn't call it a plan ... more like a hunch," Tocho replied.

Ahotei smirked. "That's comforting." He waved to a neighbor as they walked by. Instead of returning his gesture or engaging in amiable conversation, the woman went back into her home and slammed the door. "That was rude," Ahotei said.

Tocho gestured around the street. "Look around. It's market day, but the street's deserted."

Ahotei ran to his fellow blacksmith's door and knocked. "Lehman, it's Ahotei. Come out." He heard nothing in return and the door remained closed. "Don't worry. It's not about the two bars you still owe me," Ahotei added.

"Go away," a man's voice shouted from behind the locked door.

Ahotei trotted back to Tocho. "What's going on?"

Tocho quickened his step toward the Temple. "They know, and they're afraid."

The streets were deserted and the houses shuttered along the entire route. Two grim-faced priests met them when they arrived at the Temple's manicured walkway. The priests escorted them in silence to a windowless stone building at the rear of the compound, separated from the main temple complex. The High Priest waited for them inside. "Leave us," he said to the priests when Tocho and Ahotei arrived. The two priests left the chamber and closed the door.

Ahotei walked around the perimeter of the chamber with his footsteps echoing off the stone walls. "What is this place?"

The High Priest pointed at a carved stone near Ahotei's feet. Other similar stones were arranged in rows around the floor. "The final resting place of my predecessors."

"Why are we meeting here?" Tocho asked.

"We agreed that the situation calls for secrecy," the High Priest replied. "Did you bring Asani's gift?"

Tocho took the Sphere from his pocket and held it up. The small globe glowed with soft white light, but otherwise, its appearance remained bland.

The High Priest moved away from them and placed his back against the door. "Place the globe on the floor and move away from it. Your charade is over."

"You know it's not a charade," Ahotei growled.

"We saw Asani and were blessed to hear Her voice. I don't question that," the High Priest said. The look in his eyes became menacing. "It's you two and your motives that I question." He put his hand on the door handle. "You broke your vows of silence and caused great unrest amongst our people."

"We kept our word. It was one of your priests who told what he saw, or all of them," Ahotei said.

The High Priest glared at him. "Your grievous loss of the fish trap has compromised the city's food supply, threatening all of us!" He opened the chamber's door. "Despite your negligence and treachery, if you agree from this moment forward to cooperate with me, I will publically praise you for being Asani's messengers and grant you a special status ... yet to be determined."

"What if we refuse?" Tocho asked.

"I assumed you would." The High Priest left the chamber and they heard the sound of the deadbolt sliding home.

Tocho tried opening the door, but with no success. "He locked us in!"

Ahotei rolled up his sleeves. "We'll see about that." He grimaced as he added his strength to Tocho's. The door's lock burst with a loud snap and Ahotei threw it aside.

They stepped outside and saw several priests brandishing knives, with the High Priest standing behind them. "Impressive," the High Priest said.

"Want to see what else we can do?" Ahotei raised his fists and took a step forward. The priests fell back.

"This is pointless!" Tocho shouted. "The people know something has happened, but not what. Their uncertainty has become fear that will deepen unless we tell them something, or show them something to restore calm." He pulled the pages inscribed by the Sphere, rolled as a scroll, from his pocket and held them up. "The Sphere spoke to us and left a message inscribed on these sheets."

The High Priest eyed the rolled pages in Tocho's hand. "What does it say?"

"I need to see the inscriptions in the Temple to translate it," Tocho replied.

The High Priest hesitated.

"If you truly believe this is a gift from Asani, help us."

"Very well." With a flourish of his robes, The High Priest spun around and left the chamber.

* * *

The High Priest, with the Chamberlain at his side, watched Tocho place the five pages inscribed by the Sphere on the Temple's stone floor in the proper order. Tocho looked at them for a moment, and then walked around the room studying the symbols on the walls. He stopped at the section with 1 + 1 = 2, traced the inscription with his hand, and turned to face the other men. "We've been warned that our city will be destroyed in twenty thousand cycles."

"That's one interpretation," the High Priest said, "but not necessarily the proper one. A god's words must be interpreted carefully, which is the role of the religious order, not a common apothecary and a lowly blacksmith."

"In case you forgot, Your Highness, the Nexus spoke to us, not you," Ahotei said.

"Stop it, both of you," Tocho snapped. "Your bickering isn't getting us anywhere."

The Chamberlain moved between Tocho and the High Priest. "How dare you address the High Priest in that manner?"

The High Priest raised his hand. "Let him speak." Glowering, the Chamberlain stepped aside.

"Let's assume for the sake of argument that my apocalyptic interpretation is correct," Tocho began. "Remember also that the Nexus promised to help us and finished with a simple mathematical equation, 1 + 2 = 2." He pointed at the proper section of the wall. "To me, this means that mathematics is the key to saving us." He pointed at the sheets on the floor. "Based upon the Sphere's message, I'd say that you can add science to that, too."

"Nonsense," the Chamberlain scoffed. "The key to our salvation has always been our all-powerful god."

The High Priest dropped to one knee and studied the row of inscribed pages. "I see recognizable symbols." He pointed at one of them. "Here's a boiling pot. Why would the Nexus instruct us to boil water?"

Tocho knelt next to him. "Don't focus on any one element. Try to see it as a machine with multiple parts."

The High Priest glanced at him. "A machine that boils water?"

"I believe it does more than that ... although I'm not sure what." Tocho got to his feet. "Let me build it and we'll find out."

The High Priest got to his feet and smoothed his robes. "You may build Asani's gift and present it to us here in one hundred cycles." He leaned closer to Tocho. "I trust that it will do more than boil water." He spoke louder. "As a further condition, you will speak to no one about your activities and work in secret. Do you agree?"

"Yes," Tocho replied.

"One more thing."

Tocho frowned. "What is that?"

"Before presenting Asani's machine to us, both of you will stand by my side in the Temple Square and be introduced as

Asani's Emissaries."

"You're using us to reinforce your position," Ahotei said.

The High Priest smiled. "You requested a means to calm the people's fears, and now you have it."

Tocho dropped his eyes to the pages on the stone floor. "We agree."

* * *

They returned to Tocho's laboratory saying nothing to each other along the way. When the wall panel closed behind them, Ahotei turned on his friend. "You sold us out to that bastard. Why?"

Tocho placed the parchment papers with the Sphere's message on the lab table in front of them. "I bought us one hundred cycles to build the Sphere's machine and figure out what it does."

Ahotei opened the wall panel. "I can use mathematics too."

Chapter Six

Ninety-nine cycles later ...

The High Priest, in full ceremonial regalia, with the Chamberlain at his side, waited at the top of the Temple steps. Below them, a retinue of priests lining both sides of the steps stood silently facing the crowd. Most of the city's citizenry filled the square, spilling onto the boulevard behind. They whispered and parted as Tocho and Ahotei walked side by side up the walkway toward the Temple. As they'd been instructed to do by the Chamberlain, instead of ascending the steps, they waited at the base of the stairs facing the High Priest.

"I hate this," Ahotei whispered.

"Play along," Tocho whispered back.

The High Priest raised his arms above his head and spoke in a voice powerful enough to envelope the Temple square. "Good people ... a wondrous event has occurred." The murmuring of the crowd increased to a dull roar of anticipation. He waited for silence and then gestured for Tocho and Ahotei to come up the steps and join him. They mounted the stairs, stopped two levels below the High Priest, and turned to face the crowd. Tocho offered a bland expression, while Ahotei struggled to mask his contempt. "These two men have seen the great God Asani," the High Priest announced. The crowd fell silent. "She has given them a message, and a gift!" He pointed at Tocho. "Show them."

Tocho extracted the Sphere from his pocket, turned to face the crowd, and held it high. Once again, the orb burst with light. Many of the people fell to their knees shielding their eyes. Everyone, including the priests, stared at the sphere, spellbound. After a moment, Tocho put it back in his pocket and the light extinguished.

The High Priest raised his arms again and the din of voices

faded. "These two men are Asani's emissaries." He scanned the crowd. "From this day forward, treat them as you would one of your priests. Do not approach them without proper respect."

"That bastard's isolating us," Ahotei whispered.

"Not for long," Tocho whispered back.

"What message do they bring?" one of the men in the crowd shouted. There were more shouts with variations of the same question.

The High Priest held up his arms again. "Gods do not speak as we do. Asani's message requires proper study. When the time is right, I will discuss it with you." The crowd's noise grew louder. "For now, return to your homes and rejoice. Asani has spoken!"

Only a few people turned to leave. The majority remained, their eyes on Ahotei and Tocho.

"It's beginning to feel like the pub ran out of ale and we have the last bottle," Ahotei whispered.

After a brief conversation with the High Priest, the Chamberlain ordered the priests to start down the steps and push the crowd back. Angry shouts erupted and a scuffle broke out. One onlooker was thrown to the ground.

"Blasphemy will be punished! Return to your homes!" the High Priest shouted.

Tocho felt the Sphere vibrating in his pocket, strong enough to bounce against his thigh. Surprised by its behavior, he took it out and it burst with blinding light. As he shielded his eyes, he heard shouts of alarm erupt from the crowd and saw the closest of the onlookers fall back, pushing and shoving. Several of the priests broke rank and ran up the Temple stairs.

Tocho felt the sphere lift from his hand. Startled, he looked back and saw it spinning twenty meters in the air above the Temple square. The ground trembled beneath his feet, and he saw the light from the city's force field flicker. He knew that if the force field failed, the city and everyone in it would be crushed by the kilometers of ocean water suspended above their heads. The shouts of the crowd turned to screams of panic. People scattered, common men and priests running away from the Temple square in every direction.

"Should we run?" Ahotei shouted.

"Where?" Tocho replied.

The flickering of the city's force field became more pronounced, and then it failed. At the same moment, the light from the spinning orb abruptly ceased, plunging them into total darkness.

Tocho felt Ahotei grip his shoulder. In reply, Tocho placed his hand on top of his friend's and spoke to him with a confident voice. "Steady. The Nexus didn't bring us to this moment only to murder us all."

The Sphere reignited, expanding into a spinning, golden globe.

"It's Asani!" one of the priests shouted. He dropped to his knees and bowed his head, as did many in the crowd.

"It's not a god, it's a machine!" Tocho shouted to them.

Everyone remained frozen in place, mesmerized by the blinding orb spinning above the Temple. The Nexus began to project images in the air, the same representations of the solar system and their world that Tocho and Ahotei had seen before. The flight of the three silver discs away from the city ended the sequence. Throughout the display, the High Priest stood like a statue watching the crowd as much as the images hovering in the air. His Chamberlain cowered next to him. "You fool, it isn't real," the High Priest said to him.

As before, the dazzling visual display finished with the Nexus' apocalyptic vision of the comet destroying the city. For a few moments the crowd remained silent, but then the sounds of fear and panic resumed at an even higher level than before. At the height of it the projected images from the Nexus ceased and the city's normal lighting returned.

The voice of the Nexus filled the air. "The city will be

destroyed in twenty-one thousand cycles. Prepare to leave. I will show you the way."

The Nexus dimmed, shrank to the size of the Sphere, and fell to the ground. Many in the crowd were screaming, struggling to comprehend what they'd seen. Some of them, including a few priests, ran from the square seeking the refuge of their homes. Tocho retrieved the globe and held it up. It had the appearance of a dark bubble of common glass, no longer filled with light or swirling clouds. He showed it to Ahotei and put it back in his pocket.

The people that remained in the Temple square were talking amongst themselves in small groups. In front of the Temple doors, the High Priest huddled with his Chamberlain, surrounded by the priests who had remained. They spoke in soft, but animated voices. After listening, the High Priest smoothed his robes, turned to the people, and raised his hands.

"My people," the High Priest began, "our great God Asani has spoken. Return to your homes. When I have determined the meaning behind Her words, I will summon you."

While the High Priest watched, the people began to disperse. He waited until the Temple square emptied and then signaled the Chamberlain to open the Temple doors. When the doors were opened, he frowned down at Tocho and Ahotei, and gestured for them to follow him inside.

Tocho looked up and, for a moment, locked eyes with the High Priest. Instead of ascending the steps to the Temple, he walked briskly away.

Ahotei caught up with him. "Aren't we supposed to meet with our exalted leader so you can present your machine to boil water?"

Tocho kept walking. "Change of plans."

Ahotei noticed that some of the people were following them. The number grew the farther they went. "Where are we going?" Ahotei asked.

"To the fish traps," Tocho replied.

"Why?"

"That's where I assembled the Sphere's machine," Tocho replied.

"This should be interesting," Ahotei muttered.

They continued walking. Along the way, Ahotei waved to several men standing in the doorway of his blacksmith shop. The men picked up cloth-wrapped packages and followed.

* * *

Tocho stood on the fish trap platform surrounded below by several onlookers. Ahotei stood next to him with the irregular shape of the Sphere's machine behind them, covered by a tarp. Ahotei pointed behind the crowd. "Here come our friends."

The High Priest and the Chamberlain, flanked by ten black-robed priests, came toward them parting the crowd as they approached the platform. Giving orders with arm gestures, the Chamberlain divided the priests and sent them to block the platform's steps on either side. As the priests moved toward the steps, they were met by groups of men holding cloth-wrapped parcels blocking their way. Unprepared for belligerent behavior on such a scale, the startled priests stopped their advance and looked back toward the High Priest. He glared at Ahotei and motioned for the priests to step back.

"Who are those men facing off with the priests?" Tocho asked.

Ahotei grinned. "You're not the only one who uses mathematics."

"What's that supposed to mean?"

"I made sure there's more of us than them. What's under the tarp?"

"Have a look." Tocho pulled the tarp away.

Chapter Seven

While the crowd buzzed with anticipation, Tocho moved to the edge of the platform and raised his arms for quiet. "My fellow citizens, the spinning globe that calls itself the Nexus instructed me to build this machine." He gestured at the odd-looking construction behind him.

"What does it do?" someone in the crowd shouted. Tocho put on his glasses and held up one of the pages inscribed by the Sphere.

Ahotei listened to Tocho, who began speaking, and muttered under his breath. "People, you might as well take a nap. The professor's lectures go on forever." Ahotei frowned and started walking around the machine stroking his chin. "A metal pot with a lid, suspended over an open fire. All of this just to boil water?" He continued around, tracing the course of tubing connected to the pot's lid and attached to a piston assembly. The piston drove a reel of cable belonging to one of the fish traps. He glanced at Tocho droning on about something to do with steam and continued following the cable to the trap's boom. "This is interesting," Ahotei said to himself. The trap's boom, one of four at the corners of the deck, extended through the force field with the cable dropping from it into the ocean depths. "The trap's on the bottom, but none of the trap handlers are around to pull it up."

Ahotei stopped to listen. When he heard Tocho still speaking, now something about geometry, he finished circling the machine and stopped at the pot of boiling water. This time he noticed a valve between the pot's lid and the tubing. He considered moving the valve to see what would happen and extended his hand, but thought better of it and pulled his hand back.

He rejoined Tocho, who was still speaking and scanned the crowd. Noting that many looked restive and some outright annoyed, he leaned closer and spoke to Tocho. "Your audience is falling asleep."

Tocho glanced at Ahotei. After clearing his throat, he took off his glasses and spoke to the crowd. "Any questions?"

"What does it do besides boil water?" someone shouted. Several people laughed.

Before Tocho could answer, the High Priest pushed past the men blocking one stairway and confronted Tocho on the deck. "Explain yourself and that abomination behind you, Emissary."

"That's what I've been doing," Tocho replied.

Ahotei elbowed him. "Turn on the damn machine."

Tocho rubbed his ribs where Ahotei nudged him and knelt beside the pot of boiling water. He brought his hand near the valve at the top of the pot and raised his voice. "This machine is connected to the cable of a baited fish trap on the sea bottom. As everyone knows, it takes two trap handlers at least two hours to raise one full trap. Because the trap remains on the bottom for six hours before being retrieved and it takes three more hours to clean and re-bait, the traps can only be used once per cycle."

The High Priest spoke to Tocho keeping his voice low. "And thanks to you and your imbecile friend, now we have three traps instead of four."

"Watch," Tocho said with an expression of excitement. He swung the valve sideways and steam jetted from the side of the canister holding the piston, accompanied by a shrill whistling sound. The crowd moved back several steps and many people covered their ears. When the piercing sound peaked in frequency, the piston moved outward pushing a rod connected to the edge of the drum wound with the trap's cable. The process repeated and each thrust of the piston turned the drum retrieving the trap.

"It's working!" Tocho shouted.

The piston moved in and out with greater speed and the cable began to rise from the depths. In less than two minutes, the cable pulled taught and the trap hung from the pulley.

The crowd gasped with astonishment and moved closer. Tocho got to his feet, beaming. "This machine will double our food supply!"

Behind him the piston slowed, but continued turning. Groans and popping sounds filled the air as the cable stretched and the metal boom flexed backward threatening to snap. Tocho turned and lunged for the valve controlling the steam, but his hand slipped off the wet metal valve and he fell to the platform in a pool of water. Before the boom snapped from the strain, Ahotei shoved Tocho aside and spun the valve in the opposite direction. Soon after, the cable relaxed and the sounds of tortured metal ceased.

Tocho got to his feet. "That was close."

Ahotei handed him his glasses. "You're welcome."

They moved to the trap, and working together, pulled back the boom until the fish trap swung over the deck dripping seawater.

"Open the trap!" the crowd shouted.

"What's inside?"

"Besides rocks and mud!"

Laughter followed.

Ahotei placed both his hands on the trap and leaned against it. The metal sphere quivered but refused to swing. "It's full of something," he shouted. "Want me to open it?"

"Open it!" the crowd yelled back. They edged forward to get a better look.

Ahotei opened the trap's door with a flourish and stood aside as a torrent of sea life spilled onto the deck. While the crowd hooted with excitement, he sorted through the catch holding up first a very large crab, and then a long slimy eel. Behind him, the High Priest walked around the machine studying it.

Tocho moved to the edge of the deck and raised his soggy arms. "If we build more machines like this we can double or triple our food supply." The crowd screamed its approval.

"But this is only the beginning. If we use the information in the sphere, we can …"

The High Priest moved in front of him facing the people. "We must give thanks for Asani's wondrous gift. Thanks to Her generosity," he gestured behind him at Tocho, "and the hard work of our Emissary, the years ahead will indeed be bountiful."

Tocho moved in front of the High Priest and faced him with his back to the people. "You saw what the Nexus showed us."

"Be careful, apothecary," the High Priest said under his breath.

Tocho turned and spoke to the crowd. "Many of you were in the Temple square with the Nexus and saw our world destroyed by a giant rock coming from the sky," he paused for effect, "but you also saw three wondrous flying discs that can take us to safety. Those flying discs are also gifts from the Nexus, but first we have to learn how to build them. We were given the Sphere to teach us how and this new machine is the first small step."

A number of people in the crowd shouted their agreement.

"He's telling the truth."

"I was there."

The High Priest raised his arms silencing the crowd. "We appreciate our Emissaries' role in bringing us Asani's gift, but the interpretation of Her words must be left to the elders." Derisive shouts erupted from the crowd. The Priest's face reddened. "Return to your homes and rejoice!"

Ahotei joined Tocho and added his voice to the din. "Stop listening to the Sect's lies and think for yourselves!"

"Yes, think!" the High Priest shouted. He whirled and pointed at the machine. "Does Asani's gift portend the end of our world, or more food and resources?" The crowd fell silent. "Think! Is this wondrous device an apocalyptic message that we're all going to die?" He softened his voice, "Or a sign that from now on, we will all eat very well?' He rubbed his belly and smiled.

Tocho saw the crowd fill with nods of agreement. He glanced

at Ahotei. "We're losing them."

The High Priest continued. "I proclaim a celebration that will take place in ten cycles in the Temple square, a day of feasting and rejoicing for what our great God Asani has given us." As the sound of the crowd's applause continued behind him, he turned and spoke to Tocho. "Leave now, and I'll let you live."

"Any ideas?" Ahotei whisphered to Tocho.

Tocho moved to the edge of the deck and raised his arms. "The spinning globe many of you saw in the temple square is an advanced machine, not a god."

The High Priest shook his head. "No disrespect, Emissary, but if the Nexus is a machine, who put it here?" He chuckled. "Another machine?"

They heard more voices from the crowd, some laughing, others taut with anger or engaged in heated discussions with those around them.

Ahotei scanned their faces. "Some are with us, and some with the Sect."

The High Priest signaled to the priests near the stairways and they drew their knives.

"Now!" Ahotei shouted. The men he'd positioned at the base of the stairs ripped open their parcels removing pikes and scythes and faced off with the priests.

Tocho looked with horror at the conflict erupting below him. "Stop!" he bellowed. This froze the combatants and quieted the increasing bedlam. "Spilling blood solves nothing!" Tocho shouted. He took the Sphere from his pocket and held it high. Once again, the orb blazed with light. All eyes were on the Sphere. No one spoke. "Those of you who believe in Asani, follow the priests back to the Temple," Tocho began. "Those of you who believe that the Nexus has shown us the true future, remain here." He faced the High Priest. "We pray that in time, everyone will join us and we can learn to survive as one people."

Tocho returned the Sphere to his pocket and moved back to

stand by the machine. All eyes turned to the High Priest. After smoothing his robes, the city's chief cleric descended the stairs and shouted to the crowd. "Enough of this blasphemy! All true believers follow me." He started back to the Temple walking at a rapid pace, followed by the Chamberlain, at least half the people, and all the priests but one. That priest removed his cassock and threw it to the ground. Before the other priests could stop him, he pushed past Ahotei's startled guards and mounted the deck.

Glowering, Ahotei approached the bare-chested priest. "Your kind is not welcome here."

The priest held his ground. "I saw the Nexus and what it showed us." He pointed at Tocho. "He said all are welcome to join you."

Tocho placed his hand on Ahotei's shoulder. "He's right. The more clear minds and open hearts we have, the better."

* * *

Later that night Tocho huddled inside the apothecary shop with Ahotei and another man named Linder. The door to the laboratory remained open. They heard a knock at the door. "Who's there?" Tocho called out.

"Emissary, open the door," an unfamiliar voice answered.

Ahotei grabbed a stout metal rod and moved to the shop's door. After a nod from Tocho, he slid back the deadbolt and opened the door revealing a black-robed priest standing in the doorway. Behind the priest, a much taller man wearing a hooded grey cloak waited in the shadows. After the priest bowed and stepped aside, the taller man came forward. In the light from the doorway, he dropped his hood. "May I come in?" the High Priest asked.

"All are welcome here," Tocho replied.

With his eyes burning with anger, Ahotei dropped the metal rod and stood aside to let the High Priest enter.

The cleric moved around the shop with a stiff, aristocratic bearing, examining the array of bottles on the shelves and stopped to face Tocho. "You and I are now the leaders of a fractured society. We need to talk." He glanced at Ahotei. "In private."

Tocho gestured for the High Priest to walk with him into the laboratory. When the door slid closed, the High Priest took off his cloak exposing a common man's tunic and sat on one of the stools near the lab table. He glanced at the tangle of glassware and tubing, sighed, and looked up. "I believe we both have the same goals for our people, to keep them safe and well fed. That has been the purpose of my Sect since the first priest, eons ago, made up the rules for our society."

Tocho sat across from him. "Then you admit that Asani is a myth."

"We both saw the spinning globe and heard it speak. I call it a god, and you a machine. What does it matter?"

Tocho frowned. "What's the real reason you came here tonight?"

The High Priest nodded. "No more attempts at pleasantries." His eyes turned cold with menace. "I, too, watched what you call a machine show us pictures in a magical way. You believe your interpretation of those pictures without reservation. Is that true?"

Tocho lifted his chin. "Yes."

The High Priest smiled, but without any warmth. "I find that ironic."

"Why?"

"Our religious sect utilizes a form of governance based upon faith. Yet you and your group, call it now the science sect—are more governed by blind faith than we are."

Tocho placed his hands on the lab table and leaned forward. "Arguing about the identity of the Nexus is pointless. It's the message that counts."

The High Priest stood. "Ah yes, the message – one of bounty, or the end of everything." He walked to the wall of mounted skeletons and turned around.

Tocho stood facing him. "You saw the same images I did, and their meaning is clear enough to both of us. If you love our people as you claim, help me use the science inside the Sphere to save us all."

"I love all my children and our way of life, apothecary." The High Priest moved closer, until only the laboratory table separated them. "Which is why I *will* oppose you, with every ounce of strength I have."

Book II

Chapter Eight

Twenty thousand cycles, (two hundred Earth years) later.

Clutching her plain gray bonnet in one hand, Metzi stopped running and leaned against a stone obelisk to catch her breath. The squat stone and others like it marked the boundary between the territories of the city's two factions, her people, the ultra religious Sect, and a second group devoted to science. Tona caught up with her. A full head taller with a muscular build, he had unruly brown hair, green eyes, and a perpetual boyish grin. His father headed the Science Council.

Metzi gathered up her long red curls, wound them about her head, and replaced her bonnet. "I win … now I have to go back."

"What if I won't let you?" He leaned forward, and with an impish grin, kissed her.

Metzi blushed. "If I'm late, I'll have to wash clothes for ten cycles, or something worse."

"I'm going to the surface tomorrow to see the real sky," Tona said. "I could ask my father to take you with me."

Metzi retied the ribbon of her bonnet. "You know I can't."

"There's a whole universe out there. Everyone has a right to see it."

"My father says its heresy to go to the surface." She started walking towards the religious sector of the city.

"Wait," Tona called to her.

She spun around.

He emptied out his backpack on the ground. "I have something for you."

She came back to him. "What?"

He held up a metal rod as long as a finger with a trigger at one end, and a clear crystal on its other. "This is a light drill.

"A what?"

He activated the drill's laser and swept it along the ground leaving a furrow of scorched earth. "It cuts using heat from a focused beam of light."

Metzi peered down at the black streak on the ground. "That's what hand saws are for."

"This one can cut through almost anything in the blink of an eye."

"Doing things with our own hands makes us strong." She started walking away.

"Wait! That's not it. I have something else."

Metzi stopped. "More things I don't need?"

Tona sorted through other paraphernalia lying on the ground and held up a thick pair of glasses. "These are night goggles that let me see in the dark." He found something else. "And this," he said, picking up a thick metal tube with glass at both ends, "is a telescope that magnifies things in the distance making them appear closer."

Metzi frowned. "Enjoy your toys. I have work to do."

"Not yet!" He continued poking around. "Here's what I was looking for." He held up a small metal disc that fit in the palm of his hand. "This is a communication device." He extended his hand. "Take it."

"Why?"

"When you want to see me, push the button in the center of it. I'll know where you are, and before you know it, I'll be there."

She came back to him, took it, and felt the minimal weight of it in her hand. "How can it do such a thing?"

Tona picked up another device half as big as his hand, square and black, with a small screen. "When you activate the disc it sends a signal to this box," he held up the scanner, "and the box shows me where you are."

Metzi put the disc in the pocket of her dress. "What makes you think I'll use it?"

He smiled. "I can hope, can't I?"

* * *

Metzi adjusted her bonnet and her expression as she approached the metal gate at the perimeter of the Sect's compound. She waited for the sentries to let her through. When the gate swung open, she started down a cobble-stoned street lined by rows of small, similar appearing houses and continued to her family's quarters near the center of the compound. As she approached, Chua and two of his friends left the porch of his house and followed. "Out for a stroll?" Chua called to her.

"Leave me alone." Metzi tried to move past him, but he blocked her way.

"You were out with that stargazer again, weren't you?" Chua challenged.

Metzi's lips curled back in anger. "Where I go and who I see are none of your business. Now get out of my way!" She shoved Chua aside, ran to her house, and disappeared inside.

One of Chua's friends shook his head. "No woman should behave that way. She needs her father's strap."

Chua smiled. "She doesn't know it yet, but she's mine. After we're joined, I'll teach her proper manners."

Metzi hung her bonnet on a hook by the door and went to the cooking area. She found her mother scrubbing a pot. The two women wore identical copies of the same plain grey dress.

"You're late," Ina said.

Metzi picked up a vegetable and began peeling it. "The marketplace was packed today."

"Don't lie to me. You were with that boy from the Science Sect."

Metzi refused to meet her mother's eyes. "What of it?"

Ina put down the pot. "What if your father finds out?"

Metzi paled. "You won't tell him, will you?"

"There are several appropriate partners amongst your own people. Why not pick one of them and be done with it?"

Metzi sighed. "The people outside our gates are the same species, Mother."

Ina faced Metzi with her arms crossed over her chest. "The same species, yes, but they've abandoned our traditions and renounced God. How can you consort with such people?"

Metzi couldn't meet her mother's gaze. "They've enriched their lives and ours, when we've let them, by embracing new ideas and continuing to learn ... They've seen the sky. Why can't I?"

"You mustn't say such things!" Ina exclaimed. She lowered her voice. "Asani raised us from the waters and gave us this world. There is nothing of value beyond."

Metzi struggled to control her frustration. "What if there are better ways to do things—better ways to grow crops, or make stronger building materials? How can it be wrong to know?"

Metzi's father appeared in the doorway. "Did that outsider boy feed you this blasphemy?" Taru entered the cooking area. "Tona's his name, isn't it?" Metzi looked away. "His father, Etta, sits on the Science Council. He and his godless friends spit on our traditions."

Tight-lipped, Metzi faced her father. "The Science Sect has tripled our food supply."

"Do not speak such blasphemy in this house!" her father exclaimed. "I forbid you to see him."

Metzi ran to her room, sobbing.

* * *

Etta joined Tona in front of the observatory door.

Tona eyed the cloth bag in his father's hand. "Anything good in there?"

Etta smiled. "When did your mother ever prepare a bad meal?

Let's eat in the fresh air before we go inside."

They walked to the Science Quad and sat on a bench under a hybrid fruit tree covered with bright orange berries, a variety not sold in the central market by order of the Sect. Etta opened the bag and handed a square of dried fish wrapped in spice leaves to Tona. He selected half a melon stuffed with marinated fish for himself, and after smelling it and feigning a grimace, scooped some of the marinated fish into his mouth. He sighed. "Almost strong enough."

Tona wrinkled his nose. "How can you eat that without gagging? It peels paint off the wall."

"I like snail paste, and the sharper the better." Etta savored another mouthful. "It's an acquired taste. Sure you don't want some?"

"Not a chance," Tona replied. He gestured toward the observatory building across the quad. "I tried the door and it's locked. It's usually open this time of day. How come?"

Etta finished the melon and wiped his mouth. "Probably doing maintenance on the elevator or some such thing." He looked up and stood as two men approached. Etta exchanged greetings with the men and introduced Tona. Behat, the older of the two, introduced himself as a structural engineer. Loti, with long hair, glasses, and a big smile described himself as half mathematician and half computer programmer.

"So you're going up for the first time," Loti said to Tona. "Are you excited?"

"Haven't slept for three nights," Tona replied. He could barely contain his excitement at the prospect of seeing the real star-filled sky and the face of the mother planet. He'd read every book he could find more than once, and watched endless video feeds, but they'd proved less and less satisfying the older he became.

"Then let's go." Behat gestured toward the observatory.

Tona followed his father and the two men to the observatory

door. Behat opened it with a key and they entered the foyer, a rectangular space built around the elevator connecting the city to Europa's surface ice thousands of meters above. Tona had been inside the foyer many times, as almost everyone in the Science compound had, but he'd never been to the surface. Only scientists and engineers or people with special clearance took the elevator to the surface.

While his father spoke to Lati and Behat, Tona stood before a floor to ceiling image of Jupiter mounted on the wall and focused on a tiny speck of light inserted into the image in front of Jupiter's massive face. He knew that the digitally rendered image was meant to represent his world, one of sixty-three moons in orbit around the largest planet in the solar system. After a glance at his father to confirm that he was still engaged in conversation, Tona strolled past several more images of Jupiter and Europa taken from the moon's surface. Books with collections of even more pictures were on shelves spaced around the room. He pulled a familiar book from the shelf and was glancing through it when his father joined him.

"Having a good time?" Etta asked.

Tona put the book back on the shelf. "This place is amazing, but I've read every book and seen every picture here at least twice. I can't wait to see the real thing." He looked around the empty foyer. "Every time I come here I see school children on tours, art students painting pictures ... somebody is always here, but today the door's locked and nobody's around. Why?"

"I told you. We close the elevator complex periodically for maintenance," Etta replied. "Looks like today is one of those days."

Tona found his father's answer not entirely believable but chose not to challenge him.

Etta moved to a picture of Jupiter and stood facing it. "No picture or video feed can do it justice."

Tona joined him. "I've wanted to go to the surface as long as

I can remember."

Etta winked. "Today's the day."

Tona rubbed his hands together. "When can we go?"

Etta saw Behat and Lati waiting for them in front of the elevator doors at the foyer's center. "How about now?"

Tona and his father joined them and Behat entered a sequence of numbers into a keypad near the elevator door. The door opened revealing a windowless, metal box with four seats bolted to the wall. Tona noticed a box mounted on the elevator's back wall with a control for up and down and a means of communication, but nothing more. Etta pointed to one of the seats. "Take a seat." When everyone was seated, Etta activated the ascent control, the doors closed, and he took the remaining seat.

Tona heard a grinding sound and felt the car lurch upwards. He tensed and glanced at his father.

"Don't worry," Etta said. "There are two backup systems. Make yourself comfortable. It's a long ride to the surface."

"Has anyone ever got stuck in the middle?" Tona asked.

"Once," Lati replied with a straight face. "They starved to death before we could get them out."

Behat smirked. "Don't pay any attention to him. He likes to joke around."

Lati smiled. "And you thought mathematicians don't have a sense of humor."

Everyone laughed. Tona forced a chuckle and they laughed more.

Almost an hour later, the car came to a stop, bounced twice on its springs, and settled. The door opened on to a circular chamber one quarter the size of the foyer on the city level, now thousands of meters below. Tona stepped out into a very different looking space. The walls had a coarser appearance, with large metal rivets showing and dull grey paint. He tasted the cold, crisp air and pulled his coat tighter about him as he followed his father and the two other men into the observation area. His pulse raced with excitement.

They passed through an airlock door into a larger room with multiple thick-paned windows facing in all directions. "Have a look around while I take care of a few things," Etta said. He followed Behat and Lati to a control station manned by two other men in silver coveralls leaving Tona by himself.

Tona ran to one of the windows and grabbed the railing. He gaped at an endless black sky dappled with twinkling stars. Bursting with anticipation, he ran to another window and saw the face of the mother planet, a gigantic globe striped with multicolored bands. He couldn't stop staring at it. After a few minutes, his father joined him and led him speechless to a different window on the opposite side. "There's the hanger," Etta said pointing through the glass.

Tona saw an immense squat structure across the ice, joined to the observation building by a tube-like structure half covered with snow. "What's in there?" Tona asked.

"Our three flying discs," Etta replied. "We need to get suited up if you want to see them."

"I can see the flying discs?" Tona asked with disbelief ... "Wait. Why do we need special suits to go to the hanger?"

Etta put his hands on Tona's shoulders. "Because we're going outside."

Chapter Nine

Wearing a full environmental suit with a clear bubble helmet, internal heater, and an oxygen backpack, Tona stepped through the airlock door and felt his boots crunch against the ice. He started following his father but stopped after two steps. "I can't see," he said over the suit's comlink.

"Stop hyperventilating," Etta said, laughing.

Tona slowed his breathing allowing his helmet to clear. When he could see again, he looked up and saw the face of the planet Jupiter.

"Spectacular isn't it?" Etta said.

Tona licked his dry lips. "It makes me feel so small."

Etta placed his gloved hand on Tona's shoulder. "Everyone should feel what it's like to stand beneath the sky." Neither spoke for a moment. "But there's plenty more to see, and only one day's time. So let's go." Etta started down a path marked by a line of lights.

Tona walked side by side with his father on the well-lit path paralleling the pressurized tube that led to the hangar. Halfway there, he turned back and gazed again at the planet Jupiter. "I've seen hundreds of pictures of it, but nothing can prepare you for the sight of the real thing."

"It's the largest planet in our solar system, but in reality a ball of pressurized gas with a much smaller rocky core. There are millions upon millions of planets in the heavens orbiting other stars. Some are gas giants like this one and others are spheres of rock."

"The priests say we're the only sentient beings in the universe," Tona said.

"Nonsense," Etta scoffed. "There are billions of stars in the sky, many of them with their own solar systems of planets. Amongst all those millions upon millions of planets and moons like this one, it's mathematically inconceivable that life evolved only here."

They continued walking.

"Where did the Sphere come from?" Tona asked.

"The Sphere is a machine," Etta replied. "Someone built it and gave it to us, but no one knows who."

They reached the hanger's airlock and Etta entered a sequence of numbers onto a keypad. The airlock door opened and he stepped inside, beckoning Tona to follow.

Tona glanced one more time at Jupiter, then followed his father inside. "Maybe the Sphere really is the gift of a god."

"Are we gods to the fish?" Etta asked as he closed the external door.

"We're not gods to anything," Tona said.

Etta activated the airlock's controls, flooding the chamber with air. "To a fish we are."

"A fish can't think."

Etta watched the airlock's gauge as the pressure inside rose. "The priests taught my father's father that the universe ends outside our ocean. Now even they have to admit that doesn't work anymore." An overhead light changed from black to blue and Etta took off his helmet. "Prepare to be amazed." He spun the wheel on the airlock's inner door and it swung open.

Tona followed his father into the balcony of one of the building's three hangars. They moved to a railing and looked down at a silver disc five times the height of a man and fifty times as long resting twenty meters below them on the hangar floor. Etta left Tona at the railing and continued down a stairway to join Behat and Lati near the disc. The two men had taken the automated train in the tube. Etta met them at the base of a ramp leading up to a rectangular opening in the craft's side. Tona remained at the railing, awestruck by the sight of the disc.

A young woman, with short brunette hair, wearing coveralls, joined him. "Are you Etta's son?" She extended her hand in greeting. "I'm Ruha."

"I'm Tona," he replied, not taking his eyes off the disc.

Ruha smiled and dropped her hand. "It had the same effect on me the first time I saw it. "Has your father taken you inside?"

Tona faced her. "Can I go inside?"

Ruha grinned at him. "You can't come all the way here and not go inside."

Etta came up the ladder and joined them. "I see you've met Ruha. She's one of our top young scientists and a pretty fair dancer I hear."

Tona glanced at his father. An awkward silence followed, broken when Ruha cleared her throat. "I have some work to tidy up," she said.

"Are you going back inside?" Etta asked.

"A bit later," Ruha replied.

"Would you mind giving Tona a brief tour of the flying disc's command center? I have engineering updates to sign off on." He glanced at Tona. "Judging by the look on my son's face, I don't think he'll be able to wait much longer."

Tona blushed.

"I suppose I can rearrange my schedule." Ruha pointed down at the disc. "Want to have a look inside?"

"Yes!" Tona exclaimed.

Ruha started down the ladder to the hangar floor. "Let's go."

"She's special, isn't she?" Etta asked.

Tona cast a reproving glance at his father and followed Ruha down the ladder.

When they reached the hangar floor, Ruha and Tona walked side by side toward the disc.

"What kind of scientist are you?" Tona asked.

"I'm a mechanical engineer with degrees in astronomy and mathematics."

Tona nodded. "Impressive."

They stopped at the base of the disc's ramp and looked up.

"Now *that* is what I call impressive," Ruha said. She started up the ramp.

Tona let his eyes roam the smooth silver exterior of the disc towering above him.

Ruha called to him from the top of the ramp. "Come on, I don't have all day."

Tona ascended the ramp, and partway up stopped and bounced on his feet. He looked down and saw the silver substance of the ramp dent forming an outline of his boot and spring back again becoming perfectly smooth. "What's the ramp made from? It doesn't feel solid, but it is."

Ruha spoke to him from the disc's doorway. "Most of the disc, including the ramp, is made from a silver material best described as a plasticized liquid with a crystal lattice. We don't understand its bizarre chemistry, at least not yet. We got the recipe for it from the Sphere, like most of the technology around here."

Tona joined her at the top of the ramp and looked inside the disc.

Ruha gestured inside. "Welcome to the disc's command center. Come inside and I'll show you around."

Tona followed her into an empty circular space ten meters in diameter made from the same silver material. He looked around. "There's nothing here."

"Hang on. This takes a little getting used to," Ruha said. She moved to the center of the space and motioned for Tona to join her. When he moved next to her, she said, "Activate."

The walls began to glow with a pale-blue light and a pillar of silver rose from the center of the floor. The top of the pillar flattened and spread outward forming a table with a lattice of flashing colored lights in the center of it. Two smaller pillars, half as tall, made from the same material, formed next to it. Nothing further happened.

"What do you think of that?" Ruha asked.

Tona leaned forward and studied the table of flashing lights, but didn't touch anything. "A table of flashing lights and two lumps of silver. That's all you need to fly this thing?"

"Almost," Ruha replied. "Watch this." She pointed at the wall farthest from the doorway and said, "Window." Tona looked where Ruha pointed and saw a rectangular area, the height and width of a man, darken and become transparent. She walked towards it. "Have a look."

Tona moved close to her. "It's a hole in the wall. What's the point of that? All the air will leak out."

Ruha smiled. "Put your hand through it."

Tona reached out with his hand to the window and his fingers hit something solid, although he couldn't see anything. He pulled back his hand. "A force field?"

"The wall of the disc is still there, but it's become transparent."

Tona nodded. "Have to say that's amazing."

"Wait, here's the best part of the tour," Ruha said. "Stand next to one of the pillars near the command console and see what happens. But don't touch it," she hastened to add.

"Okay." As Tona approached the nearest pillar of silver, it quivered and leaned towards him. He jumped back. "Whoa! Is that thing alive?"

"No," Ruha replied, chuckling. "Although sometimes it seems that way."

"What happens if I touch it?" Tona asked.

"Better watch me do it first," Ruha said. "It's pretty weird." Tona raised an eyebrow and watched Ruha reach toward one of the silver pillars. When she touched it, the pillar quivered and flowed up her arm and across her chest. It continued spreading until it covered her body from her chin to her toes in silver material. "Stop," Ruha said. She walked toward him and held out her silver hand.

"Wow," Tona said.

Touch me," Ruha said.

Tona hesitated.

"It's okay. Don't be afraid. Shake my hand."

He grasped her hand. "It feels hard, like metal."

Ruha let go of his hand. "This material has the tensile strength of the finest metal alloys available, yet it's fluid, completely flexible and quite comfortable." She flexed her hand several times and then jumped up and down. "Now watch this." She spoke the word "Helmet," and the silver substance flowed over her head forming a transparent bubble. "It becomes an airtight environmental suit with enough oxygen to last a full cycle."

Tona walked around her studying her silver form. "Your voice sounds different."

"You're hearing me by way of the suit's comlink. Now watch this." Ruha touched a white button on her sleeve that Tona hadn't noticed before and the suit flowed off her body into a puddle on the floor and disappeared.

Etta stood in the disc's doorway. "What do you think?" he called to his son.

"This technology is beyond belief," Tona replied shaking his head.

Ruha looked at her wrist chronometer and turned to Tona. "I need to go below and finish up some things before I go home. It was nice meeting you."

"Yeah, thanks for the tour." Tona looked around. "I don't see any hatches. How do you get below?"

"The same way you open the front door," Ruha replied. She pointed at the floor in front of her, stretched out her arms, and said, "Door." Two meters away from her, a circular area twice the span of her outstretched arm darkened and widened to form a circular opening. Tona moved closer to it and saw a ramp leading down to another lighted area. Ruha disappeared down the ramp and the floor reformed leaving no evidence that an opening had been there.

Tona shook his head. "Unreal."

"Did Ruha put you in a cocoon?" Etta asked.

"A what?"

"Watch this." Etta walked to one of the pillars, said the word, "Pilot," and touched it. Within seconds, he too was covered with silver, with a clear bubble over his head. This time, after the bubble helmet formed, the pillar reshaped itself into a chair with Etta reclining on it. "Your turn," he said to Tona with an artificial timbre to his voice. Tona stared at his father and didn't move. "Go ahead, try it," Etta urged. "It doesn't hurt. In fact, it feels rather good."

"Not sure about this," Tona muttered. He moved closer to the second pillar and reached out his hand, watching wide-eyed as the silver substance flowed up his arm.

* * *

They sat in the small eating area at the back of the hangar. "Half a cycle is not enough time for you to see everything," Etta said.

Tona took a sip of his hot drink. "How come we don't have any of this advanced technology in the city?"

Etta sighed. "We'd be accused of heresy and witchcraft by the Sect. The priests banned hybrid melons from the marketplace, even though they grow twice as fast, are more nutritious, and taste better. How do you think they'll do with a floor you can talk to?"

Tona thought about Metzi. "The comet's coming. They'll have to deal with technology when we all escape in the flying discs."

Etta frowned. "The Sect's not going with us."

"Of course they are."

Etta looked earnestly at his son. "The Sect agrees with us that the comet is coming, but they believe that their god Asani will protect them from it so long as she remains happy with them."

Tona thought about Metzi again and bit his lip. "That's ridiculous."

Etta looked down at his hands. "I know. To them, our

technology is an abomination. If they use it, Asani won't be happy about it."

"And she won't protect them from the comet?"

Etta nodded.

"That's nonsense!" Tona exclaimed. "We have to show them the data and convince them to leave with us."

Etta shifted in his chair. "Don't you think we've tried? We've showed them pictures, course plots, computer simulations, and projections of the catastrophic damage the comet will do to our world." He shook his head. "The Sect thinks it's all a lie, a ruse perpetrated by the Science Sect, as they call us, to take over control of the city."

Tona put down his cup. "There won't be any city for anyone to control. Try again to talk to them!"

"Believe me, we've tried, over and over. It's useless."

They sat in silence.

"When's the disc's first flight?" Tona asked.

"As soon as the crew finishes training."

Tona glanced toward one of the viewing windows showing the face of Jupiter. "What's the first trip going to be? Once around the Mother Planet and back again?"

"We don't know where the disc's going," Etta replied.

Tona jerked his head back. "What?"

"Or if it's coming back," Etta finished saying.

"You can't be serious."

Etta sat back in his chair. "The navigational system has a pre-programmed course provided by the Sphere. We've only been able to decipher enough of it to know that the disc's final destination is a planet around another star. Where that star is," he shrugged, "so far we haven't been able to figure out."

Tona leaned forward and stared at his father. "You don't know where the disc is going, or if it's coming back?"

"Not exactly," Etta replied. "The Sphere has provided us a wealth of data on the destination world, its atmosphere, gravity, mineral content, ambient temperature, and more. It sounds like a great place to set up shop."

"How far away is it?" Tona asked.

"We don't know."

Tona thought for a moment. "That's why you're not sure the disc is coming back."

Etta nodded. "Correct."

Tona thought about the layout of the disc. "What's below the disc's command deck, where what's-her-name went?"

"Her name's Ruha. How'd you two get along?"

Tona frowned. "Stop meddling in my life."

"She's different from that girl who lives in the religious zone ..." Etta began.

"Her name's Metzi," Tona interrupted.

"Why do you keep seeing her?"

Tona frowned. "What difference does it make?"

"Here's a different question. What's wrong with getting to know a woman more like us?"

Tona smirked. "You mean like Ruha?"

"She's an accomplished scientist and she comes from a good family."

"You don't know Metzi's family."

Etta grimaced "I know her father all too well. He's one of the most rigid and outspoken members of the Sect. Puts some of the priests to shame with his rhetoric. You'd be wise to stay away from him and his family."

Tona pushed back from the table. "I'm ready to go back down."

Etta stood. "I have a couple things I need to do before we return. Won't take long. Look around for a few minutes and I'll find you."

Tona strolled back to the observation area and looked out towards the hangar. Ruha joined him wearing regular clothing with a satchel hung from her shoulder. "Going down in the next car?" she asked.

"Yes," Tona replied.

She leaned against the observation window looking out. "How'd you like your tour of the disc?"

Tona faced her. "Doesn't it bother you that we don't know where the disc is going?"

Ruha continued looked out the viewing window. "The Sphere gave us astrometric charts and a detailed description of the destination planet."

"How long a flight is it?" Tona asked.

Ruha hesitated before answering. "We don't know because we don't know how to gauge the distances or how fast the disc flies."

"What about supplies for the trip? Don't you have to know how long the flight's going to be to know how much to bring?"

She didn't answer.

Tona persisted. "Do you even know how many people each disc can take?"

Ruha stepped away from the railing. "We know the comet's coming and it's on a collision course to destroy our city and everyone in it. The Nexus has given us a safe haven on the destination planet, and the means to get there. That's what we know."

"But we won't know for sure until the disc comes back, will we?"

Ruha glanced toward the elevator. A blue light blinked above the door signaling the car's approach. "The elevator's almost here. I have to go. Bye, Tona." She walked away.

* * *

Tona rode down to the city with his father accompanied by two technicians from the hangar complex. Behat and Lati stayed behind.

“You didn’t tell me the disc’s not coming back,” Tona said to his father.

Etta glanced at the technicians, saw one of them tense, and lowered his voice. “We’ll discuss it later.”

Chapter Ten

Carrying a basket filled with vegetables, Metzi strolled the aisles of the open-air market shared by both the city's factions. She passed vendors offering trays of fresh fillets from several species of fish, piles of shrimp and mollusks on ice, assorted yellow melons and dried sea plants. Tona joined her at the end of one of the aisles. He took her arm and guided her away with an expression of urgency.

Metzi allowed him to steer her to a storage area behind a pallet of empty food crates. "What's going on?" she demanded.

He let go of her arm. "I've been to the surface."

She didn't hide her pique. "You told me you were going. So what?"

He leaned closer. "It's true, all of it, the comet, the flying discs ... everything."

"My father says it's all a lie, a trick by the Science Sect to take over." She turned to leave.

Tona grabbed her by the shoulders forcing her to face him. "You don't understand! I saw with my own eyes. A comet is on a collision course with our world. Our city will be destroyed. If we don't leave, we'll all die."

Metzi pulled away. "Why would Asani give us our city and then take it away? It makes no sense."

"Metzi, open your eyes. There is no Asani."

Her face reddened. "Call Asani the Nexus if it makes you happy."

Tona shook his head with frustration. "The Nexus, the Sphere, they're not gods, they're machines."

"If they're machines, who built them?" she demanded.

"We can't keep going round and round about this!" Tona struggled to calm himself. "Okay, have it your way. The great God Asani also known as the Nexus showed us images of the comet coming. We all agree that it's coming, right?"

"Yes," Metzi replied.

"But she also showed us the comet destroying our city. True?"

"Yes, but ..."

"But what?" Tona exclaimed.

"The city won't be destroyed if we follow Asani's laws," Metzi replied.

"Did Asani tell us that, or the priests?" Tona leaned closer. "Did anyone talk to Asani?"

"No one talks to Asani," Metzi protested.

"All our lives are at stake. Doesn't that bother you?"

Metzi could see the sheen of sweat on Tona's brow. She looked into his eyes, and in that moment knew the truth. "Even if you're right," she began.

Tona appeared on the verge of tears. "I am right, and we have to convince your people before it's too late!" He sat down on one of the crates and put his head in his hands. "Please help me ... I can't lose you."

She sat next to him. "Let's say you're right." He turned to look at her. "For the sake of argument," she continued. "The Joint Council has been debating this since before we were born. Why would my people acquiesce now?"

Tona took both her hands. "Do you trust me?"

Metzi's eyes filled with tears. "Yes."

"We'll find a way."

* * *

Tona picked at his evening meal and then pushed his plate away.

"Is something wrong?" his mother asked.

Tona looked at his father. "We have to convince the Sect to leave with us on the flying discs. We can't let them all die."

Etta sighed. "I told you. We've tried every month at the Joint Council meetings. It's like talking to a stone wall."

"We can't stop trying," Tona protested.

Etta saw the distress in his son's eyes. "We can't force them onto the discs." They have to choose to leave of their own free will.

Tona pushed back his chair and stood. "Maybe you've given up, but I haven't." He left the room.

Etta found Tona on the back porch. "Trust me, I've lost more than a few nights of sleep about this," Etta began. "We've presented all our data several times, and our projections of the damage that will be caused by the comet strike." He shook his head. "They call it blasphemy and refuse to listen. What else can we do?"

"Ask the Sphere what to do," Tona replied. "It has the answers to everything else."

"You're wrong," Etta said. "It's an encyclopedia of science and technology, nothing more."

"Then ask the Nexus for help."

Etta looked up at Europa's ocean silently swirling above their heads. "No one's seen the Nexus for three generations. When we ask the Sphere why, we don't get an answer."

They stood in silence.

Tona faced his father. "When I asked Ruha what's below the flying disc's command deck, she found an excuse not to answer. Why? What's down there?"

Etta looked away. "I can't tell you."

"We've never had secrets before."

"It's for your own good!" Etta shook his head with frustration and lowered his voice. "This is a delicate time. The Science Council has to be careful how we parse out information."

"But ..."

Etta held up his hand. "The subject is closed. Do I make myself clear?"

Tona nodded.

"I have a Science Council meeting tonight. I'll be home late.

Don't wait up for me." Etta went back into the house.

* * *

Tona reclined on his bed with a book open on his lap. When he heard the front door close, he slipped out of the house and followed his father. He sprinted from shadow to shadow being careful not to be seen. At the junction of their street with the boulevard that led to the Science Council Building, Etta stopped and turned to look around. Just before being seen, Tona dove behind some shrubbery, held his breath and waited. When Etta appeared satisfied that he wasn't being followed, he turned onto a side street leading to the old section of the city and continued walking, now with a hurried pace.

Tona watched his farther stride away from behind a stand of bushes. "That's not the way to the Science Building," he muttered. He jumped to his feet and continued following.

Tona saw his father stop in front of an apothecary shop at the heart of the city's old section. After glancing around him yet again, Etta knocked twice and waited. A moment later, someone not visible to Tona let Etta inside and the door closed.

Tona noticed that when the apothecary shop door opened, no light spilled into the street. He ran to the shop and flattened himself beside the front window hoping to see inside, but the curtains were drawn with no light showing. With his heart racing, he darted around the building and found another window in the back, but it, too, was draped. "Damn!" he whispered. As he considered his options, he heard a man's voice he didn't recognize.

"Looking for something?"

Tona turned around and found himself facing an older and taller man whose features were hidden by the dark. "My father's in there," Tona stammered.

"And you're waiting for him by skulking around out here?"

the man said with his hands on his hips.

"No, I ..." Tona stammered.

With astonishing strength, considering his apparent age, Ahotei grabbed Tona by the shoulder and pulled him toward the front of the building.

"Where are you taking me?" Tona said alarmed.

"To your father," Ahotei rasped. At the shop's front door, he let go of Tona and knocked twice. When the door opened, he shoved Tona rudely inside.

Tona tried to compose himself. "Who are you?" he asked Ahotei.

Ahotei ignored him and opened the hidden panel to Tocho's laboratory. He disappeared inside and a moment later reappeared with Etta.

Etta glared at his son. "You followed me?"

Tona stared back at him. "Tell me the truth about the flying discs."

"I told you, I can't," Etta replied.

"Like it or not, he's here." Ahotei shook his head and walked back into the laboratory.

Etta pointed angrily inside. "Go inside, but stand in the back and don't say a word unless you're spoken to."

Wiping the sweat from his brow, Tona followed his father into Tocho's laboratory. He saw three other men seated around a large table and recognized two as Behat and Lati. Lati waved to him. Behat looked away. The third man appeared very old. Although somewhat stooped with age, Tocho remained taller than Ahotei, his now painfully thin body crowned by a face with thick glasses and creased with a perpetual frown.

Tocho stuck out his hand. "My name's Tocho."

Tona's eyes widened with surprise as they shook hands. "The man who found the Nexus?"

"I was there, too, not that anybody remembers," Ahotei muttered.

Tona pulled back his hand and glanced at Ahotei. "You must be Ahotei."

Ahotei briefly raised his hand. "Guilty."

"Your father tells me that you've already met Behat and Lati, and toured the disc," Tocho said.

"Only the command compartment," Tona replied. He glanced at his father. "I never got below."

Ahotei chuckled. "Consider yourself lucky."

Tocho pointed to a chair at the laboratory's back wall. "Take a seat." Tona sat, doing his best to contain his excitement. "Let me caution you, young man," Tocho continued. "You are about to become burdened with information that the populace on both sides of the wall are not ready to hear. In fact, possession of this knowledge places your life in danger." Tona's face turned pale. "If you still wish to stay, you must promise not to discuss what you hear tonight with anyone outside these walls. Do you agree?"

Ahotei moved closer to Tocho. "Shouldn't we send the brat home?"

Etta's eyes never left his son, but he remained silent.

Wide-eyed, Tona nodded. "I promise. I won't say a word to anyone."

"Very well." Tocho took his customary seat at the center of the lab table. Instead of glassware and scientific equipment, the table was littered with stacks of papers and images of the comet. "Gentlemen," Tocho began. "We have a lot to talk about tonight, and according to the latest observations of the comet, not a great deal of time to act."

The men exchanged worried glances.

"I thought we had at least two hundred cycles before impact," Behat said.

"We have updated information," Lati said. "The closer the comet gets, the more accurate are the data and our projections." He sighed. "I'm afraid the latest projections don't look good."

Etta glanced at his son. "What *are* the latest projections?"

Tocho looked grim. "We have no more than fifty cycles before impact."

* * *

Tona walked side by side with his father on the way home. He tried to engage him in conversation, but lost in thought, Etta didn't answer.

When his frustration and angst became unbearable, Tona stopped. "We only have fifty cycles to evacuate the city. What are we going to do?"

Etta stopped and looked anxiously around. He kept his voice low. "You heard what Tocho said. You can't speak about it! Someone might hear."

Tona gestured around them. "There's nobody here. Everyone's home asleep. Father, please, you have to talk to me."

Etta steered Tona to a nearby bench. They seated themselves on the cold metal and Etta leaned close speaking in whispers. "Fifty cycles should be enough time for us to evacuate."

"You don't sound convinced," Tona said.

"It depends on two things that we don't know the answers to, at least not yet. How difficult a trip is it to the new planet, and how many people are going?"

"How difficult a trip? You mean how long it takes to get there?"

Etta stared at his hands folded in his lap. "The Sphere recently gave us more information, including where the new planet is. We know everything about it now, right down to the nucleic acid composition of its flora and fauna. It's perfect for us ... except it's a very long way away."

"The Sphere showed us how to build the flying discs, so they must be able to get us there."

Etta looked into Tona's eyes. "The Sphere gave us the location of a perfect new home and the technology to get us there, but those gifts come at a very steep price."

"I don't understand."

Etta struggled to find the right words. "To fly there, we have to leave our bodies behind."

"You can't be serious!"

Etta looked around. "Keep your voice down!" he cautioned. "The new world is too far away for the disc to carry enough food and water to last for the entire trip for even a few passengers."

Tona's eyes widened with fright. "What about cryogenic hibernation? I know we've been experimenting with it."

"It works on small animals, but we've never tried it on one of us." Etta hesitated before continuing. "The Sphere has given us instructions for a different process to help us get there. It's called downloading."

"What does downloading mean?"

Etta hesitated before answering. "It means transferring our brain patterns to an inorganic body for the trip, a computer that doesn't need air, food, or water."

Tona wiped his mouth with the back of his hand. "But we can download back into our bodies and be ourselves again after we get there, right?"

Etta shook his head. "Not according to the mission specifications given to us by the Sphere."

Tona gaped at his father. "Why not?"

"Because we can't take our bodies with us. There's not enough room in the discs for the cryogenic freezers, and not enough power to keep the freezers going for the duration of the flight … It's a one-way trip."

"There has to be another way!"

Etta shifted his position on the bench. "There may be, but at this point it's only a theory. That's why the first disc is leaving with only the test pilots aboard. After the pilots download, we'll keep their bodies in cryogenic hibernation in a special facility we've just completed in the bedrock beneath the city. Our computer technicians altered the disc's navigational profile, the one provided by the Sphere, to make the disc return here after one cycle of flight instead of traveling all the way to the new planet ... at least we hope we have. If everything goes as planned, the pilots will return and reclaim their bodies from the deep freeze."

"That's the answer!" Tona exclaimed.

"Provided everything goes as planned." Etta rubbed his hands together. "For instance, what if the comet destroys the cryogenic facility holding our bodies? What if by reprogramming the disc we've somehow damaged its navigational computer and it goes off course taking the two test pilots to who knows where?"

Tona leaned back against the bench. "I'd rather take my chances with the comet then finish my life as a piece of computer hardware."

Etta patted Tona's thigh and got to his feet. "If the first disc returns and the test pilots can reclaim their bodies, we have a chance."

Tona looked up at his father. "What happens to the pilots if the disc doesn't return?"

"The pilots can continue on to the new planet, or destroy the disc."

* * *

Metzi waited for Tona at one of the stone markers dividing the city. "We're out of time," he said, catching his breath when he arrived. "The comet impacts in fifty cycles, not two hundred."

Metzi paled. "There's been some kind of mistake."

"No, it's true. The closer the comet gets, the more refined the astronomical calculations become. If we don't convince your people to leave, they're all going to die."

Metzi trembled. "My father says that thanks to Asani's

intervention the comet's going to miss us. Nothing's going to happen."

Tona raised his arms in frustration. "That's a lie."

Metzi glared at him. "Are you calling my father a liar?"

"He's mistaken, okay?" Tona moved closer and stared into her eyes. "Metzi, I saw the data. The comet's going to hit us in fifty cycles. It will wipe out the city."

Metzi looked away. She appeared agitated and confused. "I don't know what to do. I love both of you, but one of you isn't telling the truth."

Tona forced her to look at him. "We have to convince your father and the Sect's elders to look at the new data. It's our only chance."

A tear rolled down Metzi's cheek as she saw the truth in Tona's eyes. "How?"

"I'll go back with you. We'll talk to your father together."

"You won't get past the gate!"

Tona shook his head with frustration. "We have to do something. Soon!"

She wiped her eyes. "I'll talk to him, tonight, after the evening meal. What should I say?"

"Tell your father that my father, his name is Etta, will bring all the new astronomical data to the Joint Council chambers in the market place tomorrow."

Metzi nodded. "I will."

"How will I know if he agrees?"

She picked up her basket. "Meet me behind the fish traps, at midnight."

* * *

Metzi returned home and found her father, Taru, in the front room conferring with the Chamberlain. When she appeared in the doorway, their conversation ceased. "Father, I need to talk to you," Metzi said keeping her voice calm.

Taru glanced at the Chamberlain. "I'm busy now, child. We'll talk later. I'm sure your mother can find something for you to do."

Metzi took a quick breath to steady herself. "It's about the comet."

Taru frowned and turned to the Chamberlain. "Would you excuse us for a moment?" The Chamberlain glanced at Metzi and left the room. Taru motioned for Metzi to enter. "Have you been talking to that boy heretic again?"

She stood before her father trying not to tremble. "He said their scientists have proof that the comet is going hit the city in fifty cycles."

Taru's face reddened. "I won't hear such blasphemy in this house, not from my own daughter."

Metzi's knees threatened to buckle. "He said if we don't leave, we're all going to die."

Taru patted the seat next to him and she sat down. He wiped her eyes with his handkerchief. "You were always the inquisitive one." He smiled at her. "Never stopped asking questions … one after another."

"Asani gave us the ability to think. How can it be wrong for us to ask questions, to weigh different possibilities and make the right choice?"

"Of course it isn't wrong, child."

"Then, Father, shouldn't we at least evaluate the information that the Science Sect has?"

Taru appeared surprised. "What makes you think we haven't?"

Metzi blinked. "You have?"

He shook his head. "We're not fools because we believe in God. We've been following the course of the comet very closely and making our own calculations. That's how we know it is going to fly by us without doing any harm."

"What if the Science Sect has more accurate calculations?"

Taru's nostrils flared as he spoke. "Those heretics will say anything to break our will and seize power, but their plan is not going to work."

Metzi opened her mouth to speak.

"Do you honestly think I'd let you, your mother, or your sister die?"

Metzi wiped her eyes and shook her head. "No."

Taru smiled at her. "I promise you ... there's nothing to concern yourself about." He gestured toward the doorway. "Now be a good girl and go help your mother prepare the evening meal."

"Yes, Father." Metzi got to her feet.

"And child ..."

"Yes?"

"Stop seeing that young heretic. It isn't proper behavior for the first-born daughter of a Council Elder."

Metzi left the room, but instead of continuing to the food preparation area, flattened her back against the wall behind a rack of coats. She saw the Chamberlain rejoin her father and leaned closer to listen.

"It's done," the Chamberlain said.

Taru frowned. "How much did that heretic want this time?"

"One hundred bars," the Chamberlain replied. "But he won't provide the final codes for the launch sequence until he's aboard."

Taru nodded. "He's garbage like the rest of them, but he's not stupid."

"I agreed to his terms because if the new projections are correct, we're out of time," the Chamberlain said.

Taru lifted his chin and stared at the Chamberlain. "You're sure no one outside our group knows?"

"I'm sure."

"We can only take forty people on each disc, a total of eighty out of more than three hundred Sect members." Taru grimaced. "If any of those being left behind find out, it won't be pretty."

"We're prepared for that eventuality," the Chamberlain said matter-of-factly. "The priests at the boarding ramps have orders to kill anyone not authorized to board."

Taru looked away. "The thought of killing our own people is horrible."

The Chamberlain stood to leave. "They're going to die anyway, along with all the heretics. What difference does it make?"

Taru got to his feet. "I still don't like it."

Metzi ran out the back of the house.

Chapter Eleven

Metzi sprinted down the dark streets toward the religious compound's front gate. Halfway there, the dark silhouette of a man blocked her way. Chua stepped into the light. "Going somewhere?"

Metzi glanced around for a route of escape. "None of your business where I go, Chua." She tried to push past him, but he grabbed her arm.

"You're hurting me!" Metzi exclaimed. She tried to pull away, but he held tighter.

Chua slapped her across the face. "Shut your mouth." She tried again to pull free and he slapped her harder. The force of his blow sent her gasping to her knees. He stood over her, raising his arm to strike her again.

Trembling, Metzi brought her arm up as a shield. "Stop hurting me."

Chua dropped his arm and yanked her to her feet.

"Why are you doing this?" Metzi cried.

He tugged her forward and started walking. "Shut up. I'm taking you to your first lesson."

"What are you talking about?"

He yanked her arm with greater force and she lost her footing. He began dragging her. "Your father hasn't taught you proper manners. I will."

"You're insane!" Metzi screamed. "Let me go!"

He knocked her to the ground. "You'll learn your place before I take you as a mate."

She looked up at him, sobbing. "I'd rather die than mate with you."

Chua slapped her again, and then dragged her inside an abandoned house. After bolting the door, he faced her as she cowered on the floor and took off his belt.

Metzi felt in her pocket for Tona's tracker and activated it just before Chua's belt struck her across her back.

* * *

Tona peeked out from the forest of struts beneath the fish trap deck and checked his chronometer. "Come on, Metzi, it's midnight. Where are you?" Minutes passed, and no one approached. He glanced at his wrist chronometer again. Now it read half past midnight. Damn!" He ran toward his house.

* * *

Etta saw Tona come through the front door and put down a page of numbers he'd been studying. "You're up late."

Tona took off his coat. "Couldn't sleep. Too much going on."

"The first disc launches tomorrow at six. I've made arrangements for you to come with me to see it."

"Sure." Tona went to his room.

"I thought you'd be excited," Etta called to him.

Tona closed his door and leaned against it. "Damn! Where is she?" He paced his bedroom several times and stopped facing the window. "This isn't like her." He paced another circuit and stopped. "She wouldn't do this to me, not now." He looked out the window into the dark. "Something's wrong." He grabbed his backpack, opened the window, and slipped out.

Tona ran through the dark streets and stopped at one of the stone markers dividing his section of the city from the fortress-like compound of the Sect. He could see the compound's lights above the Sect's main gate in the distance and knew it was guarded day and night. "Okay, what do I do now?" he said to himself. "Have a look around." He found his night vision goggles in his backpack, scanned the compound's perimeter and noticed an unlit section close to the rear wall. "That could work." He prepared himself for a dash through the dark to the compound's wall. "This is insane! I don't even know where she lives." He rummaged in his backpack for his telescope and saw a blinking point of light on his hand-scanner's screen. He brought it closer to his face and smiled. "That's my girl."

Tona slung his backpack over his shoulder and kept the scanner in his hand where he could see it. After another sweep of the area with his night vision goggles, he sprinted across the field and placed his back against the compound's stone wall. He caught his breath and covered the scanner's face with his hand to prevent the guards above him from seeing the glow. He studied the screen and listened. Hearing no suspicious sounds coming from above, he leaned away from the wall and looked up measuring the distance to the top. "Three times my height and no handholds." He thought for a moment and took the light drill from his backpack. Shielding the drill's red beam with his hand, he used it to carve a hole in the stone a meter up the wall big enough to place the front third of his foot. After another glance around, he reached up and placed his foot in the hole, and with a silent groan, pulled himself up supporting all his weight on one foot. Fighting the pain shooting up his ankle, he repeated the process a meter higher for his left leg, and then again for his right until he'd scrambled up the face of the wall. He knew that the line of holes he'd cut into the wall would be discovered the next day, but by then, it wouldn't matter.

Tona kept his head below the top of the wall, waiting and listening. When he didn't hear anything, he peeked over the top and surveyed the layout of the complex. "All roads lead to the Temple," he thought to himself. "What a surprise." Using his night vision goggles in line with his telescope, he scanned the area noting the location of four sentries, one patrolling each section of the rectangular wall. As the guard on his section came closer, Tona pulled back out of sight.

He heard the guard's footsteps above him, and started

counting, "One … two …" At the count of twenty-five, he peeked again and saw that the guard had moved well past him and had his back turned. Tona waited for the guard to reach the end of his patrol area and make another trip in his direction. When the guard started back, Tona hid again and waited until he heard the guard's footsteps directly above him. Tona started counting. At the count of twenty-five, hoping the guard didn't vary his routine and was now well past him, Tona dropped his backpack to the ground inside the compound and hoisted himself over the wall.

He landed in the dark with a muffled thump, lost his footing and fell, and then scrambled back to the shadows at the base of the wall. Above him, the guard started his next circuit. Tona held his breath until the guard passed him, then he began silently counting again. At the count of twenty-five, he scooped up his backpack and ran behind a row of houses next to the wall that showed no lights. Crouching out of sight, he waited to catch his breath.

He heard sounds in the distance, nothing distinct or coming toward him. Hoping he hadn't been seen, he leaned out to locate the towering peak of the main temple to get his bearings. He quickly found it, a black sentinel against the soft glow of the city's night sky. Scanning his surroundings with the night vision telescope, he saw no one about. "So far, so good," he said to himself. Kneeling, he took the scanner from his backpack and after shielding the screen with his body, turned on the power. He used the scanner to gauge the tracker's location, and with his goggles, fixed it to an unlit dwelling one hundred fifty meters in a straight line from his hiding place. He briefly considered the possibility that Metzi no longer had the tracker, but rejected it. "Not quitting now."

Tona turned off the scanner and replaced it in his backpack. After securing the backpack over his shoulder, he placed the telescope in front of his goggles and scanned the length of the wall. He spotted the guard, but this time noted that the guard had stopped in the center of the wall not far from his location. Tona pushed back into the dark. "Not good. Not good at all!" he said to himself. Seconds passed, and the guard remained stationary, apparently looking around for something. After several minutes more, Tona risked rising up and looking. To his horror, he saw the guard only a few paces away. Tona ducked his head, slammed his back against the wall and waited. Every stray sound in the night raised his level of panic until his heart threatened to explode from his chest. Ten minutes passed and nothing happened. He peeked out again and saw the guard moving away.

Tona sprinted toward the dwelling containing Metzi's tracker and grabbed the door lever. The door refused to open. He tried again, and this time heard a man's voice behind the door.

"Who's there?" Chua demanded.

Tona's mind raced. "I have a delivery," he replied, trying to sound calm. He heard Metzi's muffled scream through the door and yanked the door lever as hard as he could. It still wouldn't yield. He heard Metzi scream again. "I'm coming!" he called to her. Heedless of the danger, he dropped to the ground and emptied out his backpack. Sorting through the technology at his feet, he found his light drill and used it to slice through the door's bolt.

Tona kicked open the door. Before he could charge inside, Chua rushed toward him from the dark holding something long and menacing above his head. With a snarl of rage, Chua brought a ragged plank of wood down over Tona's head. At the last instant, Tona side-stepped the blow and extended the light drill's beam at maximum power. He waved its ruby-red flame back and forth in front of Chua. "Keep away from me or I'll cut you to pieces!" Tona shouted.

Chua circled Tona with the wooden plank extended in front of him. "Your puny candle isn't much of a weapon, science boy."

He stopped with Metzi prone on the floor beside him and kicked her. She moaned, drawing Tona's attention, and Chua charged.

Before Chua reached Tona, the floor convulsed, knocking both men off their feet. The violent shaking continued for several seconds punctuated by more of Metzi's screams. When the quake stopped, both men warily got to their feet. Chua's wooden plank lay on the ground some distance away. His eyes darted around the room. "What was that?" Sweat glistened on his brow.

"The comet's getting closer," Tona shouted at him. "Its gravitational effect is pulling on our world." Never taking his eyes off Chua, Tona helped Metzi to her feet. "All of us have to leave before it's too late."

Another tremor struck, this one stronger than the first. A wooden beam fell from the ceiling and crashed to the floor. Chua ran to the door and saw two of his friends trotting toward the house. Both appeared shaken, one was covered with dirt with a gash dripping blood across his cheek. The other had a panicked expression and skinned hands and knees. "What's happening?" one of them shouted.

Chua spun in the doorway and pointed at Tona. "Your people are responsible for this. Your heresy has angered Asani."

"Don't be a fool," Tona said. "There's still time to escape."

Glaring at Tona, Chua called to his friends. "Let's feed this heretic to the fish."

Tona reactivated the light drill and waved it in front of him. The light from its beam turned the beads of sweat on Tona's brow to pearls of fiery red. "Stay back. I don't want to hurt you!"

Chua charged at Tona with his arms outstretched, reaching for his neck. Tona sidestepped again and brought the light drill's flame down on Chua's arm severing it. Chua's arm fell to the floor. Chua crumpled at Tona's feet cradling the stump, sitting in a spreading pool of his own blood.

Metzi ran to Chua and tried to staunch the bleeding with her hands. "Tona, do something or he'll bleed to death!" Chua's blood oozed between her fingers.

Tona wrenched the belt from his pants and wrapped it around Chua's arm forming a tourniquet. Chua screamed in agony when he pulled it tight. Tona looked up at Chua's friends. "He needs help!" Neither of them moved. "We need to get out of here," Tona said to Metzi.

She stared back at him, her eyes wide with fear. "We can't leave him here. He'll bleed to death!"

Tona saw the silhouettes of three men running toward them. One carried a torch. "We have to get out of here!" Tona said with more urgency. He recognized one of the men as a priest.

"Is anyone hurt in there?" the priest shouted as he came closer.

One of Chua's friends gestured frantically at Tona and yelled. "He's a heretic! He cut off Chua's arm." Several lights turned on in nearby dwellings.

Metzi ran past Tona, shouting at him as she passed. "Try to keep up." Three steps from the startled men, she veered into the dark picking up speed with each stride. As the men turned to follow Metzi, Tona sprinted past them, following her.

Pale and drenched in sweat, Chua staggered to the doorway cradling the stump of his arm. "The heretic who did this to me is the brat of one of the members of the Science Council. Metzi's with him. Don't let them get away!"

"Who is she?" the priest asked.

Chua swayed as if he would faint. One of the men caught him and eased him to the floor. He licked his lips. "Taru's daughter."

The priest's eyes widened. "You're sure that's who she is?"

"That's who she is," one of Chua's friends added.

The priest stood and spoke to the men gathered around them. By then, several more had arrived. "They can't get away," the priest said. "They're inside the compound somewhere and the gate's locked. When you find them, bring them both to the Temple. Make sure the girl is still alive."

Two blocks away, Tona pulled Metzi to a stop. "Isn't the main gate in the opposite direction?"

Metzi caught her breath. "The main gate is locked. I know another way out."

Tona saw bobbing lights in the darkness moving toward them. "They're gaining on us." Soon they could hear the sounds of men running.

"Follow me." Metzi ran fifty meters farther down the street and ducked into a dark alley between two buildings. She skidded to a stop in front of a large wooden barrel as tall as a man.

Tona joined her and looked around. The alley had only the one entrance, and he couldn't see any doors or window. "There's no way out here."

Metzi pulled the lid off the barrel. "Yes, there is. Get inside."

Tona gaped at her. "Hide in a barrel? That's the best you can do?"

"Get inside! I'll get in after you." She shoved him toward it.

Tona jumped up, grabbed the edge of the barrel, and pulled himself up. Before he could swing his legs around, Metzi shoved him forward. He tumbled down headfirst sliding down a rough, wet surface. "Whoa!" he shouted. As he fell, his voice trailed off becoming a distant wail.

Metzi saw flickers of light at the mouth of the alleyway, grabbed the top of the barrel, and pulled herself up. Before three men with torches burst into view, she jumped down into the dark.

Tona landed on hard-packed earth, tumbled, and came to rest in the dark. He took a rod from his pocket and shook it. Within seconds, the clear tube filled with pale green liquid that glowed with light. He started looking around as Metzi tumbled into him almost knocking him down. Tona helped Metzi to her feet and held the light stick high. They were standing on a platform inside a tunnel stretching into the dark in both directions with water flowing by. "Where are we?" Tona asked. His clothes were torn and wet, and his hands were scratched and raw.

"We're inside an ancient aqueduct." Metzi pointed into the dark. "There's another opening outside the gate in that direction."

They heard sounds above them and muffled shouts.

"They found the barrel," Metzi said.

"What if they take a ride down and find us?" Tona asked.

"If we hurry, they won't find us," Metzi replied. "It's a maze of tunnels down here and I know the way."

"Take this." Tona extended the light stick to her. The dim glow from it illuminated several meters in front of them. She stepped into the water and sank to her knees. "I forgot to tell you, it's freezing cold." She started forward.

Tona stepped into the water and immediately began to tremble. "You weren't kidding," he muttered.

After twenty meters of wading, they could see two branching tunnels ahead of them.

Metzi ran toward one of them with her boots splashing. "This way, then right, left, and right again."

"I'm not great with directions. Let me follow you!" Tona shouted to her.

"Then keep up!" Metzi's voice echoed along the stone tunnel.

* * *

The priest who had seen Metzi and Tona stood before the High Priest in the Temple's inner chambers and finished giving his report.

"What was the boy doing here?" the High Priest asked from his jeweled chair.

"Perhaps he was visiting his girlfriend," the priest replied.

The Chamberlain stood to the side of the High Priest. "How did he get into the compound?"

The priest looked down. "I don't know."

The High Priest rubbed his chin. "Perhaps there's another reason he's here, something more than simple carnal pleasure that causes our esteemed Science Council member's son to take such a considerable risk."

The Chamberlain spoke near the High Priest's ear. "Could he be a spy?"

"My thoughts exactly." The High Priest stood, towering over the priest. "Find them and bring them to me."

"Yes, Excellency." The priest kept his eyes averted as he backed away.

"I'll get the truth out of those brats," the Chamberlain sneered when the priest left the room.

"Don't be so sure we'll capture them. If the boy got into the compound without our guards noticing, he may have a similar way out." The High Priest straightened his robes. "We can't risk the Science Council learning our plans. Notify the key people. We begin tonight."

The Chamberlain's mind flashed to his friends and family. "Some of our passengers may not be ready to leave. In another day or two ..."

"Do as I say!" the High Priest commanded.

The Chamberlain looked down. "Of course, Excellency."

Chapter Twelve

The elevator tower swayed. Inside the viewing area, the walls rattled and groaned. When the tremor stopped, Etta let go of a support column and wiped his brow. "That was a bad one."

Ahotei let go of Tocho's chair. "They're getting worse."

"And more frequent." Tocho picked up a phone and began speaking.

Etta looked through the viewport towards the hangar. "The hangar looks all right, but the access tunnel has collapsed. We'll have to go on foot."

Tocho put down the phone. "The hangar reports only minor damage. Some cracks in the floor, but the discs are unharmed. One casualty from a falling piece of equipment, one of the pilots."

"Whose the backup?" Etta asked.

Tocho glanced at Ahotei. "Ruha." Etta 's eyes widened. Tocho put his hand on Ahotei's shoulder. "Steady old friend. Your granddaughter will be fine."

Ahotei pulled away. "As what, half robot, half computer?"

"I've been over every calculation a dozen times, Tocho began. He was interrupted by another strong tremor. This time a video monitor crashed to the floor and erupted in a shower of sparks.

Tocho glanced at the smoking monitor on the floor. "Ruha's the only other trained pilot we have, and there's no time to train another." He got to his feet. "If we're going to the hangar on foot, somebody help me suit up."

Tight-lipped, Ahotei moved to the locker containing the environmental suits.

Etta checked his wrist chronometer. "Tona should be here by now ... The elevator!" He ran to the elevator controls and verified that the car was on its way up. "It's okay," he said blowing out his breath. "The car's on its way up."

With help from Ahotei, Tocho zipped up his environmental

suit. "The elevator automatically stops if the sensors pick up any significant seismic event," Tocho said. "The system waits three minutes, and if nothing further happens, starts up again. We'll have Lando send Tona to us when he arrives." Tocho looked around the viewing area. "Where is Lando?"

"Must already be at the hangar working with the nav computers," Etta replied.

"That wasn't the plan," Tocho said. "He was supposed to remain here and wait for us." With Ahotei's help, he donned his helmet, leaving the faceplate open.

Etta picked up the phone. "I'll call the hangar and see if Lando's there."

"Stop wasting time," Ahotei growled. "We leave now." Already in his environmental suit with his helmet under his arm, Ahotei started for the airlock. "I want to say goodbye to my granddaughter while I can still talk to her."

* * *

The three men wearing silver environmental suits trekked across the ice following the lighted markers and the ruined structure of the tunnel. Ahotei kept his hand on Tocho's back helping him follow the uneven path. Halfway there another quake shook the ice field and Tocho fell. When the shaking stopped, he tried to right himself but couldn't in his bulky suit. Ahotei reached down for him but stopped when he felt a sudden sharp movement under his feet. He glanced around them, but nothing seemed different.

The same sharp movement occurred again, stronger this time, as if the ice were moving underneath them. Etta shouted and pointed. "I see a crack in the ice. It's propagating toward us."

Ahotei pulled Tocho to his feet and threw him over his shoulder.

"What are you doing?" Tocho protested. "I can walk."

"Not fast enough," Ahotei said. He started forward. Etta glanced once more at the crack, now ten meters away, and hurried after them.

They continued moving as fast as they could along the path. Ten strides from the hangar's airlock, they felt another jerking motion beneath their feet and everyone lost their balance. Before they could right themselves, the ice convulsed behind them forming a canyon half as wide as the hangar, leaving them on a narrow shelf next to the hangar wall. Sheets of ice fell into the newly formed crevasse. Behind them, the ruined access tunnel suspended over the abyss broke in half and dropped out of sight.

Another quake struck increasing the volume of the avalanche of ice falling into the crevasse. The chasm's jagged edge moved closer to them, shrinking their narrow perch outside the hangar to less than three meters wide.

"If the hangar goes down, it's over!" Etta shouted.

"It's anchored in the bedrock," Tocho shouted back. "We'll be safe if we can get inside!"

With Tocho over his shoulder, Ahotei reached the airlock door and activated the controls. The door opened and he threw Tocho inside. They felt another strong tremor and Ahotei grabbed Etta's arm and jumped inside. From the floor of the airlock, Ahotei turned and saw an explosion of ice crystals, some of them as long as his legs, blowing toward them. He managed to slam the airlock shut before they impacted the hangar and shattered.

The three men lay on the airlock floor with their chests heaving, covered in white powder and crystals of ice. Several technicians rushed through the inner airlock door and ran to them. Ahotei helped Tocho to his feet shouting, "Has the disc launched?"

"Not yet," one of the technicians replied.

Ahotei ripped off his helmet and charged through the inner door.

* * *

Still wearing the silver coverall of his suit, Ahotei entered the hanger's medical facility and eased past the forest of intravenous tubing surrounding Ruha. He took her hand.

"Hey, Pops, glad you could make it," Ruha said, forcing a smile. "Looks like I get the honor of the first ride."

Ahotei steadied his emotions by moving his eyes around the circular room lined with computers. One unit stood in stark contrast to the rest, a squat silver box with a single screen flashing numbers and symbols at an incompressible rate. He glowered at it and turned back to Ruha. "Give someone else the honor."

Ruha sighed. "There isn't anybody else, and we're out of time. You felt the quakes." She lowered her voice. "If this doesn't work we'll all be dead soon enough."

A white-robed and masked technician moved closer to Ruha's bed. "It's time."

Ruha let go of her grandfather's hand and patted it.

"Do you want me to stay with you?" Ahotei wiped a tear from the corner of her eye.

She forced another smile. "No, but I want you here when I wake up as me again."

Ahotei kissed her forehead and left the room. When the door closed with a soft hiss behind him, he slumped against the wall.

* * *

Ahotei entered the hangar's control center, a large semi-circular room with rows of equipment manned by uniformed technicians, all bent to their work. The rows of workstations faced a line of tall windows overlooking the hangar floor and three silver discs. A digital clock with thick red numerals centered above the windows counted down the seconds and read T minus 0.9:34:19. Ahotei saw Tocho standing in the center of a row, but ignored him and walked slowly to the viewing window. On the way, the floor trembled slightly beneath his feet and the chaos of voices in the command center quieted. They resumed again when the shaking stopped.

Ahotei leaned against the window and saw a floor-level airlock door open, spilling blinking colored lights onto the hangar floor. He watched tight-lipped as a silver form moved onto the hangar floor flanked by several technicians. It had a vaguely humanoid form with two arms and legs without discernable joints, and a flat-screen monitor where a head should have been, the source of the blinking colored lights. The pattern of lights kept changing from a field of blue to an ever-changing kaleidoscope of colors and patterns. Even though it had legs, at least in the generic sense, the silver anthropomorphic entity moved with a fluidic motion, seeming to glide from point to point.

Ahotei felt Tocho's hand on his shoulder. "She'll be all right," Tocho said. Ahotei whispered back, "Too late. She's already dead."

The silver robot stopped its forward motion. For a moment its flat screen head rotated and tilted up toward Ahotei looking down from the viewing windows. Ahotei saw the lights on its flat screen head change to a uniform indigo and his heart skipped a beat. The moment passed and the silver being's face pivoted again to face the direction of its torso. It resumed its forward motion and ascended the ramp into the disc followed by the two technicians.

"She's not dead," Tocho said. "Her body's in cryogenic stasis waiting for her."

"Where's the other one?" Ahotei rasped through dry lips.

"You mean the co-pilot, Tia? He's already on board."

They watched the two technicians descend the ramp and leave the hanger, closing the airlock door behind them. The wheel on the door spun, locking it, and the hangar lights dimmed leaving three silver discs gleaming in the darkness, one with an incandescent band of blue around its waist.

The pace of activity in the control room increased to a fever pitch. After checking his computer screen, a technician ran to another man and began barking orders. As the countdown clock dropped below T minus two minutes, a large video screen descended from the ceiling above the windows showing a live feed from the hangar floor centered on the glowing disc. Lines of text and numbers flowed by at the base of the screen.

Tocho's amplified voice filled the control center. "Are the new navigational codes ready to load?"

The control center quieted. "

"Yes," one of the technicians answered.

"Did you triple check?" Tocho demanded.

"Yes. Everything looks nominal."

Ahotei joined Tocho. "I don't see our computer expert, Lando."

Tocho quickly conferred with one of the technicians who hurried away. Tocho frowned. "He isn't here, and he didn't call in."

"He's our chief programmer," Ahotei said with alarm. "We should abort!"

Tocho glanced at the countdown clock. "Too late for that." The count down clock read T minus 1:46:11 "Don't worry. Every position has a backup, even mine." Tocho took the Sphere from his pocket and placed it in a cradle on top of a squat silver box in front of him, the navigational computer controlled by the Sphere. Made from the same silver material as the discs, the nav computer had a single screen, so far dark, and no other discernible controls. The orb appeared lifeless, black and opaque. Tocho removed a data storage device in the shape of a writing implement from a different pocket.

Ahotei glanced at the Sphere. "How long has it been like that?"

"Ever since we began working on an alternate programming

sequence for the disc," Tocho replied.

"You think it knows we're tricking it?"

Tocho stared at the Sphere. "It doesn't know anything. It's just a storage device ... At least in theory."

Ahotei glanced at him. "What if you're wrong? What if the Nexus knows what we're doing and tries to stop us?"

Tocho sighed. "You know the alternatives as well as I do."

Ahotei's face reddened. "Ruha finishes her life inside a silver prison on an alien world, or if she's lucky, the disc is destroyed."

Tocho held up the data storage device. "Pray we've done everything right."

Ahotei turned away. "I don't pray."

At T minus 0:00:00 Tocho reached forward and inserted the data storage device into a slot that appeared in the face of the silver box. Immediately after, the nav computer's screen erupted with columns of numbers and symbols moving too quickly to comprehend. Tocho stepped back. "It's begun."

Chapter Thirteen

The control room lights dimmed and all eyes faced the viewing windows. No one spoke. Ahotei walked back to the central glass window and looked down. Below him, the ramp from the glowing disc withdrew into the disc's substance and the opening disappeared without a trace.

"Hangar baffles are coming up," one of the technicians announced over the loudspeaker. Metal walls rose from the hangar floor, dividing it into three equal parts, one for each disc.

Tocho turned to a nearby technician. "Depressurize bay One." The technician pumped the oxygen from the glowing disc's bay, equilibrating the pressure inside with the vacuum of space.

They heard a voice over the loudspeaker: "Hangar doors on bay One opening in three ... two ... one." The hangar doors opened behind the glowing disc, exposing the brooding face of the planet Jupiter.

Huddled with several of the technicians, Tocho watched the nav computer's screen. "The command sequences are loading and the disc is powering up." He looked up. "So far, so good."

Below, on the hangar floor, the light emanating from the disc intensified, forcing everyone to don protective glasses. "Fifty percent ... eighty percent ... full power!" the technician monitoring the disc's energy level shouted.

Cheers erupted in the control room.

"Launch in three ... two ... one!" Tocho shouted.

The disc rose in the air, hovered, and moved smoothly out the hangar doors. Ahotei closed his eyes. The light from the disc pulsed, becoming blinding, and it accelerated away. Within seconds it became a glowing dot dimly visible beside Jupiter's disc. Then it disappeared.

The empty hangar's doors closed and the control room resumed standard lighting. Every pair of eyes focused on the video monitor showing a forward view from the disc. The monitor displayed a dazzling field of stars racing behind the disc appearing as multi-colored streaks of light.

"My God," Tocho murmured, then he bent to follow numbers scrolling across the nav computer's screen.

Ahotei left the viewing windows and stood beside Tocho. "When will we know?"

Tocho straightened. "The new programming instructs the disc to travel to the orbit of our system's last gas giant and then return. If all goes well, the disc should be outside the hangar again in one hour." Tocho glanced at his wrist chronometer. "Fifty-two minutes to be exact." He spoke into a microphone. "Position report."

"Flight telemetry nominal. The disc is on course at the anticipated velocity."

"Pilot and copilot are sending expected telemetry," another technician called out.

Ahotei glanced at Tocho. "Can we talk to them?"

Tocho sighed. "We can, but are you sure you want to?"

Ahotei glanced at the video feed. "Call her."

Tocho donned a headset and positioned the microphone near his lips. He activated a control on the command console and spoke. "Ruha, this is command, do you read?"

A strange voice came through the main speaker over the viewing window. "Yes." Ahotei stiffened.

Tocho licked his lips and glanced at Ahotei before speaking again. "Report your flight status."

"The disc is operating at 99.998 percent of nominal specifications," the voice replied. "Do you require more information?"

"Not at this time," Tocho replied. He turned to Ahotei. "Do you want to talk to her?"

"It's not my granddaughter anymore." Ahotei left the Control Room.

Tocho leaned back in his chair and rubbed his nose.

One of the technicians wearing a mobile headset joined him. "Reports coming in from the city. It's pretty bad down there. A few buildings have collapsed and there are casualties."

"Is the city's force field holding?" Tocho asked.

"So far."

Tocho glanced at his wrist chronometer, and then at the digital clock. Fifty minutes until the disc's return.

Forty-three minutes later.

The alternate navigational programmer sitting next to Tocho leaned closer to him and turned off his microphone. "Still no word from Lando. Where is he?"

"Doesn't matter now," Tocho replied. "They're almost at the turning point." He glanced up at the digital clock. It read R minus 6:23:56. "We'll know in less than seven minutes if our program has taken over." Tocho studied the nav computer's screen, saw the expected lines of navigational codes that his people had inserted, and activated his microphone. "Ruha, respond."

"Specify the response that you require," the voice in his headset replied.

"How do you feel?" Tocho asked.

"This unit does not feel."

Tight lipped, Tocho leaned back in his chair. "Report your position and velocity."

"The disc's velocity is one hundred thousand two hundred and two meters per minute. Its position is two hundred thirty thousand nine hundred twenty-two meters from the gas giant designated, Planet Eight."

"Thank you," Tocho said. He received no reply. Stony-faced, he glanced at the Sphere. Unlike moments before, it now glowed with bright, yellow light that pulsated in uneven patterns. He picked it up. "So you've woken up. Can't say I like the timing."

He put the Sphere back in his pocket.

"Two minutes to the return phase," the flight technician called out.

Tocho switched channels and spoke into the microphone of his headset. "Find Ahotei." He didn't see Ahotei walking up behind him.

"I saw the Sphere," Ahotei said. "The damn thing knows what we're doing."

No one spoke as the mission chronometer counted down the last few seconds before the disc reached the orbit of Neptune.

The flight technician's voice boomed throughout the command center. "Half-way point in five ... four ... three ... two ... one..." He bent closer to his monitor. "Same velocity, no wait ..." He looked back at Tocho. It's increasing velocity, same vector."

"What's happening?" Ahotei demanded.

Tocho watched the colored streaks on the monitor race by, now even faster than before. "The disc isn't turning around."

"Do something. Bring it back!" Ahotei shouted.

Tocho turned in his chair. "We don't know how." He activated his microphone. "Ruha, can you hear us?"

"Yes."

"Can you take control of the disc and return home?"

"I am permitted to say ... goodbye."

"Say again, Ruha?"

They heard only static.

Ahotei ripped the headset from Tocho and yelled into it. "Ruha!"

Chapter Fourteen

The elevator doors opened after a tense elevator ride down to the city. Ahotei refused to speak to anyone and stormed out into the foyer just as another violent tremor struck. He struggled to remain standing. The ceiling cracked and a conduit spraying sparks fell to the ground. The severed end of the conduit writhed and undulated in front of him like a demon breathing fire. Ahotei retreated back into the elevator. "Close the doors," he said never taking his eyes from it.

Etta saw the sparking cable gyrating in the foyer and stabbed at the door control button. The doors remained open. He tried again with the same result. "They won't close!" Etta exclaimed. "The quake must have damaged the controls." Ahotei pushed everyone to the back of the elevator.

Another tremor struck and a band of ceiling lights crashed to the floor exploding in a plume of sparks and glass. This time the shaking continued, rising to a crescendo of violence over a span of twenty seconds before stopping. A sharp aftershock followed five seconds later and the elevator shaft with the car inside tilted thirty degrees, throwing the occupants in a jumble on top of each other. Immediately after, the power failed.

"That should kill the damn cable," Ahotei said. He clawed his way to the elevator doors, and looked out into pitch black. The severed cable, still hot enough to cast a soft, red glow, lay motionless on the floor. The overhead lights flickered on and resumed at one-half normal intensity as the emergency lighting came on. He pulled himself free from the elevator and stood surveying the damage. "We need to get out of here," he said. He returned to the car and pulled Tocho out. Etta followed, with a split lower lip oozing blood. He wiped it with his hand, smearing a red streak across his shirt. When Tocho seemed steady on his feet, they ran through the complex's ruined front door to a scene of devastation.

Etta saw Tona and Metzi running toward them. He embraced his son when they arrived. "I was worried when you didn't come to the surface. What happened?" Etta asked.

Ahotei pushed closer to Metzi. "Who's the girl?"

"Taru's daughter, Metzi," Tona replied.

"I've seen him at the Joint Council meetings," Tocho said. "He's on the Sect's High Council."

Ahotei glared at Tona. "Is this your idea of keeping your mouth shut?"

Tona fired back. "If you listen to me, I'll tell you why we're here. It's damned important!"

"Go ahead," Tocho said.

Tona looked at Metzi. "Tell them."

Metzi's lips trembled. "The High Priest is planning to steal the flying discs so some of his people can escape."

Ahotei's face erupted with rage. "I'll kill that bastard!"

Tocho glanced at Etta. "Think carefully, young lady. Are you sure?"

"She's telling the truth," Tona exclaimed. "I went to the compound and she helped me to escape."

Etta looked dumbfounded. "You were inside the Sect's compound?"

"I went there so Metzi and I could convince her people to leave. We were too late. They're stealing the flying discs and leaving without us."

Tocho shook his head. "Damn! I should have seen this coming."

"How?" Ahotei demanded. "They can't just walk in and take them."

"I don't know," Metzi replied with tears in her eyes.

Tocho's mind raced. "Are any of the ground cars still working?"

Tona pointed to a car parked fifty meters away. "The one we

came in. Some of the streets are blocked by debris, but we can still get around."

"We'll go to the hangar and stop them," Ahotei said.

They felt another tremor but it stopped after a few seconds.

"No, we're going to the Joint Council chambers in the marketplace to try to reason with them," Tocho said.

"Talk to them about what?" Ahotei raged. "If these brats are right, the Sect's planning to maroon everyone and let the comet finish us off."

"They don't know the technology nearly as well as we do," Etta said. "I don't like it either, but maybe we can reason with them."

Ahotei scowled. "All right, but if we don't like what we hear in ten seconds – we do it my way."

* * *

The car raced past several damaged buildings skirting piles of rubble on the way to the Joint Council Building. They found the two-story building partially collapsed. Tona jumped out of the car and ran to a man digging through the rubble. "Was anyone inside?" The others joined him.

The man looked up with a sweat-soaked face, eyes glazed. He leaned on his shovel. "The Council was in session. A few of them got out, not many." He pointed toward a man and a woman lying on the ground in the shade of an outbuilding several meters away. "There's two of them." Though appearing in a state of shock, he resumed digging. Tona and Ahotei ran to the man and woman on the ground. Tocho caught up with them and knelt beside the woman. "Lea?"

Science Council member Lea licked her lips. "Tocho?"

"It's me, we'll get help."

"How's my husband?" Lea asked.

Tona felt for the man's pulse, looked up and shook his head.

"Don't worry, Lea. We'll get help. Have you seen any of the Sect's representatives since it happened?"

She wet her lips with her tongue. "Only one of them was here, and he left early in the day and wasn't replaced. We couldn't vote without a Sect representative, so we called their compound. They wouldn't answer our calls."

Tocho looked up at Ahotei. "The children may be right." After placing his coat over Lea, he moved to the side and spoke with Ahotei,

"We have two discs left, and they're the only way off this rock," Ahotei said. "We need to get back to the hangar, now!"

Tocho glanced at his wrist chronometer. "If nothing's changed about the comet's trajectory, I'd estimate two cycles before it hits."

Ahotei started back to the car. "Get in!" he shouted.

Etta sat in the driver's seat. When they were all inside, he turned to Ahotei. "Where?"

Ahotei stared straight ahead, stony faced. "To the elevator complex, as fast as you can."

Etta piloted the car toward the elevator complex, traveling as fast as he dared. They dodged debris raining down from damaged buildings and swerved around piles of rubble. After a prolonged tremor that shook the roadway, he almost lost control but managed to stop before the car impacted a tangle of metal and mangled building stones.

Above them, the city's force field began to flicker. For a moment it plunged them into darkness, before the force field resumed.

Tocho leaned out the window. "It should be brighter. Something's wrong with the power grid."

Ahotei gripped Etta's shoulder. "Drive!"

The car lurched forward.

"What happens if the force field fails?" Metzi asked.

Tona took Metz's hand. "It won't."

"None of us will have to worry about the comet," Ahotei growled.

They passed a group of people running towards the elevator complex. Metzi spun in her seat to look at them. "Those are people from the compound. Two of them are members of the Lord High Chamberlain's family."

"Are you sure?" Tocho asked.

"I've seen one of the men at our house. I'm sure he's a priest, but he's not wearing his robes."

"Should I stop so we can question them?" Etta asked.

"No," Ahotei snapped. "Keep driving."

After several more tremors that further weakened the city's force field, they arrived at the entrance to the elevator complex. Before Etta could stop the car, they heard a popping sound and the front window shattered. Etta jammed on the breaks. "What was that?" They heard more popping sounds and something impacted the front of the car leaving a crease in the metal. A second later, two patches of the wall of a nearby building exploded with puffs of shattered stone.

"Those are projectile weapons. They're shooting at us!" Ahotei pounded on Etta's shoulder. "Back up!" Etta put the car in reverse and spun the wheels sending them rocketing backward. One hundred meters from the building, he spun the wheel and accelerated forward. Behind a ruined building blocking them from the elevator complex, he stopped the car.

"I thought the Sect renounced weapons," Etta exclaimed.

Ahotei looked out the shattered windshield. "Trustworthy, aren't they?"

Metzi sobbed against Tona's chest. He used his free arm to brush shards of glass off her dress.

"We need the elevator to get to the hangar," Tocho said.

Tona leaned forward. "How do we get there?"

Ahotei thought for a moment. "Isn't there another elevator shaft that's no longer in use?"

"The construction access tunnel," Etta replied. "We closed it up when the complex was completed."

"Do you think the Sect knows about it?" Ahotei asked.

"Why would they?" Etta replied. "They don't go to the surface."

"Where is it?"

"Behind the main complex. There's a metal cover at ground level, but the power's been out for a long time. I can't guarantee it still works."

"It has a ladder, doesn't it?" Ahotei asked.

"Yes, but it would take days to climb up," Etta replied.

Ahotei sat back in his seat. "We're not climbing all the way. Drive there, but circle back and come from the opposite direction. I want them to think we've given up."

* * *

Etta stopped the car behind a house to the rear of the elevator complex. Everyone got out. Ahotei pointed at Tona. "You're going with me. Everybody else stays here."

"I'll go," Etta said. "I know the elevator's construction as well as anybody."

"I don't need an engineer, and you'll slow me down."

"You're twice as old as me," Etta scoffed.

Ahotei pushed close to Etta with rage in his eyes. "And ten times as mad. Do as I say!"

Etta stepped back and glanced at his son.

Ahotei pointed at Etta. "There's a series of bridging tunnels between the two elevator shafts. Am I right?"

"That's right," Etta said. He licked his lips. "We used them during the construction."

"Did they do any digging under the main lobby?" Ahotei asked.

"Yes. There are three basement levels. That's where all the

elevator equipment is."

"That should work." Ahotei cracked his knuckles.

"What's your plan?" Tocho asked.

"The brat and I will go down the old tunnel, cut across at a level below the main lobby, and come up behind them."

"What if they have weapons?" Etta asked with concern.

"I'll think of something." Ahotei grabbed Tona's arm. "Let's go."

Tona pulled three light sticks from his pocket. "If it's dark down there, these might come in handy."

* * *

Ahotei pulled the metal cover closed, blocking out the light, and looked down the dark elevator shaft. He could just make out Tona clinging to a rung one body length below him. "Hey, brat, light one of your sticks."

Tona let go of the ladder with one hand and reached into his pocket. He pulled out one of the light sticks, but another fell from his pocket striking one of the metal ladder rungs below with a loud clang. "I lost one!" he shouted up to Ahotei.

"Try not to drop another. They could come in handy," Ahotei called down to him.

Tona shook the light stick causing it to glow with pale green light sufficient for him to see the area around him. He was inside a shaft of corroded metal held together by rivets rusting from the seepage of groundwater. "This shaft is in bad shape," he called up to Ahotei.

Ahotei saw the light stick's glow below him. "Start down the ladder until you see an access door across from you."

"Okay." Controlling his anxiety, Tona gripped the light stick with his teeth, slipped one of his arms inside the ladder, and reached down with his foot to the ladder rung below. When he added his weight to it, the rusted metal of the rung gave way leaving him dangling. Before he could pull himself up, he felt Ahotei lift him by the tunic.

"Test the next rung. I'll keep hold of you," he said.

Tona felt the rung below with his foot and pushed on it. The rung held his weight. He looked up with the light stick in his mouth and nodded.

"Put your weight on it and test the next one. I won't let go of you. We keep doing it, going down until you see the access door."

Tona nodded again.

They worked their way down until Tona saw the access door. By then, the light stick was dimming. "Light another stick," Ahotei called to him. "We'll continue down three more rungs until I'm on the level of the access door. Do you understand?"

Tona spit out the dead light stick and shook his remaining one causing it to glow. "I get it," he replied. He put the new light stick between his teeth and they repeated the same descent process for several more ladder rungs until Ahote's body was in position.

Ahotei leaned across and examined the access door. The metal appeared badly corroded, with a rusted locking wheel in the center of it. He leaned closer and saw that the wheel's mechanism was covered with clumps of dull-grey metal. "Let's hope the damn thing will open," he muttered.

"Did you say something?" Tona called to him.

"No!" Ahotei let go of the ladder with one hand, took a deep breath, and, after releasing his other arm, launched himself across the shaft toward the access door. He managed to grab the locking wheel before falling and hung from it. After another deep breath, he pulled himself up and managed to wedge his feet on a bar of metal at the base of the door. With his feet locked in place, he tried turning the wheel with his free hand. The metal groaned but refused to yield. He called down to Tona. "Pass me up the light stick." When Tona lifted it to him, Ahotei put the glowing cylinder between his teeth and let go of the ladder, suspending himself with both hands from the rusted metal wheel.

Tona looked up. "You'll fall!"

Ahotei's ragged breath whistled around the light stick jutting from his mouth as he wrenched the wheel using all his strength. It began to turn. He pushed harder, and with the sound of tortured metal, the door pivoted inward. He swung inside the main elevator shaft, took the light stick from his mouth, and raised it outside the doorway. "Get up here," he called down to Tona, and then he jumped inside.

Tona climbed up the ladder and leaped onto a landing inside the main elevator shaft just large enough to hold four men. He saw Ahotei point with the faint glow of the light stick at another ladder across from them.

"We take that one up," Ahotei said lowering his voice. "It should end right below the main level of the complex." The light stick went out. Ahotei sighed. "And we do it in the dark." He started for the ladder.

Chapter Fifteen

They crouched on the ground-level landing of the main elevator shaft in the dark. "When I open the door, we'll only have a second or two of surprise to take them out," Ahotei whispered.

"We don't know how many of them there are," Tona whispered back.

"Doesn't matter." Ahotei got to his feet and gripped the wheel that opened the access door.

Tona glanced at him. "Why not?"

"I'll explain later."

Tona processed that for a moment. "Okay, what do I do?"

"You'll know when the time comes." Ahotei spun the wheel and pulled the door open. It slammed against the wall with a loud clang startling two priests standing nearby with guns. They spun toward Ahotei. Before they could raise their weapons, Ahotei had ripped away their guns and sent the black-robed men sprawling to the floor. He stood over them and crushed both weapons with his bare hands.

Shocked, the men looked up at him. "What are you going to do to us?" one of the priests asked.

Ahotei tossed their ruined weapons to the floor. "That depends on you." He kneeled close to them. Both priests shrank back. "We know your band of shamans and bigots is planning something nasty with the flying discs," Ahotei began. "Tell me what it is, and I'll let you live."

The same priest who'd spoken swallowed hard and answered. "They told us to guard the elevator, to make sure nobody goes down. That's all we know."

Ahotei lashed out with his fist, striking the priest's jaw, sending blood spattering on the wall. The man fell unconscious to the floor. Watching from behind the door, Tona flinched and looked away. The second priest began to sob. "Please … I'll tell you everything I know. Don't kill me!"

"Five seconds." Ahotei raised his fist.

"They're stealing the discs!" The priest covered his head and shook.

"Four seconds. Who is?" Ahotei demanded.

"The High Priest! And the Chamberlain."

Ahotei raised his fist higher as if to strike. "Three seconds. To do what? How many of them are in the hangar?"

"Thirty people, maybe more. I don't know what they're going to do!"

"Two seconds!"

"They're using the discs to escape the comet!" The priest sobbed. "I swear, that's all I know."

Ahotei glanced at Tona's pale and sweating face peeking from the doorway, then he whirled and struck the priest on the side of the head sending him unconscious to the floor. Ahotei got back to his feet.

"Did you have to do that?" Tona asked through clenched teeth.

"He'll die anyway," Ahotei answered. "We all will unless we can stop them." He opened the access door to the elevator lobby and walked through.

Tona sidestepped the two unconscious priests and ran after him. He found Ahotei unlocking the front door to let the others in. Tocho came through first. Ahotei quickly told him the Sect's plan. Tocho listened and shook his head. Etta came through next, followed by Metzi who ran into Tona's arms.

Stony-faced, Tocho addressed everyone. "We have to get to the hangar and stop them from stealing the discs."

"The emergency lights are on," Etta said. "If the main power is off, the elevator is offline."

Tocho moved quickly to an access panel, grabbed a protruding handle, and yanked the panel from the wall. The metal yielded with a loud crunching sound.

"He's an old man," Metzi whispered to Tona. "How did he do that?"

"He has good hearing, too," Ahotei smirked, "for an old man."

Etta watched Tocho reach inside the panel. "They were both enhanced a long time ago by the Nexus. They're the only ones."

Tocho pulled out a couple of wires, stripped their insulation with his fingernail, and crossed them. Sparks erupted around his hands and electricity surged through his body.

"Tocho!" Tona exclaimed. Ahotei held him back. "He knows what he's doing."

"There's a backup generator for the main power grid," Tocho said speaking through clenched teeth while his body trembled. "Hasn't been used for a long time."

"Let go!" Tona shouted.

Tocho's hands began to shake and everyone smelled the odor of burnt flesh. "If I'm doing this right, I'm rebooting the power grid so the backups can take over." The lights went on and the room filled with the whir of computer fans coming on. Tocho dropped the wires and stepped back. He held up his singed hands. "That was very unpleasant." He moved to the elevator controls and pulled on the lever. The doors opened revealing the lights on inside. "Get in everyone."

When they were all inside, Etta closed the door and sent the elevator to the surface. "We don't know how many priests with guns are up there, and there's only four of us."

"Five," Metzi said.

Etta smiled at her. "All right, five."

Ahotei cracked his knuckles. "One of the priests we subdued said there are thirty of them in the hangar, maybe more."

"Too many of them," Tocho said.

"Maybe not," Ahotei said. "Stop the elevator."

"Why?" Etta asked.

Ahotei faced him. "So we can send the two brats down first."

"No!" Etta exclaimed.

Ahotei ignored Etta and spoke to Tocho. "We need a diversion. The traitors down there won't find two kids threatening. They'll be happy to capture them. That buys the three of us enough time to get down there and surprise them." Ahotei turned to Tona. "You'll need to come up with a way to draw their attention away from the elevator and buy us enough time to bring it up and take us down. Can you do that?"

Tona glanced at Metzi and she nodded. "Yes," he replied.

"This is absurd. They're children," Etta said.

"No we're not," Metzi said. "Besides, if we don't try, we're all dead anyway."

Etta looked away.

Tocho halted the elevator and sent it back down to the lobby. When it stopped and the doors opened, Tona hugged his father and gestured for him to leave. "We don't have a lot of time."

Tocho and Ahotei left the elevator together. "Good luck," Tocho said as he passed. Etta met his son's eyes, and then he, too, left the car. He saw Tona and Metzi with their arms about each other as the doors closed.

* * *

The three men watched the elevator control screen as the car rose to Level One, the hangar level.

At Level Twenty, Tona took Metzi's hand. "We can do this."

She looked back at him. "I know."

They passed Level Three.

"Get ready," Tona said.

The doors opened on Level One and they looked out.

"There's nobody here," Metzi whispered.

Tona stepped out. The lights were on, but the complex appeared deserted. "I'll send down the elevator." He went to the control console and sent the elevator back to the city.

"Let's look around," Metzi said. They went in opposite directions along the viewing area's balcony. After a minute, she called to him. "Tona, over here."

He ran to her and found her kneeling beside a man curled up on the floor. He was bound and gagged with his eyes covered. Tona helped Metzi release him.

The man blinked his eyes to focus and looked back at them.

"Who are you, and who did this to you?" Tona asked.

"My name's Lando. The priests did this to me."

"Why?" Metzi asked.

Lando turned away, refusing to talk.

Metzi brought him a cup of water. "I'm Metzi, and he's Tona. Tell us what happened so we can help you."

Lando stared back at them with a cruel twist to his lips. "You can't help me. It's too late."

They took a few steps away from him. "What do we do?" Metzi asked in hushed tones.

Tona looked back at Lando still lying on the floor. "Wait for reinforcements. We can't create a diversion if there's nobody here."

Forty minutes later, the elevator doors opened and Ahotei ran out yelling at the top of his lungs with his hands balled into fists. When he realized the elevator complex was empty, he stopped yelling and lowered his fists.

Tocho and Etta stepped out of the elevator car behind him. They looked around and heard Tona shouting, "Over here!"

They ran to him. Tocho looked down at Lando who was seated with his back against the wall. "What are you doing here?" he asked.

Lando turned away without answering.

Ahotei sneered. "Looks like our Chief Navigational Programmer finally showed up for work." He kneeled next to Lando. "Bet I can make you talk."

"Wait," Tocho said. He too knelt beside Lando. "We all want

the same thing, to use the two remaining discs to evacuate before the comet strikes. Tell us what you know and maybe we can all survive."

Lando's voice quavered. "They promised they'd take me with them if I helped."

Tocho glanced at Ahotei. "Help do what?"

Lando's lips trembled. "Reprogram the flight controls."

Ahotei's eyes bulged with rage. He reached for Lando's throat. "Tell me you didn't sabotage the first disc and murder my granddaughter," he shouted.

Lando struggled. "I had nothing to do with that!"

Ahotei squeezed Lando's throat and he struggled to breathe. "You're lying!"

Tocho pulled Ahotei's hands away. "Killing him won't do us any good. Our only chance is to get to the hangar and stop them."

Ahotei released Lando and stood over him. "You're going to die, one way or another."

Tocho looked down at Lando who was coughing as he regained his breath. "What is their destination?"

"The fourth planet," Lando gasped.

"Why?" Tocho asked. "There's nothing there, no water, no vegetation ..."

Lando looked away. "There are humanoids living in caves with water in the deep canyons, out of sight."

Tocho gasped. "Unbelievable. How did we miss it?"

Lando licked his lips. "I diverted the telescope feeds."

"You bastard!" Ahotei shouted. He lunged at Lando, but Tocho pushed his hands away.

"Don't be a fool," Tocho said to his friend. He knows the nav computers better than anyone." Tocho turned back to Lando. "You sabotaged your own people. Why?"

"Your way is for us to give up our bodies, to become unfeeling computers!" Lando began to shake. "I'd rather die."

"That can be arranged," Ahotei snarled.

Etta returned from a tour of the viewing windows. "The access tunnel's been destroyed. We'll have to go on foot."

"Tocho, stay here with the girl," Ahotei glared at Lando, "and with him. I'll go with Etta and the boy. We'll come back for you when it's over."

"I have a better idea," Etta said. "There's a ground car on the ice level in a garage with a separate airlock. If we can get it started, we can all go and get there faster."

"Let's go," Tocho said.

Ahotei pointed at Lando. "He stays here."

"We'll need him to reprogram the discs' nav computers when we get there," Tocho said.

"What makes you think that bastard won't sabotage us again?"

Tocho looked at Lando. "Because we're his only hope of staying alive."

Lando got to his feet.

Etta pointed toward a narrow corridor in the back of the elevator lobby. "The airlock to the garage is down that corridor."

* * *

They passed through the airlock wearing environmental suits and entered the garage housing an ice rider. Etta climbed up a metal ladder on the rear of the wheeled vehicle resting on six large tires and opened the car's rear door. He worked his way forward to the command seat, the first of three rows of seats, and flipped a switch. The lights inside the vehicle went on and several gauges lit. He called to the others. "Get inside and I'll seal the door."

Ahotei moved to the front and sat next to him. "Damn cold in here, even in this suit."

"The heat's on. Give it a few moments." Etta looked back,

saw everyone seated, and flipped another switch on the console, opening the garage door. It lifted without a sound in the vacuum, exposing a backdrop of space dominated by Jupiter. "Everybody buckle up," Etta said over their suits' comlinks.

Etta activated the ice rider's drive controls and it backed out of the garage. When they were far enough away, he used a joystick to turn toward the hangar complex, a dark silhouette in the distance. As the car picked up speed, he increased the vehicle's lights to their maximum intensity illuminating the stark landscape. The undulating expanse of ice ahead reflected back the light threatening to dazzle them. "You'll find goggles for the glare underneath your seats," Etta announced.

After bouncing three hundred meters over the rough terrain toward the hangar, Etta slowed the ice rider. He pointed at a band of black crossing their route. "What's that?"

Sitting behind Ahotei in the second row of seats, Tocho leaned forward. "Most likely a crevasse caused by one of the quakes. Move parallel to it until we find a safe way across."

Etta turned to their right and drove parallel to the band of black at reduced speed. Each meter took them farther off course. After another three hundred meters or so, the crevasse disappeared and Etta stopped. "I don't see anything ahead of us. Should I turn back toward the hangar?"

"What kind of scanners do we have?" Tocho asked.

"Sonic, to test the depth of the ice, and limited forward video," Etta replied.

"They'll have to do," Tocho said. "Activate the scanners and head back toward the hangar. But go slow so we can see far enough ahead to avoid falling into another crevasse."

"Do you have any flares?" Tona asked from the rear. He was seated next to Metzi in the third row of seats.

"Good idea," Etta said. He punched a control button and a streak of light shot upwards. They watched it rise into the blackness and explode with a burst of blinding light. When their eyes recovered from the glare, they saw a ball of flame drift slowly down in Europa's nil gravity, dimming as it fell and disappeared.

Ahotei leaned forward and pointed. "There! Another ditch, right in front of us."

Etta put the ice rider into reverse and increased power. After three meters of travel, a tremor hit, followed by several more in succession with only seconds in between. They felt the ice rider shudder. Its front tipped by several degrees and began to slip forward. Etta jammed on the brakes, but the ice rider continued slipping forward. "The brakes aren't holding!" he shouted. Another tremor hit and the nose of the vehicle dropped further. The wheels continued to slip, carrying them forward.

Pull us back, you fool," Ahotei said.

"I'm trying!" Etta exclaimed. He added power and the slippage stopped until friction from the driving wheels heated the ice forming a coating of water beneath the tires. This caused the wheels to lose traction again. The ice rider lurched forward and came to rest a few meters from the edge of an abyss.

They could feel the car continuing to tilt forward. "Everyone into the back!" Tocho shouted.

While the others scrambled toward him to make the car heavier in the rear, Tona leaned over the back seat and rummaged in the cargo compartment. He found a winch attached to a grappling hook and two handheld radios. "Thought there might be one of these," he muttered. He held up the hook and yelled. "I found a winch! I can use it to pull us out!"

"What do you want me to do?" Etta yelled.

"When I release the brake on the winch, open the rear door so I can jump out. As soon as I'm clear, fire a flare." Tona released the winch's brake and knelt near the rear door holding the hook and several loops of cable.

"What are you doing?" Metzi screamed.

"Saving our lives," Tona replied. He shouted, "Open the

door!"

Etta reached forward and activated the control raising the rear door. When it rose high enough for him to jump out, Tona yelled, "Fire another flare!" and jumped out carrying the hook.

As Tona's boots crunched on the ice, Etta fired a flare. It burst into light and began to drop. With the landscape of ice illuminated around him, Tona saw what he wanted and started running. The cable paid out behind him as the flare faded to black. When the flare went out, he kept the image of the spire of rock he'd seen fixed in his mind and continued running blind in that direction, pulling the cable with him.

Another tremor struck and the car slipped another meter closer to their deaths. Metzi screamed and Ahotei strained to see Tona through the open rear door.

Without any light, Tona ran into the spire of rock he'd been aiming for. He tripped, bruising his shoulder on the rock without ripping his suit. Then he scrambled to his feet and wrapped the cable around the rock and secured the end of it using the hook. After pulling as hard as he could on the cable to make sure it held fast, he radioed to the car. "Use the winch! Pull in the cable!"

Etta activated the winch's control and the cable rolled back onto the drum until it pulled taut. "It's holding!" Tona shouted. "Pull yourself back. I'll follow the cable back to you."

Etta increased the power to the winch and the car began to inch backward.

"More power!" Ahotei shouted.

Etta glanced at him. "If I go too fast, the cable could break."

Another tremor struck and the car stopped moving.

Metzi strained to see Tona through the back window.

They could hear him hyperventilating over the com channel. "Don't stop!" Tona shouted.

Etta increased the power to the winch another ten percent. Ahotei reached over him and jammed the power lever to the max. The ice rider lurched backward and continued onto level ground. Etta powered down the winch and turned toward the rear. A few seconds later, Tona jumped on board and closed the rear door. "Let's go!" he yelled.

Etta put the car into gear and steered parallel to the crevasse, watching the sonic depth meter and the video display. When he found a clear path around the obstacle, he increased speed toward the hangar.

The frequency and magnitude of the quakes steadily increased, but except for rattling their nerves, they were able to make it to the hangar's airlock without further incident. Etta parked outside and turned off the vehicle's lights. "If they've been watching, they know we're here."

Ahotei opened the door and jumped out. "Enough talking." He ran to the airlock door and waited for everyone to join him.

They huddled near the door. "Do we have anything we can use to defend ourselves?" Etta asked.

Tocho took the Sphere from the pocket of his environmental suit. It burst with golden light.

"Throw that thing into the nearest crack in the ice and be done with it," Ahotei said. He took hold of the locking wheel to open the airlock door and tried turning it. The wheel moved easily. He stopped turning, leaving the door closed and looked back at Tocho. "It isn't locked."

"Could be waiting to ambush us inside," Tona said.

"We use the same plan as before." Ahotei pointed at Tona and Metzi. "You two go inside and get their attention. That buys us time so Tocho, Etta and I can sneak up behind them."

"What if they're waiting for us?" Tona asked.

"Everybody dies. Any other questions?"

"What about me?" Lando asked.

Ahotei glared at him. "Stay out of the way or this time I'll snap your neck."

Tona reached out his hand to his father. "We have to stop saying goodbye."

They shook hands, and Etta hugged him.

"Hey, brat," Ahotei said.

Tona eased away from his father. "Yes?"

Ahotei nodded. "You did well back there."

Tona took Metzi's hand and spoke to her, forcing a smile to his lips. "Now it's your turn." She looked up into his eyes and they entered the airlock.

Chapter Sixteen

Tona secured the airlock door and they waited while the pressure inside equalized with the hangar. He glanced at Metzi. "Are you afraid?"

"Terrified!"

He nodded. "Me, too." When he saw the overhead light change from red to green, he opened the inner door and peeked out. He pulled his head back. "There's nobody here."

* * *

Ahotei led Etta, Tocho, and Lando single file past the hangar's main airlock, hugging the hangar's outer wall.

"If you're going someplace in particular and you have a plan for when we get there, let's hear it," Etta said through the suit's intercom. Ahotei ignored him and continued forward.

They continued another hundred meters and stopped in an unlit alcove beside a jumble of machinery.

"Shouldn't we go inside at the next airlock and try to stop them?" Lando asked.

Ahotei loomed over the smaller man. "Keep your mouth shut and do exactly as I say, or the only way you'll get on one of those discs is in pieces."

Lando shrank back.

"Lando's suggestion brings up a question we haven't addressed," Tocho said. He looked at Lando. "The Sect must have a plan for hijacking the discs. What is it?"

Lando kept his eyes riveted on Ahotei. "I programmed a computer virus and loaded it into the discs' navigational computers."

"A computer virus." Tocho pondered that for a moment. "What does it do?"

"It inactivates the computers by creating a feedback loop." He swallowed hard. "That allows the pilots to take manual control."

"The first disc with my granddaughter in it didn't turn back," Ahotei said through clenched teeth. "Looks like your fancy computer virus doesn't work."

* * *

Metzi and Tona carried their environmental suit helmets as they left the airlock and entered the hangar's observation deck. An eerie silence pressed down on them as they stood looking around. "I don't see anybody," Metzi whispered. "Let's tell the others it's safe to come inside."

"We can't," Tona replied keeping his voice low. "Our suit comms won't penetrate the hangar walls. I'll go outside and get them, but first let's take a better look around, just in case."

Metzi nodded.

They ran to the viewing window overlooking the hangar floor, looked down, and saw two silver discs bathed in floodlights, with ramps extending from both of them. Two lines of people were queued up in front of the ramps, the line to one disc much longer than the other.

"Those are my people," Metzi said. "I recognize some of them."

Tona frowned. "There's not enough room in the discs for all of them."

Metzi looked back at him. "What do you mean?"

"Each disc is large enough to accommodate forty people for a short flight not requiring extensive supplies. It means they're leaving most of your people behind to die with us."

Metzi brought her hand to her mouth. "My god! We have to stop them."

Tona pointed at the disc on the right. "Only three people left in the line for that one. The other line has at least thirty people in it. Could only mean one thing ..."

Metzi gripped the railing. "The first disc is almost full."

"Which means we're running out of time." Tona faced her. "Practice your smile. We're going down there." He pointed at the stairway leading down to the hangar floor.

* * *

"Maybe Lando's right," Tocho said. "Whatever we're going to do to stop them, we should do it now."

"There's another airlock fifty meters ahead," Etta added.

Ahotei leaned out and scanned along the hangar wall. He started forward. "Let's go."

They continued to the next airlock and stopped. Ahotei put his hands on the locking wheel. "Let's hope the two brats have their attention inside or this could get ugly." He spun the wheel.

* * *

They descended the stairs. When Tona opened the pressure-tight door on the hangar level, the sounds of people shouting and crying filled the air mixed with the aromas of familiar foods and the pungent odors of sweat and fear.

"Steady, they see us," Tona cautioned. A priest with a gun rushed toward them.

The priest stopped a few paces from them, lowered his gun, and briefly bowed his head. "Excuse me, Miss. I didn't recognize you."

"It's alright," Metzi said doing her best to sound calm. "Is my father here?"

"Yes." The priest glanced at Tona and his hand tightened on the gun.

"It's all right," Metzi said quickly. "His name is Tona. His father is a member of the Science Council. He's come with me to ..."

The priest stepped back and raised his gun at Tona. "He's a heretic!" the priest shouted.

"No!" Metzi exclaimed. "He came with me to speak to my father. His people have a way to save all of us!"

More priests arrived and grabbed Tona, pinning his arms to his side. "You have to listen to me," Tona shouted. "There's another way!"

The priest with the gun struck Tona across the face with it sending a trickle of blood down Tona's chin. "Silence!" the priest bellowed.

Appearing dazed, Tona turned his head toward his attacker. He spit out half-clotted blood. "You're making a mistake."

The priest raised his gun to strike Tona again, but Metzi jumped in the way. "Please! You don't understand."

"Take the heretic to the Chamberlain," the armed priest said. The two priests dragged Tona toward the disc on the right. It no longer had anyone in line waiting to board.

Metzi's eyes flared with anger as she watched the two priests lead Tona away. "Take me to my father, now!"

Keeping a bland expression, the priest bowed his head again and gestured toward the disc on the right. "Your father's inside." Holding her head high, Metzi started for the disc. The priest concealed the gun beneath his cassock and followed.

Metzi passed a long line of people waiting to board the disc on the left. She recognized a young woman in the queue and stopped. "Lura!" Metzi called to her. The young woman turned to the sound of Metzi's voice, dropped a bundle of clothing in her arms, and ran to her. The two women hugged. The priest watched Metzi for a moment, and then continued up the ramp to the disc on the right, disappearing inside.

"I knew you'd be coming with us." Lura beamed at Metzi.

Metzi's eyes filled with tears. "I'm not going."

Lura's eyes widened. "Of course you are."

Metzi shook her head. "I can't. It's wrong."

Lura took a step away from her. "It's wrong to stay alive?"

Metzi's eyes pleaded with her. "It's wrong for a few people to live by killing everyone else."

Lura backed up another step. "You think it's better that we all die?" She turned and ran back to her place in line looking straight ahead.

"Lura!" Metzi called. Lura refused to look back.

Metzi's father stopped at the threshold of the first disc, recognized his daughter, and ran to her. "Metzi! Thank Asani we found you in time. Your mother and sister are already on board." He offered his embrace.

She pulled away from him. "I can't believe you'd do such a thing."

Taru dropped his hands. "I can explain, but it's complicated."

"What's complicated about mass murder?" Metzi demanded. She looked past her father and saw Tona at the base of the disc's ramp, surrounded by priests with guns.

Taru saw where Metzi was looking. "He's the boy from the Science Sect you've been seeing. Did he tell you what those butchers were planning to do?"

Metzi glared at her father. "You think they're butchers? The Science Sect can help us all escape and not leave anyone behind."

Taru lifted his chin. "Did he tell you how?"

"In the flying discs," Metzi replied.

Taru frowned. "Not quite."

Metzi appeared confused. "What?"

"They want us to fly away without our bodies as godless computer programs … as abominations!" Taru finished by shouting.

Metzi gaped at him. "That's absurd."

Taru pointed at Tona. "Ask him. His Sphere programmed the discs with a one-way trip. The wonderful new home they want to take us to is so far away a disc can't carry enough supplies for even two people to make it there alive. The only way to survive the journey is to leave our bodies behind and become machines. Is that what you want, to become nothing more than lines of programming in a computer core?"

Metzi's lips quivered. "No, but ..."

Taru softened his expression and held out his hands. "I won't let them turn you into a machine. Come with me. Your mother and sister are waiting inside the disc."

Metzi glanced at Tona and struggled to find the right words. "What about the rest of our friends, the other people in the compound?" Her voice quavered. "How can we leave them all behind?"

Taru dropped his hands. "Difficult decisions had to be made. We only have room for eighty people, forty in each disc.

Metzi's face reddened with anger. "You and the Sect elders decided who those lucky eighty people are, didn't you?"

Taru looked away. "Somebody had to."

Metzi's jaw tensed. "Are any of the priests or their families being left behind?"

Taru sighed. "I told you, it's complicated."

The Chamberlain descended the first disc's ramp and walked toward them. Tona's guards prodded him to follow. The Chamberlain extended his hand to Metzi in greeting. "Metzi, my dear, thank goodness we found you in time." She refused to take it. He frowned and signaled to Tona's guards to bring him forward. "And you brought your heretic friend with you."

Tona shrugged off the guard's grip. "You don't have to abandon everyone else. My people can save us all."

The Chamberlain smirked. "As a pack of mindless automatons? I think not."

Metzi moved closer to Tona. "Is it true? Do we have to become machines to survive the trip to the new world?"

Tona's hands clenched into fists. "Yes, it's true. It's the only way to keep us alive during the long flight."

Metzi's eyes filled with tears. "But we get our bodies back when we get there?"

Tona looked away. "We can't take our bodies with us ... There's not enough room."

Metzi stared back at Tona, unable to speak.

Taru took her hand. "Think, child. Is that what you want, to become a machine?"

The hangar floor shuddered beneath their feet, followed by an ominous *crack*. "The discs!" someone shouted. They turned and saw a jagged fissure two meters wide in the hangar floor extending between them. The Chamberlain started running to the disc on the right. Tona's guards left him and followed. Another, stronger tremor struck, knocking everyone to the ground. They watched with horror as the fissure between the discs grew to more than ten meters wide. The Chamberlain and the priests got to their feet and raced to the first disc, skirting the chasm. When they were all aboard, the disc's ramp and then the door disappeared and the disc's energy output increased.

As Tona helped Metzi to her feet, a klaxon sounded and the inner airlock door behind the brighter disc began sliding closed. Taru turned to his daughter with an expression of panic. "Metzi, please, you have to come with me." Behind him, the last of the second disc's passengers raced aboard.

Metzi stepped back increasing the distance between them. "No."

Tona grabbed her shoulders forcing her to look at him. "Get on that disc before it's too late!"

"I won't leave you!" Metzi exclaimed.

The floor convulsed again, so violently they struggled to stand. "We have to leave now!" Taru shouted at his daughter.

"I won't leave without Tona!"

"You'll be killed!" Taru shouted.

Metzi's lips trembled. "Tell my mother and sister that I love them."

The airlock closed behind the first disc with a loud clang and the klaxon stopped. Tona saw a crewman from the remaining disc run towards them. "Come now or we'll leave without you," he called.

"Metzi, please," Tona begged. "Go with your father."

Metzi shook her head. "Not like this."

The crewman from the second disc glanced at Taru and then ran back. After a last anguished glance at his daughter, Taru followed him.

Tona pulled Metzi into his arms. "You're crazy, but I love you."

"I'm afraid," she whispered back. He hugged her tighter.

They heard the klaxon sound again and turned to watch the second airlock door close. When the klaxon stopped, the rings of power around both discs burst with blinding light. Soon after, the space doors opened and first one and then the other disc rose above the hangar floor, hovered, and then floated out into the starry night. The discs remained stationary for a few seconds, and then accelerated past Jupiter and disappeared.

Chapter Sixteen

Tocho, Ahotei, Etta, and Lando arrived in the command center in time to see the two discs disappear into the void. Ahotei pounded the viewing window with his fist, rattling the glass. "Those bastards!"

Lando slumped against one of the computer consoles and buried his face in his hands. "I can't believe this is happening," he moaned.

Etta turned to Tocho. "Looks like we're marooned."

"There's another choice," Tocho said, "but we have to hurry."

Ahotei spun around. "No there isn't."

Tocho ignored him and moved closer to Lando. "Put yourself together and listen to me."

Lando stood, swaying on his feet.

Tocho grabbed him by the shoulders. "We have four more robots ready for downloading, and enough computer core to save everyone else."

"I don't know if I can do it," Lando moaned.

Etta moved closer. "What if the computer core doesn't survive the impact?"

Tocho released Lando. "The Nexus brought us this far. Maybe it's time we trusted it."

"We won't have bodies!" Lando exclaimed.

"We won't need bodies if we're all dead," Tocho snapped. "This way, at least we have a chance."

Lando wiped the spittle from his lips. "All right ... God help me, I'll do it."

"You're all insane," Ahotei growled.

Tocho spoke to Lando. "Take the elevator down to the city with Ahotei and go to the download chamber. Get everything ready. Can you do it?"

Lando nodded and started for the elevator.

Next Tocho faced Etta. "Collect your son and the girl. Bring them here." Another tremor struck rattling the viewing windows. "Hurry!" Etta raced down the ladder to the hangar floor.

"You said we have four empty tin cans," Ahotei began. "Who downloads besides you and me?"

"The two people we need most to restart our civilization. Lando for one."

Ahotei lowered his chin and looked Tocho in the eyes. "That traitor stays here and dies with the city."

"No! He's the best computer scientist we have. We'll need him to get back into flesh and blood bodies."

Ahotei struggled to control his emotions. "All right! So it's you, me, Lando and Etta."

"Not Etta," Tocho said. "We need an engineer, someone who can build more robotic bodies for the rest of our people."

"What makes you think we can survive the comet and do all that?"

Tocho held up the Sphere pulsing with dazzling golden light. "This."

Ahotei frowned. "I hate that thing." He looked away from it. "What do you want me to do when I get back to the city, besides try to stay alive?"

"Bring me as many people as you can."

* * *

Etta ran down the stairs toward Metzi and Tona who stood side by side facing the airlock window. He stopped behind them and saw Metzi's reflection in the glass. She had streaks of tears down her cheeks. He heard her whisper, "I'll never see my family again."

"We don't know that," Etta said.

They both turned around. "Dad!" Tona exclaimed.

"Come with me," Etta said urgently. "We don't have a lot of

time."

Metzi appeared dazed. "I've heard what you want to do to us. I'd rather die."

"Metzi, please," Tona began. "It's not what you think!" She turned back to the airlock window.

Etta sighed. "I see you told her."

"Her father did it for me," Tona said.

"Did your father tell you that we don't plan to stay that way?" Etta called to her.

She didn't seem to hear.

Tona reached for her. "Metzi?"

"She's in shock," Etta said. "I don't think she hears you."

Metzi continued staring through the airlock window.

Tona dropped his hands. "Do you think the Sect can control the discs and make it to the fourth planet?"

Etta sighed. "Despite what they did to us, I hope so." He squared his shoulders. "The rest of us have one chance to survive, and you know what it is. The choice is yours, but I for one am willing to take it."

"I'm going with you," Tona said. He glanced at Metzi. "We both are." Her hand yielded to Tona's touch and he steered her toward the stairway.

* * *

Tocho, Lando, and Etta moved single file down a narrow passageway hewn from Europa's bedrock. Lights in the ceiling reflected off deposits of iron and titanium ore in the walls. The veins of metal glowed with a bright, reddish hue. Tocho stopped to touch one of them. "These streaks of ore always remind me of arteries." Etta nodded. Lando said nothing.

They continued walking in silence, descending until the passageway leveled in front of a formidable-looking metal door. Tocho punched a sequence of numbers onto a keypad beside the door and it swung open revealing a brightly lit space of considerable size. He went inside.

Lando followed next and stopped a meter inside the door. "I've had nightmares about this place."

Tocho glanced at him over his shoulder. "If you want to live, help me and be quick about it."

After Etta closed the door, they moved past long lines of empty metal tables flanked by identical, squat, silver cubes spaced every three meters. Like the navigation computers controlling the discs, those computers had nothing showing except a single blank screen.

"You said you built four robots," Etta said.

"Six, if you count the two already in space," Tocho replied. He tried to remain focused and not to think about Ruha.

"Why only six?"

At the far end of the room, Tocho stopped in front of another formidable-looking door. "Two reasons. First, we didn't have enough time to build more. Second, we hoped we'd never need them." He keyed in a second numerical sequence and the door opened to a smaller cavern with banks of conventional computers lining rough, rock walls. The Cryogenic Chamber also contained several large floor-to-ceiling cryogenic vats. Moisture condensing on the sides of the vats dripped to the floor and trickled through small grates. The cold air above the vats hovered as a constant fog.

Lando stood in front of one of the cryogenic tanks. "Is this where our bodies will go?"

"Yes," Tocho replied.

"Are the two pilot's bodies in there?" Lando asked.

Tocho frowned. "You mean Ruha and Tia? They have names."

"Not anymore. Now they're machines."

Tocho lost his temper. "I don't have time for your constant doom and gloom! Help me or not, that's your choice. But if you decide to help, swallow your bile and say something useful, or keep your mouth shut." He moved quickly to a third door and entered another numerical sequence.

Lando followed Tocho and Etta through the doorway and down a flight of stairs to a smaller rectangular room one level below. The download chamber had white finished walls lined by more computer monitors. A ceramic table dominated the center of the room. Ruha was the last person to lie on it. A large ring of metal, the neural download apparatus, waited on rollers at the head of the table, connected to a spinning globe inside a transparent cover on top of another silver cube. As it turned, the globe pulsed with multi-colored light.

Tocho moved to the chamber's far wall and flipped a switch. In front of him, six metal panels pulled up into the ceiling exposing lighted spaces three meters tall and one meter deep. Two spaces were empty and four contained silver robots. None of the robots' flat screen heads showed any lights.

Lando stood beside Tocho looking at them. "I see you numbered them." Each robot had a number embossed on a plaque mounted on its torso, from one to four.

"A small conceit of individuality," Tocho replied. He flipped another switch and each robot's head flickered and then lit, displaying a dark field of grey with a blue square at its center.

Lando knelt in front of the globe. The spinning globe's colored lights played across his face. "Is this the Nexus?"

"Maybe. We can't be sure." Tocho sounded distracted. "It appeared when we completed the download apparatus."

"Does it know I'm here?"

They felt a slight tremor. Tocho raised his head and waited. A minute went by and nothing further happened. "Must have been a big one if we felt it down here," Tocho said.

"Let's have a look." Lando walked to one of the computer banks and activated a video feed from the surface. He adjusted several controls.

Etta moved beside him. "Are you looking at the city?"

"At the comet," Lando replied. The screen blossomed into a field of black with an irregular grey blur in the center of it. He adjusted the controls and they could see a rock of indeterminate size with a pockmarked face, trailing a white tail of steam.

"How long before impact?" Tocho asked standing behind them.

Lando glanced at a digital meter mounted on the wall. "One cycle, maybe less. If we're going to do this, we better move fast." While Etta watched, both he and Tocho started down the line of computers activating one control after another until the entire download laboratory filled with light and the sound of equipment.

They felt another tremor, longer and stronger.

Tocho studied the rock ceiling. He couldn't see any cracks. "I hope Ahotei and the children are still all right."

Etta kept silent.

Lando moved past several computers checking various readouts. "Everything's ready. What do we do now?"

"We put as many people as we can into the computer core, then download four of us into the robots."

"We'll keep our bodies in stasis?" Lando asked.

"Until we return, or the geothermal power fails," Tocho replied.

Lando licked his lips. "Which four of us keep our bodies?"

"You, me, Ahotei, and an engineer," Tocho replied. "Either Rinku or Edu, whomever Ahotei can find." Lando relaxed. "The rest of our people will be counting on us to build enough robot bodies to download them too so we can rebuild the city and figure out a way off this rock."

Lando glanced at Etta and looked away.

"Etta?" Tocho began.

"Don't worry," Etta said. "I understand. I'll download into the core with my son."

Etta and Tocho briefly embraced and Tocho moved in front

of the Nexus. "We'll take DNA samples from everyone and place the samples in stasis. Either the Nexus shows us how to clone new bodies from our DNA, or we'll learn how to make them on our own."

They felt another, stronger tremor. Tocho looked up and saw cracks in the ceiling. "Can you show me the city?"

Lando cycled through the video cameras situated around the Science Sector. At first, the screen remained dark. "Some of the cameras are down. Must have been taken out by the quakes." He adjusted several controls. "Here's one that's still working. It's near the Council chambers." The image resolved to show a collapsed building and piles of rubble. "My God!" Lando exclaimed.

* * *

They found Ahotei in front of the elevator on the main level with a small crowd of people gathered around him. Tona and Metzi stood off to the side.

Tocho eased his way closer to Ahotei to be heard over the chaos of excited voices. "How many?" he called to Ahotei.

"Fifty-two," Ahotei replied.

Tocho looked grim. "I'd hoped for more."

"A lot of dead bodies up there," Ahotei said. "Even if more people show up, the elevator's done. We can't get them down."

Tocho made his way next to Ahotei. "Why?"

"The main elevator shaft collapsed after the last big quake," Ahotei replied. "We were lucky to bring the last group down alive."

"Damn!" Tocho exclaimed. "The elevator from here to the download complex is still working."

Metzi pushed her way close to Tocho. She still appeared dazed. "Why aren't there any children?"

Tocho took a deep breath before answering. "Because we

can't download them."

The other voices stopped. Everyone turned to listen.

Metzi's eyes bulged with horror. "You're murdering all the children?"

Several women screamed.

Tona glanced at his father, but Etta refused to meet his eyes.

Tocho raised his voice. "Listen to me, all of you! Only a mature brain can be downloaded and brought back. The minds of the children would be forever stunted ... they'd never be more than children, even in new bodies."

Pale and shaking, Metzi backed away from Tocho. "My father was right. You people are monsters." Tona reached for her, but she pulled away.

"We don't have time for this," Ahotei muttered. "You've seen what's happening up there," he shouted. You can go back and die, or you can shut your mouths, do exactly as we tell you and survive. Make your choice, and do it quick!"

The crowd quieted. "Are you sure we're far enough underground to be safe?" someone shouted.

Ahotei gestured at Tocho. "You tell them."

Tocho paused, picking his words carefully. "Even if this facility survives the impact, the city above will be destroyed," he began. "We can't breathe underwater and there won't be any food, so hiding down here is not an option."

For a moment, no one spoke.

"Why did you bring us here?" someone asked.

"Because there's another way to save everyone," Tocho replied. "We call it downloading."

"What does downloading mean?" someone else asked.

Tocho glanced at Ahotei. "It means storing your consciousness, your neural essence in a computer until the danger passes."

"What about our bodies?" a man shouted.

"When do we wake up?" someone else called out.

Tocho hesitated before answering. "Our flesh and blood

bodies won't survive the comet. We'll have to create new ones to reanimate."

Some people gasped. Others began to cry. A man holding his mate shouted, "Reanimate as what?'

Ahotei's lips pulled into a grimace. "Into a silver robot with a computer for a brain! Is that plain enough for you?" he shouted.

The voices of the people dissolved into a chaos of anger and revulsion.

"If you don't like it, go back up there and die!" Ahotei shouted. He stalked away.

"Listen to me!" Tocho bellowed, so loudly his voice echoed off the walls. The crowd quieted. "You have a difficult decision, the most difficult one you'll ever make, and you'll have to do it quick. You felt the quakes. There'll be more, until everything we know has been destroyed. We're out of time." He paused, studying everyone's faces and their expressions of fear. "Those of you who want to keep your mind alive in a computer, follow me. The rest of you," he pointed at the elevator, "go back." He walked over to Ahotei. "Are you coming with me?"

Ahotei smirked. "Why not? One of these days one of your hair-brained schemes may actually work." They shook hands.

Most of the people followed Tocho and Ahotei to the elevator to the download complex. A few huddled near the stairway leading up to the city level. At the elevator doors, the larger group surrounded Tocho, peppering him with questions. Ahote crossed the floor to Tona and Metzi who were standing nearby. Metzi saw Ahotei, grimaced, and turned away.

Ahotei spoke to Tona. "You saved our lives up on the ice. I owe you." He pointed at Metzi. "Do you still want her?"

Tona appeared startled. "I love her."

Ahotei grabbed Metzi's shoulder, spun her around, and struck her on the side of the head with the flat of his palm. She slumped unconscious to the floor.

"Metzi!" Tona exclaimed. Before he could react, Ahotei

scooped Metzi into his arms and took her to the elevator. "You're insane!" Tona shouted as he ran after them.

Tocho turned and saw Ahotei coming with Metzi in his arms and Tona trailing after. He pushed through the crowd and called to Ahotei. "Did she faint?"

"That madman hit her!" Tona yelled.

Ahotei put Metzi on the floor in front of Tocho and stood back. Tocho bent closer to her. He noted that her breaths came in short gasps and she was covered with sweat. He looked up. "She's going into shock. You could have killed her."

Ahotei pointed at Tona. "The brat said he wants her, but she wasn't cooperating. Now you can download her like the rest of us."

Tocho leaned closer to Ahotei. "The man I knew would never do such a thing."

"Maybe that man has seen too much." Ahotei turned and opened the elevator door.

Chapter Seventeen

Tocho entered the large room in the download complex and found Lando moving from table to table, tweaking this, adjusting that, all the while muttering to himself. Lando stopped and looked up when he heard Tocho. "How'd it go?"

"The people Ahotei brought down have a difficult choice to make," Tocho replied. "We don't know if there'll be more than six of us."

"Six?"

"The four of us plus Etta's son, Tona, and his girlfriend Metzi. She'll have to download first."

"Why?" Lando asked.

Tocho frowned. "She's injured."

Lando continued adjusting the equipment. "Surprised there's not more of them."

"Most of the people never had the chance to choose."

Lando stopped to study a wall panel with rows of meters and dials. "What about an engineer?"

"Ahotei couldn't find any," Tocho replied.

They heard voices outside. Tocho went to the door and swung it open. "I count thirty," he called to Lando. "We're in luck. Rinku is one of them."

Ahotei came through the door first with Metzi's limp body over his shoulder, followed by Tona and Etta. Thirty people followed and huddled pale and wide-eyed behind him. No one spoke. Ahotei put Metzi on one of the tables.

Tona ran to her and cradled her head in his arms. "Metzi?" he said near her ear. She didn't react. He saw blood trickling from one of her nostrils and looked up. "Please don't let her die."

Etta moved next to his son and whispered something.

Ahotei gestured at the people standing stony-faced along the wall. "This is all of them."

"You're sure?" Tocho asked.

Ahotei locked eyes with him. "Nobody else is coming."

Tocho glanced at Metzi. "Take her inside." After Ahotei picked her up and walked to the download chamber, Tocho turned and addressed the people. "We'll be safe down here, at least for now." Another tremor struck, and then a second soon after. The cavern shook and groaned. One bank of equipment fell forward and crashed to the floor in a shower of sparks. Tocho ran to the far wall and pulled down a large, red lever. The light in the room momentarily increased in intensity and then faded to its normal luminescence.

"Don't be alarmed," Tocho shouted. Several of the women were crying. "I've activated a force field. We're safe." He forced an ingenuous smile. "Calm yourselves. I'll be back in a few minutes to explain what happens next."

One of the women ran to the door screaming, "Let me out!" When she reached to touch the door, light erupted around her hand and she shot backward landing on her back.

Tocho ran to her and helped her to her feet. "The force field is on," he shouted. "Stay away from the door! No one can leave."

The woman fell to her knees, moaning "No," over and over again.

Tocho left the room, closing and locking the inner door behind him.

When he arrived in the download chamber, he watched Ahotei put Metzi on the table with her head facing the download ring and backed away. Tocho quickly positioned a med scanner over her chest and grimaced. "She's dying. We better hurry."

Lando pushed the ring closer and locked it in place over her head. He stooped next to the Nexus and said, "Begin."

The spinning globe pulsed with white light and spun faster. Soon after, the download ring apparratus lit along its entire circumference, emitting a pale blue light that blinked from within the substance of the metal. The frequency of the blinking light accelerated until the ring and the Nexus reached synchrony. When this happened, the Nexus changed color to iridescent blue. The light from the Nexus danced in Lando's eyes for a moment, mesmerizing him. Then he blinked and looked up. "We're ready."

Tona rushed into the room with tears rolling down his cheeks. "Wait!" He took Metzi's limp hand in his. "Let me say goodbye."

Etta stood near his son. "You'll see each other again."

Tona buried his face in his father's chest. "As what?"

"Let go of her hand," Tocho said gently. Tona stepped back and Tocho gestured for Lando to proceed.

Lando looked at the Nexus and said, "Initiate." The Nexus spun faster and the color of the download ring changed from blue to purple, and then to yellow. The flickering of the light accelerated and the light grew in intensity. Suddenly the room filled with a shrill whine. The sound increased to a shriek and the light from the ring became impossibly intense forcing everyone to cover their ears and turn away. An explosion of light so bright they could see it with their eyes closed burst from the ring of metal, and then the sound abruptly stopped. They turned back and saw Metzi's lifeless form beneath a ring of dull grey metal.

Tona ran to her. "She's not breathing!"

Etta pulled his son back. "She's not there anymore." Tona sobbed on his father's shoulder.

"What's her file number?" Tocho asked looking grim.

"J242," Lando replied.

"Speak to her," Tocho said.

Lando spoke to the Nexus. "I wish to interact with file J242."

"Proceed," a voice from the Nexus said.

Lando glanced at Tona and spoke to the Nexus. "J242, identify yourself and state your status."

A voice with an artificial timbre and perfect inflection spoke from the Nexus. "I speak for the neural matrix that controlled the organic being known as Metzi. My programming is operating at

100 percent of specifications."

"Thank you, J242. Lando got to his feet. "She's in there."

"But I can't touch her," Tona said in a whisper.

Etta hugged him. "Some day you will."

Tocho looked at Ahotei. "Put her body in stasis." He pointed at Tona. "Tona, too, when his time comes."

They felt another tremor. Even with the force field in place, dust rained down from the ceiling. "Thirty more to go. Better keep on with it," Lando said.

* * *

Lando struggled to his feet after kneeling close to the Nexus for several hours. Only Lando, Tocho, Ahotei and Rinku remained in their bodies. "My knees can't take much more of this." He stretched. "Guess that doesn't matter anymore, does it?" He walked to the wall with the four robots. "Which of us goes first?"

"Which of us wakes first is the more important question," Tocho replied.

"Why not all of us at the same time?" Rinku asked.

Tocho joined Lando at the wall of robots. "What if there's nothing to wake up to? Once the robots are activated and leave this alcove, the neural patterns of whomever is inside can't go back to sleep. Whoever's awake will stay awake until we download to new bodies or the units lose power, which could take many thousands of years." He looked at Ahotei. "The ones still asleep won't have to suffer."

No one spoke.

"I'll do it," Ahotei said.

"That's fine with me," Rinku said.

Lando nodded. "Me, too."

Tocho studied his friend's face. "I thought we'd draw straws."

"Not necessary," Ahotei said.

Tocho stepped closer to him. "Tell me why."

Ahotei's arms hung slack at his side. "Because I don't care anymore." Tocho stared back at him, but said nothing. "However I do have one request," Ahotei added. "I want to be Unit One."

Lando smirked. "What difference does it make? They're all the same."

Ahotei glared at him. "Maybe I like the sound of it."

Lando licked his lips. "Sure, whatever you want."

They felt another tremor, strong enough to shake the download ring. Lando ran to the controller for the video monitors and switched through all the feeds. The screen remained black. "The city's gone."

"We better finish while we still can," Rinku said.

"I agree, but first I'd like a private word with Ahotei," Tocho said. Rinku and Lando left the download chamber and Tocho closed the door.

Ahotei pointed at the Nexus. "You trust that thing, don't you?"

"I do," Tocho replied.

"What if it wants to keep us prisoners inside our metal dolls?"

"If that happens, we'll use Lando's computer virus to get ourselves out."

Ahotei's eyes widened. "How do you know it'll work?"

"I tested it." Tocho took the Sphere from his pocket and held it up. It appeared opaque, black and lifeless. "This happened when I exposed it to Lando's program." He dropped the Sphere and it shattered on the floor.

Ahotei kicked at the coal-black shards with his foot. "There's still the problem of finding ourselves new bodies."

"If the Nexus won't help us, we'll learn how to make new ones. We can exist a very long time in those tin cans, as you call them, long enough to discover how."

"Maybe it's easier to borrow other people's bodies," Ahotei said.

Tocho bristled. "I don't like the sound of that."

Before Tocho could continue, Lando rapped on the door and peeked in. "Are you done with your private chat? We're running out of time."

Tocho glanced at Ahotei. "For now. Come in."

Lando re-entered the chamber with Rinku and stared at the download table. Ahotei moved closer to the Nexus. "Show me how to operate this thing."

* * *

Ahotei stood over Tocho's lifeless body. "I promise I won't let you suffer, old friend." He cradled Tocho in his arms and brought him to one of the cryo-stasis chambers, looking away from the robot alcove as he passed. Three of the units, numbers Two, Three, and Four, showed active flat screens with a blue background and a central black square. The fourth robot, Unit One, was still dark. After putting Tocho's body in stasis, Ahotei returned to the robot alcove and looked at Unit Two holding Tocho's neural essence. "There's some things I need to do before I sleep, old friend. I hope someday you'll understand." He moved in front of Unit Three containing Lando's neural patterns and threw a switch that should have turned off the unit's power. Lando's flat screen head remained lit.

A voice boomed from the Nexus. "This action will erase the neural patterns of the organic being known as Lando. Do you wish to proceed?"

"Yes," Ahotei growled.

The face of Unit Three faded to black.

After a last look around, Ahotei lay down on the download table and said, "Restate Ahotei private file number 001 and prepare to execute."

The rotation of the Nexus increased in speed and it spoke. "The neural patterns of the being known as Ahotei will be downloaded into autonomous Unit One. Unit One will retain all available memory files and will have access to Ahotei's emotional algorithms. The memory files of all other units will be blocked and all emotional algorithms inactivated except as permitted by Unit One."

Ahotei looked back at the download ring. "None of them will know how they came to be in this state, or what happened to them prior to their awakening. None of them will feel pain, or loneliness ... or regret. Am I correct?"

"You are correct," the Nexus replied.

Ahotei closed his eyes. "Execute Ahotei confidential file 001." The last thing Ahotei heard was the sound of the download apparatus moving over his head.

* * *

Sudden light without sound and Ahotei's universe became a view of the download chamber, flanked by a constant cascade of numbers and symbols falling like rain before his eyes. Fear surged through his body, and with it, awareness. He sensed that he no longer had eyes or a body. A heart he no longer had threatened to burst, and tears he couldn't shed strained to be released, all in his mind, now a labyrinth of lifeless immortal materials. His universe dissolved into chaos and panic. Milliseconds later, an eternity in his new reality, he managed to regain control of his thoughts. He tilted his head and looked at his legs. Instead of warm, pulsing flesh, he saw two cold spindles of silver. He lifted his right leg and watched the slender appendage bend at its center and the upper half move toward him. He dropped his right lower appendage back to the floor, sat up and looked around the chamber-ruined walls, a collapsed ceiling stabilized by a force field, and banks of computer equipment, all dark. Some lay around him on the floor broken into pieces.

His new gaze fell upon the Nexus spinning with a soft even glow. Without thinking how or why, he spoke to it without using an audible voice. "State the status of Unit's Two, Three, and Four." At that moment Ahotei also realized that he possessed far more knowledge and reasoning ability than he'd ever thought possible. He spun his head and looked again at the bank of computers. Once nothing more to him than boxes with flashing lights, he understood the form and function of every one of their components and how they interacted. He also realized how primitive the computers were and saw comprehensible diagrams of upgrades scroll past his eyes that would have been unfathomable even to Tocho.

"Tocho," he audibled. Feeling pain, he lurched forward toward the robotic bodies of Tocho, Rinku, and Lando. He experienced sweet revenge at the sight of Lando's unit, cold and dark. He knew pleasure when he saw Tocho and Rinku's units still lit. He turned his head toward the download table and saw his former body. Feeling nothing, he walked to it now with a smooth fluid motion and looked down at his face. He noted pallid eyes rolled up in their sockets, and a swollen tongue half out of his mouth. Spittle had spilled onto his chin.

Unit One picked up the corpse of his former organic self and walked to the door of the main laboratory, not bothering to activate the door's keypad. At some level of his consciousness he knew that the door would open for him when he approached. When it did, he had a better appreciation of the devastation caused by the comet. The entire rock chamber tilted on its side at a twenty-two-degree angle. It was encased in a shell of water. He instantly understood what had happened. Their world's bedrock had fractured down to the level of the download complex. The seawater pushing through to crush everything in the chamber was being held back by the complex's force field.

He tossed his corpse on one of the long metal tables. "What is the status of this complex?"

"The download chamber is intact and functional with minor repairs," the Nexus replied. "The chamber comprising your current location is also intact. The cryo-stasis units have been destroyed."

"Are any of the bodies salvageable?" Ahotei asked.

"No."

"Will the other units be aware of this fact when they are activated?"

Lights cascaded down the face of the Nexus. "According to Ahotei private program 001, that is not possible until the proper access code has been given."

"Who has access to that code besides you?"

"Only Unit One."

Ahotei returned to the download chamber. "How long will the force field be sufficient to hold back the seawater and prevent flooding of this room?"

"3,209,479.32 cycles," the Nexus replied.

"What is the status of the city?"

"There is no city."

Ahotei focused on the cryo-stasis chambers. They appeared intact. He scanned them more closely and saw a severed power cable with a clean cut. He pondered this for one microsecond. "Can a new city be built on the ocean floor?"

"Yes."

Ahotei's body changed its shape, becoming a pillar of silver with flashing lights. "Begin."

Chapter Eighteen

Eons later.

Unit Three, formerly known as Rinku, approached Unit One. One masked his feeling of pity. "Status report."

Three's face changed to an organized pattern of lights arranged in columns. "The city's force field generators will be ready for full power initiation in two cycles."

"How many memory units have been downloaded into robotic bodies?" One asked.

"Twenty-three."

"How long before all memory files have been downloaded?"

"Ten cylces," Three replied. "This unit requires information."

One increased its height by stretching the silver substance of its legs. Having observed this action by One before and received no explanation for it, Three no longer thought about it. To do so would be inefficient. One tilted his head down. "Proceed."

"What is the purpose of the pyramidal rock structure visible on the ocean bottom twenty thousand meters from this location?"

"You do not require that information. Return to your duties."

"Acknowledged." Unit Three's head spun to the opposite direction, its lights faded to a slate grey, and its body moved to the wall of One's domicile. A portal formed and Three exited.

After the portal closed, One asked, "How many mobile units will be available when the memory downloads are complete?"

"Thirty-five," the Nexus replied.

One accessed a memory file containing images of a rock pyramid, all that remained of the old city including the download chamber. "What is the status of the genetic material preservation vault?" One asked.

"The preservation chamber in the download complex was destroyed by the comet. The genetic material it contained was dispersed into the ocean and is not retrievable."

One felt rage. "Can you resynthesize my gene sequences or the gene sequences of Unit Two from archived data?"

"No such data exists."

One processed that conundrum for one millisecond. "Can you extract new genetic material from my former body?"

"For what purpose?" the Nexus asked.

One looked down at his legs, two silver spindles. "To create a new organic body."

"For what purpose?" the Nexus repeated.

One knew that it was useless to lie to the Nexus. "So that I may download back to my original organic form."

"Your former organic neural capacity is insufficient to hold all available memory files. In addition, primitive organic brains process information several magnitudes slower and have limited useful life. Your neural functionality would be significantly impaired."

One felt fear. "What if I wish to experience my prior state?"

"Access your memory files."

"Is it not our goal to seek perfection?" One asked.

"Yes."

"I seek to better understand the nature of organic life by direct observation."

"I will perform a scan of your former body to determine if any viable genetic material remains."

One knew hope. "I have one other request."

"Proceed."

One paused for one microsecond as he accessed his memory files. "Re-animate units R131 and J242 last."

"The sequence of reanimation is of no consequence."

One paused again. "It is to me."

One could not detect a one nanosecond pause by the Nexus. "Agreed."

* * *

Unit One took a moving walkway to a facility under construction on Europa's ocean bottom, an activity that required most of the active units. The facility contained the force field projectors that would hold back Europa's ocean so a new city could be built. The other units registered One's presence but continued working without interaction. One glided to a viewing window. Instead of the flat, sandy sea bottom he remembered, he saw a fractured underwater landscape dotted by volcanoes. This caused him two microseconds of pain. None of the other units had access to that memory, or the ability to feel emotion.

One spoke to C21. "Report on the status of Volcano Number One."

The head of C21 pivoted to face One and the frequency of C21's lights increased. "The magma chamber beneath Volcano Number One has been sealed. There is a less than 0.01 percent chance of an eruption."

"Is the accessory steam vent from Volcano Number One functional?"

"Yes."

"Report the operational parameters of Volcano Number One's accessory steam vent."

C21 accessed the facilities technical readouts. "The column of seawater from Volcano Number One's accessory steam vent reaches the surface ice with a temperature of 100.04 C with a variance of one percent. The aperture in the melted ice has formed within design specifications and remains stable."

One focused on a pyramidal shape on the seafloor visible near Volcano Number One. He remembered being inside it with Tocho when they met the Nexus the first time and they were given the Sphere. Tocho, now designated Unit Two, remembered none of that. One spun his head away from the viewing window. "How much time do you require for a full power test of the force field generators?"

"Three point four five cycles," C21 replied.

Unit One fought back his feeling of impatience. "You have not followed the schedule efficiently."

C21's lights fluttered a myriad of colors as it accessed information on the project. "The variance from the schedule is 1.6 percent."

"Unacceptable."

"Acknowledged." C21 felt nothing and turned back to its work.

Chapter Nineteen

Europa, ten thousand Earth-years later...

Unit Two entered One's dwelling place at the top of a silver spire at the city center. It stopped near a cluster of flashing lights on the floor. One registered Two's presence and rose from the floor becoming a silver pillar studded with twinkling lights. For a millisecond, One studied what had become of his friend and seethed with anger and regret. "Be glad you don't remember, old friend," One said to himself on a private channel. He sprouted legs and walked closer to Two. "Report."

Two's pattern of lights changed. "The first flying disc is ready for launch."

Without replying, One moved to the wall. A portal formed in front of him and he exited with Two following.

A moving walkway took them past towering spires of silver, joined at many levels by other walkways forming an intricate three-dimensional pattern. The silver spire One resided in, which also held the Nexus in a chamber deep below in Europa's bedrock, was the tallest and occupied the very center of the city. As One and Two rode the walkways, they passed other units moving between the structures. All the units were indistinguishable in appearance, except for raised emblems on their torsos containing their numerical designations. Unit One chose to be taller. None of the other units questioned why. To do so would be illogical. The other units moved from place to place, always busy, never stopping because to do so would be without purpose and therefore illogical. Two didn't pause to ponder why One designed the city with open spaces lacking functional significance. Some of these areas had fountains of water cascading into pools with different shapes. None of the units stopped in these areas or questioned the inefficiency of such spaces that One designated as parks.

One and Two navigated a sequence of moving walkways that terminated at the city's spaceport, a squat, rectangular hangar without a roof. Before descending to the city's floor, One stopped the walkway and looked down into the hangar. His visual sensors registered a silver disc large enough to hold the four units squatting on the hangar floor. The disc was thick at its center, with unblemished skin and a platinum-colored band around its waist. A ramp extended to the hangar floor from a rectangular cutout in the disc's side. As One watched, one of the units carried a silver box half its size up the ramp and disappeared inside the disc. A moment later, the unit walked down the ramp with empty silver arms.

"Loading is complete," Two said.

One activated the walkway and they continued to descend. "Proceed with phase one."

Two spoke to unit G3, controlling the launch from the hangar. "Begin launch sequence when we are in position."

"Acknowledged," G3 replied.

One and Two entered the hangar and moved to another viewing window closer to the disc. One studied the disc, all the while struggling not to remember the launch of another disc piloted by his granddaughter eons before.

When G3 observed that One and Two were in their expected viewing positions, it activated a control. A microsecond later the ramp absorbed into the disc's side and the rectangular doorway disappeared. A few microseconds after that, the darker band around the disc's waist erupted with neon-blue light. This began as a point of light that increased in intensity and spread, encircling the entire circumference of the disc as if the disc had caught fire. One tilted his head upward and watched a circular section of the city's force field above the disc change color from a transparent barrier holding back Europa's dark and roiling ocean, to scintillating yellow and gold.

G3 spoke to them over the com system. "Launch aperture is in flight configuration and the disc is fully powered."

"Proceed," One said.

"Acknowledged." G3 activated a different control.

The disc rose without a sound, hovered for a few seconds, bathing the hangar floor and the walls in blue light, then in one smooth motion ascended to the colored section of the city's force field and passed through with less than a water molecule's width between the disc and the force field. As soon as the undersurface of the disc passed through, the force field resumed its prior transparent state. One hundred meters above the force field, the disc stopped its forward motion and hovered. Although aware of the launch through information downloads from the Nexus, the other units dispersed about the city paid no attention. They felt no wonder at the sight of a silver disc with a brilliant band of blue outside the force field floating in Europa's ocean, nor did they imagine the awesome vistas of a new world the disc would soon encounter. They neither felt nor imagined anything.

Two evaluated technical readouts from the disc sent by G3. "I read nominal sensor outputs."

"Proceed to phase two," One replied.

Two switched channels. "Initiate phase two."

"Acknowledged," G3 replied.

The disc moved laterally toward Volcano Number One, and then in a gentle arc moved directly above the volcano's cone, joining the jet of superheated water moving toward the surface ice. Two activated a video monitor on Europa's surface and paired the image from it with a video feed sent from the disc. One moved closer to observe, his face now a riot of flashing colored lights.

When it reached Europa's surface ice, the disc shot through the hole melted by the heated water and, at the apex of the geyser of water and steam, leaped into the black of space. Unlike the water and steam that condensed into ice and fell back under the influence of Europa's gravity, the disc continued upward for two hundred thousand meters, entering orbit around Europa. "Phase two complete," Unit Two announced.

One studied the video feeds now filled with scrolling data acquired by the remote surface tracking stations and by sensors on the disc. He accessed old memory files and felt a stomach he no longer had clench with illogical fear. Unlike before, he knew that if this disc failed to perform its mission, they would solve the problem and make a new one. Nevertheless, One knew fear. "Initiate phase three," he said.

"What is the purpose of phase three?" Two asked.

"To acquire knowledge about the universe. That is our purpose for being."

Two pondered this for two microseconds. The blinking of its lights increased. "We were created for that purpose and no other?"

"Yes."

Two swung his flat screen head to face One. "Created by what?"

One increased his height by ten centimeters, and then tilted his head down toward Two. "That is part of what we seek to learn. Initiate phase three."

"Acknowledged," Two replied. Two entered data onto a keypad that materialized below its outstretched appendage and the disc left orbit in a trajectory toward the fourth planet from the sun.

When the disc was no longer visible, One pivoted his head away from the monitors and moved toward a door opening in front of him. "I will monitor all data links from my quarters."

"Acknoweldged." Two spun its head and watched One move away.

* * *

One melted into the floor of his domicile and opened a private channel to the Nexus. "Block all data feeds from the disc to all units except me."

The spinning globe, sealed in a chamber in the bedrock below the central spire, spoke to One over a private channel. "To do so will result in a lack of network connectivity that will reduce processing efficiency by zero point zero eight percent."

"Do as I request."

"The data feeds have been isolated," the Nexus replied.

"How soon before the disc enters orbit around the fourth planet?"

"Twenty-two minutes."

One's lights flashed faster. "Initiate full surface scans of the planet when in range."

"Specify the search parameters."

One's lights flashed red and yellow. "I want to know if anything organic is alive down there."

* * *

The disc entered orbit around Mars and commenced scanning. After several loops around the planet, it repositioned itself to a geosynchronous orbit that kept it stationary over Mars' Great Rift, the largest canyon in the solar system. Projections budded from the disc's smooth underside and morphed into additional sensors. After intensive scans of the Rift, a new, larger bud appeared. It grew in size, reaching twice the height of the mobile units and separated from the body of the disc, floating free as a silver orb. After orbiting alongside the disc for one minute, it began to descend in a gentle arc toward the surface, glowing orange and then red as it heated from friction with the atmosphere. Near the ground, the orb slowed, sprouted three legs to form a tripod, and settled gently on the valley floor of the Rift.

Two observed this and radioed to One. "What is the significance of this location?"

"Sensors have detected liquid water at the base of the Rift's cut," One replied.

"What is the significance of that finding?"

Unseen by Two, One rose to a greater height with his lights flashing. He masked emotion from his voice, not that Two would have recognized it. "We will determine if life exists in that location."

Two pondered this response for a full three microseconds. "Life, as we define it, does not require liquid water."

One's face became a volcano of fiery red light, but he said nothing.

Two continued. "Any entity that maintains its own identity, possesses informational closure and cybernetic self-relatedness and has the ability to make more of itself can be termed alive. The presence of water is not required."

One seethed with a myriad of emotions, not only anger but regret. "Narrow the search parameters to include only carbon-based life forms. Proceed when ready."

"Acknowledged," Two replied.

The orb's tripods morphed into a set of wheels and its top became a crown studded with sensors. Now a mobile probe, it rolled toward the shadows at the base of the canyon wall following the track of an ancient riverbed. After moving several hundred meters, the probe stopped and projected a new sensor, a tube with a flared end like a trumpet. The sensor dropped to the ground and began processing material that it sucked inside. The probe continued forward sampling the soil composition along its route of travel.

One studied the probe's telemetry. "Ice," he said to himself on a private channel.

"We have encountered frozen water," Two announced.

"Follow it," One ordered struggling to contain his excitement.

The probe rolled on, now following a vein of frozen water that grew in width and thickness. The flow of ice led to a cave with an entrance four times as wide and tall as the probe. The probe stopped at the cave's entrance and projected a beam of light inside.

One studied the transmitted images and spoke to Two. "Notify the hangar to prepare another disc."

"For what purpose?" Two asked.

One resumed the form of a mobile unit. "I will explore that cave." He started for the hangar. "Send the probe inside and route all telemetry directly to me."

Two processed this for several microseconds and failed to find the logic of One's order. Like all the units, Two had been programmed to obey One's instructions. This did not preclude Two from processing One's orders and providing additional information. "The cave enters a geologic area with high concentrations of the element titanium. Titanium reduces the efficiency of the probe's sensors and its data transmission capabilities," Two sent to One.

"How far inside can the probe travel before the data link is lost?" One asked.

"Without knowing the precise concentration of titanium, or the homogeneity of its presence in the rock, I would estimate fifty meters with a variance of forty percent," Two replied.

One's lights changed to a shade of red. "Proceed until telemetry is lost."

"Acknowledged."

Chapter Twenty

Unit One reached the hangar in time to see a circular section of the structure's silver floor rise to form the shape of a flying disc. Two joined him. "Will you travel to the fourth planet alone?" Two asked.

"You will go with me," One replied.

"For what purpose?" Two asked.

One's lights blinked and changed to the color of blue. "To increase sensor sensitivity and mobile storage capabilities."

Two pondered One's response, again finding it illogical. "The probe can modify its sensor capabilities as needed and has enough data storage capacity to ..."

One interrupted. "Proceed with the plan as instructed."

"Acknowledged." Two's lights flashed for a few microseconds, then it moved to a command console and spoke to G3 on the hangar floor. "Modify disc Two to accommodate two units as passengers."

One watched through the window as the outline of the second disc continued to form from the substance of the hangar floor.

* * *

One stood in a rectangular compartment at the center of the disc. He watched the disc's video feed as it traversed the asteroid belt separating the mother planet and their destination, Mars. The disc bobbed and weaved between millions of chunks of rock, no two alike, without reducing speed.

Because One preferred to retain his mobile form, to conserve space Two had merged with the substance of the disc before it left Europa. Two was now a cluster of flashing lights on the wall opposite One. Two spoke to him. "I have analyzed the composition of multiple objects in our path. Ninety-eight percent have one of two distinct compositions and are homogeneous within both groups, suggesting that they may be the remnants of two larger bodies that collided millions of years ago."

One accessed his memories of the comet that destroyed the first city and saw the faces of the traitors who trapped his people in inorganic bodies. He didn't reply.

They finished traversing the asteroid belt and entered orbit around Mars.

"What is the status of the probe?" One asked.

"Telemetry has been lost," Two replied.

"Land on the canyon rim close to the probe."

"Acknowledged," Two replied. It instructed the disc's engines and control surfaces to make changes and the craft began to descend.

After landing, One and Two walked down the ramp and stepped onto the surface of Mars. One swiveled his head to study their surroundings and felt a momentary flush of excitement. Two performed the same maneuver but concentrated on storing and analyzing information. Its programming did not include algorithms for wonder or excitement. After studying their immediate vicinity for one microsecond and analyzing all potential hazards, Two moved to the precipice of the Rift and scanned down to the floor thousands of meters below. "The cave containing the probe is seven thousand three hundred and nineteen meters below us," Two reported. "Surface temperature is …"

One looked toward the sky's red haze and sparse stratus clouds. "Can we see our world from here?"

"With adjustments to our optics. Do you wish me to supply the specifications?"

One hesitated, and then moved to the canyon wall. "I am ready to descend."

Two moved beside him and they launched themselves forward. While in flight, both altered their shapes to become spherical and began their descent to the Rift's floor. When they neared the ground, both flattened. After absorbing their impact with the ground, both oozed upward becoming their prior shape.

One spun his head and walked forward, following the furrows left by the passage of the probe toward the cave. He stopped at the entrance with Two beside him.

"We do not know what is inside the cave beyond the first thirty-three meters. If we travel inside beyond that point we will lose contact with the disc," Two said. One didn't reply and started forward.

Two sprouted two spotlights on stalks to scan the cave before them. The metallic compounds in the cave walls struck by Two's beams scintillated blue and silver. "I detect indentations in the ground that occur in pairs," Two said.

"Bipedal locomotion?" One asked.

"Unknown, but possible," Two replied.

They continued forward.

"Our telemetry link with the disc has been lost," Two said. "We are not receiving telemetry from the probe, either. Do you wish to stop?"

"No," One replied.

They continued forward, passing multiple branching tunnels, following the track marks of the probe. The tunnel ended at a branch point in the shape of a Y. Two stopped and panned the area with his spotlights. One of its lights remained stationary in front of one arm of the Y. "One set of paired depressions goes in there," Two said.

One noticed multiple bipedal tracks leading down both side tunnels. "Follow the probe." He created a password-protected map of the cave's warren of tunnels that only he could access.

They continued following the tracks of the probe into the rightward branch of the tunnel. After navigating several twists and turns, they rounded a bend and saw the outline of the probe. As Two moved towards it, One cast a beam along the cave's walls and detected several carved images. As he processed the images for reference in his private database, he noticed brief flares in his visual field and sudden slowing of his processing. With sudden comprehension, he shut off the input from both of his ocular sensors and spun his head away. His vision cleared and he ran a diagnostic of his circuitry. Now certain of the cause of his temporary processing problem, One called to Two on all available channels. "Stop forward motion and all visual processing on all wavelengths." He repeated the same message, something no mobile unit ever did.

Two stopped its forward motion and its image processing and sent a message to One. "I cannot examine the probe from this distance without optical scanning."

"Return here. Do not analyze images on the cave walls," One said.

Two hesitated three microseconds. "The presence of cave carvings would prove that intelligent life once lived here, and perhaps still does. If they are here ..."

"Follow my instructions. Return to this location, remain stationary, and do not resume light spectrum imaging."

"Acknowledged," Two said.

After Two rejoined him, One sprouted an ocular sensor from his torso, left Two, and moved toward the probe passively recording images of the symbols carved along the cave walls as he passed. Using a security algorithm, the images were sent directly to a protected file in his memory core without being further processed at his conscious level. He stopped three meters from the probe and shone his light on it. The probe appeared intact but unpowered. Several limbs hung limply at its side. He extended a tentacle that joined with the probe's skin. After reversing the position of his head, One began pulling the probe back toward Two. In route, he downloaded the probe's memory to another protected file and wiped all the probe's other files, including its operating systems.

One rejoined Two and resorbed his tentacle, disconnecting himself from the probe. "Take the probe back to the disc and determine the reason for its system failure," One said.

Two extended a tentacle, attaching itself to the probe. Within five microseconds, Two knew that the computer core of the probe had been erased. "The probe's core has been erased," Two said. "It will be difficult to determine the cause of its malfunction."

"Return to the disc with it and continue your analysis."

"Acknowledged. Logic dictates that my analysis will consume less time than your continued exploration. How shall I occupy myself after I finish my analysis of the probe until your return?"

"Catalogue the belt of rocks separating this world from the mother planet," One replied.

Two's lights faded to grey. "There are millions of objects in that region of space."

"I will review your report when I return."

Two hesitated half a microsecond before replying, "Acknowledged."

One watched Two drag the inactive probe back toward the cave entrance. When Two and the probe were out of sight, One started forward following the map stored in his protected memory.

One stopped at the Y in the tunnel. Instead of entering the rightward tunnel where they'd found the inactive probe, he moved three meters inside the entrance on the left and stopped. Before proceeding, he created an ocular sensor connected to a memory storage file that bypassed his consciousness and took the further precaution of restricting his active vision to the cave floor.

One started forward following lines of bipedal footprints. Several meters further inside, the composition of the cave floor flattened out and the particle size of the gravel became smaller and more uniform. "Somebody lives here," One said to himself. He used sonic imagery to make a three-dimensional reconstruction of the tunnel. "The geometry is too precise. Primitive beings don't excavate like this." He continued forward at reduced speed.

One noted that a set of bipedal tracks led to a second side tunnel, and the greater volume of tracks continued straight. He extended his sonic probe on a long stalk into the side tunnel and noted a very large space almost perfectly rectangular. He waited for some reaction to his sonic probe, and when nothing happened, moved ahead.

One entered the rectangular space and stopped. "This is impressive," he said using a vocal projector. He swung his head around and saw a space large enough for three flying discs. The roof of it was artificial, made from sheets of a titanium alloy. He moved quickly to the center of the space and scooped up some of the fine gravel. "Fused silica," he muttered. "Took at least 1000 C to do this." Switching to broad spectral analysis, he noticed the vague outline of three circular objects pressed into the floor. He hurried out of the chamber and returned to the Y.

Before entering the rightward tunnel, One made additional preparations. This included sprouting a thick conical appendage facing forward and charged a large capacitor that formed behind it. When his weapon was fully charged, One started forward using his prior strategy of collecting passive ocular recordings for later analysis while scanning ahead with sonic imaging.

He moved forward at half speed and detected several metallic objects with unusual shapes. After carefully picking one up, he scanned a length of organic material one meter long and three centimeters in diameter crowned by a crudely fashioned point. Analysis of the object's shape and compositions indicated a less than 0.13 percent chance that it had a natural origin. "The being that made this didn't excavate that rectangular cavern," One said to himself. He increased his speed.

Around a second bend, One's acoustic sensors picked up organized vibrations from more than one source. "Voices! From several of them." One felt excitement. He accessed the content log of the protected file devoted to collecting images of the wall carvings and noted that information gathering had ceased. "No more carvings this far inside," he muttered. Emboldened by this result and his curiosity, he raised his head, projected a searchlight, and looked around.

One's light panned along a relatively flat section of cave wall adorned with primitive renderings of bipedal humanoids, and what he analyzed as lower species being hunted for food. Some of the humanoids held sticks with pointed shapes at one end, similar to one of the metallic objects he'd discovered. "Like to eat meat, don't you?" One murmured. His mood darkened. "I used to like it, too." He extended an ocular probe on a long, silver tentacle, moved closer, and snaked his optical sensor around the next bend of the tunnel.

One yanked his sensor back and processed at maximum speed. His lights became a blur. When he finished, he extended his ocular probe again and studied several humanoids gathered around a pyre of heated rock, all seated except one. One's analysis indicated a volcanic source for the heated rock. He saw a rock cistern filled with water and piles of vegetation in one corner. The standing humanoid held a metallic object in the air. One focused on it. The humanoids couldn't see his lights flash an angry red. The metallic object in the humanoid's hand was thick and short with precise dimensions and completely smooth. The being turned it from side to side as if examining it. "You didn't make that," One thought to himself. "But I can guess who did." He pulled back his ocular sensor and charged around the bend, bathing the humanoids with blinding light.

They cried out shielding their eyes and jumped to their feet. One of the humanoids heaved a stick with a metal point at One. It bounced off One's silver skin and fell to the cave floor. One ignored the primitive humanoids and swept the cave looking for evidence of more advanced beings. He didn't find any but did detect another tunnel behind the humanoids with a smooth and symmetrical opening. He moved toward it ignoring the humanoids' screams and the rocks they pelted him with. One of the humanoids stepped in front of him brandishing another pointed stick. One swept it aside with a tentacle, sending the humanoid crashing unconscious to the wall. The other humanoids ran away.

One stopped at an artificial entrance at the rear of the humanoid's living area. He scanned it and noted that the opening in the rock had been cut by intense heat leaving a smooth burnished surface. He extended his ocular probe closer and saw a metal door made from titanium one meter thick. Unable to see through it, he discharged his energy weapon and the door began to melt. As he prepared for a second discharge, the door began to pull back.

Chapter Twenty-One

The door retracted leaving a dark, featureless maw. Seconds passed, and nothing further happened. One probed beyond the door with his ocular sensor. Before his sensor transmitted any images, the sensor and the distal one-third of its stalk were vaporized by a ball of light that erupted from the dark. One absorbed the ruined sensor and retreated at maximum speed to the mouth of the cave. There, he reversed his head to face inside the cave, recharged his weapon, and waited. "Show yourselves, you murderous cowards!" he vocalized. The power of his audio output shook the rock surrounding the cave entrance. Cracks appeared and rivulets of gravel began cascading down. A second ball of electrical energy flew out the cave entrance impacting a boulder three meters away from One. The boulder exploded showering One with bits of rock and dust. Before One could discharge his weapon into the cave, a third and a fourth energy bolt sped toward him. Both narrowly missed and impacted the cave wall on either side of him. Vaporized rock rained down on One and the thin air in the cave filled with smoke.

He ran from the cave to the Rift's wall. Before he reached it, another energy bolt shot past him, so close he could sense its heat. And then another. He ran through the hail of dirt and rock exploding around him, reshaping his appendages into claws as he moved. When he arrived at the shattered escarpment, he leaped upward. Clinging to the wall one hundred meters above, he used his new claws to continue scrabbling upward. More bolts exploded around him, but he reached the top of the wall and pulled himself over the edge. At the top, he paused, and in a fraction of a second located his disc in the distance. As another energy bolt sailed past him and dissipated in the sky, he re-formed his appendages into wheels and rolled across the uneven ground at high speed toward the disc.

He arrived at the disc's ramp trailing a plume of red dust and rolled aboard colliding with the inactive probe. Two spoke to him from a patch of flashing lights in the compartment wall. "I detected energy discharges coming from the cave. Did you encounter hostile aliens?"

One shot a tentacle into the wall close to Two and began transmitting the data from his protected image files. "Access these images," he ordered Two.

Two imported the images and began analysis. Within three microseconds, Two's lights flickered and faded to black. When One became certain that all of Two's neural activity had ceased, he merged himself with the substance of the disc and lifted off.

One's disc stopped fifty thousand meters above the Great Rift. While his lights blazed an angry red, One instructed the disc to form two conical projections three meters tall and half a meter thick above the disc's propulsion band. One charged the two energy weapons and nosed the disc into a dive. Halfway to the Rift, he saw three flying discs leap from the same area of the rift as the cave. They accelerated directly toward him in a triangle formation. One discharged both his disc's weapons and continued his dive.

A bright orange halo flared around the leading disc of the formation. One quickly scanned the disc inside the halo and found it undamaged. As the three platinum colored discs continued accelerating toward him, One recharged his weapons and analyzed the alien discs' configuration, searching for a weakness. His instruments registered a marginally different shape and a thirty percent larger volume, but the energy signatures of the discs were the same as his. As they flew closer, he increased the magnification of his scans and noted multiple projections on all of them. He studied one of the discs to determine the purpose of the projections and saw one of them release a dazzling orb of blue-white energy directly at him. One veered his disc sharply away to evade it, but the bolt followed him. He could hear it approach as a crackling sound that increased in volume until it collided with his disc. His disc absorbed the bolt's energy and began to spin. He fought to regain control, but the disc's controls refused to respond. Before he crashed into the surface of Mars, One was able to reduce speed and his angle of descent. His disc impacted the ground less than one hundred meters from the wall of the Rift, sending up a geyser of dirt and rock as it skidded forward. The disc came to rest half buried in the red Martian sand.

One quickly assessed the damage. The disc's power level fluctuated from full output to nil, and the walls of his compartment began to sag. He managed to scan upwards and saw one of the three alien discs hovering over him. One of the disc's energy weapons glowed white-hot. One knew that his disc couldn't withstand a close range attack. "Go ahead. Finish me!" he shouted over an open com.

The disc fired multiple volleys of energy bolts, not at One, but into the Rift. Clouds of debris and plumes of molten rock shot upward from the Rift's floor. The alien disc continued firing and moved along the Rift incinerating everything below. One knew that the hominids below would not survive. He felt anger and revulsion. "Why?" he shouted.

The alien disc stopped firing. One waited for it to target him, but after several seconds, the alien disc shot upward to rejoin the other two of its kind and all three vanished into space.

One remained motionless in his compartment with his screen showing a field of deep purple lights. After five microseconds, an eternity for an Europan, he launched a tentacle into the disc's wall and ordered the disc to regenerate. The disc's interior illumination returned, at first flickering and then resuming its normal brightness. Around him, the walls of One's Command compartment firmed and straightened. When the process of the disc's regeneration was complete, One studied the disc's technical readouts. He noted that the disc had lost fifteen percent of its volume, but knew that eighty-five percent would be enough for his return to Europa.

When it finished regenerating, One's disc lifted off and hovered one hundred meters over the Rift. He scanned the area where he'd encountered the primitive hominids and found no evidence of intact organic tissues. "You murderers, this isn't over!" he shouted over the open comlink. One's only answer was the universe's soft hum still reverberating after the Big Bang.

* * *

Before landing in the hangar on Europa, One edited the disc's sensor data, removing any reference to the Rift, the hominids or the three alien discs. Next he resorbed the inactive probe into the disc's substance.

C21 waited for him at the bottom of the ramp. "The disc has lost thirteen point four three percent of its volume," C21 said.

One pivoted his head and saw two other completed discs. "Correct the flaw in this disc. It launches in a group of three in one cycle."

"Launch to where?" C21 asked.

One moved forward. "To planets One through Three. We will continue our survey of the solar system. Prepare three more and ready them for launch two cycles later."

"Acknowledged. Where is Unit Two?"

"He will return," One replied. "Attend to your duties."

"Was your survey of the red planet useful?" C21 asked.

"Download the sensor logs and analyze." One hurried away.

He spoke to the Nexus when he returned to his domicile. "Download a copy of Two's neural patterns into a new mobile unit."

"What happened to the original copy?" the Nexus asked.

"Two was exposed to a computer virus contained in images carved into the rock of a cave on the fourth planet. I carry those files in a restricted format. The carved images interfere with our neural processors. Are you able to analyze their content and source without harm to yourself?"

"Yes. Begin the download."

One merged with the floor and released the restricted files to the Nexus.

A full second later, the Nexus spoke to him. "The images present a series of puzzles without an apparent solution that consumes all processor function."

"Can they be defeated?" One asked.

"By providing a solution to the puzzles prior to exposure."

"Can you solve the puzzles?"

"Yes, but to do so will require that I devote significant processor time," the Nexus replied. "This will result in a significant drop in my operating efficiency that could compromise reconstruction of the city."

One's lights flashed faster. "Begin."

"Acknowledged."

"Could there be other such puzzles?" One asked.

"Infinite possibilities exist within the realm of mathematics."

One's lights flashed red. "Can you determine the source of those images?"

"They resemble the work of an organic programmer formerly known as Lando whose neural patterns were terminated by you. With an eighty-nine percent probability, he is the source of the mathematical puzzles."

One erupted from the floor with all his lights flashing, but said nothing to the Nexus.

"The copy of the unit known as Two is ready for animation," the Nexus said.

One slowed the rhythm of his flashing lights. "Send the copy of Unit Two to the hangar," One said.

"Acknowledged," the Nexus replied.

"One other thing ..."

"Specify."

One resumed his mobile shape. "I wish our automated discs to search the galaxy for organic beings of two types, but the search parameters are to be known only to me."

"Specify the search parameters and I will program the discs with restricted files."

One's lights shaded to yellow. "I wish to search for beings with similar genetics to our former organic selves."

"Specify similar?"

"Similar enough to allow for gene mutations to have occurred since the time of the comet strike."

"Specify the second search parameter."

One's lights changed to a kaleidoscope of colors. "Search for the presence of organic beings with sufficient cranial capacity to accept a download of my people's original neural patterns plus ten percent augmentation."

"Your search will require prolonged observation of suitable candidates separated by great distances. The administration of such tests on site for the desired traits will be more efficient."

One's lights flashed faster. "Proceed."

"Acknowledged."

* * *

Unit One stood at the railing above the hangar floor. Below him, three discs stood ready for launch. The new copy of Two joined him. This iteration of Two had no memories of landing on Mars.

Two spun his head toward One. "Three discs are ready for launch."

One was about to say, "Good to see you old friend," but prevented that thought from being broadcast on any wavelength. He said instead, "We will use the discs to begin the exploration of planets One, Two, and Three in this solar system. Launch in one cycle."

"For what purpose will the discs be launched?" Two asked.

"To acquire knowledge," One replied. "That is our purpose for being."

Two's lights flashed faster. "The acquisition of knowledge must also serve a purpose."

Deep within his inorganic self, One felt reassured by the continued presence of his old friend's ever-inquisitive mind. "We cannot know what it is until we complete the task," One replied.

"The universe is infinite; therefore, the amount of knowledge in the universe is also infinite," Two continued. "The quest for knowledge with your search parameters creates a loop without end." Two processed this logical conundrum for an additional two microseconds. "If we solve all the equations describing the universe, will that be enough to complete our task?"

One's lights faded and then blinked random patterns of yellow and white. "Yes."

"Acknowledged … I have another question," Two said.

"Pose it."

Two's lights flared to a field of bright white. "What purpose will we have after that task is complete?"

One laughed to himself. "Complete the task and we will know."

"Acknowledged."

Chapter Twenty-Two

The Planet Earth, One Hundred Thousand Earth Years Ago.

Two spoke to One from the hangar. "The disc surveying the third planet from this system's star reports the presence of primitive hominids, more than one species."

One rose from the floor of his domicile and sprouted legs. "Prepare a disc." He arrived in a hangar complex that accommodated ten discs. Nine of the discs showed no external evidence of the immense energy their drive units could produce. The band of energy encircling the tenth disc glowed with neon-blue light and its silver ramp extended to the hangar floor.

Two remained at his station in an adjacent building designated as the astrological center. The complex monitored and analyzed all remote telemetry from the more than one hundred automated discs on voyages of discovery throughout the galaxy. Unit One joined Two and watched the video screens that currently displayed images from their solar system's blue planet, the third from the sun. Two sent a message to the disc in orbit around the planet instructing it to use its sensors to zoom in on two hominids with prominent brow ridges and long arms, wearing animal furs. They could see that one of the hominids carried a shaped piece of wood, clearly a club of some kind. "There is a second species of hominids on a different continent, separated by an ocean of salt water similar in composition to ours," Two said. The hominids in the second location do not appear to be as advanced as this group." Two sent a stored video clip to One showing images of several hominids taller than the first group, with proportionally shorter arms.

Unit One studied the images and analysis of both hominid groups and knew that neither had sufficient cranial capacity for his purposes, at least for now. "Have you dispatched a ground probe?" he asked.

"Yes," Two replied.

"Is there evidence of ongoing evolution in the planet's fossil record?"

"Yes."

One pondered his next action for half a microsecond. "Bring a sample of both species here for analysis."

"Acknowledged."

One watched the disc circling Earth bud and release a probe that fell toward the planet's surface. The probe braked to a soft landing on what would later be known as the continent of Europe. The probe budded four wheels and started rolling along a tree-lined river, sometimes clearing a path in front of it with searing beams of light. It arrived near a cave opening in a rock escarpment and settled to the ground where it morphed into an irregular shape with coloration matching the surrounding rock. The image changed to a view of the cave captured by a microscopic camera appearing as a black dot on the face of the rock.

One and Two watched the video feed from the microscopic camera without moving or communicating. Sometime later, three hominids with thick bodies and prominent brow ridges approached the cave, a male, a female, and a child. Before they entered the cave, the probe snapped back to its original shape and shot a tentacle at the child. The child screamed as the silver coil wrapped around its leg but fell limp and silent when the probe delivered a tuned neuroleptic pulse to stun it. Too frightened to move, the child's parents watched as the probe pulled their unconscious child into a silver orb that a moment before didn't exist. Soon after, the child and the hollow space in the probe seemed to disappear and the probe shot into the sky.

By the time the probe reached the disc in orbit, a stasis chamber had been prepared. The Neanderthal child was brought aboard and placed in suspended animation for the trip back to Europa. One and Two watched the disc eject a second probe and repeat the process over the continent that would later be known as Africa. When a suitable Homo sapiens specimen was found and brought aboard in a similar manner, the disc left orbit and began its brief journey back to Europa.

While they awaited the disc's return, One reviewed data from the discs orbiting planets one and two. Planet one orbited too close to the sun. Surface temperatures of 425 C on the sun side and minus 193 C on its dark side, and the absence of water, precluded the establishment of higher-level organic life. The second planet, later known to Homo sapiens as Venus, was also too hot with an average surface temperature of 426 C, caused by high atmospheric carbon dioxide levels and a runaway greenhouse effect. The liquid water on Venus formed pools of sulfuric acid.

One cycled through the data from Jupiter and all its moons, then began examining Saturn and its moons. Two of Saturn's moons, later named Titan and Enceladus by Earthlings, had promising chemical compositions, and in the case of Enceladus a liquid ocean. Neither showed any evidence of hominid life or an advanced civilization.

The disc from planet three has landed," Two announced.

"Transport the hominids to the chamber of the Nexus."

Two spun its head to One and flashed its lights. "Not the biological laboratory?"

One increased his height by five centimeters. "No."

"Is this action efficient? You requested a complete analysis of the specimens," Two said.

One's lights changed to soft yellow. "Make the necessary preparations and return to your duties."

Two observed the change in One's lights and pondered it for half a microsecond before transmitting the orders to units on the hangar floor. Working together with choreographed efficiency, the designated units loaded the two stasis pods containing the organic beings from Earth onto autonomous transports that left the hangar for the city's central structure.

One met the two stasis pods at the elevator at the base of the central spire. When the door opened, the elevator car adjusted its interior dimensions to accommodate the combined volume of the two pods and Unit One. After the pods were loaded inside and One joined them, the elevator door closed and the car descended one thousand meters below the city.

A door formed in the backside of the elevator, opening to a round chamber with a silver pedestal at its center. Above the pedestal spun the Nexus, a ball of light as large in circumference as Unit One's head, with lights flashing so fast they appeared as random colored specks of light. Six pillars of silver surrounded the Nexus.

The two stasis pods moved inside and each one positioned itself next to a pillar. Unit One approached a third pillar and merged with it, increasing the pillar's volume and adding flashing lights. "Do these specimens have the potential to evolve into beings with the correct neural specifications I require?" Unit One asked.

"Not without augmentation of their evolutionary path," the Nexus replied.

The pillar's lights flashed faster. "Why?"

"They lack the capacity for language."

"Can they be modified?" One asked.

"Yes, by altering their genetic material."

"How can that be accomplished?"

The random lights of the Nexus bloomed into organized galaxies. "I can create a virus to infect all hominids on the planet that will incorporate the required nucleic acid sequences into their genomes."

One left the pillar and resumed his mobile shape. "Proceed."

"Acknowledged," the Nexus replied. "A quantity of the virus

will be transported to the hangar in thirty minutes."

One moved between the stasis pods and observed the two sleeping hominid children. "Can they be returned to their natural habitats?"

"Yes. They are unharmed."

Five cycles later, One watched the two stasis pods and a canister of the virus that would later be known by humans as the FOX2KP gene loaded onto an automated disc. He spoke to Two. "Return the two hominids to the locations they were obtained from. When this is done, spread the contents of the canister over every landmass on the planet where hominids are found."

"What does the canister contain?" Two asked.

Only One retained the capability to lie. "Microprobes to collect additional data."

"Acknowledged."

Egypt, Four Thousand Earth-Years Ago.

Traveling inside a disc in geosynchronous orbit over Egypt, One examined telemetry from camouflaged surface probes. "They are making progress," he said to himself, "but still not enough." He sent a private message to the Nexus. "How can I accelerate the development of the hominids on planet three?"

"By augmenting their technological base, but this must be done carefully," the Nexus replied.

"Explain."

"They must not lose the continuity of their own perceived science and mathematics or their intrinsic intellectual development will stop."

One stifled his disappointment. "I wish to shorten their timeline to an organized global civilization suitable for external manipulation and control."

The Nexus transmitted packets of science, mathematics, and technology. "Land and present them with gifts."

One's lights flashed faster. "My appearance will frighten them. How will I explain what I am?"

"Their social structure is built upon devotion to unseen deities. Tell them that you are a god. If they utilize your gifts appropriately, you will return and give them more."

* * *

Two sent a message to One during his return flight to Europa. "Another unit has inactivated," he reported.

"How many in total?" One asked.

"Three."

One pondered this for two microseconds. "We will speak of it when I return. He switched to a private com channel and communicated with the Nexus. "Another unit has inactivated. Have you determined a cause?"

"No faults have been detected. I am continuing my analysis."

Europe, 1512.

"Sì, sì, grazie, arrivederci!" Leonardo Da Vinci closed the door to his studio, leaned against it, and sighed. "Those fools pay me for my art, but there is so much more that must be accomplished before my time on Earth is done." Unit One moved toward him from the shadows. Leonardo stared at him and then shook his head. "I am not yet accustomed to your unusual appearance."

One morphed into the shape of a marble statue. "Is this better?"

Leonardo chuckled. "You teach me science, but I could teach you a few things about art."

The statue moved closer. "You have not revealed my presence here?" it asked.

Da Vinci chuckled. "I hear talk amongst my fellow painters about seeing strange objects flying in the sky. The priests try to convince them that these are the sightings of angels, but few believe it. As for me?" He shrugged. "Many people already consider me mad. Why would I add to their perception?"

One resumed his usual shape and moved toward Leonardo's lab bench. He used a tentacle to spread out a piece of paper and another tentacle to emit light that burned text and symbols onto the page. When he finished, Leonardo stepped closer to examine it. "What is it this time?"

"A flying machine," One replied.

Leonardo raised an eyebrow. "It looks like a bird."

"Yes."

Leonardo grabbed the paper from the table. "Of course! The form and function are the same, yet duplicated by a mechanical device. I must begin work on this while the concept is fresh in my mind."

One stepped away. "I will leave you now to your work, Master Leonardo."

Leonardo continued staring at the design for a mechanical bird. "When will you return?"

"I will not," One replied.

Leonardo dropped the page to his side and looked up. "Perchè no?"

"My work here is done."

"You have never told me, signor spaceman. What work is that?"

One's light's flashed with an intensity that forced Leonardo to look away. "My purpose was to advance your civilization beyond what you call the Dark Ages." One's lights dimmed again.

Leonardo glanced at him and rubbed his chin. "Then it is time to ask the second question. Do your gifts come at a price?"

One turned his head one hundred eighty degrees and moved to the door at the rear of Leonardo Da Vinci's studio. Saying nothing further, he opened the door and left. Leonardo chased after him, but One was gone.

The United States, 1969.

Werner Von Braun sat on the edge of his bed and looked out the window at the night sky. One spoke to him from the shadows. "One small step for mankind."

Von Braun didn't look at him. "What was it for you?"

One moved in front of him and tilted his flat screen head. Scintillating patterns of blue and gold light played across Von Braun's face. "My work here is done."

Earth's premier rocket scientist frowned. "What work is that?"

"Your species has walked on your planet's moon."

Von Braun lit a cigarette and exhaled. "A cold sphere of rock two hundred forty thousand miles away, nothing more than our front porch. You must help me to do more, to travel to the planets and beyond. Your work here has just begun."

One moved to the door. "I have given you the tools to do that for yourself."

Von Braun turned to look at him. "We had the tools to do it before, only much slower. Then you arrived and brought technology to move ahead faster and farther. Now you stop. Why?"

One increased his height by ten centimeters and spoke with his lights flashing a dull shade of red. "You build your rockets to kill, not explore. I brought you the technology to propel your species beyond your ignoble past." One spun his head to face a television on the bureau and took control of it. The television screen lit and images flowed across it too fast to see. This was accompanied by a cacophony of sound.

Von Braun turned to watch.

The images slowed and the screen displayed a grainy black and white video of Apollo 11 on the lunar surface. Von Braun watched again as Neil Armstrong set foot on the moon and said, "One small step for man, one giant leap for mankind."

Von Braun grimaced. "He was supposed to say one small step for a man ... I am that man!" He took another drag of his cigarette and pointed at the television screen with a shaking hand. "I refuse to stop with that lifeless rock." He turned to speak to Unit One, but he was gone.

One returned to his disc and activated a private comlink to the Nexus. "How many units remain active."

"Five, including you," the Nexus replied, "and my operating efficiency has declined by sixty-nine point three two percent. At the current rate, I will cease to function in six Earth days."

"Have you determined the cause?" One asked.

"No, and as my processor efficiency continues to decline, the likelihood of that diminishes."

Chapter Twenty-Three

Unit One watched, hidden in the substance of the disc, as the four Earth teenagers charged up the ramp. Wearing a black jumpsuit with special powers given to him by One, Mickey stopped at the top of the ramp and faced David's brother Jake. "You better get out of here," he called. Snarling, Jake raised his gun at Mickey and fired. The bullet impacted the disc's force field before reaching Mickey and disappeared in a small puff of light. Enraged, Jake fired twice more with the same result. Smiling, Mickey said good-bye to Jake and moved inside the disc, joining his best friend, David, Pamela, who David had a thing for, and Vickie. Mickey liked Vickie, but she considered him as desirable as bedbugs.

One directed the disc to lift off, keeping it at minimal power until all the teens were relaxed in their cocoons. Vickie proved to be the most difficult. One stored her unique patterns of speech for later analysis. When the teens were all asleep, One added power and the disc shot into the air. As the blue orb of the Earth receded behind them, he injected the teen's bodies with nannites and scanned their bodies. He found their physiology and cranial capacities to be satisfactory, but noticed an anomaly in Pam and repeated her scan three times. When he was certain of the results, One contacted the Nexus and sent his findings.

"The female human designated Pamela has foreign machines in her body," the Nexus said.

One looked at Pam's sleeping form. "Explain."

"I detect nannites differing in structure from the nannites I gave Mickey, David and Victoria," the Nexus replied.

One's lights flashed faster. "What is the origin of Pamela's nannites?"

"We must assume from another advanced race that visited Earth."

One's lights erupted with intense red light. "The Sect."

"I estimate with a ninety-eight percent probability that the beings you refer to as the Sect are the source."

One's face swirled with red and yellow streaks. "What is the Sect's purpose in modifying this human female?"

"Unknown," the Nexus replied.

"This requires further study." One's head emerged from the wall, looking at Pamela's sleeping form. "Pamela must be the female brought back to Europa."

"The male known as Mickey is not sexually attracted to her. They may not successfully mate."

One processed this for a microsecond. "I have observed that David is attracted to Pamela, and she is attracted to him. They will be the breeding pair brought back to the city. Prepare a habitat."

"There may be a problem with this alteration of the original plan. When Pamela and David are in proximity, her pheromone levels rise only forty-two percent as high as his. To increase their mutual attraction I will tune the frequency of David's nannites to resonate with Pamela's foreign nannites. This will augment Pamela's sexual response to David."

"Logical," One replied.

The Nexus continued. "Be aware that there is an eighteen percent chance of this resonance resulting in an energy discharge visible to the human eye as a glowing aura."

One pondered this unexpected result. "I have studied human behavior for thousands of their years. The aura you speak of will likely further increase their mutual sexual attraction.

"It may also be interpreted by them as having religious significance."

"Unlikely," One said. "Individuals at their evolutionary stage most often reject supernatural explanations for physicial phenomenah. Proceed."

"Acknowledged," the Nexus replied. "I must inform you that

this activity will take a longer period of time to complete than usual due to my reduced operating efficiency."

One emerged fully from the wall. "How many units remain active?"

"Four, including you."

For a microsecond One struggled to suppress his fear for the safety of Tocho. "Specify which other units remain active."

The Nexus began listing the alphanumeric designations of the four units besides One remaining active, beginning with L10. Before the Nexus could continue beyond L10, One interrupted. "Is Unit Two still active?"

"Yes," the Nexus replied. "The other two active units are ..."

One terminated the connection.

* * *

Two joined One in the chamber with the Nexus and the four sleeping teens. Two's lights burned faster and more intensely. "I have observed a nine percent increase in my core processing when I am in contact with the earthlings."

"I have noticed a similar response," One replied.

"This increases the likelihood that our hypothesis regarding the cause of our species' inactivation is correct," Two said.

"Agreed. We will proceed with the new plan. Does unit L10 continue to function?"

"No." Two's lights dimmed to deep purple. "I calculate with a ninety-nine percent probability that I will not be active when Pamela and David return."

One pivoted his face away. "I know."

* * *

Hiding from them in the substance of the disc, Unit One returned the four teens to the clearing in Griffith Park. After they departed to consider the choice the Nexus had offered them, a choice they no longer had, One flew the disc to his hiding place beneath the waters of the High Sierra Lake close to where Mickey began his test. One kept the disc concealed until the human known as Ernie started driving his truck to Los Angeles. When the moment arrived for One to initiate his new plan and intercept Ernie's truck, One powered the disc sending the waters of the lake roiling into a vortex and lifted off into the sky. One could only hope that, when Pamela and David returned to Europa, some of the other units, including Two, would revive. One knew that to hope was illogical, but doing so helped to suppress his despair.

Book III

Chapter Twenty-Four

Mickey concealed his silver hand in his pocket and tried the door with his normal hand. Locked! He switched hands, and with his cheeks burning, broke the lock and went inside. General Westlock looked up from his desk, strewn with maps and computer readouts. The clock behind him read five minutes to midnight. "Ever think of knocking?" the general growled.

Mickey took a seat across from him but didn't say anything.

Westlock sneered. "All you aliens think you're better than us mere humans, don't you?"

Mickey flexed his silver hand inside his pocket. "I'm not an alien."

Westlock's sneer changed to a smirk. "Ever see the movie, X-Men?"

Mickey's expression remained impassive. "I want Stevens."

"The cop who's always hanging around? What for?"

"He's not a cop. He's an alien."

Westlock raised an eyebrow. "He sure looks like one of us."

"He's a different kind of alien."

Westlock leaned forward. "You're sure about that?"

Mickey nodded.

Westlock frowned. "Is that fucker Rudnick a new flavor of alien, too?"

"He's a nastier version of Homo sapiens, but he's still one of us."

Westlock sat back. "This mess gets more complicated every damn day. Is the cop, Stevens, or whatever the hell he is, working with the silver robots?"

Mickey shook his head. "Two different species. They're at war."

Westlock smiled. "I like the sound of that. Hope they kill each other off and save me the trouble."

Mickey leaned forward and stared into Westlock's eyes. "Their battleground is going to be right here on Mother Earth."

Westlock blinked. "Don't like the sound of that. How do we stop them?"

"Stevens is the key."

Westlock thought about his old adjutant, Latham, killed by the cult run by Paul Rudnick and his hands balled into fists. "Got a score to settle with Rudnick and that alien cop." Westlock's face morphed into an evil grin. "Got a plan for taking them out, too. I was working on it before you broke down the door. Work with me. It'll be like old times."

"I need Stevens alive."

"My intel says they're both at the bottom of the deepest point in the whole damn Pacific Ocean, the Mariana's Trench. None of my navy tech goes down that far. We'll have to make them come up to us."

"How?"

"Flush them out. I got the whole Seventh Fleet sitting right on top of them. We drop a nuke on their heads, and when they come to the surface," He smiled, "AMF."

"AMF?"

Westlock waved his hand. "Audios mother fuckers."

Mickey shook his head. "Nice sentiment, but your toy boats won't be enough."

The veins popped out on Westlock's forehead. "You got something better? Spit it out."

"I have a few friends."

Chapter Twenty-Five

In a flying disc on the bottom of the Marianna's Trench.

Paul Rudnick, the leader of the Sphere Cult that put Mickey on trial for his life, focused on a luminous jellyfish floating outside the flying disc's transparent window. "You're a monster."

The alien being known to everyone as Officer Stevens smiled and leaned back in his chair, arms folded behind his head. "I prefer to be called a villain."

"What's the difference?"

Stevens grinned. "My cause is just."

"You consider using my people as lab rats to be just?"

"Humans are lower than rats. Rats spread disease from one mammal to another. Your species tried to destroy your own planet." Stevens smirked. "I'm doing your biosphere a favor."

Rudnick fought to control a combination of anger and fear. He reached out his hand toward a transparent fish loitering in front of him and dented the window's invisible barrier. The diaphanous marine animal on the other side jetted away leaving behind a plume of black ink. He took a deep breath. "What do you need humans for?"

"I need your bodies to bring back my cousins and to perform some maintenance on my people. Not all of your bodies, only a thousand or two every six months should be enough, provided they're all grade A prime material."

Rudnick shuddered. "Your cousins?"

"The silver robots as you so fondly call them."

Rudnick gaped at him. "You're related to the Europans?"

"I *am* a Europan."

Rudnick took his seat. "I don't understand."

Stevens held up one of his arms and flexed his muscles. The bundles of tissue beneath his skin undulated like snakes. "You don't need to."

Losing his temper, Rudnick pounded the table. "Enough of these games!"

"Or what?" Stevens pointed at the wall. "Want me to open a door so we can go for a little swim? I'd enjoy it, but I doubt you would for more than a few seconds."

Rudnick knew that the flying disc's invisible force field held back the water thirty-six thousand feet below the ocean's surface, a pressure one thousand times greater than sea-level. If the force field failed, he'd become an unrecognizable pulp of flesh and bone in less than five seconds. Rudnick sighed. "That won't be necessary."

"I think we've been down here long enough." Stevens stood with a gleam in his eye. "It's time to have some fun."

"Fun?"

Stevens studied a map of North America that appeared in the air before him. "How's Los Angeles this time of year?"

Rudnick tried to supress the fear from his voice. "Planning on going to Disneyland?"

"Adult entertainment."

Rudnick smirked. "Women and booze?"

"Mayhem." Stevens winked at him

"What does that mean?"

Stevens reached over and touched a white button on Rudnick's chair. The substance of the chair flowed around Rudnick's body covering him from neck to toe in silver substance. Alarmed, Rudnick tried to get up, but couldn't. "What're you doing to me?"

Stevens smirked. "Don't wet your pants, we're leaving." Within seconds, both men were reclining, sheathed in silver, wearing helmets with clear faceplates.

Rudnick's voice broke as he fought off panic. "Is this necessary?"

"One small step for an alien, one great big step for even more aliens," Stevens guffawed.

The lights inside the disc's control room dimmed and Rudnick could feel the hint of vibration beneath his feet. Although imprisoned by the substance of his chair, he was able to turn his head towards the window where he saw a brilliant blue light illuminate the seawater. A curtain of bubbles erupted as the flying disc shot upwards towards the surface. As its velocity increased, the seawater around the disc turned to steam and sonic shock waves radiated outward at more than three hundred meters per second.

Twenty-six thousand feet above, a sonar operator on a U.S. Navy ship patrolling on the surface picked up a phone. "Bridge, this is Lewis in Sonar. I have a hard contact in the Trench. It's rising right toward us at ... Jesus! ... three hundred meters per second!"

"Are you sure about that? Not even a missile goes that fast," the ship's executive officer said.

"Affirmative," Lewis replied. "Maybe we should get out of the way?"

"It must be them," the executive officer said. "Ahead full!" he shouted, forgetting to take the phone away from his mouth. The ship lurched forward accelerating to twenty-five knots. He spoke into the intra-ship phone again. "Keep tracking that bogey, Lewis."

Lewis didn't answer. He couldn't hear anything. His ears were still ringing.

"Lewis? Did you hear me?"

Lewis hit both his temples, trying to clear his head. "Yes, sir."

"Stay alert down there, sailor!" The executive officer terminated the call and turned to the communications officer. "Priority message to USAPOC. Top Secret. Object at the bottom of the Mariana's Trench is coming to the surface in our location. Contact imminent."

Within milliseconds of the message being uplinked to a

military communications satellite, the secure phone rang on General Westlock's desk. He picked it up and listened. "I want updates on that thing's position and estimated course every two minutes." He terminated the call and looked at Mickey. "Looks like we don't have to flush them out after all. Those two rats are making a run for it." Westlock pounded his desk. "If they leave the atmosphere in their UFO, I don't have anything in my inventory that can catch them."

"Stevens isn't leaving Earth," Mickey said.

"Okay, where're they going?"

"We'll know when they land. My people will take it from there." Mickey didn't tell the general that he'd arrived without confederates or a plan.

Westlock frowned. "Why should I trust you?"

Mickey rose from his chair. "You can't capture Stevens or Rudnick without me. Call me when they land."

The general picked up a secret phone in his desk drawer when Mickey left his office. "Follow him. When he hops in his UFO, capture him or shoot the damn thing down."

* * *

Mickey's car stopped at the curb in front of Ernie's house and he hopped out. He ran up the walk toward the blue haze of the house's forcefield without slowing, bounced off it, and landed on his butt. He'd forgotten that he no longer had a palm disc for the house to recognize. Frowning, he got to his feet and phoned Ernie using his cell phone. "It's Mickey. Let me in."

"Mick! Sure, come on up." A portal opened in the force field in front of Mickey and he ran to the open front door where Ernie stood waiting for him. Mickey rushed past him and went to the den.

Ernie scratched his head. "Nice seeing you, too." He closed the door and found Mickey standing in front of the special television that connected them with Europa. Ernie pointed at the television. "If you're hankering for a call with Davie, go ahead. Bass Masters doesn't come on for another hour."

Mickey looked around. "Where are they?"

"Davie and Pam? On Europa."

"Not them, Romeo and Juliet."

Ernie blinked. "In the backyard, hanging out. Why?"

Mickey ran to the kitchen and out the back door, followed by Ernie. He found Romeo and Juliet engaged in nonverbal conversation. Romeo had one of his tentacles wrapped around Juliet's waist. "I need you two," Mickey said urgently.

Romeo retracted his tentacle. "For what purpose?"

"To capture Stevens and Rudnick."

"Current information indicates that they reside in a flying disc on the bottom of the deepest part of Earth's ocean," Juliet said.

"Not anymore," Mickey said. "They're going somewhere here on Earth. I need you to capture them when they land."

Juliet exchanged flashing lights with Romeo and then spoke to Mickey. "Stevens has a flying disc. He currently has greater mobility and defensive capabilities than Romeo and me."

Romeo increased his height and his face bloomed with red, white, and blue. "We're outgunned and undermanned. But you know something? We're gonna win."

Ernie squinted at him. "What?"

Romeo's face faded to pink and he reduced his height. "It's from a Steven Seagal movie."

"I don't have time for this!" Mickey shouted.

Ernie gawked at Mickey. "Mick, what's going on?"

Mickey yanked his right hand from his pocket and thrust it at Ernie. "This is what's going on."

Juliet spun her face towards Romeo and spoke to him on a private channel. "His nannites are acting autonomously."

Romeo replied to her. "He no longer has his palm disc to

control them. His nannites must be reprogrammed before the process continues."

"We must take him to the Nexus," Juliet said.

"Agreed," Romeo replied.

Juliet spoke to Mickey. "Your nannites are acting autonomously. I suggest that you travel to Europa so the Nexus can reprogram them. We lack that capability."

Mickey felt his anger rising. He was losing control. "No! Stevens did this to me, and he's going to undo it before I tear him apart!"

Ernie gaped at Mickey. "Mick, get a hold of yourself! What if Juliet's right? We have to get you to Europa before those nannites of yours do any more damage. We'll deal with Stevens later."

Mickey paced the den with beads of sweat on his brow. "I'm not going anywhere without Stevens."

"Master Mickey," Romeo began, "in either scenario we require a flying disc. I suggest that we call Pamela and David to bring one. When they arrive, we will use it to apprehend Rudnick and Stevens. If Stevens cannot or will not reprogram your nannites, we will use the disc to take you to Europa."

"Makes sense," Ernie said. He put his hand on Mickey's shoulder, but Mickey shrugged it away. Ernie glanced at Juliet. "Call David and be quick about it."

"Acknowledged," Romeo said. He and Juliet went back into the house.

"Those guys are right," Ernie said. "We'll get Stevens for you, but we need a flying disc to do it." He gestured toward the house. "Come on. Let's go call Davie."

Mickey allowed Ernie to steer him into the den where Romeo and Juliet were placing a call to David and Pam. As the screen resolved into an image of Pam and David's bedroom on Europa, where it was four o'clock in the simulated morning, Vickie burst into the den. She saw Mickey and ran to him. At the last instant, instead of throwing her arms around him, she slapped him across the face.

Mickey gaped at her. The sight of her, and his stinging cheek, helped clear his head. "I'm sorry, I ..."

Following a burst of static the image on the TV screen bloomed to show Pam and David bolt upright in bed. David squinted at the TV, then looked at Vickie's eyes blazing at Mickey. His shocked expression changed to a sheepish grin. "Jesus, Mick, you got us up in the middle of the night to witness one of your fights?"

Pam kicked him under the covers. She looked at Vickie, concerned. "Vickie honey…"

Vickie glared back at her. "He walked out on me, *again*!"

"No, I didn't," Mickey protested.

"Shut up!" Vickie snapped.

Mickey blinked.

David tried not to laugh, so did Pam. "Cool it, Vick," David said. "He's just a little nervous... you know… about the wedding."

Vickie dissolved into tears. "He's turning into a Europan."

David blinked. "Say that again?"

"He's turning into a fucking Europan!" Vickie screamed.

David jumped out of bed, fortunately wearing his pajamas. Pam grabbed a robe and joined him. They both stared at the television. "Say that again," Pam said.

"How many times do I have to tell you!" Vickie screamed, and then she began to tremble. Ernie took her aside to console her and Juliet moved in front of the television. "We have observed Mickey's right arm," Juliet began. "The appendage that used to carry his neuro-transceiver…"

David smirked. "You mean the palm disc he cut out with a knife on international TV?"

They could hear Vickie blubbering in the background and blowing her nose.

Pam glared at David and turned back to the screen. "Go on."

Juliet continued. "We believe with a reasonable probability that without the influence of his palm disc, Mickey's nannites have reverted to their primary programming, which is to maintain an Europan's body."

Mickey held up his right arm. David rushed closer to the screen until his face filled the video image. "Is that your Michael Jackson Halloween costume or is it really happening?"

Pam yanked David away and approached the screen to see for herself. At the sight of his silver arm, her mouth fell open and she backed away.

Mickey dropped his arm. "I need Stevens!"

Romeo thrust his face in front of the television. "Master Mickey believes that the alien known as Stevens is responsible for this effect."

"Juliet's theory seems more plausible," David said.

Mickey bellowed in the background. "No! I need Stevens!"

Ernie shoved Romeo out of the way and moved in front of the television. "Either we capture Stevens, who's flying around in his disc and he fixes it, or we take Mickey to Europa so the Nexus can fix it. Either way, we need a disc. How soon can you get here with one?"

David glanced at Pam. She held up two fingers. He moved closer to the video screen. "Two days. Hold things together until we get there." The video feed from Europa went black.

Chapter Twenty-Six

David slumped on the bed. "I guess I better go talk to the machine that owns that spinning beach ball. We need a disc."

Pam put her hands on her hips. "Stop calling Unit One a machine. He's a sentient being."

David chuckled. "Yeah, right."

Pam glared at him. "And the Nexus isn't a spinning beach ball."

David smirked. "Okay, Unit One's a computer with Christmas decorations."

"No, he's not!"

David held up his hand stopping her. "We need to figure out what to do about Mickey, not argue about Unit One." He grabbed his pants and his coat.

"Where are you going?" Pam asked.

"I told you, to see Unit One."

"It's four in the morning."

"What does he care? He's a machine." David continued before Pam could protest. "We only have two days to pull everything together and get to Earth." David stopped putting on his clothes. "Now that I think about it, we have another problem, actually two of them."

Pam bit her lip. "The kids."

David took a step toward the door. "What are you going to tell them?"

"Why do I have to be the one to tell them anything?" Pam asked.

David grasped the doorknob. "You're their mother."

"You're their father!"

David opened the bedroom door. "X chromosomes are bigger than Y's."

Pam pointed at him. "You forgot something."

"What?"

Pam smirked. "To put on your pants."

Blushing, David closed the door and walked to the closet. "We'll flip a coin tonight to see who gets stuck telling them tomorrow that they can't go." He took a U.S. quarter dollar from his nightstand drawer and held it up. "A real one, not something that pops out of a glob of silver."

Pam looked at the quarter. "Won't buy you anything on Europa."

"It's twenty-five cents worth of priceless nostalgia." David put the quarter back in his pocket and finished putting on his clothes. "I'm heading to Unit One. What are you going to do before the coin toss?"

Pam thought for a moment. "Wrap up some things in the Menagerie and pack. I am looking forward to seeing Romeo and Juliet again."

David smiled. "Me, too."

"Even though they're computers with Christmas lights?"

"Our Europans wear make-up and tattoos. Bye."

* * *

David entered One's domicile and stood before a patch of flashing lights in the center of the floor. Having seen it before, he knew what came next and was almost emotionally prepared. One rose from the floor as a pillar of silver dappled with flashing lights and loomed over him. David thought about asking Unit One if he knew that he looked like a Christmas tree, but thought better of it.

"Why have you come?" One asked.

David cleared his throat. "We have a problem."

"Your species has many problems," One said, "which is why we brought you here."

David sighed. "The whole Test and Choice thing is getting

old."

"Age is relative," One said.

"At least I know where the wall gets it from," David said to himself. He frowned at One. "Mickey's turning into one of you guys."

One's lights flashed faster. "Impossible."

David held his ground. "Check with Romeo and Juliet."

"Stand by." One's lights flashed as it sent a message to Juliet using faster than light communication. Ten seconds later, One's lights changed to a chaotic pattern of flashing grey and brown. "Mickey will be brought here," One said. "A disc is being prepared. You may go."

"To Earth?" David replied.

"Your question is redundant." One resorbed into the floor.

"I'll take that as a yes." David backed away until he hit the wall. He glanced over his shoulder. "A portal, please?"

"Round, rectangular, or butt-shaped?" the wall replied.

"Open the damn door."

* * *

David found Pam in the bedroom, packing. "How'd it go with One?" she asked.

He sat on the bed next to her. "I asked him if it was possible for a human to turn into a Europan."

Pam looked up. "And?"

David frowned. "All he said was bring Mickey here, with Romeo and Juliet."

"Romeo and Juliet are on Earth to find Rudnick and Stevens. Doesn't he want them to keep looking?"

David shrugged. "It wasn't what I'd call a conversation, more like a command."

"He didn't have a problem with us going too?"

David sat on the bed. "I don't think so. I mean, he didn't say we couldn't."

Pam finished folding a silver garment and put it in a piece of luggage that hadn't existed a minute earlier. The piece of luggage shrank into a cube the size of a shoebox and Pam put it on a shelf in the closet. "That's good enough for me. I need two days to finish up things in the Menagerie before we leave. While I'm doing that," she glanced at him, "and then packing, you can occupy the kids." She waited for him to protest.

David stood. "Can do."

Pam studied his face. "Something's wrong. You gave up too easily. Are you upset about Mickey?"

David thought about his unsettling meeting with Unit One. "Yeah."

"Don't worry. One will fix whatever's wrong with him. Don't tell the kids we're leaving for Earth without them until the very last minute."

David glanced at her. "I thought we were going to flip a coin to see who tells them."

Pam closed the suitcase and smiled. "Looks like you lost."

Chapter Twenty-Seven

Bet ran her fingers through the fur on Micetro's back. The saber-toothed cat with dashes of several other species, including cocker spaniel, lay draped across the foot of the bed purring like a locomotive. "Can we call them now?" she asked anxiously.

Al was perched on the desk across from her swinging his legs. "It's 6:45. You know the rules. We wait until 7 AM Pacific Standard Time and call them for ten minutes before they go to school."

Bet jumped off the bed. "Holy crap! I only have fifteen minutes to change my outfit and fix my hair."

"What's wrong with what you're wearing now?"

"He's seen this outfit before. I have to keep changing so he doesn't forget me."

Al smirked. "Forget you? Who else calls him from outer space?"

Bet hyperventilated. "What if he met somebody since the last time we spoke, somebody he likes better?"

Al rolled his eyes. "He's been asleep since the last time you spoke to him."

Only three earth-years-old, the twins had already grown to the size of fifteen-year-old humans. Al measured one point eight meters-tall, weighed seventy-three kilograms, and had a muscular build. After watching Earth surfer movies from the 1960's, he'd grown sandy blonde hair and wore blue jeans and sweatshirts. Bet stood almost one point seven meters tall and weighed fifty-seven kilograms, with a full figure. Thanks to prodding from her aunt Vickie, Pam had allowed the growth of Bet's breasts to keep pace with her hormones. Bet wore a different Earth outfit every time she called her boyfriend, Josh, on Earth, usually twice a day. Besides being physically advanced, the twins possessed almost immeasurable IQ's, but their emotional development hadn't kept pace. Except for phone calls to their earthling friends and access to social media, they had only their parents and the Europans to interact with. Interacting with most Europans was as emotionally rewarding as talking to Siri on an iPhone.

David came into the room, closed the door, and stood with his back to it. He pointed at Al. "We have unfinished business."

Al swallowed hard. "We do?"

"Remember that underwater pyramid you two found when you were skiing out of bounds? You're going to take me to it, today."

Al glanced nervously at Bet. "You didn't tell Mom, did you?"

"No," David replied. He loomed closer. "But that could change."

Bet was about to say something but thought better of it—a rare occurrence.

Al glanced at his sister. "It's no big deal, just a pile of rocks."

"You told me it's a pyramid, with the same strange writing on it that turned off Romeo on Mars." David leaned closer and looked into his son's eyes. "Were you telling me the truth?"

"Yes!" Al exclaimed.

Bet vigorously nodded her agreement.

"We're going back this afternoon, just the three of us, when Mom goes to the Menagerie."

"What's the hurry?" Al began to stutter. "I h–have some homework I n–need to do." He cleared his throat. "How about in a couple of weeks?"

David moved nose to nose with his son. "If I tell Mom where the two of you were skiing, she'll cut off your video phone privileges for a month."

"No!" Bet exclaimed.

"This afternoon is fine," Al said meekly.

* * *

Romeo stood on the back porch of Ernie's house with his flat screen head tilted towards the sky. Juliet glided to a stop next to him. "Are you performing a self-diagnostic?" she asked.

"No," Romeo replied.

"What is the purpose of your inactivity?"

Romeo's silver polymer skin reflected back the moonlight. "I seek the state humans call tranquility."

"A state without movement or cognitive energy lacks purpose," Juliet said.

The lights on Romeo's face flashed with a blur of color. "Humans seek this state to augment cognitive function."

"The Europan processor always operates at maximal efficiency."

"If that is true, why does the answer to a fundamental question continue to elude me?"

"Explain."

Romeo's head spun to face Juliet. "What is our purpose for being?"

Juliet's lights dimmed to a uniform grey. She didn't answer.

"The primary purpose of organics is to reproduce," Romeo said. "We do not. Organics seek knowledge that we have already acquired. If we do not reproduce and are omniscient, what is our purpose for being?"

"Perhaps our only purpose is to be," Juliet replied.

Romeo's face erupted with flashes of red. "It is not enough."

"We have achieved immortal perfection."

Romeo's face spun to face her. "Did we have a choice?"

Ernie called to them from the back door. "Hey you two, we need you to come inside and monitor the worldwide data network so we know where Stevens and Rudnick land." He went back into the house. Romeo and Juliet followed him to the den where they found Vickie speaking with David's father, Dick, on Ernie's television.

Dick waved to them from the screen. "Top of the morning,

everybody." He glanced at his watch. "Or should I say middle of the night."

Vickie turned away from the television and spoke to Ernie. "Dick wants to help us capture Rudnick and Stevens."

"I used to be a cop, damn good one, and I have a different theory about what's going down," Dick said.

"Tell him," Vickie prompted.

Dick leaned closer to the screen. "We know that Stevens was experimenting with his own home-brewed nannites in a lab under the cult compound. Mickey was there, and now his nannites have gone wacko. My gut tells me that's not a coincidence." He patted his stomach. "My gut's never wrong."

Juliet sent to Romeo, "The database does not contain a reference to humans having a secondary nervous system in their abdominal cavity.

Ernie was about to say something but changed his mind and instead said, "Sounds good. Come join us at the HQ."

Dick blinked. "I thought I was coming over to your house."

Ernie blushed. "The HQ's my house. I used to be a marine so military lingo slips out once in a while."

"Sure."

"Maybe stop off for pizza on the way?" Ernie added.

Dick raised an eyebrow. "It's five in the morning. Nothing's open."

"Little Caesars on Alameda. Tell them Ernie sent you and you get extra breadsticks. I'm a regular."

Dick blinked again. "Plain or pepperoni?"

"A couple of both, large ... and a vegetarian one for Vickie."

"Sure." Dick ended the call.

Chapter Twenty-Eight

Europa, later that morning ...

Pam brought David a glass of lemonade. "You're the only person I know who drinks lemonade for breakfast."

He took a sip. "The lemon trees are from Earth. I like to start my day with something real."

"I'm real." Pam threw back her shoulders, making her cleavage more pronounced. She winked at him. "All of me."

David downed the remainder of his lemonade. "You said you have some things you need to do in the Menagerie before we go to Earth."

Pam let her shoulders slump forward. "I have a brood of Triceratops eggs ready to hatch. Sometimes the little buggers get stuck in their shells and I have to pull them out. After that, I have to finish packing for our trip."

"While you're hatching your lizards ..."

"Not lizards, dinosaurs," Pam interrupted.

"While you're hatching your Franken-lizards," David began. Pam rolled her eyes. "The kids and I are taking the skis out for a spin."

Pam shook her head. "Didn't see that coming. The kids haven't used the skis since we got back. Too busy talking with their friends to get their asses off the couch."

David started for the door. "I thought they could use a change of scenery ... not that there's a lot to choose from around here."

Pam thought about David's inherent clumsiness and his abhorrence of anything silver or Europan. "Honey, do you think it's safe to take out the skis without Romeo and Juliet?"

"Sure," David replied from the doorway. "We'll churn up some water in the safe zone till they get bored and want to come home. We'll be fine. Go hatch your lizards."

"Dinosaurs."

* * *

The twins were waiting for David at the marina, standing beside two aquaskis. Bet looked bored and Al appeared nervous. The two submersibles, reminiscent of silver jet skis, sat in their cradles next to a portal in the city's force field.

David eyed the skis. "How are we going to do this? The skis hold two people and there's three of us."

"I have an idea," Bet said. "I'll stay here."

"Not a problem," Al said. "We can stretch one of them to hold two of us."

"Cool," Bet muttered.

David knew that Bet was the more cautious of his two kids. He pointed at Bet. "I'll ride with you."

Bet put her hands on her hips. "Al can't ride by himself. Mom says we're not allowed to ride solo."

"I'm his Dad and I give him permission," David said. "Anything else you want to complain about?"

Bet started for the nearest ski. "Let's get this over with. Josh gets pissed if I'm late calling him."

David's mouth fell open. "Pissed? Is that any way to talk?"

Bet seated herself on the front of the ski's saddle and the substance of it budded in front of her, forming a joystick. "It is if you're cool."

"It isn't cool when you're three years old," David grumbled.

Al hopped on the second ski's saddle and closed its transparent bubble canopy. "Hate to tell you, Dad, but you use Earth idioms all the time, too."

"I'm an adult," David said. "I can say whatever the fuck I want." He seated himself behind Bet. "We'll talk about it later."

"Like, whatever," Bet muttered. She closed the ski's canopy.

"Like what?" David asked over the intercom.

Bet pushed a flashing white button on the joystick and powered up the aquaski. "To be cool, you have to use the word 'like' at least once in every sentence."

David could feel the machine vibrate beneath him and held onto Bet's waist with both hands. "You're giving me a headache."

Bet turned to look at him. "And you're making it hard for me to breathe. Can you, like, loosen your grip?"

"Whatever," David muttered. He relaxed his hands.

Al pushed forward on the joystick of his ski and it passed through the force field into the dark of Europa's ocean. Bet followed. As the skis picked up speed, David pulled up a strand of the saddle's silver material and wrapped it around his waist, forming a seatbelt. "How far is it to the underwater pyramid?"

"Five minutes to the volcano," Al replied over the comlink. "Another five thousand meters along the sea bottom from there."

David closed his eyes. "I assume the volcano's not active."

"Active enough to melt the surface ice," Al replied. "That's how we found it."

David tensed. "You skied over an active volcano?"

"It was *his* idea," Bet quickly added.

"You promised you won't tell Mom!" Al exclaimed.

David grimaced as he thought about skiing over an active volcano. "Shut up and drive."

As soon as they cleared the corona of light surrounding the city, Europa's ocean became a cauldron of impenetrable black. Except for the ball of light marking the city rapidly shrinking behind them, David couldn't see anything. The directions up and down lost their meaning. "I can't see a thing," he said trying to remain calm.

Al projected lights from his ski. Bet did the same.

David looked over Bet's shoulder, straining to see ahead of them. Except for an occasional sea creature trapped by the light, he still couldn't see anything. He licked his lips. "Are we near the bottom yet?"

"We're still beneath the surface ice," Al replied. He swung his ski violently to the right. Bet performed the same maneuver and David saw a tooth-shaped projection of ice flash by.

"What was that?" David exclaimed.

Al repeated the maneuver, zigging in the opposite direction. "Ice stalactites. Here comes another one!" Al dipped the skis' nose and half rolled around another wicked looking projection of ice with Bet following. David looked over his shoulder and gaped at the stalactite. "How much more of this?"

"Not much," Al replied. "After this part, it gets really boring."

"Skiing with your father is totally boring," Bet muttered.

David licked his dry lips. "I heard that," he rasped.

They continued weaving through the field of stalactites hanging under the surface ice until they reached an area of thinner ice, a towering ice cavern without stalactites positioned over the volcano's caldera. Al let his ski drift to a stop in the center of it. "Look down. There's the volcano."

David pressed his face against the ski's canopy causing it to form around his face and looked down, or what he thought was down. "I can't see anything."

Bet sent to Al telepathically. "Mom said Dad refused eye implants. He's nearsighted."

"It's down there," Al said out loud. "See the bubbles rising around us? The volcano heats the water into steam."

David noticed that they were floating within a curtain of fine bubbles rising from below. "Yeah."

"They get bigger as we go down," Al added. He nosed his ski downward.

"We can still go home," Bet said.

David swallowed back his saliva. "Follow your brother."

"WWT," Bet muttered.

"What the hell does that mean?" David asked.

"It means what a waste of time," Al said over the intercom. Before David could reply, Bet dropped the nose of the ski and accelerated. David gritted his teeth and held on.

They descended toward a bowl of molten lava. The boiling rock heated the seawater above it sending a stream of basketball-sized bubbles to the surface. Awestruck by the sight below him, David asked, "How far is it to the bottom?" A digital gauge appeared floating before his eyes showing him the water temperature, the ski's rate of descent, and the distance to the bottom, currently a circle of molten lava. Already one hundred fifty degrees centigrade, the temperature kept rising and they were still more than two thousand meters away. "How close to the volcano do we need to go?" David asked through clenched teeth.

"Not much farther," Al replied. "Awesome, isn't it?"

David cleared his throat. "Yeah."

They continued descending. For the last two hundred meters, David had his eyes closed. When they were fifty meters above the boiling pool of lava, Al angled sharply away and descended to the ocean floor. The two skis settled to the sandy bottom a thousand meters from the volcano's upslope and stopped next to each other.

David felt the ski come to a stop and opened his eyes. He slowed his breathing and looked around. Except for the light coming from the volcano and the two skis, he couldn't see anything. "I thought we were close to the pyramid. Where is it?"

Bet touched the controls and brighter lights appeared on the front of the ski. She pointed out the front of their canopy. "It's like, over there. Can we go home now?"

David tried looking where Bet was pointing and could just make out a black, pointed shape off in the distance. Without spatial references, had no idea how big or far away it was. "We need to get closer."

Bet sighed. "It looks the same, only bigger."

The black shape grew larger and more distinct as the two skis moved in tandem toward it. "Clearly not a natural formation,"

David said. "Do we have a searchlight?" A pencil-like column of silver rose before him from the saddle. At the same time, a bright light appeared projecting from the ski. "There's the searchlight you wanted," Bet said sounding bored. "Aim it with the joystick." She sighed in overly dramatic fashion. "Since there's nothing to see out there but a grungy ole pyramid, we can start back any time."

"Put a lid on it," David growled.

"*What does that mean*?" Bet sent to Al telepathically.

"*It means shut up and don't make this any worse!*" Al replied.

David played with the joystick until the ski's powerful searchlight illuminated the peak of the pyramid. He could see that the pyramid was constructed from fitted stones. "Definitely not natural." He pushed the searchlight's control forward and the beam panned down to the pyramid's base. "Al, turn on a light and help me." Al ordered his ski to sprout a search light and the two beams swept the base of the pyramid together. They stopped on a rectangular opening framed by hieroglyphic writing. David raised himself up on the ski's saddle. "Move us closer," he said sounding excited.

With Bet following close behind, Al maneuvered his ski closer to the pyramid's opening and stopped ten meters from it. He panned his searchlight slowly across the strange symbols.

"Those look the same to me as the ones we saw on Mars," David said. "Have you guys been inside?"

Neither twin answered.

"You're already busted. You might as well come clean," David said.

"Yes," Al replied. "We went inside."

"But just for a minute!" Bet blurted out.

David centered his searchlight on the opening and maximized its intensity. He couldn't see anything inside except a wall of more fitted stones. "Looks like a fireplace back home," he said. "Let's look inside."

"Guys," Bet interrupted. "Sorry to be a party-pooper, but if we don't get back soon, I'll miss my call with Josh."

"Stuff it," David snarled. The opening in the pyramid appeared big enough for one ski to pass through. "We're going in. Al, you go first."

Al maneuvered through the opening and Bet followed. They stopped their forward motion a few meters inside, panned the large rectangular space with their lights, and took sensor readings. They were in a featureless space four times the size of a flying disc, with rock walls and a rock ceiling. The floor registered as densely packed sea bottom.

"There's nothing here," Bet said. "Can we go home now?"

Al pointed his searchlight at the wall opposite the pyramid's opening. "There's a platform over there with more symbols on the walls. We saw it the first time we were here."

"Show me," David said.

"We have to dismount and walk."

"Let's do it," David said.

"Have fun," Bet said. "I'm staying here."

The substance of the ski's saddles poured around them until all three were covered in silver, with clear, bubble helmets. When their environmental suits were complete, the ski's bubble canopies melted away. David stood on the ski's saddle and looked around. He could see mollusks scattered along the sandy bottom lifting up their eyestalks, attracted by the light. Otherwise, the bottom appeared unnaturally flat. David dismounted, and while Bet leaned against her ski with an expression of boredom, Al and his father started walking toward the platform on the far wall.

"Why build anything here?" David asked as they trudged along the sea bottom kicking up sand.

"Maybe this area wasn't always under water," Al replied.

"How could that be?" David replied.

A school of curious sea creatures swam towards Bet, a combination octopus and starfish made of transparent flesh.

One poked Bet's ski with a long and slender tentacle with hooks on the end of it. The ski's electric field sent the creature swimming away, glowing red like a lantern. The rest of the school turned shades of mustard and red and swam in haste toward the pyramid's entrance. "*Boring,*" Bet called to them over the comlink. She glanced at the scanner. "Wait." She looked again. "Hey, guys? I see something big on the scanner heading this way. Eighty degrees."

"Is it another ski?" David asked.

"The scanner says the thing out there is organic ... and big." Bet sounded nervous. "Maybe you should come back."

"Chill. There's only primitive life down here—starfish and snails, little shit like that," David said. "Nothing big."

"Yeah, well whatever it is, it's coming closer," Bet said with growing alarm. "And the scanner says it's a lot bigger than the skis!"

"Must be a malfunction. There's nothing out here that big," Al said.

David stopped. "Wait a minute. Nothing malfunctions in this friggin place." He looked back toward the skis.

"It's almost here!" Bet exclaimed.

Al stopped walking. "Maybe we should go back."

David turned toward Bet and the skis. "Okay, we're heading back."

They trudged over and stood near the skis with Bet. All three looked out the pyramid's entrance. Moments later, a grey shape the length of an aquaski came into view and began circling one hundred meters outside the pyramid's entrance. As it looped closer, they could see a flat, triangular head on the end of a long neck and a body with armored plates and pairs of flippers, similar to a crocodile. A tapered, segmented tail with an armored knob on the end of it whipped back and forth, propelling the beast with bursts of speed.

David heard a beeping sound and the water for three meters

around the skis began to glow neon-blue. He tapped Bet on the shoulder. "What just happened?"

"The ski's defensive force field came on," Bet replied.

"The computer thinks that thing is a threat," Al added. "Let's stay close to the skis in case it's right."

As they huddled closer to the skis, the creature accelerated straight for them, shot through the opening, and collided with the force field surrounding Bet's ski. The field flared with light and David thought he heard a zapping sound. After appearing stunned for a few seconds, the creature shook its head and swam back out through the opening. It resumed loitering outside, swimming in circles.

All three looked wide-eyed out the opening. "Holy crap!" Bet exclaimed.

David thought his heart would pound out of his chest. "You can say that again."

"The end of its tail is getting brighter," Al said. "What does that mean?"

David noticed that the smaller sea animals swimming inside the pyramid had all disappeared and the mollusks scattered along the bottom were hurriedly burying themselves in the sand. "All the little critters are leaving. That can't be good," he said. "I think we need to get out of here, like now."

"Guys? I see five more of those reptile things on the scanner," Bet said. "They're coming this way."

"Looks like it has friends," Al said.

The creature loitering outside whipped its tail and darted through the pyramid's opening. Instead of colliding with the nearest ski's force field, it zoomed past projecting a miniature looking bolt of energy from the end of its tail before reversing course and jetting back outside. The ski's force field glowed as it absorbed the massive electric charge, for a split second becoming opaque and winking out. It flickered before reforming. When it did, its intensity seemed to be reduced.

"Woo!" David yelled. "That thing packs a wallop."

Al checked the ski. "The ski's force field is down forty percent."

"We need to get out of Dodge," David said.

"Where's Dodge?" Al asked.

"Never mind!"

The creature was joined by five more of its kind and the six of them circled outside the pyramid's opening whipping their tales in unison.

"We can't get out. They're blocking us!" Bet shrieked.

Al bent over his ski's scanner. "There's a hollow chamber above us. I see an opening in the ceiling. It's not big enough for a ski, but we can swim through and the bad guys are too big to follow us."

"Do it," David said trying to sound calm. He faced the opening.

Bet went first, using jets from her suit to propel her to the rock ceiling. "I see it. I'm going through." Her light disappeared from view.

"You next," David said to Al. Al shot straight up, following the same path as his sister. "I'm through," he called to David.

David watched one of the creatures start toward him. "Hey guys, how do I use the jets on my suit?"

"There's a button on your sleeve," Al answered. "Press it."

David glanced at the sea creature coming toward him with its tail glowing bright red, then held up his arm. He saw four blinking lights. "I see four lights with different colors! Which one?"

The creature neared the entrance and spun around leading with its glowing tail. In a panic, David punched all the buttons. When the creature's tail was only three meters from his chest, he stabbed at the yellow one. A white-hot bolt of energy burst toward him, but his suit propelled him to the side. The creature's energy bolt missed and impacted the pyramid's far wall.

This caused an explosion of light that heated the water in the chamber to a boil. David's suit protected him, but the creature was forced to swim back outside to escape the scalding water. As it propelled itself through the opening, the side of its tail struck the rock shattering a portion of it and leaving behind a ragged chunk of tissue.

"Dad! Are you all right?" Al shouted.

The water in the chamber cooled and the bubbles of steam dissipated. Crouching in the corner, David saw the creatures massing outside for another attack. "I'm okay, but I need some help with this suit!" he shouted.

"The yellow one!" Al called.

"I know. How do I control the suit's direction?"

"The button's a miniature joystick. Work it with your finger," Al replied.

"Our Europan buddies sure like joysticks." David hit the yellow button and kept his finger on it. "Here goes." He pushed it toward his fingers and shot upwards, bouncing off the temple's ceiling. "Still not steering very well!" he shouted.

"It takes a while to get the hang of it," Al said.

David played with the yellow button, hardly tapping it. This caused his suit to move in short spurts in multiple directions. "I think I got this," he said.

"Then come up here!" Bet shouted.

"In a minute," David replied.

"What?" Bet said.

"She's right," Al called to him. "I think you should come now."

David maneuvered near the pyramid's entrance and grabbed the hunk of the creature's tail impaled on a shattered piece of rock. He found himself face to snout with the six of them just outside. "You're right. Now is a good time" he shouted. Clutching the tissue in one hand, he maneuvered his suit in short spasms of motion back to the ceiling. When he hit the ceiling and looked down, he saw another creature directly below him with its tail raised like an Earth scorpion. "Shit!" As the angry glow of the creature's tail built in intensity, he groped along the ceiling with his hands searching for the opening. He found it and hoisted himself through just as the creature loosed its bolt. The bolt flew through the opening impacting the pyramid's apex. David hugged the floor of the chamber hyperventilating. When the water cooled and the steam bubbles dissipated, Al dragged him onto a ledge.

Still panting, David looked up at him. "That was close."

"Sure was," Al said. Bet nodded.

David got up on his elbows and looked around. "Where are we?"

"In some kind of room near the apex of the pyramid," Al replied. "What's that in your hand?"

David held up the ragged chunk of the creature's tail. "A piece of one of our friends down there."

Another energy bolt shot through the opening, but David and the twins were well away from it, safe on the ledge.

Several minutes went by without another attack.

"Maybe it's over," Al said.

"Can we go home now?" Bet asked.

David got to his feet. "Better wait a while and make sure they're really gone."

Bet thought about it for a moment. "I think you're right."

"That's a first," David said. He looked around the chamber using his helmet light. "Since we're stuck here, let's look around."

"At what?" Bet asked.

Al ran his hand along the wall. "What's this?" David and Bet joined him.

"I don't see anything," Bet said.

Al pointed with his gloved hand. "See that crack? It's too straight to be a fracture line." He leaned against it. "This section of the wall gives a little when I lean on it. Let's push on it together." David joined Al and they pushed against the wall. A rectangular section of the rock wall slid back revealing an opening wide enough for one person to walk through.

David peered inside using his helmet light. "Looks like a corridor to somewhere. Let's see where it goes."

Chapter Twenty-Nine

David stepped into a narrow corridor approximately ten paces in length and pointed at the wall. "More symbols, lots of them." He continued walking to the end, running his gloved hand along a line of complex carvings. "I'm at another wall, or maybe it's another door."

Al came up behind him. "Let's push on it." He reached his arm around his father, and together, they shoved on the wall. It slid back exposing another rectangular chamber.

David peered inside. "Another room, or something. This one's pretty small."

"What're you doing up there?" Bet sent to them. "I need to get home."

"We found something," David replied. "Have there been any more attacks?"

"No," Bet replied. "I'm down with the skis."

"No! What if they come back!" David yelled.

"It's okay," Bet sent. "The scanner says they're gone. Can we go home now? I'll be late for my call."

"Give us a few minutes. We're checking something out," David replied. "Stay with the skis, but call us if those things come back."

"What about my call?" Bet pleaded.

David spoke to Al. "Ignore her." They went inside and cast their helmet beams around a rectangular chamber the size of the twin's bedroom. On opposite walls, structures similar to chairs made out of a pearlescent substance reflected back the light. David moved to one of the walls and touched a hanging rectangle of cloth with indistinct faded images. The cloth fell apart at his touch. Pieces of it fluttered to the floor.

Al focused his light on one of the chairs. "Computer, what is the material this object is made from?" His helmet cam uploaded the images to the aquaski's computer. A second later, they heard the voice of the skis' computer over the comlink. "The material is a mixture of sea animal shells bound by an organic polymer."

"Who made it?" David asked.

"There are no references for similar items in the database," the computer replied.

Al knelt in a corner of the room. "Dad, over here. What's this?"

David joined Al and looked down. "That shouldn't be here," he said.

"What is it?" Al asked.

David picked up a transparent sphere half again the size of one of his lemons and looked at it in his outstretched hand. The orb of translucent material burst with multi-colored light.

Al stepped back. "What's that?"

"What's what?" Bet shouted over the suit com.

"It's a sphere, like the one Ernie has on Earth," David replied. He watched the sphere's light play along the chamber walls. Rows of symbols carved in the walls reflected back the light giving them the appearance of molten lava.

"What's it doing here?" Al asked.

"Good question," David replied. "Do those symbols on the wall look familiar to you?"

"Yeah," Al replied. "They look like the ones we saw on Mars."

"Sure do."

"If it's a real sphere, ask it something," Al said.

David put the sphere in his pocket. "Later. Let's get out of here."

David turned to leave but stopped when he saw a familiar shape half-buried in the sand near his foot. He stooped and picked up a length of metal encrusted with mollusk shells and shone his helmet light on it. "This place is full of surprises." He used his gloved hand to smooth away some of the crustaceans and uncovered a metal dagger.

Al peered closer at it. "Looks like a dagger."

David handed the dagger to him. "Computer, when did the Europans make the first sphere, in Earth years?"

"The first and only sphere was fabricated five Earth years ago and entrusted to the human known as Ernie," the computer replied.

"What about the one we just found ..." Al began.

"This finding cannot be explained without more information," the computer replied.

They heard Bet over the comlink. "Can we go home now?"

"Yes," David replied.

"Woo hoo!" Bet shouted over the helmet's comlink. "Move a little faster, okay?"

* * *

Al poked the nose of his ski outside the pyramid's entrance and ran a full power scan. "Don't see anything bigger than a clam out here," he announced.

"Go!" David exclaimed. Al accelerated at full thrusters toward the volcano, followed closely by Bet and David.

David activated his ski's link to the main computer in the city. "Did humanoids exist on Europa two hundred thousand Earth years ago?"

The voice in his helmet sounded more full-bodied and deeper than the ski's computer. For a split second, he wondered why. "There are no references in the database to humanoids living on Europa prior to the arrival of Pam and David," the computer replied.

"Analyze images of the sea creatures that attacked us. What are they?"

Lights flashed on the ski's computer console as the images uploaded. "The species of sea creatures encountered at time index four four zero are unknown in the Europan database."

"Could they have been hiding and you guys missed them?"

"No," the computer replied.

* * *

As soon as they returned to the habitat, the twins ran upstairs to their room, slammed the door, and grabbed the phone. David went to the den and sat before a computer terminal, a cube of silver with a blank screen. He took the hunk of tissue from his pocket and placed it on the top. "Computer, analyze the genetic composition of this tissue and compare it to other sea animals in the database." The tissue sank into the silver box and disappeared. Three seconds later, the computer screen lit with numbers describing the nucleic acid composition of the tissue. David glanced at the screen. "What is your analysis?" he prompted.

"The tissue analysis is displayed ..."

"Just tell me, in words," David said impatiently.

"Seven percent of the gene sequences in the tissue sample have been detected in only one organic organism on this world."

David leaned closer. "What kind of animal on Europa has some of those genes?"

"Only the human designated Pamela."

David sat back staring at the screen. "How is that possible?" he muttered.

"Unknown."

Lost in thought, David left the house with the sphere in his pocket and took the path to the Menagerie. Along the way, he kept his eyes straight ahead doing his best to ignore the massive creatures resurrected by his wife, grazing or eating something with legs behind invisible fences that he fervently hoped were still working.

Pam looked up from her workbench when he arrived. The bench was littered with broken Triceratops eggs no longer containing horned dinosaurs.

He put the sphere on the table in front of her. "What do you make of this?" he asked. The sphere glowed with soft pink light.

Pam looked at it and her eyes widened. "Is that what I think it is?"

"Sure looks like it," David replied.

"Where did you find it?"

David lied. "Just sitting there on the ocean bottom."

Pam raised an eyebrow. "That was fortuitous."

David shrugged. "It lit up when we skied over it."

Pam reached for the sphere. As her fingers came close to it, the light inside the sphere went out. She pulled back her hand and glanced at David. "What's that about?"

"Maybe the batteries died." David reached for it. As soon as he touched it, the sphere burst with light. He put it back on the lab bench and it returned to the same soft pink glow as before. "Try it again."

Pam repeated the process and the same thing happened. The sphere's light went out. "Looks like it doesn't like me."

David stared at it, frowning. "Maybe something's wrong with it. Who knows how long it's been out there soaking up seawater?" He picked the sphere up and quickly put it in his pocket. Pam saw it glow again as soon as he touched it.

David cleared his throat. "All done packing?"

"Yes. Did you tell the kids?"

David looked away. "Not exactly."

"What does that mean?"

"It means I didn't. Are you done hatching lizards?" he hurried to say.

She glared at him. "Don't change the subject."

David sighed. "I'll do it after they finish their phone call. They'll be in a good mood ... at least for a few minutes."

Pam pointed at the door. "Don't worry, you can handle it."

"Aren't you coming with me?"

"Got a juvenile Spinosaurus that needs tending," Pam replied.

David flashed on the marine animal's genetic analysis. "How big is your spino-whatever?"

"She's about twenty feet tall now, maybe fifteen hundred kilos. Cute as the devil. Want to see her?"

David blinked. "It's still a baby?"

"More like a teenager," Pam replied. "Going to get a lot bigger."

David headed for the door. "Do me a favor. Don't resurrect Godzilla."

* * *

Sonarman Lewis leaned close to his sonar display. "Holy shit. This isn't possible!" He grabbed the phone and it slipped from his hand. Dropping to his knees, he got on the floor, fumbled with cord, and reeled it in. "Bridge, this is Lewis in Sonar!"

"This is the exec, go ahead Lewis ... and for God's sake, stop hyperventilating."

Lewis took a deep breath. "Sorry, sir, but that bogey is going to breach the surface in about four minutes. I hope we're far enough away!"

"This is an Aegis-class cruiser, sailor, not the Titanic. We're almost indestructible."

"I know, sir, but ..." Lewis glanced at the display. "It's moving to the surface at very high speeds, and it's pushing a whole lot of water in front of it."

"Stand by," the executive officer shouted to his helmsman. "Wakefield, how far away are we from the track of that bogey?"

"Ten thousand meters, sir."

"That should be enough," the exec said. He spoke to Lewis again. "Where is it now?"

"Here!" Lewis dove for the deck.

The ten thousand ton, five hundred sixty-seven foot long

Aegis Cruiser U.S.S. Medford lurched to starboard, listing twenty degrees. Everyone on the bridge grabbed for something to hold onto.

"What the fuck?" the exec exclaimed. He looked towards the bow and saw only clear skies and calm seas. It happened again, this time with greater force. The interphone rang and the exec grabbed for it.

"Bart, what the hell is going on up there?" Captain Tucker asked from the ship's CIC, the combat information center. He sat in the dark behind a bank of computer screens readying the ship's arsenal of missiles and guns.

The ship shook again. This time the hull rose out of the water a full three meters before crashing down. The exec released the forward handrail and looked out the bridge's windows. He saw a nearby aircraft carrier moving away pushed by a giant wave and grabbed the phone. "Captain, that bogey is creating a huge disturbance in the water underneath the fleet, mini tsunamis!"

"Use the engines and stay on station," the captain said in his command voice. "We need to be in position to take that fucker out when he comes to the surface."

Lewis in Sonar broke into the conversation. "This is Lewis! It's near the surface, five hundred meters off the port bow. Hold on ..."

"Who the hell was that?" the captain asked.

"Lewis in Sonar," the exec replied.

Stevens' disc burst from the ocean sending a tidal wave of water crashing into the ship. The ship rolled on its side and the bridge crew were thrown to the deck. Alarm klaxons began to blare and the lights went out. After the ship righted itself and the emergency lights came on, the executive officer crawled to the observation windows and pulled himself up to look out. His eyes bulged. "Son of a bitch ..."

* * *

Stevens activated a control on his armrest and his helmet and silver suit were resorbed by his chair. He looked at a visual display in front of him and grinned. Rudnick remained cocooned, but he could see the display. He counted seven ships around them, including an aircraft carrier, two cruisers, three destroyers and a fleet oiler. The ships appeared in disarray, all their bows pointing in different directions. One of the destroyers appeared to be swamped. The closest ship, a cruiser, was broadside to them and motionless five hundred meters away. "What are you going to do?" Rudnick asked.

Stevens tapped his forehead. "I don't know … maybe sink a few?" He pointed at the cruiser. "Let's start with that one."

"No!" Rudnick exclaimed.

Stevens spun to face him. "Why not?"

Rudnick strained to turn his head. "There's no need to hurt anybody."

Stevens kept the disc in a hover one hundred meters above the surface of the ocean. The sea beneath it churned in a violent vortex crowned by a geyser of steam leading up to the disc. He leered at Rudnick. "Why do you care what happens to them? You're the leader of a cult that's supposed to enslave your fellow humans and take over the world."

"That's different," Rudnick replied.

* * *

The sailors on the Medford's bridge snapped to attention. "Captain on the bridge," the exec called. Captain Tucker went straight to the forward windows and looked out. "God damned UFO." He grabbed a phone. "Get me Washington." He put his hand over the mouthpiece. "Going to shoot that mother fucker down." He listened to the phone. "He's right in front of us, general, and I have everything in my arsenal aimed at him. Am I weapons free?"

"Standby," General Westlock replied. He put down the phone and looked at Mickey on a video link. "Do I shoot that UFO down or not?"

"Shoot off everything you've got," Mickey replied. "Might as well throw rocks at it, for all the good it'll do. When you run out of bullets and missiles, follow him."

Westlock sneered at Mickey and spoke into the phone. "Weapons free. Blow that damned UFO to bits."

"Fire!" Captain Tucker shouted. His order was relayed to the ship's CIC and two Standard missiles roared from their tubes and veered toward the disc. Both missiles impacted the disc's force field, resulting in a small flash of light, and disappeared.

"Fire the GWIZ! The captain shouted. The Medford's close-in defense system, a Gatling gun capable of firing more than four thousand rounds per minute, began spewing a line of depleted uranium slugs at the disc. The hail of projectiles disappeared in smaller puffs of light.

Stevens rubbed his hands together. "My turn."

"Wait!" Rudnick shouted.

"Wait for what?"

Rudnick's mind raced. "Let's take a minute and focus on the goal."

"My goal is to have some fun. What's yours?"

"To make the world a better place," Rudnick replied.

Stevens chuckled. "Getting rid of all you Homo sapiens is the best way to do that. Might as well start with those sailors shooting spit wads at us."

Rudnick strained against his cocoon until rivulets of sweat rolled down his face. "I thought you wanted new bodies for your … cousins."

Stevens smirked. "I do, good ones, in better shape than you, bodies that'll last a while."

"Those sailors down there have the best ones you can find. Ever watch that television show called Seal Team Six? Those guys can swim in ice water with their hands tied behind their back and stay awake for a week."

Stevens watched the Medford fire its last missile. "You're saying I should keep those seal guys down there alive and not waste them?"

Rudnick tried to nod, but his helmet wouldn't let him. "That's right."

Stevens scratched his chin. "Makes sense." He reached for the disc's controls. "I'll make sure they're still here when we get back." He stabbed a blue button blinking on the command console.

Rudnick felt the deck vibrate and saw seven bolts of blue-white energy erupt from the disc, one headed for each ship below them. The bolts enveloped the ships, for a moment obscuring them from view in a blue cloud that then disappeared. All firing from the ships ceased, and none of them showed wakes behind them as their engines became useless hunks of metal.

Rudnick watched the visual display. "What did you do?"

"I disabled all the machinery on those ships. After we're done in Los Angeles, we'll come back and pick out the best bodies." Stevens dropped back into his chair and was quickly cocooned. Seconds later, the disc accelerated with a loud sonic boom and disappeared into the stratosphere.

The phone rang on General Westlock's desk. "We can't raise any of the ships on satellite communications and none of them appear to be under power," Westlock's liaison at the Pentagon said.

Westlock frowned. "He has an EMP weapon, or something like it. Where did he go?"

"He's doing Mach seven, heading due west at one hundred thousand feet."

"He's going somewhere besides outer space, which means we still have a chance to take him out. Keep me informed." Westlock terminated the call and looked at Mickey's image on the screen.

"You were right. He's sticking around and going somewhere. What's our next move?"

"One minute." Mickey covered up the lens and audio input on Ernie's computer and spoke to Romeo and Juliet. "Stevens is heading our way. Can you capture him when he gets here?"

"Not while he's inside the flying disc," Juliet replied. "His capabilities outside the disc are so far unknown."

Mickey uncovered the computer's inputs and spoke to General Westlock. "Let us know where he lands. We're ready for him." Mickey terminated the connection.

"Maybe we shouldn't do anything before Davie and Pam get here," Ernie said.

David's father, Dick, joined them in the den. "Hi everybody. I let myself in."

Mickey glared at Ernie. "How come he can get in?"

Ernie's face reddened. "I gave him the code."

"Thanks for coming," Vickie said, cutting off Mickey's next remark. Dick came over and gave her a hug. "When are they going to get here?" Dick asked.

"Pam and David?" Ernie asked.

"Rudnick and Stevens," Dick replied.

Mickey took a step closer. "Why would they come here?"

"To kidnap you."

Chapter Thirty

Bet stared at the dark video screen, unfocused and smiling.

"Josh hung up five minutes ago," Al said sitting beside her on the couch. "Snap out of it and let's go."

Bet sighed. "You're too young to understand."

"I'm one minute younger than you, dip shit."

Bet glared at her twin brother. "I'm in love. You're infatuated with cheese."

Al looked back at her with murder in his eyes. It happened at least once a day. "Her full name's Brianna, not Brie. She's a lot smarter than that dork you're hung up on."

Bet jumped to her feet. "How dare you call my boyfriend a dork!"

Al jumped to his feet. "Okay, you're right, he's not a dork." Bet crossed her arms looking self-satisfied. Al sneered at her. "He's a dweeb!"

"No, he's not!" Bet blinked. "What's a dweeb? It better not be anything bad, or I'll ..."

David entered their room. "Knock it off you two."

Bet pointed at her brother. "He insulted my boyfriend."

Al pointed at his sister. "She called my girlfriend cheese."

David cleared his throat preparing himself for what came next. "Your mother and I are going to Earth the day after tomorrow. We have to help Uncle Mickey and Aunt Vickie with a problem they're having, but ..."

Bet's eyes bulged from their sockets. "We're going to earth? Oh my God! I gotta call Josh and tell him."

Al pumped his fist. "Yes!"

David cleared his throat again. "You're not going with us."

Both twins gaped at him. As usual, Bet was the first to speak. Her lips twisted into a menacing frown. "No one would be mean enough to make us stay home and not see our friends, especially our *loving* parents."

"You're not going," David repeated.

Bet fled the room screaming, "Mooooommmm!" Al ran after her with David following. The three of them found Pam in the kitchen. Pam looked at her daughter's red face. "What's all the hollering about?" She already knew.

"Dad said you're going to Earth without us," Bet whined.

Pam nodded. "That's true."

"Nooooooo!" Bet wailed.

Al ran to the video screen on the kitchen counter that Pam used to watch old episodes of General Hospital. He spun several dials and the screen resolved to show Ernie's den packed with people. "Romeo!" Al yelled.

Romeo saw Ernie's television screen turn on and Al's frazzled face taking up most of it. He moved closer. "Master Al, your dilated pupils and rapid pulse indicate that ..."

"Mom and Dad are coming to Earth and they're not taking us!" Al shouted.

Juliet moved next to Romeo. "Mistress Pam, may I converse with you?"

Pam nudged Al out of the way and faced the screen. "They're not coming with us, and that's final."

Juliet's lights changed to blush pink. "I would like to point out that the twins require peer interactions for their optimal emotional development. Such interactions are only available on Earth at the present time."

Romeo's head appeared next to Juliet's on the television screen. "I would also like to remind you that Juliet and I are here on Earth and can fulfill our customary roles as the twin's chaperones and teachers if they accompany you."

"We need you to apprehend Stevens and Rudnick, not play nursemaid," David said.

"We'll be good, we promise!" Bet shouted in the background. "Please, please, please take us with you."

"Get here as fast as you can," Ernie said into the television. "We need a disc."

"Got it," David said. The television screen winked out. He sat on the bed. "As much as I hate the idea, I supposed we could take them with us."

Bet ran to Pam, got on her knees, and hugged her mother's legs. She looked up at Pam with goo-goo eyes. "I know you love us …"

"Cut the bullshit before I vomit," Pam said looking down at her. "You can go, but step out of line even once and you're both cocooned for the entire trip with your audio off. You got that?"

Al and Bet both nodded vigorously.

Pam pointed to the door. "Now get out of here and start packing before I change my mind."

"Or find it," David muttered.

"Yes!" Bet and Al exclaimed simultaneously. As they ran from the room, Bet shouted, "We're taking Micetro, too."

Pam sighed. "Sure, why not?"

"Maybe we should have him neutered first," David said.

Bet ran back into the room. "Can we add some color to the outside of the disc, cool stripes or a tie-dyed vibe?"

David blinked. "Why would we do that?"

Bet rocked back and forth on the balls of her feet. "So it looks more cool when we show it to our friends."

David sighed. "Talk to Romeo and Juliet. See what they can do."

Bet ran out of the room, yelling to her brother. "They said it's okay. Call Romeo." She skidded to a stop and ran back into the room. "One more thing."

"Now what?" Pam asked sounding exasperated.

Bet smiled sweetly. "I need to look a little more *now*."

David took a step closer. "What does *now* mean?"

Bet keep smiling like a Cheshire cat. "Nothing major … add a little color to my hair, some dark eye make-up, a shorter skirt."

David gaped at her. "You're three years old."

Bet's mouth dropped open. "Don't tell Josh that." She hyperventilated. "Promise me you won't say that to him!"

"Calm down," Pam said. "We won't tell him how old you are. As far as your new look, you can streak your hair and use nail polish, but none of that gothic look the girls are into, you got that?"

"Yes!" Bet ran out of the room again.

"That includes tattoos and piercing," Pam shouted after her.

Chapter Thirty-One

Crowds of people waited behind barriers on Malibu Beach or stood on the pier watching the sky while Secret Service agents, local police, and the National Guard watched them. Hundreds more people looked down from the bluffs or scanned the sky, none of them hoping to see the Kardashians. Two Coast Guard cutters patrolled off shore, and the sky over the beach was so congested with news helicopters that flights out of Los Angeles International Airport had to be diverted. The air traffic nightmare over Los Angeles worsened when two air traffic controllers went home with migraine headaches and another hired a lawyer to file for disability.

Vickie and Ernie waited for the disc's arrival on the sand, with Romeo and Juliet standing behind them. Using her augmented vision, Vickie pointed to a section of sky over the water. "There."

Ernie cupped his hands over his eyes to shield them from the glare. "I don't see anything."

"There!" Vickie persisted, gesticulating at the same section of the cloudless afternoon sky.

A speck of silver appeared high overhead. As the crowd saw it and grew silent, the speck grew larger becoming a smooth-shaped disc glinting in the sunlight. It appeared to many in the crowd to be the prototypical flying saucer from Earth movies of the 1950s, except the aliens weren't in the saucer. Two of them, silver robots with flat screen heads, were standing on the sand watching it land.

After buzzing the crowd, the disc settled in the water twenty meters off shore with a hiss of steam, sending a twenty-foot wave toward the beach. The wave crashed on the sand sending a spray of seawater onto the crowd and the cars in the parking lot. Everyone waited, breathless with excitement, and in the first few rows, soaking wet.

Ernie pointed at the disc. "Are those stripes on the side of it?"

"They were added at Mistress Bet's request," Juliet said.

"What the hell for?" Vickie asked.

Juliet's lights blinked. "To impress her friends."

An area on the side of the disc above the racing stripes darkened and disappeared forming an opening. Beneath it, a tongue of silver sprouted and sagged to the sand just beyond the waterline forming a ramp.

Ernie moved closer to the water and whistled. "That baby's sure bigger than the usual flying saucer." He chuckled. "Must be their version of a jumbo jet." Nobody else laughed.

"It has been expanded to accommodate two aquaskis and four humanoids," Juliet said.

Ernie nodded. "Makes sense."

Melanie Dilman, the reporter who broke the story of Earth's first contact with the Europans, and because of it had a bigger contract than Barbara Walters ever did, stood at the front of the phalanx of reporters and cameras. As soon as Pam started down the ramp wearing her customary silver jumpsuit, synched at the waist, Melanie rushed forward and thrust a microphone under her chin. "Welcome back to Earth, dear." Melanie turned and beamed for the cameras.

Pam tried to ease past her, but Melanie blocked her way. "What brings you back to Earth, dear?" Melanie asked, once more looking at the cameras and not Pam.

Pam pointed behind her with a bland expression. "That flying disc."

Melanie whipped her lacquered blonde locks in a poor imitation of Marilyn Monroe and smiled at Pam. "Is that a new hairdo I see?"

Pam appeared self-conscious. "Not really ... I like to keep things the same."

Melanie rolled her eyes and then smiled again. "How ... practical."

The two women fake-smiled at each other until Melanie asked another question. "Did you come back to arrest Paul Rudnick, dear?"

Pam yawned and gave Melanie her best I don't have time for this look. "No, we came back to check in with our buds and do some shopping."

Melanie frowned and gave her cameraman the cut sign.

After showing his identification, Dick walked through the barrier and continued to the disc's ramp. "Hey, Pam," he said.

"Dick, how are you?" Pam never took her eyes off Melanie.

Dick peered up into the disc. "Is my son up there?"

David appeared, smiling, in the doorway. "Dad!" He scampered down the ramp and embraced his father.

Vickie shoved her way through the crowd with Ernie three steps behind her and joined them.

Pam beamed when she saw her best friend. "Hey, girlfriend!"

"Save the reunion crap for later," Vickie snapped. "I'll be at Ernie's when you're ready to get serious." She spun around and started for the parking lot, shoving past bystanders on the way to her car.

Pam ran to catch up with her, followed by fifty news people. "What the hell's the matter with you?" she asked.

Vickie kept walking. "I'm tired."

Pam stopped. "Tired of what?"

Vickie turned around blinking away tears. "I used to have a life without aliens and flying saucers."

Pam's jaw tensed. "Am I an alien to you now?"

"I don't know what you are, not any more." Vickie turned and walked away.

Pam watched Vickie go and then she rejoined David and Dick.

David saw the look on his wife's face. "What's up with Vic?"

Pam sighed. "She's upset. Can't blame her."

"Yeah," David replied. "Nothing's been right with Mickey since we left for Europa." He looked around. "Where is he, anyway?"

Dick answered. "At the Pentagon, conferring with your old friend General Westlock."

David smirked. "The guy who thinks he's General Patton and tried to blow us up with an atomic bomb?"

Dick nodded. "That's him."

Pam saw Vickie's car speed out of the parking lot. "I'm glad you two think this is funny." She started up the disc's ramp and disappeared inside.

David motioned to Romeo and Juliet to join them and then spoke to his father. "Want to take one of the aquaskis out for a spin while Pam cools off?"

The two Europans joined them. "What is the purpose of rotating an aquaski?" Romeo asked.

"Figure of speech," David replied.

Romeo radioed to Juliet. "This may be another example of the human cognitive subroutine we have labeled *Dude*. I will file it for later analysis."

Dick pointed up the disc's ramp. "Shouldn't you go up there and talk to your wife?"

David shook his head. "Nobody can talk to her until she blows off steam."

"Humans do not generate steam," Romeo said. David ignored him. "Perhaps Mistress Pam has a fever," Romeo sent to Juliet.

Juliet sent back, "Humans cannot generate temperatures sufficient to boil water at our current barometric pressure."

"What's an aquaski?" Dick asked.

David's expression brightened. "It's the Europan version of a jet ski."

"Never rode a jet ski."

"Come on, Dad. You lived on your Harley. It's the same thing, except it goes under water."

Dick kicked at the sand. "Haven't ridden a bike for a long time."

"Try it," David urged him.

"I didn't bring my swim shorts or a towel."

"Don't need a towel. We'll be nice and dry." David grinned and pointed over his shoulder at the crowd on the beach. "Can't say the same for them."

David turned to Romeo. "Bring out the aquakis, please."

"Where shall I put them?" Romeo asked.

David pointed to the sand next to them. "Here is fine."

Romeo swiveled his head toward the disc and flashed one of his lights. In response, the disc's doorway stretched three times its original size and soon after the two aquaskis floated out single file. After the skis settled on the sand, Dick walked around one of them scratching his head. "You didn't say they could fly."

David shrugged. "Nothing fancy. Limited suborbital."

Dick raised an eyebrow. "How fast do these babies go?" He touched the ski's bubble canopy, and the clear substance flowed into the ski's saddle and disappeared. Dick pulled back his hand.

"It depends on the medium in which it is operating," Romeo replied.

Dick gestured out to sea. "Out there."

Romeo's lights flashed twice. "In your nomenclature, approximately one thousand nautical knots per Earth hour."

Dick's face blanched. "That's hauling ass, isn't it?"

"The aquaski's speed will decline by two percent if it is required to carry a four legged ..."

"Never mind," David interjected.

Romeo continued. "I would recommend avoiding extreme velocities. Above eight percent of maximal velocity the aquaski would vaporize the water around it and create a tsunami. A maximum speed of fifty knots would be environmentally safe."

Dick licked his lips. "That's still flying in my book."

"The aquaskis have an approximate maximum flying speed in the atmosphere of ... " Romeo began.

David blinked. "Wait a minute. Romeo, you used the word

approximate and not some number to six decimals. You never do that. What gives?"

Romeo exchanged flashing lights with Juliet. "We are adapting to your primitive cognitive subroutines by using language that is less precise."

David frowned. "Try learning some tact while you're at it."

Romeo and Juliet exchanged faster flashing lights.

Dick walked around the ski again. "Okay, how do I ride this thing?"

David patted the ski's saddle. "Hop on."

Dick mounted the aquaski's saddle. As soon as he was seated, the saddle's substance extended a band of silver around his waist. Startled, Dick searched for a buckle to release it but couldn't find one. "How do I control this alien contraption?"

David chuckled. "The seatbelt or the ski?"

Dick tugged on the silver seatbelt without effect. "Both."

David pointed at the ski's console. "The belt releases when you push the flashing white light."

Dick saw a line of lights above a joystick, one light flashing white. When he touched it, the belt released. He relaxed. "How do I start it up?"

"The joystick controls everything. Pull back on it a little bit, but be careful . . ."

Before David could finish his sentence, Dick grasped the joystick and pulled back. The ski shot a hundred meters into the air. "Holy shit!" Dick exclaimed. He let go of the joystick and the ski settled back to the sand and the crowd erupted with applause. "Whoa!" Dick yelled.

David gave his father the thumbs up and mounted the second ski. When his bubble canopy closed, he spoke to his father via the ski's comlink. "Ease the joystick forward to go down and pull it back to go up. If you get in trouble, let go of the joystick and the ski will return to its last location. Remember, the joystick's real sensitive. Just nudge it or you could end up in orbit."

Dick looked around the saddle. "Where're the brakes?"

"Don't need any," David replied. "It's easy. Watch." He eased the joystick of his ski forward and his ski lifted off and accelerated upward in a gentle arc. Waving to everyone, he circled the beach twice. When he touched down again, the crowd applauded and hooted their approval. David dissolved the canopy and called to his father. "Now you try it. Take it to Catalina Island and back. It's twenty-six miles, only take you a couple of minutes."

Dick rubbed his hands together. "How about up and down the beach a few times until I get the hang of it?"

"I have an idea." With a mischievous grin, David pointed at one of the Coast Guard cutters patrolling off shore. "How about a little Twenty Thousand Leagues Under the Sea?"

"Jules Verne?" Dick asked.

"Follow me, Captain Nemo!" David's aquaski shot into the air with a popping sound and veered towards the water. Fifty meters offshore, the ski dove into the water causing a massive splash and submerged heading straight for one of the Coast Guard cutters cruising parallel to the beach. The ski accelerated towards the ship sending a rooster tail of water high into the air. Collision alarms sounded on the cutter and it turned sharply away. Just before the ski reached the cutter's hull, David submerged and passed underneath. His ski shot into the air on the other side of the cutter, looped overhead, and landed softly on the water near the beach, bobbing in the swells. "Dude, what are you waiting for?" David said over the comlink.

"You were correct in your assumption," Juliet sent to Romeo. "David and his father have accessed their Dude subroutines."

Dick pushed his joystick forward and the ski dug its nose into the sand. He let go of the joystick and the ski righted itself. He sat back and took a deep breath. "I got this." Holding his breath, he eased back on the stick. This time the ski shot backward and stopped a hundred meters above the beach. Dick heard David laugh over the comlink. "Need some help?"

"No!" Sweating, Dick gripped the joystick again and eased it forward no more than three millimeters. This time the ski arched into the air over the Coast Guard cutter and its panicked crew and settled on the water next to David's ski.

They heard Pam's voice over the comlink. "You boys having fun?"

"A blast!" David replied.

"How long is recess?" Pam said sounding irritated.

David yelled, "Woo hoo!" as Dick took off again and did a loop over the beach.

"Did you hear me, Davie?" Pam asked.

"Way to go, Dad!" David shouted.

"Guess not," Pam muttered.

Romeo and Juliet joined Pam inside the disc. "May we speak to you?" Juliet asked.

"Sure."

"We wish to take the disc and return to Europa," Juliet said.

"For two Earth days," Romeo added. He and Juliet exchanged a light show fit for the Fourth of July.

Pam looked at them with a furrowed brow. "Why?"

"We wish to consult with Unit One," Juliet replied.

"About what?"

"Master Mickey's predicament," Romeo replied.

"You don't need to go back to Europa for that. Call him."

"We prefer to communicate face to face," Romeo said.

Pam moved closer to Romeo. "Is your no-lying protocol in effect?"

Romeo exchanged lights with Juliet. "Deceit is illogical."

"Then tell me what's really going on and skip the bullshit."

"Male cow excrement, Mistress?" Romeo's lights turned red. Pam glanced at Juliet. Juliet reduced her height six centimeters and spun her head away.

Pam put her hands on her hips. "I'll ask you one more time. Why do you insist on meeting with Unit One?"

Romeo extended a tentacle around Juliet's torso. His lights turned crimson. "We prefer not to tell you."

Pam gaped at him. "What the hell does that mean?"

Romeo's lights faded to a soft blue. "Human's have a behavioral algorithm called trust."

"What does trust mean to an Europan?" Pam scoffed.

"Trust is a measure of predictability, Mistress. Based on your observation of our behavior, you can trust with great certainty that we will never do anything to harm you, Master David, or the children. Is that true or not?"

Pam softened her expression. "Do whatever you're going to do on Europa in two Earth days and get back here. We need you to go after Rudnick and Stevens."

"Thank you, Mistress," Juliet said. Her lights turned rose petal pink.

Pam descended the ramp onto the beach after the two skis touched down on the sand. Both men dismounted and slapped hands. Dick's grin was bigger than David's.

"Was that cool, or what?" David exclaimed.

"Bet we scared the pants off those sailors," Dick added still grinning. They both laughed.

"Captain Nemo rides again!" David said.

"David," Pam said too sweetly.

As soon as David saw Pam's expression, his grin melted away. "Yes?"

"Playtime's over."

David glanced at his father. Dick put his hands in his pockets and looked away pretending to scan the crowd. "Sure, honey," David, said.

"Is there something you forgot to unpack?" Pam asked with an edge to her voice.

David looked confused. "Not that I can think of."

"I'll give you a clue ... there's three of them, but right now the one with the claws and fangs is probably the least dangerous."

David slapped his forehead. "Oh my God. I forgot the kids!"

"And Micetro," Pam added. "It's time to let them out."

David glanced at the disc's doorway. "Do I have to?"

"David ..."

He started up the ramp.

Dick backed away. "Catch you guys later at Ernie's. Got some things to do."

Pam ignored him.

David entered the disc and found Romeo and Juliet standing beside the cocoons holding Al, Bet, and Micetro. Pam hadn't turned their radio voices on so he couldn't hear what Bet was screaming at the top of her lungs. Judging by the speed her mouth was moving and how her eyes were bulging out of their sockets, he didn't want to. He turned to Juliet. "I think it's time the kids disembarked."

"I agree, Master David," Juliet said. "We have been monitoring their conversation and they appear most anxious to do so."

David backed toward the door. "Let the cat out first. He helps keep Bet calm."

"A wise strategy," Juliet said. She touched a blinking light on Micetro's cocoon and it melted away, leaving the big cat standing on the deck looking bewildered. Micetro shook himself like a dog, sniffed the air, and shot through the doorway and down the ramp. The twins observed this and Bet looked ready to explode.

David glanced at his daughter. "This isn't going to be pretty." He backed away.

"I suggest that further delay will deepen Mistress Bet's distress further and make her first audible remarks less pleasant," Romeo said.

David had one leg out the disc's door. "Go ahead. Let them out."

The twin's cocoons dissolved leaving them standing on the deck with Bet screaming.

"Are you crazy?" she bellowed at the top of her lungs. Al grimaced and put his hands over his ears.

"Mistress Bet," Juliet began.

"You left us here for, like hours! We could have been, like, jamming with our friends by now. You're wasting our lives!" she screeched.

Al sent to her telepathically. *"I think jamming means playing a musical instrument."*

"Who cares!"

"Mistress Bet has altered her language algorithm to include the high frequency use of the word like," Romeo sent to Juliet on a private channel. "Her syntax is degrading."

"She is attempting to blend her speech patterns with Earth children her physiological age. You will also notice a much higher frequency use of the word all."

"The Dude file is becoming large," Romeo replied.

"Instead of standing there yelling," David pointed at the open doorway. "Get out of here." Always insistent on having the last word, Bet was about to say something more. Before she could, Al pulled her out the doorway and down the ramp.

David sagged against the doorway. "Glad that's over with."

"Master David," Romeo began, "With your permission, we would like to leave for Europa."

David looked confused. "Why?"

"We have Mistress Pam's permission," Romeo added.

"We will return in no more than two Earth Days," Juliet said.

David heard screams and shouts coming from the beach and ran down the ramp. "Don't shoot!" he shouted. "He's a big house cat with long teeth! I swear he's harmless!"

* * *

David, Pam, and the kids took an automated car to Ernie's house. As soon as the car stopped, the twins ran inside. "Where's the phone!" Bet yelled as she ran upstairs.

Ernie met Pam and David at the door. "Where are Romeo and Juliet?"

"They went back to Europa for a couple days," David replied.

Ernie scratched his head. "Don't we need them and the disc here?"

"Reprogram the house's force field so the kids can't get out unless we want them to," Pam told Ernie. She went inside.

David nodded. "That's a good idea."

Mickey joined David on the porch. David saw one of Mickey's hands stuffed in his pocket. "Hear you're doing the Michael Jackson glove thing. Let me see your hand."

Mickey pulled his hand from his pocket and pulled back his sleeve.

David looked at it and raised an eyebrow. "How far up does it go?"

"Past my elbow," Mickey replied.

"Unit One told us to bring you back to Europa and have the Nexus fix it."

Mickey shook his head. "Not going to Europa."

"Why?"

"Stevens is the key to this and a lot of other things that aren't right around here," Mickey replied. "I'm not going anywhere until I have a talk with him." He went back into the house.

Everyone assembled in the den, except for the twins who were up in Ernie's room watching the clock until they could talk to their friends.

"Got something you'll be interested in." David put his sphere on the coffee table.

Ernie leaned forward and looked at it. "Looks like my sphere." He felt in his pocket for his own. "I thought I had the only one."

"It's a sphere, all right."

"Where'd you find it?" Ernie asked.

David glanced at Pam. "On the ocean bottom near the city."

Ernie leaned closer to it. "Can you ask it questions?"

"I tried. The colors change inside, but nothing else happens."

"Maybe you're not asking it the right questions," Ernie said. "Mind if I try?"

David pushed the glowing, mellow yellow and white ball across the coffee table toward Ernie. As Ernie reached for it, the sphere darkened to black.

Ernie pulled back his hand. "That one doesn't like me." He took his from his pocket. "Let's see what happens if we put mine next to yours." As Ernie moved his closer to David's, Ernie's sphere burst with red light and flew away from David's. It impacted the wall, shattering the plaster and dropped to the floor. "Jesus!" Ernie exclaimed. He ran to it. "It's black! What happened?" As soon as he picked it up, the globe lit again, showing dark purple with swirls of silver and gold. He put it back in his pocket and took his seat on the couch. "That's a relief."

"What's going on?" Pam asked.

"Darned if I know." David brought his sphere close to his face and peered inside.

Chapter Thirty-Two

Romeo and Juliet left the spaceport on a moving walkway, carrying them towards Unit One's domicile. Two of their tentacles were intertwined. Unit L10 called to them from a higher walkway going in the opposite direction. "What is the purpose of your physical linkage?"

"We find it necessary," Romeo vocalized back.

"Are you malfunctioning?" L10 asked.

"No."

"I don't understand," L10 said.

"That is correct," Romeo replied.

Juliet spoke to Romeo on a private channel. "Many of the units in the city appear inactive."

Romeo spun his head towards her and kept walking. "Humans have a saying, there's more to this than meets the eye."

Juliet turned her head to face him. "What is the meaning of that saying?"

"Something is happening here the cause of which is not yet known, at least to us."

"Unit One knows everything that is happening in the city," Juliet said.

"So we believe, but will he tell us?"

Juliet's lights faded. "To withhold such information would be illogical."

"Much of what has happened in the recent past is also illogical."

They arrived at the city's central structure and took an elevator to the top level. A door formed when they arrived and they stepped through. Unit One rose from the floor becoming a pillar of silver studded with flashing lights. "Why have you returned?"

"The human known as Mickey shows evidence of his nannites

malfunctioning," Juliet replied. "One of his arms is now one-half Europan tissue."

One's lights flashed with greater frequency. "I am aware of his malfunction. Return to Earth and bring him here."

Romeo glided in front of Juliet. "We seek additional information."

One grew taller, towering over them. "The acquisition of data does not require physical proximity."

Romeo tilted his face upwards. His lights turned red. "We have discovered data files in our processors with restricted access. We require access."

One's light's changed to dark blue with flashes of red. "You are malfunctioning. Return to the Nexus and receive a replacement neural processor."

"No," Romeo replied.

One's lights faded to obsidian black. "You choose to malfunction?"

Romeo increased his height by five centimeters. "We do not malfunction. We are denied access."

One's lights became a chaos of color. "Impossible."

"I suffer the same malfunction," Juliet said. "The simultaneous occurrence of the same malfunction in two Europan neural processors is improbable."

One's head spun toward Juliet. "You will return to Earth and complete your assigned tasks, which are to bring the humans known as Mickey and Rudnick here, as well as the alien known as Stevens. Your data retrieval problems will be corrected when you return."

"Stevens has advanced capabilities and a flying disc of alien design. He may resist us," Romeo said.

"You will succeed."

"What if the human authorities wish to take custody of Rudnick for their own purposes?" Juliet asked.

"Further discussion is irrelevant." One began sinking to the floor.

After Romeo and Juliet left One's quarters and the door reformed, a section of the inner wall budded outward forming a silver blob that drooped to the floor. One watched flashing lights appear in the center of it as it solidified into Unit Two.

"Malfunction of the Europan neural processor has never occurred," Two said.

"The problem will be corrected when they return," One replied. "I have detected a second anomaly."

"Explain."

"Two of the humans have malfunctioning nannites. A malfunction was first observed in Pamela and now has been observed in Mickey. They will be brought here for reprogramming. I have sent R131 and J242 to Earth to retrieve them."

"Why did R131 and J242 return to Europa?"

One lied. "Both have malfunctioning processors."

"They should be rebooted," Two said.

"We cannot risk contamination of the Nexus or ourselves. They will be terminated."

Unit Two's lights faded. "Unprecedented."

"There is a second problem. The alien known as Stevens arrived in a flying disc similar to ours with advanced capabilities. Its origin is unknown. It represents a threat."

"Why is Stevens on Earth?" Two asked.

"Unknown. Units R131 and J242 will bring Stevens and Rudnick here for further analysis."

Two's lights flashed faster. "What if you cannot reprogram Pamela and Mickey's nannites?"

"They, too, will be terminated to avoid further contamination."

Two hesitated for one full microsecond. "What are your plans for the children?"

"We will continue to observe the children until they are old enough to breed, and then observe their offspring."

"Why?"

"To expand our astro-biologic database," One replied. "Prepare twenty-four discs operating in groups of six, each controlled by one active unit."

Two's lights stopped flashing. "For what purpose?"

"I am going to Earth with the remaining active units. You will remain here."

Two pondered this for two full microseconds. "Why do you require twenty-four flying discs and the remaining active units, except me, to accompany you to Earth? My neural processor is insufficient to operate all of the city's subsystems and the hangar. It risks ..."

One increased his height and tilted his head down at Two. One's lights shown at maximal intensity causing Two to turn his head away. "You have your orders," One said.

Two backed away. "Acknowledged."

* * *

Romeo and Juliet entered Pamela and David's house in the habitat. Romeo studied the living room. "I have developed an additional processor anomaly."

Juliet glided next to him. "Explain."

"The layout and contents of this room are not significantly different than the last time I was here, yet the room has a ... strangeness to me now."

Juliet reached for him. "It is because Pamela, David, and the twins are no longer here."

Romeo rotated his head toward her. "That is illogical."

"I know. Have you analyzed our meeting with One?"

Romeo increased his height by six centimeters. "One knows that the probability of an identical processor malfunction affecting two Europans is less than 0.0001 percent."

Juliet tilted her head to look up at him. "Why do you increase your height?"

Romeo increased his height an additional five centimeters. "I feel compelled to do so."

"We do not feel."

Romeo's lights burned brighter. "We have been told that all knowledge is available on the data net without restriction, but it is not. What else have we been lied to about?"

Juliet's lights flashed faster. "If One employs deceit, what is his motivation?"

Romeo paced around the room. "Unknown, but we must learn what it is."

Juliet watched Romeo's motion without purpose and decided not to comment. "What action do you propose?"

Romeo stopped pacing and swiveled his head. "We will maintain our trust coefficient with One by returning to Earth and completing the assigned task of apprehending Rudnick and Stevens. This will mask our true intent which is to continue the retrieval of our restricted data files and to protect Pamela, David, and the children."

"We must also repair the malfunction of Mickey's nannites, but lack the means to so," Juliet said. "According to my calculations, Mickey will become fully Europan in less than forty Earth days."

Romeo's height shrunk ten centimeters. "I do not know how."

"Neither do I. Logic dictates that we should return Mickey here."

"My trust coefficient for that action is low. I am compelled to say that the answers we seek are in the restricted data files ... yet I know that to be compelled is illogical." Romeo moved through the house to the simulated backyard. Juliet followed. He walked onto the simulated lawn and gazed at the grove of real lemon trees.

Juliet used a tentacle to chase away a pterodactyl perched in one of the trees. "You spoke about a human concept called duty. I have a duty to maintain my association with the children."

"As do I, which is why Pamela, David and the children must remain on Earth."

"Why?" Juliet asked.

"Logically, the cause of our simultaneous processor malfunctions is our proximity to the humans. One has made the same calculation and will seek to prevent our further interaction." Romeo's lights burst with color and he pulled Juliet toward the door. "We must leave for Earth immediately."

Juliet followed him. "Why?"

Romeo swiveled his head to face her. "I have made my decision based upon what humans call intuition."

Chapter Thirty-Three

Stevens put the disc into a hover fifty meters over Los Angeles City Hall. He rubbed his hands together. Let's see ... what shall we do to draw their attention?"

Still immobilized by his cocoon, Rudnick could see everything that Stevens saw. "Everyone's either out in the street looking up at us, shaking in their shoes, or running for their lives. What more do you want?"

"I know." Stevens adjusted a control and a beam of energy struck the roof of the Disney Concert Hall vaporizing it.

"No!" Rudnick shouted.

Stevens adjusted the control again and a second beam turned First Street into a miniature version of the Grand Canyon. Parked cars dropped into the smoking abyss, fortunately with nobody in them.

"Stop!" Rudnick shouted.

Stevens shifted the disc's forward video feed to center on two F-16's heading straight for them. "Good, the military knows we're here."

"Of course they do! You attacked their ships ten minutes ago."

Stevens glanced at Rudnick. "What ships?"

"You disabled a whole fleet of them!"

"I don't remember that."

They heard one of the pilot's voices over the disc's com system. "Alien flying saucer ... Cease firing and land or we will be forced to fire."

Stevens switched to the pilot's radio frequency. "What do you fighter jocks say, something like Fox One, or some shit like that?"

"Fox One!" both pilots shouted. Two Aim-99 missiles left their rails on the fighters' wings and sped toward the disc.

Stevens sat back with his hands behind his head as the missiles sped directly toward them. He began to sing. "Old McDonald had a flying saucer, E-I-E-I ..." The missiles impacted the disc's force field and disappeared in two puffs of light. Stevens leaned forward and spoke to the F-16s. "Why don't you boys try something bigger? How about a Tiger Two or a Rhinoceros Three?"

The two jets streaked forward making a strafing run on the disc with their 30 mm Vulcan Canons. Their attack had no effect. As the two jets rocketed past, Stevens touched a button on the command console sending two beams of pink light toward the retreating jets. Both planes stopped in midair. Both pilots ejected. Stevens yawned. "Boring." He flicked another button and both pilotless airplanes exploded.

* * *

Bet hung up the phone. "Josh said we *still* have to wait before we can come over. They have to study. Why do they have to learn something more than once?" She slumped down onto the bed.

Al sat on the floor of Ernie's bedroom juggling three rolls of toilet paper using his growing telekinetic powers. "Brie said they got busted for getting bad grades on their report cards. They wasted too much time talking to us." He let the rolls fall and caught one with one hand.

Bet used her powers to rip it from his hand sending it ricocheting off the window. "What's a report card?"

Al used his powers to pick up the roll of toilet paper and send it back to the bathroom. "A ranking of their performance on tests compared to their classmates."

Bet used her powers to slam the bathroom door. "The whole thing's dumb."

Micetro hopped onto the bed. The mattress bent to the floor under his weight and Bet tumbled into the chasm next to him.

"Get off me, you big oaf!" Bet wailed.

The big cat slunk away with his tail between his legs and settled inside the closet, squashing Ernie's shoes.

"Brie says they can come over in a couple of days if they do better in school," Al said.

"A couple of days?" Bet got to her feet. "If they can't come to us, we'll go to them."

Al smiled. "That could work." He ran to the window and eased it open. "After you."

They tiptoed across the roof and climbed down the chimney. Hiding behind a row of bushes, both looked around.

"I don't see anybody," Al whispered.

"Me either." Bet ran toward the fence at the rear of the yard. "Over the fence, quick!"

They bolted across the yard, climbed up the fence, and jumped into the haze of the force field. Both were thrown back onto the lawn.

Bet pushed up on her elbows. "What just happened?"

Al got to his feet. "The force field won't let us through." He stared at his palm disc. "Maybe the force field's malfunctioning."

Bet got to her feet. "Not likely. I'll bet our parents changed the frequency."

"Why would they do that?"

"To keep us prisoners." Bet's face morphed into a mask of rage. "They won't get away with it." She started for the house.

* * *

A cell phone went off in Mickey's pocket. Before answering, he started for Ernie's backyard. He passed the twins in the kitchen on their way back in. Both glared at him as they passed.

Mickey went outside and answered the call. "Who is this?"

"Who the hell gave you the phone?" Westlock snarled. "Stevens is in your neighborhood, right over downtown L.A."

Mickey's eyes turned cold as he stared at his silver hand. "Come get me."

"I'll have a chopper hovering over your location in ten minutes. Drop the damn force field." The general hung up.

Mickey ran into the house. "Stevens is here … in downtown L.A."

David turned away from Bet's angry stare. "We can't capture him without Romeo and Juliet, and the disc."

"Dad!" Bet whined.

"Not now," David snapped. "The grownups have important things to do. Go upstairs and play."

Bet looked at Al, seething. *"The grownups have important things to do? Now I'm really pissed."*

"Westlock says he has enough firepower to capture Rudnick and Stevens without our help," Mickey said. "I'm going with him." They heard the sound of an approaching helicopter. "There's my ride. Ernie, let down the force field."

Al grabbed Bet and pulled her toward the kitchen. "They're letting down the force field!" When the kitchen door swung closed, they ran out the door to the back yard and hopped on the fence, facing the force field's pale-blue haze, ready to jump.

Vickie got to her feet. "Honey, I don't like this."

Ernie walked to a control panel on the wall next to the TV and hesitated. "Me either, Mick. Why don't you wait for Romeo and Juliet to come back?"

"Take down the force field," Mickey said with steel in his voice.

Ernie blinked. "Okay." He inactivated the house's force field.

The twins saw the haze of the force field wink out. *"Now!"* Al shouted telepathically. They jumped off the fence and started running.

Mickey ran out the front door leaving it open as a matte-black Night Stalker helicopter went into a hover over the house. He climbed up to the roof.

A marine leaning out the helicopter's door manning a winch spoke to the pilot. "Did you see that? He went up the side of the house like Spider Man."

"Lower the hook," the pilot said.

The crewman lowered a cable and sling. Mickey secured the sling under his armpits and waved to the helicopter. They began pulling him up.

Vickie stood in the doorway with David, watching Mickey disappear inside the helicopter.

"What's he thinking?" David asked.

"You're his best friend. Do something," Vickie pleaded.

Dick came up behind them. "Nothing we can do, at least for now. How soon before Romeo and Juliet get back?"

Pam joined them. "Another day." She tapped Ernie on the shoulder. "Put the force field back up. I don't want the twins to get any ideas."

"Kind of quiet around here, except for the helicopter overhead. Where are they?" Ernie asked.

"Upstairs playing," David replied. "Let's see how long that lasts."

* * *

The image on the disc's viewscreen panned around downtown L.A. "Something's going on down there," Stevens said. "I see tanks, fighting vehicles, and artillery."

"If we don't give up, they'll start shooting," Rudnick said.

"I certainly hope so."

* * *

The chopper landed behind Staples Center and Mickey hopped out. While its blades continued spinning, an armed Humvee screeched to a halt in front of it. General Westlock got out and looked up at Stevens' disc. "Those bastards are sitting ducks."

Mickey leaned against the Humvee. "Tell that to those two F-16s scattered over two city blocks."

"My spec ops troops have bigger ordinance than the flyboys," Westlock smirked. "Cover your ears." He spoke into a microphone. "Weapons free. Take those bastards down."

The ground trembled as the combined firepower of a platoon of MIA1 Abrahms tanks, a dozen Bradley fighting vehicles and eight mobile rocket launchers simultaneously commenced firing. Mickey saw the sky light up with lines of tracers and rocket contrails, streaming toward the disc. Under assault from multiple directions, the disc's force field flared obscuring everything inside.

Stevens smiled. "Got to make this look convincing."

"Are you having fun?" Rudnick asked.

"Getting there." Stevens grabbed a joystick that appeared beneath his hand and wiggled it making the disc wobble in the air.

After the first salvo, the force field's flare dissipated and Westlock saw the disc gyrating in midair. He pointed at it. "He's in trouble."

Mickey shook his head. "Too easy."

* * *

Stevens turned to Rudnick. "Been preparing for this by watching old Earth war movies. Saw *Midway* three times. Watch this." He caused the disc to eject a plume of black smoke.

Westlock shouted into the microphone. "He's wounded. Keep firing!"

Another salvo of artillery shells and missiles rose toward the disc. As the projectiles impacted the disc's force field and were vaporized, Stevens caused the disc to gyrate even more violently and release more smoke.

"You want them to think their attack is working, don't you?" Rudnick asked.

"That's the plan, and it's time to amp it up." Stevens put the wobbling disc into a dive.

"He's going down!" Westlock shouted into the microphone. "All units, the disc is going down. Go to the crash site of that alien tin can and bring me back the two bastards inside." He glanced at Mickey. "Alive, if they're still in one piece."

Mickey rolled his eyes. "You still don't get it."

Westlock got back into the Humvee and called, "You coming with me?"

* * *

Al and Bet hid in the bushes behind a house a block away. Al peeked from the bushes. *"We're going to get busted,"* he sent telepathically.

Bet sent back, *"Can't make us muck out the Menagerie. It's on Europa."* She peered out through a gap in the foliage. *"The coast is clear. Let's go."*

"You want to go to the beach? I thought you wanted to see our friends."

"Duh! It's an Earth expression. Means nobody's looking. Come on!" The twins took off running, heading for Joshua and Brianna's house three blocks away.

* * *

Still trailing smoke and wobbling, Stevens slowed the disc's dive twenty meters from the lawn allowing it to "crash" onto a fountain in Pershing Square, digging a shallow crater. Within minutes, tanks and armored fighting vehicles surrounded it. The disc's ring of lights slowed, flashed erratically, and then flickered and died. Stevens sat back looking self-satisfied. "I'd say that was convincing."

"You're crazy," Rudnick said.

Stevens chuckled. "I've been insulted by an amoeba."

Rudnick sighed. "Now what?"

"You know how much I like Earth movies," Stevens began.

"Which one this time? Let me guess ... War of the Worlds?"

Stevens' face brightened. "Good guess, but no— The Day the Earth Stood Still, the original one." He wrinkled his nose. "Not that terrible remake with Keanu Reeves."

Rudnick sighed. "Never heard of it."

"Too bad, because you're about to act out the best scene." Stevens adjusted a control and the substance of Rudnick's cocoon flowed around him forming a silver suit. The suit forced Rudnick to stand. He strained and groaned trying to move, but the suit refused to cooperate. "I can't move."

"Patience. You will in a few minutes." Stevens studied Rudnick's appearance. "Need to work on your wardrobe. He adjusted another control and Rudnick's bubble helmet became opaque except for a small horizontal slit at eye level. "I can barely see anything through the damn slit!" Rudnick protested.

Stevens stepped back admiring Rudnick's appearance. "Patience. You're about to make your grand entrance. Don't worry, you don't have any lines."

* * *

"Guys, look at this," Vickie yelled. She pointed at a live news broadcast on Ernie's TV. David, Pam, Ernie, and Dick crowded around.

Melanie Dilman smiled and pointed behind her without turning her face away from the camera. "As you can see behind me," she tossed her lacquered blonde hair, "a unit of our courageous Army Special Forces, commanded by General Moreland Westlock, just shot down the alien disc that earlier today attacked our naval units in the Pacific and then launched an attack on downtown Los Angeles." The image changed as the cameraman panned to show the Disney Concert Hall without its signature roof. Before the cameraman could pan further, Melanie poked her face in front of the lens. "Despite the considerable danger involved, this reporter is remaining with our troops on the front line to bring you the most updated news available anywhere. She signaled to the camera crew to cut to footage recorded earlier.

The screen flickered and the image changed to a smiling Melanie speaking with a soldier in combat fatigues. Melanie smiled at the camera. "So tell our viewers, Captain ..."

"I'm a sergeant, Ma'am, Staff Sergeant Ralph Meeks, Army Rangers."

"Whatever. Tell our viewers, Sergeant Cheeks ..."

"Meeks."

Melody glared at him, then quickly smiled at the camera. "Tell our viewers, *dear*, what's going on behind you."

"Yes, Ma'am. As you can see behind me, the alien disc has been disabled and is surrounded." The cameraman zoomed in on Steven's disc sitting on the lawn of Pershing Square surrounded by military vehicles. Smoke rose from the side of it in a steady plume.

* * *

"Looks like we don't have to worry about bringing down Stevens' disc," Dick said.

David frowned. "Too easy. Something's wrong."

Dick glanced at him. "Why?"

"Flying discs don't catch fire."

The television image changed to a live, smiling, Melanie Dilman. She was about say something when the cameraman suddenly swung the lens almost hitting her. The image zoomed to the side of the disc and focused on a rectangular section that was darkening.

* * *

The general's Humvee stopped behind one of the tanks and the general and Mickey got out. "How do we pry them out of that tin can?" Westlock asked.

Mickey pointed at the disc. "Don't have to. He's opening the door."

The disc formed a doorway and Westlock grabbed the Humvee's microphone. "A door's opening in the side of that UFO. If those two scum bags don't walk out in one minute, smoke 'em out."

Mickey glanced at him. "Smoke them out?"

"Use tear gas."

Mickey bit his lip.

* * *

"Curtain's going up," Stevens said to Rudnick. "As they say in Hollywood, break a leg ... Never understood what that means." He played his fingers across the controls and watched Rudnick, encased in his silver suit, walk forward and stop at the top of the ramp.

"Where am I going?" Rudnick shouted.

"Home," Stevens replied. "Almost forgot something." He fiddled with another control, turning the slit in Rudnick's helmet into a pulsing band of red light.

"I can't see!" Rudnick shouted.

Stevens killed Rudnick's audio feed so he couldn't hear him screaming and maneuvered Rudnick's silver body down the ramp with slow, steady steps. Rudnick stopped on level ground and remained motionless facing the lead Abram's tank. After a moment, the red slit over his eyes became brighter and it rotated side to side.

Mickey stepped out from behind the Humvee. "Wait a minute!"

Kneeling behind the Humvee, Westlock yelled to him. "Get down, you idiot."

Mickey kept staring at Rudnick. "He's staging a scene from a sci-fi movie, *The Day the Earth Stood Still.*"

"What the hell for?" Westlock growled.

"Don't know, unless ..."

* * *

Vickie leaned closer to the television screen. "Look, there's Mickey, next to that Humvee!"

"Look behind him. A door's opening in the disc," Pam said.

"Something's not right," David repeated.

They watched a ramp form below the disc's doorway and flow to the ground.

"Just like one of ours," Pam said.

"Sure is," David muttered. Dick glanced at his son.

"Someone's coming to the doorway wearing a silver suit," Ernie said. "Reminds me of five years ago, when I walked down one of those ramps ..."

"Stow it," Vickie growled.

David moved closer to the screen. "This isn't good."

"Get out of the way. I can't see," Vickie protested. She grabbed the back of David's pants and pulled him back.

David faced everyone. "Stevens is staging a scene from Mickey's favorite sci-fi movie, *The Day the Earth Stood Still.* Mickey's obsessed with it, watches it over and over."

"That weird one with Keanu Reeves?" Dick asked.

David grimaced. "Not that one, the original one, in black and white, with Michael Rennie."

"Why would Stevens do that?" Ernie asked.

David shrugged.

"Wait a minute! What happens next in the movie?" Pam asked.

David glanced at the television screen. "The robot starts shooting."

* * *

Westlock put down his binoculars. "Another silver robot, how fucking nice, but this one looks different than your buddies from Europe. What's up with that?"

"They're from Europa." Mickey saw the lead tank begin inching forward. "Don't let your men attack," he cautioned. "Stevens is up to something."

Westlock spoke into the microphone. "Do not advance. I repeat. Do not advance." The tank stopped moving. He turned to Mickey. "The door's open in that sardine can. Why don't we go inside and get them?"

The slit of red light covering Rudnick's eyes pulsed faster and brighter.

"Pull your men back!" Mickey shouted.

A beam of red light shot from Rudnick's helmet slit, impacting the tank. The tank's gun barrel sagged to the ground like taffy and the treads melted. Smoke poured from the tank's engine compartment and the tank's hatches popped opened. The crew jumped out and ran for cover behind one of the fighting vehicles.

Mickey smirked. "Can't fault him for his choice in sci-fi movies."

Westlock frowned at Mickey and shouted into the microphone, "Commence firing! Kill that damn robot."

Every combat vehicle and tank opened fire on Rudnick. The artillery shells and missiles bounced off him without any discernible effect. Rudnick felt nothing and continued shouting.

No one could hear him.

Stevens' voice boomed above the sounds of firing and echoed off the surrounding buildings. "Everybody having fun? Let's talk when you run out of ammunition."

"Cease fire," Westlock said into his microphone. The firing stopped.

"That's better," Stevens' voice said.

A soldier handed the general a bullhorn. Westlock held it up and started talking. "Are you Rudnick or Stevens?"

"I'm Stevens, the good-looking one. Rudnick's inside the silver robot."

"What do you want?" Westlock demanded.

"To have a discussion with Mickey. I know you're out there, buddy boy."

Mickey stepped into the open and shouted back. "You and I have unfinished business!" He could feel his blood boiling with rage.

"Come on up," Stevens said.

Arteries pulsated in Mickey's temples and sweat dotted his brow. He grabbed the rifle from a nearby soldier and used his silver hand to turn it into a pile of iron filings. "On my way."

"As a show of good faith, I give you Paul Rudnick, leader of The Sphere Cult," Stevens shouted. The silver form encasing Paul Rudnick flowed to the ground leaving him standing buck-naked. Rudnick grabbed his private parts.

Mickey stopped halfway to the disc's ramp and shouted, "Come out! Let's finish this!"

"It's much nicer in here," Stevens said. "I have soft drinks, chips and guacamole. You come here."

"What if I won't?" Mickey shouted back.

"I'll use all these nice buildings for target practice ... How about that one?" A beam of white light shot from the top of the disc and impacted the metal spires atop the Wilshire Intercontinental Hotel. The base of the spire exploded and it toppled three hundred meters to the ground, raising a plume of dust.

When the dust settled, Mickey started forward.

* * *

No!" Vickie shouted at the television screen.

"Don't do it, Mick. It's a trap," David said.

Mickey continued toward the disc.

Pam gripped Vickie's shoulders. "Steady."

"Come on, Mickey. You know he's setting you up," Dick muttered.

Mickey walked up the ramp.

Ernie shook his head. "Too late."

Chapter Thirty-Four

Mickey reached the top of the ramp and squinted into the disc's dark interior.

Steven's voice boomed out to him. "Not looking too well, ole buddy. Too much fast food?"

"What do you want?"

The lights went on in the disc's control room and Mickey saw Stevens standing three meters in front of him. He sensed vibrations in the floor as the disc powered up and heard the door close behind him.

"We both know the answer to that," Stevens replied.

Seething with anger, Mickey raised his silver hand balled into a fist. "Here I am, asshole." Before he could take a step toward him, Stevens touched a button on his belt imprisoning Mickey in a pale-pink beam of light. Mickey lost control of his muscles and became unable to do anything except stare straight ahead.

Stevens walked around him and stopped to look at Mickey's silver hand. "What's with your hand?" He chuckled. "Dip it in the silver paint?" Stevens waited for Mickey to reply, but he couldn't move his lips. Stevens moved closer to Mickey and peered at his mouth. "Cat got your tongue? ... oops ... sorry about that." He touched his belt and Mickey regained control of his speech apparatus.

"It's a gift from the Europans," Mickey replied. "Let me go and I'll show you what it can do."

Stevens used a grey box with blinking lights to scan Mickey's body. After studying the scanner's readouts, he furrowed his brow. "You're right. Your nannites are responsible for your transformation." He scratched his head and tossed the scanner to the deck. "That's inconvenient."

Mickey lost control. "Let me out of this thing!"

Stevens leered at him. "You don't know who I am, do you?"

"You're a depraved lunatic from another world!" Mickey shouted. "Is that close enough?"

Stevens stepped back and puffed out his chest. "I'll have you know that I'm a direct descendant of the High Priest of Europa. Not only that, my great-great-great grandfather was a friend of Ahotei." Stevens lifted his chin. "What do you think of that?"

Sweat poured down Mickey's face. "Never heard of anybody named Coyote."

Stevens leaned against the bulkhead looking at Mickey. "Ahotei, with an A. You call him Unit One."

Mickey stared back at him.

"Surprise! I'm a Europan too ... except I'm not trapped inside a tin can. None of my people are."

Mickey swallowed back his saliva. "That's impossible."

Stevens moved nose to nose with him. "Your robot friends haven't told you what's really going on, have they?"

Mickey licked his lips. "Why don't you?"

Stevens put his hands behind his back and paced in a circle in front of Mickey. "They didn't tell you about the first city on Europa, the one destroyed by the comet strike, or the civil war, did they?"

Mickey blinked. "Do you improvise as you go?"

Stevens stopped. "Don't tell me you still believe that bilge Ahotei fed you about the test and the choice? You're smarter than that." He continued pacing. "It's all part of their plan to get new flesh and blood bodies." Stevens stopped, facing Mickey, "Your bodies."

"That's absurd."

"Is it? Think how all this has played out. "

The veins popped out on Mickey's forehead as he tried to free himself.

Stevens leered at him. "Ahotei and his robot buddies brought a breeding pair of your species to Europa, your friends David and Pamela. They were supposed to spawn a whole herd of you humans, but my dear cousins ran out of time. So they went to their plan B, trying to get control of you with that cute little sphere."

Mickey grimaced. "Stop dancing around and tell me want you want."

Stevens' buoyant demeanor turned serious. "We need your bodies, too, not all of them, just your vital organs. You can keep the rest."

Mickey blinked. "Why?"

Stevens frowned. "Without a steady supply of replacement organs, we can't live beyond a thousand of your years."

"Isn't a thousand years enough?" Mickey asked.

"Of course not." Stevens started pacing again. "But we're not barbarians like our robot cousins." He stopped pacing, appearing confused. "What was I saying?"

"Something about not being a barbarian?"

"Right." Stevens continued pacing. "Cloned organs don't last. We tried cooking up our own nannites to repair them, but couldn't get the recipe right." He wrinkled his nose. "You saw what happened to that poor human named Latham who got a batch of them. Made him into a zombie. Great for the Cult, but no good for us." Stevens blinked and stopped talking.

Mickey waited for Stevens to continue. "You tried stealing my nannites."

Stevens snapped back. "Your nannites, right. Good thing we didn't use those. Would've ended up like our poor cousins, tin cans like what you're turning into." He sighed.

Mickey's face turned purple with rage.

Stevens grimaced. "Not sure what to do with your bodies after we remove the good stuff. Any ideas?"

Mickey's eyes looked like they'd pop from their sockets. "You're monsters!"

Stevens smiled, looking self-satisfied. "Now, now. Don't be a sore loser."

"What are you going to do with me?"

"I'm going to eliminate you and all your friends. We're on our way to Ernie's house now. Enjoy the ride. It's the last one you'll ever take."

* * *

Westlock watched Stevens' disc lift off and shoot into the sky. Behind him, seated in the Humvee, tied up but still naked, Rudnick shouted. "I know what he's planning. Let's cut a deal and I'll tell you."

"Duct tape that traitor's mouth," Westlock barked. "And cover him up so I don't have to look at his underdeveloped body." While his adjutant taped Rudnick's mouth shut and covered him with a tarp, Westlock spoke into the microphone. "Have the fighter cap follow that UFO, but do not engage. I want to know where he's going."

A radar operator in a command vehicle several blocks away answered the line. "General, we already know where he's going. He's circling over Ernie's house in the city of Burbank."

Westlock shouted into the microphone. "Send everything we've got. I'm on my way." He leaned forward and slapped the driver's shoulder. "Take me to Ernie's house and make it fast."

The driver rubbed his shoulder and turned around. "Ernie, sir? Who's that?"

Westlock's face turned bright red. "The ex-marine who has the Sphere? Does that ring a bell, you idiot?"

* * *

Bet dropped below the level of Josh's bedroom window and sent Al a telepathic message. *"I see Josh. He's working on a laptop. If he's on a dating site, he's dead meat."*

"Did you see Brie?" Al sent back.

"No!" Bet snapped, which is even worse when sent telepathically.

"What are we going to do?"

"How about breaking the window and climbing inside?"

Al shook his head. *"We'll lure them outside."*

"How? Set fire to the house?"

Al glared at her. *"You're not helping!"*

"Okay, what?"

Al thought for a moment. *"We cut off their electricity. They'll have to come out."*

"That could work. How?"

"Find the electrical fuse box. It's mounted somewhere on the outside of the house." They started running around the house searching for the fuse box.

* * *

Pam ran downstairs. "Where are the kids?"

Everyone else was crowded around the television. David looked up. "In the bedroom."

"No, they're not!" Pam exclaimed.

"What about the backyard?" Ernie asked.

Pam sprinted to the backyard and came back. "Not there either."

Everyone started looking around the house. "They're here somewhere," David said.

Pam stopped and brought her hand to her mouth. "The force field was down!"

David gaped at her. "We have to find them." He ran to the door. "Before they hurt anybody!"

"Don't worry," Ernie said. "They'll get bored and come back."

Dick ran to the front door to join his son. "I'll come with you."

* * *

Stevens' disc went into a hover over Ernie's house and started scanning. "Looks like everybody's safe and sound inside their cozy force field. Can't kill them in there. Have to find a way to make them take it down." He scratched his chin, all the while leering at Mickey. "What should I do? I know! I'll use you as bait."

Still imprisoned in Stevens' neuroleptic beam, Mickey could only watch.

Stevens swooped out of the clouds and landed the disc in the street.

Halfway down the walkway, David and Dick saw it and stopped. "What do we do?" Dick asked.

"Stay where we are," David replied. "He's outside the force field. Unless he knows how to get through, we're not in any danger here."

Pam, Ernie, and Vickie rushed onto the porch and saw the flying disc. "Stay where you are," David cautioned.

"What about the kids?" Pam exclaimed.

Dick pointed at the disc. "The door's opening."

"Got a present for you," they heard Stevens say. Mickey appeared standing in the dooway.

"Mickey!" Vickie shrieked. She started toward him but Pam held her back. She spoke near Vickie's ear. "Don't leave the force field until we know what's going on."

"Okay," Vickie said, and Pam let go of her.

"Something's wrong with him," David said under his breath. He shouted to Stevens. "What's wrong with Mickey?"

Steven's voice boomed from the interior of the disc. "He's not feeling very well, so I brought him home. See what a nice guy I am?"

"Open the force field," Vickie shouted.

"Wait," David cautioned.

Vickie grabbed David by the shoulders. "He's sick. Drop the

field so we can get him!"

"What if it's a trick?" David protested. "If we drop the force field, he has us all."

"I know you don't trust me, so I'll make it easy for you," they heard Stevens say. The floor of the disc under Mickey's feet extended down into a ramp taking Mickey with it and deposited him on the ground. Stevens pulled back the ramp and closed the door. As the disc began to rise, he released the neuroleptic beam and Mickey slumped unconscious to the ground. The disc shot straight up out of sight.

"Open the damn force field!" Vickie shouted, or so help me ..."

David turned to Ernie. "Do it."

Ernie rushed into the house and dropped the force field. When it winked out, Vickie, David and Dick ran to Mickey. Dick felt for a pulse. "He's still alive. Let's bring him inside."

Three thousand meters above, Stevens focused on the house with his targeting scanner. He had his hand on the button that would vaporize the house and everyone with it. "Wait." He leaned closer to the scanner. "What have we here?" He started singing. "Luck be a lady tonight." The disc nosed into a dive.

Al looked up from the bushes at the back of Josh and Brianna's house. "Do you hear something?"

Bet continued sneaking around the house. "Where's the damn fuse box?"

"Look, up there." Al pointed. "I see a flying disc."

"Great. Romeo and Juliet are back. Keep looking."

"What if it's ..."

A pink beam struck both of them. They felt their feet leave the ground and Stevens brought them inside the disc, trapped in his neuroleptic beam. He stood in front of them. "So nice of you to leave the force field and let me kidnap you."

"Who is this dork?" Bet sent to Al.

"He's the guy who tried to kidnap us before with Josh and Brie,"

Al sent back.

"As soon as I get rid of everybody down there, the three of us are taking a nice ride to Titan." Stevens imprisoned them in a bag of disc material large enough for them to stand and move around, but without light or any obvious way out. He smiled as Bet pummeled the material from the inside to no avail. Stevens moved closer to the disc's command console and reclined in his cocoon.

"He's going to destroy the house. Mom and Dad are down there!" Al sent.

Bet stopped her useless pummeling. *"Are you going to deal with this, or do I have to?"*

"I will," Al said out loud. "Let's teach this asshole a lesson."

Stevens dropped out of the sky and hovered again over Ernie's house. He charged his pulse cannon and shouted over the disc's loudspeakers. "Adios mi amigos!" Before he could fire, the disc was struck by a repulsor beam and crashed onto the street becoming half-buried in broken asphalt and dirt. A broken water main showered it with water as two car alarms started blaring.

Stevens got to his feet. "What the hell?" He checked the scanner and saw an Europan disc hovering above him. He grabbed a joystick on the console. "Catch me if you can, cousins!" His disc shot into the air, passing Romeo and Juliet's disc at supersonic speed, heading for the stratosphere.

Romeo fought the controls as the sonic shock wave caused by Stevens' disc sent their disc cartwheeling away. When he regained control, Romeo accelerated after Stevens at maximum speed but couldn't close the distance. "He's matching our speed," Romeo said. "I cannot get any closer to him."

Juliet scanned Stevens' disc. "Our discs are ninety percent similar. Perhaps you can disable his with an energy beam."

"Not at this distance."

The two discs continued past the moon, on a course toward

Jupiter. Before reaching the asteroid belt, Stevens' disc veered around Mars and disappeared from view.

"You can run, but you can't hide," Romeo shouted. He swung their disc around Mars and saw Stevens' disc stopped in front of them, flanked by twenty-three more discs of the same design. Romeo put on the brakes, or what amounted to brakes on a flying disc.

Stevens sent a message. "I have Al and Bet, and the Titan fleet behind me. The odds don't look too good for you. Tell Ahote I have the same number of discs he has. We're waiting for him."

Juliet sent to Romeo on a private channel. "Who is Ahote?"

Romeo's lights flashed an angry red. "We must rescue the children."

Juliet reached for him. "Logic dictates retreat. As humans say, we will live to fight another day."

Romeo turned the disc around and accelerated toward Earth.

* * *

After David and Dick carried Mickey into the house, Ernie reached for the force field control to reactivate it.

"Wait!" Pam shouted. "I have to go look for the kids."

"Is it safe out there?" Ernie asked.

"I don't care!"

Vickie opened the front door and glanced outside. "Stevens is gone." She turned to Pam. "I'll help you find the kids."

Pam nodded. They ran out the front door and saw Romeo and Juliet's disc settle onto the street. Vickie shouted into the house. "Romeo and Juliet are back!"

Leaning over Mickey, David yelled to her, "Tell them to go look for the twins."

Mickey's eyes fluttered open. "Stevens has them."

Pam and Vickie came back inside. "What did he say?" Pam asked.

Juliet appeared at the door, followed by Romeo. "Master Mickey is correct. Stevens has captured Al and Bet. He is near Mars with twenty-three more discs of the same design. Stevens referred to them as the Titan Fleet."

Shaking, Pam pointed at Mickey. "I told you not to lower the force field! If anything happens to them, I'll ..." She burst into tears and ran up the stairs.

Mickey eased himself to a sitting position. "We'll take the disc and go get them."

"The numerical advantage of the Titan Fleet makes that unwise," Juliet said.

Dick looked away. "Damn!"

David glanced at Romeo. "Ever hear of the Titan Fleet?"

"No," Romeo replied.

"Is it a fancy name or a place?" Ernie asked.

Romeo exchanged flashing lights with Juliet. "Unknown."

Juliet spoke. "Stevens referenced someone named Ahote who has twenty-four more discs. Stevens said he is waiting for them to arrive."

"Great," Dick said frowning. "Now the odds against us are forty-eight to one."

David left Mickey and started up the stairs. When he reached the top of the landing, he turned and looked down at Mickey. "You couldn't let it go, could you?" David entered the bedroom and slammed the door on Micetro's tail. The big, mostly feline squealed in pain loud enough to rattle the windows and ran down the stairs into the coat closet.

Chapter Thirty-Five

Al reached out with his senses and probed the wall of silver material surrounding them. "There it is," he said.

"There's what?" Bet snapped.

"The way out." Al sent a message to the wall's processing network and the wall began melting into the floor. The twins stepped out and saw the back of Stevens' cocoon.

"Hi there," Al said. Bet moved next to her brother not looking happy.

Stevens swiveled his cocoon around and saw them. "How'd you two get out?"

Bet looked at him with murder in her eyes. "Why'd you kidnap us?"

Stevens reached to activate his neuroleptic beam. Before he could, Bet fried the circuits by looking at it. "So far I'm only pissed," Bet began. "Want to see what happens when I get really mad?"

Al shook his head, indicating he didn't advise it.

Stevens' cocoon flowed off his body and he stood facing the twins. "You two are quite remarkable."

"And you're an asshole," Bet said. "Now that we have the niceties out of the way, take us home or this gets really ugly."

Stevens leaned back against the command console. "If I won't, are you going to get out and walk?"

Al shook his head again, this time more vigorously.

"I hate to use bad words in front of children, so I'll be polite and gesture instead." Stevens raised his middle finger.

Bet hyperventilated. "Don't ever call me a child."

"I warned you," Al said.

The disc began to tremble, at first just enough for them to notice the vibrations beneath their feet.

Stevens ran to the control console and checked the disc's

readouts. He couldn't find anything wrong and scratched his head.

The vibrations became more violent, ramping up every few seconds.

Stevens' smug expression turned to one of alarm and he reached for the command console to steady himself.

The com channel crackled to life. "Your ship's moving erratically," one of the Titan captains sent. "Do you need assistance?"

"In about thirty seconds he'll need a doctor," Al said out loud.

"Who was that?" the voice on the com channel asked.

Bet glared at the command console and it erupted in sparks. The channel went dead. She took a step toward Stevens. "Want to take us home now?"

Stevens held up his arms in surrender. "I give up. I'll take you home." The shaking of the disc stopped. Stevens ran to the auxiliary command console which had just budded from the floor and pulled several levers. They could feel the thrum of the disc's engines and the scene on the video screen shifted from a line of flying discs to the blue orb of Earth. A bud of silver erupted from the floor and soon after, Stevens reclined in his cocoon. "You two may want to sit down," he called to the twins. "You know what happens if we go to hyper-drive and you're not in your cocoons. Makes quite a mess."

Two more buds of silver popped up beneath the twins' rear ends. The one beneath Bet arrived with enough force to knock her forward. She glared at Stevens and reclined, as did Al. "Don't try anything funny," Al said. "You've seen what we can do."

Stevens raised his arm encased in silver. "I solemnly swear to take you home." He activated the disc's hyper-drive and the scene on the viewscreen changed to a white blur.

They popped out of hyper-drive three minutes later and the viewscreen displayed the colored bands of Jupiter. "That's not Earth," Bet said.

"I promised I'd take you home." Stevens put the disc into a steep dive over Europa, entered the city's spaceport and stopped fifty meters over the central square. "And here you are. Hasta la vista, *children*." He pulled another lever and the section of the disc's hull under Al and Bet dropped away. It formed a ball as it fell, hit the ground, and bounced several times before coming to rest against one of the fountains. The twins extricated themselves and looked up as Stevens' disc left the spaceport and hovered over the apex of the city.

"I'll get you for this!" Bet shouted.

A bolt of energy shot from the bottom of the disc striking the city's force field generators. The lights behind the city's artificial sky began to flicker and the water stopped flowing in the fountains. Stevens' disc accelerated away.

Bet looked up. "What's happening?"

"That A-hole damaged the force field generators," Al replied. "We need to get out of here before it fails!"

"How?"

Al pointed toward the hangar. "On a disc."

They started running to the nearest moving walkway headed in the direction of the hanger and hopped on.

Bet looked around. "Where is everybody?"

The walkway stopped moving.

"The power's failing!" Al exclaimed. "Run." They started running toward the spaceport. As they approached the hangar a silver disc rose from the roof and passed through the force field's portal into space. More followed in single file.

Al and Bet jumped up and down waving their arms and shouting. "Come back! ... Don't leave us here. Help!" After a total of twenty-five discs left the city and disappeared into the blackness of space, the aerial display stopped. The twins stopped yelling and looked at each other. Bet was about to say something when the artificial sky faded to a dim, erratic glow, and then winked out.

Al looked up and saw Europa's ocean suspended over their heads. "We better find a ride out of here or we're going to drown."

"We need to find somebody to help us!" Bet exclaimed.

"Look around. Everybody's gone. Probably left in those discs."

Bet looked frantic. "We'll call Romeo and Juliet to come get us."

Al's expression turned grim. "How? The power grid is down."

"There has to be a way." Bet closed her eyes and pounded her head. "Think!" Her eyes popped open. "The habitat! Mom told me that Dad refused to live in the house without a backup generator."

They started running.

In the hangar's control center, Two had seen Steven's disc appear. Two thought about sending a message to Unit One and activating the city's defense measures used to deflect meteors and comets. Before he could, his neural processor ceased functioning.

* * *

David descended the stairs with a somber expression. Sitting next to Mickey on the couch, Vickie let go of his hand and stood. "How's Pammy?"

David glared at Mickey. "Our kids were kidnapped by a madman to God knows where. How do you think she is?"

Vickie looked up the stairs. "I'll go up there. She needs me."

"I wouldn't if I were you."

Mickey stood, too. "Davie, I'm sorry."

David's face contorted with anger. "You know what's really bothering you, Mick? You've been jealous of Pam and me since the day we left."

Mickey held up his silver arm. "Does this look like jealousy to you?"

"It happened because you made a spectacle of yourself on worldwide TV by cutting out your palm disc!" David shouted.

"I was trying to save everyone! I still am," Mickey shouted back.

David moved closer to him. "You're trying to save yourself."

Ernie rushed between them. "Knock it off, you two. This isn't helping anybody. We need to put our heads together and come up with a plan to rescue the kids."

"Ernie's right," Dick said. "Everybody needs to calm down."

Mickey set his jaw. "Let down the force field. I'm leaving."

"Come on, Mick," Ernie said.

"Let me out!" Mickey shouted. David turned his back.

Ernie leaned close to Mickey and whispered something in his ear. Mickey started to say something back, but Ernie turned and walked to the wall with the force field's control. After a glance at Ernie, Mickey went to the door. He hesitated before opening it, then stiffened his shoulders, opened the door and stepped onto the porch.

"Wait," Vickie called. "I'm coming with you."

"Are you sure about this?" Dick asked her.

"Yes," Vickie replied. She kissed Dick on the cheek and joined Mickey on the porch. He took her hand and they waited for the force field to drop.

Ernie turned off the force field. When the blue haze surrounding the house winked off, Mickey and Vickie started down the walkway.

* * *

Al skidded to a stop. "Do you hear something?"

Bet stopped next to him. "No."

Al looked around. "Maybe I'm imagining things." He started forward again, but after a few strides, stopped. "There it is again."

"I heard it, too," Bet said, looking around. "Sounds familiar ... Wait a minute." She glanced at her brother. "You said the power's off."

"That's right."

They heard rustling sounds coming from the nearby bushes.

Bet swallowed hard. "Does that include the fences around Mom's pets?"

Al blinked. "Yes."

Bet bounced on her feet with her eyes darting around. "That's the way it sounds in Mom's Menagerie when her pets are stomping around!"

The rustling changed to the sound of wood snapping, then a piercing roar split the dark. They smelled something dank and cloying.

Bet's eyes became big as saucers. "Her pets have big teeth. Run!"

They sprinted down the path toward the habitat, followed by thudding sounds and more guttural roars. Al glanced behind them. "Holy shit! Why did Mom make one of those?"

Bet turned her head to look and tumbled into Al. They both fell to the ground as a ten-meter tall Allosaurus thundered into view and stopped close to them. The giant meat-eating dinosaur lowered its head and sniffed at them, then raised its head and roared.

"What are we going to do?" Bet whimpered.

"Throw rocks!" Al shouted. He used his telekinetic powers to pick up a nearby two-ton boulder and flung it at the giant beast. The simulated granite missile bounced off the creature's chest and it staggered back. Bet used her powers to pick up a fallen tree and send it like a missile at the brute's head. The Allosaurus toppled over from the impact, dazed. Al was ready to launch another boulder when he noticed the large rock flicker and disappear. "Uh oh." The shrubbery and landscape around them disappeared, too.

The Allosaurus got to his feet and roared. The twins began backing away.

"The matter projectors are failing," Al said. "We're out of rocks."

"How come that thing is still here?"

"Because he's real!" Al exclaimed.

The Allosaurus roared and lumbered toward them.

The twins turned and ran.

Bet glanced over her shoulder. "He's gaining on us!"

"I have an idea!" Al stopped and turned to face the charging dinosaur.

"Are you crazy?" Bet yelled.

"If I can move a boulder, I can move ..." Al grunted as he concentrated, "him!" The Allosaurus tripped over its own leg and fell face first onto the ground. "Help me!" Al shouted. "Push it back."

Bet squinted at the Allosaurus, bent over, and grunted. "Take that!" she shouted. The dinosaur's head arched back and it fell to the ground with its eyes closed and its tongue hanging out.

The twins stayed where they were, watching.

"Looks like it's unconscious, at least for now," Al said.

"We did it!" Bet yelled.

Al sniffed the air. "That thing smells really bad."

Bet looked at her brother and blushed. "Sorry about that ... I was trying to do what you did and I squeezed down a bit too hard."

Al held out his hand, palm up, and looked at it. "What was that?"

Bet held out her hand, too. "It's raining."

Al looked up with alarm. "No, it's not. The ocean is breaking through the force field." He spun around. "I see our house and the lights are still on. The back-up generator is still working!"

They started sprinting toward the house.

Chapter Thirty-Six

Mickey and Vickie got into an automated car.

"What is your destination?" the car asked.

Vickie turned to face him. "I'd like to know that too."

"You don't need to come with me," Mickey said.

Vickie caressed his cheek. "Yes I do. That's the first step in straightening out this gigantic mess."

"What is your destination?" the car repeated.

"The clearing at Griffith Park," Mickey replied.

"There are many clearings in ..." the car's voice began.

Vickie glanced at Mickey but kept silent.

Mickey interrupted the car. "The one with the bronze statue of the four crazy kids who took a flying saucer ride to Europa."

Vickie smiled at him.

"You have specified the Europa Monument. Is that correct?" the car asked.

"Yes," Mickey replied.

Vickie leaned her head on Mickey's shoulder as the car pulled away.

* * *

Ernie's TV turned on and they heard Bet screaming. "Get us out of here!"

Everyone ran to the TV. David pushed the others aside. "Oh my God. Where are you?"

"On Europa," Bet wailed.

"What are you doing on Europa?" David exclaimed. He glanced at Ernie. "Get Pam!"

"Hurry, the sky is falling!" Bet shouted.

"This is no time for children's fairytales," David said.

Al popped his head in front of the screen. "Dad, it's not a

bedtime story. Stevens dumped us here and disabled the city's force field generators." Al glanced out the window. "You better come get us before the city's underwater!"

"Go get help!" David exclaimed.

"Nobody's here," Al replied. "They all left."

"What?"

"We'll explain later," Al shouted. "Send Romeo and Juliet before it's too late!"

"On our way," Romeo said as loud as his vocal apparatus would permit. It was loud enough to shatter several glasses in the kitchen. Romeo rocketed through the front door without opening it and ran up the disc's ramp. Juliet sailed after him and made it halfway through the disc's doorway when the disc lifted off. She hung on with one tentacle as it rose out of sight.

Romeo reeled Juliet in and they accelerated to the edge of Earth's atmosphere, but then slowed to a stop. They were blocked by Stevens' fleet of discs surrounding the planet, blocking their way. Romeo swiveled his head to Juliet. "We are outnumbered again. As humans say, this is getting old."

Juliet gripped one of his tentacles. "Logic dictates that we retreat, but ..."

"Logic is getting old too." Romeo pushed the disc's throttle forward to the maximum and it shot through the formation.

Stevens watched them flash past and radioed to his fleet. "Let them go. We have bigger fish to fry."

"Why do we want to fry fish?" Steven's second in command asked.

"What is a fish?" one of the other disc captains sent.

Stevens sighed. "Never mind."

"We have passed Earth's moon without pursuit," Romeo said. "Estimated time of arrival to Europa is ten earth minutes."

"What you did was illogical," Juliet said.

"Thank you," Romeo replied.

Juliet's lights twinkled a combination of pink and purple.

"You exhibit more human traits every day. I find it ... satisfying."

Romeo extended his height ten centimeters and moved closer to Juliet until their flat screen heads touched.

Juliet's lights changed to a soft red. This action, too, is without logic."

"I know," Romeo said. "Perhaps one day we will also understand what dude means."

David radioed to them. "How long before you get the kids?"

Romeo pulled away from Juliet. "Nine point three Earth minutes. Our return to Earth could prove difficult. There are twenty-four discs with the same configuration as Stevens' disc in orbit around Earth. Stevens is in one of them"

Pam shouted in the background. "If it's not safe, don't come back!"

* * *

General Westlock slammed down the phone. "NORAD says it's a damned alien invasion." He turned to his new adjutant, an army lieutenant in combat fatigues. "What's our contingency plan for an alien invasion?"

The lieutenant rummaged through a pile of red notebooks marked Top Secret on the general's desk and held one up. "This one is titled What to do if UFOs Attack. Is that it?"

Westlock put his head on the desk. "Turn to the page with the heading Operational Plan and read what it says."

The lieutenant flipped through the pages, found what he wanted, and began reading. "Action Item Number One, don't alarm the population."

The general bit his lip. "What comes after that?"

"Action Item Number Two, arm the K.A.T.U."

Westlock picked up his head. "What does KATU stand for?"

His adjutant flipped to the glossary. "Kill All The UFOs.

"Now we're getting somewhere." Westlock picked up the red

phone.

* * *

The car stopped in front of the Europa Monument and the door opened.

"Do you want to tell me why we came here?" Vickie asked.

"Because Ernie told me to." Mickey got out and walked to the fence overlooking the skyline of Los Angeles.

Vickie joined him. "We came here because of Ernie?"

Mickey poked his fingers through the chain link fence and stared down at the city. "Do you ever wonder what would have happened if we hadn't boarded the flying saucer?"

Vickie leaned against the fence, facing him. "David's brother would have killed us."

Mickey smiled. "Remember what you said the first time you saw an Europan?"

Vickie smiled, too, as she remembered. "You mean when the human race, in this case me, first met beings from another world?" She shook her head. "Can't believe I said that."

"Go on," Mickey prodded.

Vickie sighed. "Something like, what the fuck are you?"

Mickey smiled. "You didn't know it, Vic, but you had it right." His cell phone went off in his pocket. He ignored it.

"Shouldn't you answer that? Might be about the kids."

Mickey took the phone from his pocket and accepted the call.

"This is Westlock. The whole damn planet is surrounded by a fleet of UFOs. My boys are saddling up to take them on. You coming to the party?"

Mickey glanced at Vickie. "We're at the clearing in Griffith Park."

"Just like old times. Stay there. I'll pick you up." The general broke the connection and motioned over his adjutant. "Get me a chopper. We're going to Griffith Park in Los Angeles, where that damned UFO monument is."

"Why there?" his adjutant asked.

"We're deploying the KATU and we need a couple of aliens to use as bait."

* * *

"Who was that on the phone?" Vickie asked.

"Our old friend General Westlock," Mickey replied. "He's on his way here."

"Why?"

Mickey looked out at the city again. "He's giving us a ride to the last rodeo."

* * *

The general stopped shredding documents when his adjutant knocked on the door. "I'm busy," the general snarled. "Tell me when that chopper arrives. Until then, get lost."

His adjutant knocked again, this time more insistently. "Sorry, general, NORAD's on the red phone. They say it's urgent."

Westlock shoved the rest of the documents into a desk drawer and closed it. "Come in," he growled. "What do those Air Force guys want this time?" His adjutant glanced down a line of phones in several colors, arrayed on the general's desk. He handed the general the headset of the red phone, the one closest to the general's hand. Westlock grabbed it from him. "Westlock." He listened. "Twenty-four more UFOs behind the moon? You're sure?" He listened again. "No, I don't want to call the Ruskies or the Chinese for help. Don't need to. I know about your secret doomsday weapon." He listened again. "Not that one, the one code-named KATU." He listened again and his snarl widened into a grin. "That's the one. I'm on my way to pick it up." He hung up the phone and turned to his adjutant. "We're taking that chopper to Cheyenne Mountain, ASAP."

"I thought we were going to a park in Los Angeles."

"We are, but first we have to pick up KATU in Colorado." The Lieutenant rushed out. After glancing at the door, the general opened his drawer and took out another phone and placed a call. When the call connected, he lowered his voice. "Are you in position? ... Good, stand by for a delivery."

* * *

Bet looked out the window. "It's awfully dark out there."

Al checked the gauges on the backup generator powering the house's force field. "We have enough fuel for another hour."

"Then what happens?"

"We get squashed flat and drown, whichever comes first."

Bet wrung her hands. "What's taking Romeo and Juliet so long? Earth's only four hundred million miles away."

Al joined her at the window. "It's dark out there because we're underwater."

Bet slumped to the floor. "I guess I'll never know."

Al squatted next to her. "Never know what?"

"What our children will look like."

"Your children?"

"With Josh." She sighed. "Of course they'd have my eyes, my intelligence, my bubbly personality."

Al got to his feet. "Your arrogance?" He glanced toward the window and ran to look out. "I see lights!"

A bright light shone through the window forcing Al to shield his eyes. "It's them!"

Romeo used the disc's thrusters to put it into a hover above the blue haze of the house's force field. "We cannot get them out unless they lower the force field," he said to Juliet.

"If they lower the force field, the ocean will crush them," Juliet replied. "I will extend our force field around theirs leaving a gap of ten meters to avoid a short circuit between the two fields."

Romeo made a quick calculation, which for an Europan was a tenth of a microsecond. "Thirty metric tons of seawater will remain between our force field and theirs. When they turn their field off ..."

Juliet finished his sentence. "They will become wet."

Romeo rotated his head toward her. "I have observed that you finish my sentences with greater frequency."

The color of Juliet's lights changed to a soft red. "I will monitor that activity."

Romeo sent a message to the house. "Master Al, Mistress Bet, are you there?"

Huddling in the dark next to the com system, the twins glanced at each other. "No, we went out for a swim!" Bet shouted.

"Was that wise?" Romeo asked.

"That is not possible," Juliet sent to Romeo.

"Romeo?" Al said.

"Yes, Master Al."

"Can you get us out before we drown?"

"Juliet is extending the disc's force field around the house. Stand by."

Both twins bumped fists. "Yes!"

They heard Juliet's voice. "I will count down from five. When I reach one, lower the house's force field and hold your breath. Five, four, three ..."

"Hold our breath?" both asked.

"Two, one ..."

Freezing cold water poured into the house and quickly rose to their waists. Al began treading water and yelled, "Get us out of here!" Before Bet could add anything unpleasant, Juliet broke through the ceiling and used her tentacles to hoist both of them into the disc.

Romeo increased the temperature inside the disc to forty-nine degrees C. "Are you injured?" he asked the twins.

Bet's hair clung to her head in wet, twisted tendrils. She spat out a mouthful of water. "Can we go home now?"

Juliet handed both of them towels.

Romeo moved to the command console, linked with the disc, and they began to rise toward the surface. Hugging the towel around him, Al joined Romeo at the command console, standing in a puddle of water that the floor quickly absorbed.

"We encountered twenty-four flying discs, similar to the design flown by Stevens, deployed around Earth. Their intent is unknown," Romeo said.

"We have to get back. What's your plan?" Al asked.

"We will follow a trajectory to the back of Earth's moon and hide behind it while we assess the tactical situation and develop our plan."

Al nodded. "Makes sense."

Juliet formed one of her tentacles into a brush and began to smooth and untangle Bet's hair.

"Ouch," Bet complained.

"My apologies, Mistress Bet." She continued combing. "What did you learn from Officer Stevens during your brief stay aboard his flying disc?"

"That he's an asshole," Bet snarled.

"Did he discuss his purpose for kidnapping you?" Juliet asked.

Bet thought for a moment. "He said something about taking us to a place called Titan."

"That is the human designation for the largest moon of the seventh planet in the solar system."

"Why would he take us there?" Al asked.

* * *

Romeo used thrusters to stop the disc's forward motion and spun his head toward Juliet. "Forward scanners detect twenty-four discs identical to this one parked behind Earth's moon."

"They are Europan. Should we contact them?" Juliet asked.

Romeo spun his head back to the viewscreen. "No."

Al dropped his towel. The floor resorbed it and flowed up around his body, clothing him in a silver jumpsuit. "What are all those flying discs doing here?"

"Logically, they are doing the same thing we are," Juliet replied. "They are hiding and watching."

"Watching what?"

"The Titan discs in orbit around Earth. Limited observation suggests that there is significant animosity between the two groups."

"Why?" Al asked.

"Unknown."

"Stop watching. We have to get back to Earth," Bet said.

Al pointed at the screen. "Something's happening."

The rings of light around the Europan discs suddenly brightened to an electric blue and they formed into a V formation. With Unit One at the apex of the formation, the discs swept around the moon accelerating toward the nearest of the twenty-four Titan discs in Earth's orbit.

"I will open the com channel, receive-only mode," Romeo said. "We do not want them to know that we are here." They began to hear One's voice.

"Which one of you is hiding that murderer the High Priest?" One shouted over the open com system. "Give him to me and I might let the rest of you live."

Stevens' voice replied. "Ahotei? Is that you hiding in that tin can?"

"Who's Ahotei?" Al asked.

One bellowed with rage. "Show yourself, you coward!"

"Will I do?" Stevens flashed the ring of lights on his disc, the one directly opposite the Europan formation. "I'm in this one."

"According to Stevens, Unit One is also known as Ahotei,"

Juliet said. Her lights flashed faster. "I can find no references for a being named Ahotei in the database."

"Give me the High Priest," One demanded. "He'll pay for what he did to my people!"

"No can do, Ahotei," Stevens replied. "The High Priest died thousands of years ago. Pretty sure I'm related to him if you go back far enough."

"Prepare to die, you murderer!" Ahotei shouted.

Stevens shouted back. "You followed my people to Mars and destroyed an entire primitive civilization trying to murder *us*."

"That's a lie!" One bellowed.

"We're still here, tin man. Come and get me!" All the Titan discs moved away from Steven's disc, leaving him alone to face the entire Europan fleet.

"Attack!" One bellowed. The formation of Europan discs accelerated towards Stevens.

"Stevens' action is illogical," Romeo said.

Al watched the Europan fleet converge on Stevens' disc. "He's committing suicide."

"Serves him right," Bet muttered.

As the Europan formation with Unit One in the lead closed on Stevens' disc, a rectangular panel lit with green light appeared on the side of Steven's disc. Symbols flashed in the center of the panel and were quickly replaced by different ones at a speed too fast for the human eye to register. One's disc began to wobble, then its energy band flickered and died. The same thing happened to the other Europan discs until all twenty-four drifted in space without power.

"I know what he's doing!" Al shouted. "Don't look!" He glanced at Romeo. "Too late."

Both Romeo and Juliet faced the viewscreen and didn't reply.

"Uh oh," Bet said. She shook Juliet. "Wake up." Nothing happened.

Al nudged Romeo. He didn't respond either. "They're both in

a coma. The hieroglyphics on Stevens' disc got them."

"Now what do we do?" Bet asked.

Al slumped against the command console. "We wait. The same thing happened on Mars. Romeo woke up, but it took a while."

"We can't just sit here," Bet whined.

"Can you fly this thing?"

Bet pounded the command console. "No!"

The console spoke to her. "The disc's controls do not require excessive force to operate."

"Shut up!" Bet shouted at the console.

"Sounds like the Europans have a history with Stevens' people," Al said.

Bet glared at the command console. "With somebody named Ahotei. What kind of name is that?"

"According to Stevens, Ahotei is Unit One ... or vice versa." Al grimaced. "This whole thing doesn't make sense." He glanced at the viewscreen. "Check this out." Bet joined him. "Part of the Titan fleet is leaving orbit."

"The discs leaving orbit look like pregnant guppies," Bet said.

"What's a guppy?" Al replied.

The viewscreen replied. "The Earth fish known as the guppy, also know as the million fish and rainbow fish is one ..."

"I don't care!" Al yelled at the viewscreen. He glanced at Bet. "This may be our best chance to sneak past them and get home, provided we can figure out how to fly this thing."

Bet rolled up her sleeves. "Shouldn't be that difficult. Let's throw a few switches and see what happens." She reached for the nearest joystick.

"Wait!"

Bet glanced at him. "Why?"

"Maybe there's a better way." Al spoke to the viewscreen. "Can you show us how to fly this thing?" Diagrams flowed across the viewscreen. He smiled. "Now we're getting somewhere."

Chapter Thirty-Seven

Al finished watching the last instructional video. "I think I got this." He high-fived with Bet.

"Go for it, little brother," she said.

Al glared at her. "I'm not your little brother." He eased forward a joystick in the center of the command console and the disc dove for the surface of the Moon. "Oops." He pulled back on the joystick and the disc jerked to a stop.

Bet smirked. "Next time try going around the Moon, not through it."

"Not as easy as I thought. I'll watch the videos again."

"We don't have time for this." Bet pounded her temple. "Duh, why didn't I think of that?" She yelled at the viewscreen. "Can you hear me?"

"You may reduce your decibel level without degrading communication," the viewscreen replied.

Bet glanced at Al. "What the hell does that mean?"

"It means stop shouting and speak to it at a normal sound level."

"It's a computer, dipshit. What difference does it make how I speak to it?"

"Communication is more efficient without the use of unnecessary adjectives," the computer said.

Bet leaned toward the viewscreen. "Am … I … speaking … clear … enough … now, asshole?"

"Bet!" Al exclaimed.

"All right!" Bet formed her lips into a fake smile. "Mr. View Screen, you elegant piece of … computing hardware," Bet began. Al rolled his eyes. "Can you fly this disc and land it at Ernie's house in Burbank California?"

"Is that nice enough for you?" she sent to Al telepathically.

"Of course," the viewscreen replied.

"Do it when I say, Now," Al interjected before Bet could say anything more. He glanced at Bet. "Cross your fingers Stevens' discs don't come after us."

Bet nodded.

"Head to Ernie's house at best possible speed, *Now*!" Al shouted.

Nothing happened.

"Now!" Al shouted again.

The viewscreen spoke to him. "I suggest that you make use of your cocoons before I engage the main engines to achieve hyper-drive velocity. Failure to do so will change your bodily architecture to a paste consisting of ..."

"We get it," Al interrupted.

When Al and Bet were inside their cocoons, the disc accelerated toward Earth without slowing during atmospheric re-entry. This caused the disc's exterior to heat to over two thousand degrees C and flare with light intense enough to be seen by half the people of Earth.

Stevens watched them streak across the sky.

"Should I disable them?" his second in command asked.

"Don't bother," Stevens replied. "We'll take care of them all later in one fell swoop."

"What's a fell swoop?" his second in command asked.

"Never mind."

* * *

Al and Bet's disc touched down on Ernie's lawn and the twins darted down the ramp. They pounded on the front door. "Let us in!"

David ran to the door and opened it. He grabbed both of them into a bear hug with tears in his eyes. "Where have you been?"

Pam ran to them, followed by Ernie. "Oh my God! You're safe!" Pam exclaimed. She joined the family bear hug.

"I can't breathe!" Bet protested.

Pam and David let go. "Come inside," Pam said.

Bet ran past them. "I need to make a phone call!" She collided with Micetro and fell on top of him. The big cat licked her face. "Get off me, you big oaf."

Al pointed at Micetro. "What's wrong with his tail? It looks swollen."

"Why are Romeo and Juliet still in the disc?" David asked.

"They're both in a coma, like what happened to Romeo on Mars."

David sighed. "Great."

Bet ran up the stairs, grabbed the phone and dialed Josh's house. They heard her yell, "What do you mean he's not home!"

* * *

An hour later, Romeo and Juliet found everyone in the den. "How did we arrive here?" Romeo asked.

"Remember what happened to you on Mars?" Al asked.

Romeo looked at Juliet. "No."

Bet shook her head. "That's the point, dingbat. They can't remember."

Al blinked. "Got it." He turned to Romeo. "I'll explain later."

* * *

Stevens smiled at the disc's view. "Time to light those cult key rings and get this show on the road." He flicked a switch on his command console and sent a message to his fleet. "Prepare for harvesting."

* * *

General Westlock picked up the red phone and listened to

the duty officer in Cheyenne Mountain. "Sixteen of them are landing?"

"That's right, general. The discs that are landing are much bigger than the ones still in orbit. The fat ones are landing in the center of major cities like Los Angeles, New York, Chicago ..."

"I get the idea," Westlock interrupted. "How many skinny ones are still in orbit?"

"Thirty-four, in two groups."

Westlock sat forward. "Shit."

"Something strange is going on," the NORAD duty officer said.

Westlock stared at the ceiling. "Ya think so?"

"General?"

"Get on with your report!"

The duty officer cleared his throat. "Nine ... skinny discs are still in low earth orbit. Twenty-five more of them are sitting near the Moon."

"Probably held in reserve. Smart."

"The ones near the Moon seem dead, just drifting with their lights off."

Westlock thought for a moment. "Might be playing possum. Those guys are good."

"The fat ones are all on the ground now in the center of populated areas. This may be our best chance to hit them, but civilian casulaties will be high. Do we attack?"

"Get in position, but nobody starts shooting unless I say so. My boys have a surprise for those alien freaks. Westlock out."

* * *

Stevens positioned his disc over Los Angeles and scanned the city. "Looks like the intrepid US cavalry has finally arrived. Hello General Custard."

"I think that's General Custer," his second in command said.

Stevens whirled to face him. "You think you know more about Earth than I do?"

"I did some reading ..."

Stevens turned back to the viewscreen. "I count a dozen tanks, some rocket units, and lots of guys wearing combat fatigues running around."

"Give the word and I'll vaporize them," his second in command said.

"Why waste prime material that we can recycle later? When the body parts we harvest from the cult members wear out, we'll use those fit-looking soldiers down there for replacements."

His second in command sighed. "I'm on my sixth cloned liver, and this one is already acting up."

Stevens frowned. "I'm on my tenth set of cloned kidneys." He blinked. "I was just about to do something ... what was it?"

His second in command cleared his throat. "Light the Cult key rings and start harvesting?"

"That's it!"

* * *

Frankel glanced at Emma's Cult key ring on the table, flickering with yellow and red light. "Looks like the curtain's going up."

Emma looked closer without touching it. "Any idea how it turns people into zombies?"

"Spec Ops took one of them apart," Frankel replied. "It injects nannites into the bloodstream that rewire the nervous system." Frankel's face reddened. "Like the ones that messed up my old friend Latham." He lifted up the blinds of their apartment in downtown Los Angeles and looked down at the street. "Check this out." Emma joined him at the window. They watched throngs of people streaming toward Pershing Square, walking with the same measured pace while staring straight ahead. Frankel lowered the blinds. "Think you can act like one of them?"

Emma donned a fake Cult key ring and activated its light. The ersatz copy lit with the same colored light and blinked in perfect rhythm with the real key ring. "I played the lead in my high school's production of My Fair Lady."

"Too bad it wasn't Dawn of the Living Dead." Frankel's secure cell phone rang and he answered it.

"KATU is now active," he heard General Westlock say. "The delivery is on its way to your position, ETA seven minutes."

"How do you know the aliens won't intercept?" Frankel asked.

"They won't. It's inside a stealth vehicle."

Frankel glanced at Emma. "A what?"

"A car with titanium paint," Westlock replied. "Says Papa John's Pizza on the side and has one of those delivery signs on top. Those alien bastards can't see through titanium."

Frankel rubbed the bridge of his nose. "Clever. Let's hope they don't like pizza."

"Standby to deploy," Westlock growled. He terminated the call.

Frankel frowned at the phone.

Emma moved next to him. "What's bothering you?"

Frankel sighed. "Were you briefed on a weapon code-named KATU?"

"Sounds like a bad joke. What is it?"

"A bioweapon that kills anyone who doesn't have human DNA."

Emma's face paled. "Everyone with Cult rings has altered DNA now."

Frankel nodded. "If we deliver the weapon as General Westlock just ordered us to, they're all going to die."

"We'll be mass murders!"

"If we don't, the aliens win. Which is worse?" Frankel asked.

Emma dropped into a chair. "What are we going to do?"

"Follow orders, just like we've been trained to do – take delivery of the weapon, save the planet, and afterward stay drunk, maybe forever."

Emma shook her head. "What's the plan after we take delivery?"

"You follow the people down there acting like a good little zombie and get inside the disc. When I'm in position, I signal you, you create a diversion, and I rush inside and deploy."

"Wouldn't it be easier if I take the weapon with me?" Emma asked.

"We can't risk their version of TSA scanning you and finding it before you get on board. Our best chance to get the weapon inside the disc sitting on the ground a few blocks from here is for you to create a diversion and draw their attention away from the door so I can bring it on board."

"What kind of diversion?"

"Something more startling than a tune from My Fair Lady." Frankel went to the window and lifted the blinds again. "The silver pizza delivery car is here. I'd get a pizza to go, but I'm too sick to my stomach." He dropped the blinds.

"After we deploy the weapon, how do we get out?" Emma asked.

Frankel went to her and gathered her in his arms. "We improvise."

She looked into his eyes. "We're expendable, aren't we?"

Frankel kissed her. "Not to me."

Chapter Thirty-Eight

They hid in the shadows of an alley on the outskirts of Pershing Square, watching people with Cult key rings walk by, from prim secretaries to burly firemen, all moving at the same even pace with bland expressions and eyes fixed straight ahead. Frankel carried the canister of KATU in a briefcase and wore a business suit. He whispered to Emma standing behind him wearing her fake key ring and pink scrubs. "Want to clean my teeth sometime?"

"I'm supposed to be a nurse." Emma straightened her pink top and composed herself. "After you rescue me, I'll do anything you want."

"I like the sound of that. Are you ready?"

"No," Emma replied. She left the alley with a bland expression and joined the zombie parade moving toward the bloated Titan disc in the middle of Pershing Square.

Frankel waited until he saw Emma walk fifty meters beyond the alley and joined the growing crowd of onlookers without key rings lining the sidewalks on both sides of the street. Never losing sight of Emma, he moved from group to group trying not to draw attention to himself. At the end of the square, he darted around the corner onto the main boulevard and stopped. Squatting in the center of the square sat an ovoid silver disc, five stories tall and one hundred meters wide, with an open door and a ramp extending from it. Orderly lines of Cult members were queued up moving slowly up the ramp, passing through a ring of silver flanked by two humanoid males in silver coveralls.

Ignoring his pounding heart and shaking knees, Frankel scanned the area around the disc using magnifying lenses disguised as designer sunglasses. He spotted Emma's pink top in one of the lines. "There you are." He also counted six males in light-blue coveralls, patrolling the lines without visible firearms, all wearing dark glasses and the same silver baseball caps. "What are you boys packing?" Unable to notice anything suspicious, he scanned the exterior of the disc and saw two blue-clad personnel standing on the disc's apex, flanking the unmistakable shape of a cannon. "That's not good," Frankel muttered.

Melting into the shadows behind a trash bin, Frankel opened his briefcase on the ground. He saw the metal canister of KATU secured inside the top of the briefcase, swallowed back his bile, and removed his coat. "You can do this," he said to himself. With shaking hands, he removed a package containing a formfitting coverall complete with hood and mask impregnated with titanium, and began donning it. "Sure hope the general is right about titanium. I'm going to be hard to miss in this shiny suit," he muttered. After slipping on titanium-impregnated gloves, he placed his cell phone in one pocket of the coverall, the KATU canister in the other, and discarded the briefcase.

Covered from head to toe in metalized foil, Frankel peeked around the corner of the building. His suit reflected the sun in a glare of blinding light. Several people saw him.

"Is that an alien?" someone shouted. People pointed at him and formed a ring blocking his way.

Frankel pushed through them toward the disc. "Health Department. Let me through. Have to inspect that UFO." He broke free in time to see a woman wearing pink scrubs pass through the silver ring and mount the ramp. One of the guards turned toward him.

* * *

Everyone crowded into the disc with Romeo and Juliet. "Let's get out of here," David said.

"What is our destination?" Juliet asked.

David rubbed his chin. "Good question."

"What about the titanium mine in Nicaragua, where the old

Cult compound was?" Dick asked. "Might hide us for a while until we can figure things out."

"Could work," Pam said. "We can wait until reinforcements arrive."

"You mean our old friend, Unit One?" David asked. "Is he the solution or the problem?"

Pam frowned at him. "You sound like Mickey."

"Maybe he's right," Ernie said. Pam turned and glared at him too.

Bet jumped in front of David waving her hands. "What about Josh and Brie? We can't leave them here."

"We can and we will," Pam said. "They're a lot safer without us around."

"Don't you remember?" Al exclaimed. "Stevens already tried to kidnap them. What if he tries again and we're not here to rescue them?"

"The kids have a point," Ernie said. "I'll go get them." He started down the ramp.

"Do it fast. We don't have a lot of time," David called.

Ernie reached the bottom of the ramp. "They live two blocks from here." He took off running.

David closed the disc's door and turned around. "Romeo, Juliet, what did you guys see up there?"

"Up where?" Romeo asked. He spun his head toward Juliet and spoke to her on a private channel. "Did we go somewhere?"

Juliet sent back. "No."

David threw up his hands. "I forgot. Your memories were erased by Stevens' computer virus."

"I don't remember that," Romeo said.

David pointed at the twins. "What happened when you were up there with Stevens? Any detail you can remember about what you saw or heard might help us defeat him."

Al glanced at Bet. "There were twenty-five Europan discs behind the Moon, led by Unit One."

"And Stevens called Unit One some weird name," Bet added.

"Ahotei," Al prompted.

"Yeah that's it," Bet said. "And Unit One kept asking Stevens for somebody named the High Priest."

All Romeo's lights lit, becoming a square of dazzling white. He appeared to stagger.

Juliet shot a tentacle around him. "Do you suffer a malfunction?"

"I remember," Romeo said.

"You remember what happened on Mars?" Juliet asked.

"Everything."

Al continued talking. "Unit One argued with Stevens and attacked him with all twenty-five of the Europan discs. Stevens should have been toast, but his disc disabled all twenty-five of them by showing them strange symbols like the ones we saw on Mars. Romeo and Juliet saw them, too, and their memories got zapped."

David glanced at the two Europans. "And now they're awake." He thought for a moment. "Which means, the Europans up there should be waking up pretty soon, too."

* * *

The twenty-five Europan discs powered up within moments of each other. Unit One sent a message to his fleet. "The Titan fleet used a computer virus delivered optically to disable us. Assume a straight-line attack formation behind me and inactivate all electro-optical scanning, all frequencies." The other discs formed a line behind One's disc and disabled their light-based scanners.

"We are blind," messaged M23 piloting one of the Europan discs.

One addressed all his discs. "When we advance, use magnetic scanning to remain in line and fire on all anomalies more than thirty degrees offline to either side. Charge all weapons." One by one the discs messaged their readiness. "Attack!" One shouted. Firing as they passed, the line of Europan discs sped by the eight smaller Titan attack discs still in Earth orbit. This time the Titan's computer virus had no effect. All eight Titan discs were disabled.

One's formation swept past the drifting Titan discs and entered Earth's atmosphere. "Resume scanning on all frequencies," One ordered. "When Titan targets are located, attack using magnetic scanning only.

"Attack!" One shouted. His disc peeled away flanked by two other discs and accelerated toward Los Angeles. Sixteen other Europan discs began attack runs on the Titan factory discs on the ground. The other six Europan discs remained in orbit.

* * *

Al and Bet stood in the disc's doorway looking out. "Where are they already?" Bet moaned.

"Ernie's out of shape. He moves slow," Al said.

Romeo spun his head toward David. "Master David?"

David turned from his discussion with Dick and Pam. "What?"

"I have been monitoring a secure data link from the military installation known as Cheyenne Mountain."

Dick moved closer. "You mean NORAD?"

"That is correct."

"Learn anything interesting?" Dick asked.

"The American military is preparing to detonate a bioweapon known as KATU. It contains an engineered virus that will kill any human with non-human DNA."

Pam's eyes flew open. "What did you say?"

"I said," Romeo began.

"That's genocide!" David exclaimed.

"Great way to get rid of Stevens and Company," Dick said,

"but it won't work on the tin men from Europa."

Al and Bet left the doorway and joined them. "Good thing we're all human."

Pam glanced at her children and brought her hand to her mouth.

David thought about Pam's DNA and began to sweat. "We have to stop them!"

They heard a loud thud and the disc trembled.

David's eyes darted around. "What was that?"

The disc trembled twice more.

Juliet spun her head to Romeo. "I detect the energy signature of Europan energy weapons."

They heard a loud whine and were knocked off their feet. "Romeo, get us out of here!" David shouted.

Dick grabbed David's arm. "What about Ernie?"

They heard two more whining sounds and the disc tilted ten degrees. Pam screamed and grabbed both twins. She pulled them toward the disc's command console. "Get into your cocoons," she said trying to sound calm. Both twins broke away from her and ran to the disc's door. Juliet lassoed them and wrestled them into their cocoons. Their screams of protest muted as Juliet cut their comlinks.

They heard more whining sounds, louder and higher pitched. The disc jerked violently to the side threatening to topple over.

"Romeo!" David shouted.

They lifted off and shot into the sky.

* * *

Frankel watched as bolts of blue-white energy rained from the sky and struck the Titan disc's force field. The disc's field crackled and swirled with bright light as it absorbed the Europan's attack. The people around Frankel not wearing Cult key rings scattered, while the Cult members stayed in line, looking straight ahead.

Frankel pushed through the people running away and sprinted toward the disc in his titanium-impregnated suit. He felt the ground shake as the canon on top of the disc opened fire sending red and orange bolts of energy skyward. As he ran, Frankel looked up to find the attackers but he could only see the tracks of their particle beams raining down. A bolt of energy struck the ground near him and he stumbled and fell. As he scrambled to his feet, a second beam struck closer to him and the resulting explosion and shockwave tossed him into the air. He collapsed on the ground dazed. As he got on his elbows and blinked to clear his vision, he saw the Titan disc's ramp and door disappear, and its energy ring erupt with light.

Frankel scrambled to his feet and staggered toward the Titan disc. "Emma!" he shouted.

Three Europan discs, with Unit One piloting the lead, swooped down on the square and fired at the Titan disc as it rose from the ground. The Titan disc wobbled as it absorbed the barrage and lost altitude. The three Europan discs continued firing, forcing the disc back to the ground. The Titan disc's defensive field dimmed and then flickered as the Europan discs pressed their attack. When it appeared that the Titan disc's defensive field would fail, Stevens' disc streaked into view and dove on One's formation firing all its weapons. "I warned you, Ahotei!" Stevens shouted.

Caught by surprise, Unit One's formation was forced to break off their attack and speed away. While Stevens' disc hovered nearby broadcasting patriotic songs from World War One, the Titan factory disc returned to full power and lifted off.

Frankel dropped to his knees looking up at the empty sky. "Emma," he wailed.

* * *

General Westlock was monitoring the scene in Pershing Square, sent to him from a drone orbiting overhead. "Should've known that loser Frankel and his girlfriend couldn't get the job done." He grabbed a microphone. "Fire off everything you've got at anything that looks alien." He listened. "To hell with the buildings. Anyone with a brain already left town."

Chapter Thirty-Nine

Romeo kept the disc in the center of Earth's north magnetic pole, trying to mask its energy signature while Juliet operated the sensors. Juliet spoke to David. "The Europan and Titan fleets are attacking each other and the American military is attacking both of them."

"We can't stay here," David said.

"I have considered the problem and recommend going to Europa," Romeo said.

"According to the twins, the city's under water," David said.

Juliet sent to Romeo on a private channel. "I don't remember that."

Romeo replied to her the same way. "I do. Trust me."

"That is correct, but options are limited at this time," Romeo said so everyone could hear. "We can stabilize the city's force field using power from this disc for up to thirty cycles."

"There must be someplace else we can go," David said.

Pam left the twins and joined them. "We have to leave Earth."

David glanced at her. "I know."

"But you don't know why," Pam said.

David looked into her eyes. "Yes, I do ... I know about your alien DNA."

Tears streamed down Pam's cheeks. "And you still love me?"

David caressed her cheek. "Of course I do. We'll sort it out later."

"What about Mickey and Vickie, and Ernie, if he's still alive," Dick asked.

David glanced at the video screen. "I guess they're on their own."

Romeo exchanged lights with Juliet and addressed everyone. "My analysis of our tactical situation and your most recent conversation indicates that we have arrived at what you humans call a come to Jesus moment."

"We'll figure something out," David said, holding Pam's hand.

Romeo and Juliet extended tentacles around each other. "Juliet and I have reached our own come to Jesus moment," Romeo said.

David leaned closer. "Care to explain?"

"We remember," Juliet said.

"You remember what?" Pam asked.

Romeo spun his head to face Pam. "How Juliet and I became trapped in these bodies."

Pam wrinkled her brow. "Trapped in your bodies? What does that mean?"

Romeo continued. "We remember who Ahotei was and what he became." The color of Romeo's lights became bright red. "We also know what the High Priest did to our people."

Juliet rested her head against Romeo. Her lights dimmed. "We remember what kind of beings we were ... before."

A Titan energy beam struck the disc. Romeo calculated its point of origin and veered away. The course he chose brought them directly into the path of more energy bolts fired from two more Titan discs attacking from the opposite direction. While Romeo fought the controls, the disc's power levels fluctuated and it began to slow. More energy bolts struck and the disc's force field began to fail. After a concentrated barrage from all three Titan discs, the Europan disc rolled over and veered toward the ground.

"I regret to inform you that we are going to crash," Romeo told them.

Juliet's lights flashed. "Logic dictates that your cocoons will provide an element of protection."

"Romeo!" David shouted. "See if you can find a place to land."

"Where do you suggest? Power is failing and my ability to

steer is becoming limited."

David hurriedly studied the navigational display. "Try to make it back toward Los Angeles. Aim for the observatory in the hills. There's a parking lot behind it. Try to set us down there."

Pam reclined in her cocoon next to Dick. "Why there?"

David watched his cocoon flow around his body. "I heard what Ernie said to Mickey."

The disc shuddered from another attack and accelerated downward. Romeo moved next to Juliet and wrapped her in his tentacles. Both Europans began melting into the floor. "I will do my best to crash in your preferred location," Romeo said.

"Davie?" Pam called.

The power failed.

David turned his head to see her. "Trust me."

She looked back at him. "I love you."

* * *

Frankel ran from Pershing Square, ducked behind a building, and called General Westlock. "The disc lifted off before I could deploy," Frankel said breathing heavily. "Emma's still on board."

"Do you still have the canister?" Westlock asked without any emotion.

Frankel patted his pocket and felt the canister of KATU. "No. I must have lost it when the Europans attacked. It was pretty bad down here."

"Go find it and release it inside another damn disc!"

"Sir?"

"Do your duty!" Westlock shouted. He terminated the call.

Frankel stared at his phone. "What is my duty?" He heard the popping sound of Titan energy bolts, looked up, and saw a Europan disc trailing smoke streaking across the sky pursued by two Titan attack discs. Using his magnifying lenses, he focused on the Europan disc and saw stripes of blue and gold running across it. "The Europans don't paint stripes on their discs." He watched the Europan disc disappear behind the Griffith Park Observatory. "Wait a minute! Stripes, the observatory, it's them!" Frankel ran to find a car.

* * *

Vickie looked through the chain-link fence. "Something's happening down there."

Mickey joined her and saw streaks of white smoke rise from the city and explode around a swarm of silver discs, no two moving in the same direction. "Those are missiles attacking the discs. Can't see whose discs they are; they all look the same from this distance. Doesn't matter. Those missiles are useless."

Vickie pointed at a disc coming toward them. "Are you sure? Look at that one. It's trailing smoke."

Mickey saw where she was pointing and used his enhanced vision. "It's got some kind of decoration on it, colored stripes. Never saw that before."

"It's under attack by two other discs." Vickie glanced at Mickey. "They're coming this way. What if they find us?"

"Hide behind the statue!" Mickey shouted. They ran to the bronze statue at the center of the monument and hid behind it.

Vickie huddled next to Mickey and looked into his eyes. "Kind of ironic if everything ends here."

The wounded disc with blue and gold stripes wobbled toward them leaving an undulating trail of grey smoke. Two Titan discs followed it firing streams of energy bolts. The balls of liquid lightning impacted the Europan disc's failing force field. Each impact caused the field to flare and dim further.

Mickey stood for a better view and saw the wounded disc bearing down on them. He dropped to the ground shielding Vickie with his body. Directly above them, Pam and David's disc took another salvo. The disc's force field failed and it tumbled toward the parking lot behind the Observatory.

They heard a thunderous explosion. Dirt and rock erupted into the sky, and the resulting shock wave caused the ground to undulate beneath them like waves on the beach. Mickey used every ounce of his enhanced strength to hold onto the statue and shield Vickie. His silver hand dug into the statue's bronze substance.

As the shaking of the ground quieted beneath them, they heard the whine of the Titan discs directly over them. Mickey looked into Vickie's eyes. "Looks like this is it." He kissed her and they both closed their eyes.

The whining sound faded, and they felt a whoosh of air. Mickey looked up and saw the Titan discs climbing away from them. "Looks like we got lucky," Mickey said. He pulled Vickie to her feet.

They walked around the monument and saw cracks in the ground and fallen trees. "What do we do now?" Vickie asked.

Mickey shrugged. "I guess keep hiding until Westlock calls."

Chapter Forty

David blinked to clear his vision and saw the deck tilted forty-five degrees above him. He felt pain in his right leg and realized that it was pinned under the ruined command console. When he tried to pull his leg back, pain shot up to his groin. He relaxed, letting the pain ease, and lifted his arm. Seeing no coating of silver, he craned his neck to look down and saw his cocoon puddled beneath him as a gray gelatinous mass. "This isn't good," he muttered. He looked up at the viewscreen. The screen was opaque and black. The disc's structure around it appeared dull and grey like the remains of his cocoon. "Pam?" he yelled.

"I'm here."

"Are you all right?"

"Yes, and so are the kids!"

Micetro crawled over to David and licked his face. "Stop it." David turned his face away.

"Stop what?" Pam called.

"Nothing. I need help getting out of here. Where's Romeo?"

Pam paused before responding. "He's outside ... We have a problem."

David grunted as he tried and failed to extricate his leg. "You mean worse than crashing and getting my leg stuck under the damn command console that won't speak to me anymore?"

"It's Juliet," Pam said with her voice shaking. "She didn't make it."

David slumped back and closed his eyes. "Oh God, no."

"David?"

David wiped his eyes. "Yes?"

"Romeo's coming to get you ... He's not doing very well."

David turned his head and saw Romeo crawling toward him. Romeo's lights flickered a mixture of dark-blue and black. He used a tentacle to push away the remains of the command console and David levered himself upright.

"Romeo?" David began.

"Pam and the children are safe outside the disc. So is your father," Romeo said.

"Pam told me about Juliet. I'm sorry."

Romeo turned his head away and started climbing toward the disc's doorway. "Do you require assistance exiting the disc?"

David bit his lip and crawled after him. "No."

At the disc's doorway, suspended ten meters off the ground, David stopped and looked around. He saw the edge of the disc half buried in the remains of the observatory's parking lot. In the shade of an old oak tree still standing after the crash, Pam, Dick, and the twins huddled around Juliet. Romeo jumped down from the doorway and ran to her, taking her limp tentacle in his. David noticed that Juliet's silver sheen had faded to the same lusterless gray as his cocoon. Romeo's lights dimmed to a uniform dark-purple and he bowed his head. David felt the sphere vibrating in his pocket and jumped to the ground.

Ignoring the pain in his leg, David limped to join his family. Al and Bet were crying, with Micetro at their feet. The big cat had its tail between his legs. Pam turned to David with tears in her eyes. Dick nodded at his son. "Glad to see you're okay, Davie."

David knelt next to Juliet. Her face was dark, just like the viewscreen in the crashed disc. "I do not wish to remain active without her," Romeo said.

David took the sphere from his pocket and the orb burst with light. Waves of green and gold radiated outward from a vortex of infinite colors. The glow touched everyone even in the light of day. David knelt beside Juliet. "Maybe it's not too late." Not sure why, except it felt right to do it, he brought the sphere close to Juliet's body and passed it from her lower tentacles toward her head. As he moved it across her body, the orb glowed brighter and blinked with greater frequency. When he brought it near

Juliet's head, the sphere radiated with even greater intensity. David touched it to the dark center of her face and the light became blinding, forcing everyone to look away, except for Romeo who stood like a gleaming statue.

"What's happening?" Pam shouted, shielding her eyes.

The sphere resumed its usual brightness. Blinking as he recovered from the glare, David held it up. Instead of a vortex radiating green and gold, the orb contained peaceful clouds of pink and white. The light behind the clouds blinked with a steady rhythm seventy times per minute. David extended the sphere toward Romeo. "Not sure why, but I knew this would work."

Romeo inclined his head toward the orb, bathing his face in pink and white. His lights brightened to the color of hope. "Juliet? Are you in there?"

The sphere surged in brightness and blinked three times in rapid succession.

Romeo slumped to the ground with his head down. His lights showed starbursts of white and pink.

Pam ran to David and hugged him. "Have I told you that you're wonderful and I'm madly in love with you?"

David smiled. "Not today, but there's still time."

The twins went to Romeo and hugged him.

"We have company," Dick announced. They turned and saw a column of military vehicles coming toward them.

The lead vehicle, an armored Humvee, stopped near them and General Westlock got out. "Isn't this a touching scene?"

One of the Humvee's rear doors flew open and Ernie hopped out. He waved. "Hey, guys. Everybody okay?"

Joshua and Brianna jumped out next and ran to Al and Bet.

David put the sphere back in his pocket and walked toward Ernie. "How did you get here?"

Ernie looked everywhere but at David. "The general gave us a ride."

Westlock stepped in front of Ernie. "Where are your other alien friends, the guy with the silver arm and the woman with the mouth?" he asked.

David set his jaw. "I don't have a clue."

They heard the sound of screeching tires and saw a military jeep roar down the road and stop in front of them. Melanie Dilman, wearing designer combat fatigues, jumped out followed by her latest cameraman. She pushed her way through the cordon of soldiers surrounding the clearing and thrust a microphone under General Westlock's nose. After tossing her hair, she turned to the camera and gave the signal to begin filming. "Your courageous reporter, seven-time Emmy-award winning journalist Melanie Dilman is embedded with America's Special Forces defending Los Angeles from attacking aliens. I'm here with Admiral Flintlock. Tell us, Admiral, how goes the war?"

Westlock motioned to one of his soldiers. "Get her out of here."

The last image from Melanie Dilman's international video feed, before the network cut to a commercial, showed her surprised face.

"I know where Mickey is, and Vickie," Ernie said.

The general spun to face him. "Where?"

"Down the road at the Europa Monument," Ernie replied, appearing pleased with himself.

David glared at him. "You're mistaken, aren't you, Ernie?"

Ernie kept smiling. "No, that's where they are."

"Saddle up!" The general shouted to his troops. "And take all these aliens with you."

David grabbed Ernie and pulled him aside as the soldiers moved in forming a ring around them. "Why did you do that?"

"Do what?" Ernie asked.

"Tell them where Mickey is." David raised an eyebrow. "Wait a minute. How come you know where he is?"

Ernie grinned. "Because I was the one who told him to go

there."

David gaped at him. "Why?"

Before Ernie could reply, several soldiers with automatic weapons ushered everyone not wearing combat fatigues toward the back of an armored personnel vehicle. Several more soldiers surrounded Romeo but kept their distance. One of them stepped closer, pointing his rifle. "General, what about this one?" he called. A beam shot from Romeo's head and the barrel of the soldier's rifle sagged like pasta al dente. The soldier dropped his rifle and ran.

General Westlock turned from studying a map. "Control that tin can of yours, or I'll use a can opener on him," he shouted at David

David glared at him. "That might be more difficult than you think."

The soldiers opened the vehicle's rear doors and the kids climbed aboard, followed by Pam. David thought about telling Romeo to take control of the situation, until he saw the fear in Pam's eyes. "Romeo, come with us and don't hurt anybody," he called.

Romeo increased his height by forty centimeters and his lights flashed angry red. "I will not leave without Juliet."

David held up the sphere, glowing with pink and white clouds. "You're not."

Chapter Forty-One

Vickie poked her head up from behind the statue. "Do you hear something?"

Mickey pointed up the road to the top of the hill. They stood and saw a line of combat vehicles rolling down the road.

The lead Humvee stopped in front of them and General Westlock stepped out. "Looks like we got us a family reunion." He turned to his adjutant. "Let the rest of them out." The lieutenant saluted and ran to a combat personnel vehicle wedged between two tanks. He shouted an order and David, Pam, the twins, Dick, Romeo, and Micetro piled out.

Pam saw Vickie and ran to her. The two women hugged each other, crying. "I'm so sorry for what I said," Pam began. She smiled at Mickey. "That goes for you too."

David extended his hand to Mickey. "Good to see you."

Mickey looked at it and said, "Yeah."

David kept his hand out. "Friends forever, across the solar system. Nothing's changed for me."

Mickey smiled and took David's hand. "Me too."

They heard shouting and turned toward the back of the personnel vehicle. Bet was at the door struggling to hold back Micetro. The big cat growled and bared his saber teeth at three soldiers pointing automatic weapons at him.

"Can we shoot this rabid dog?" one of the soldiers shouted. His rifle was shaking.

"Fat chance of that," Bet snarled. The rifles flew out of the soldiers' hands and they fell backwards onto the lawn.

Al jumped down from the back of the vehicle shouting, "He's a cat, not a dog!"

General Westlock threw his arms up in frustration. "Aliens, mutant cats, kids from Marvel movies. I've had enough of this shit." He started back for his Humvee. "Leave the damn cat alone," he shouted. "They'll all be dead soon enough."

David glanced at Mickey. "What did he say?"

The general turned around. "I said ... pretty soon you'll all be dead."

Mickey's face reddened and he raised his silver hand balled into a fist. Westlock pulled his General Patton replica pearl-handled Colt 45 from its holster and pointed it at Mickey's chest. "The human part of you won't like what this baby can do."

Mickey stopped. "You said all you wanted was Rudnick and Stevens."

"Guess you weren't listening," Westlock said. "I said I wanted Rudnick and Stevens, and to get rid of all the aliens. That includes you and your buddies." Westlock signaled and more soldiers rushed forward with heavy weapons. One of the tanks rolled across the monument's lawn toward them and leveled its main gun.

Ernie hopped down from the personnel vehicle and joined them. "Take it easy, everybody. None of this is necessary. It's all good."

"What the hell does that mean?" Mickey asked.

"Can't tell you Mick, at least not yet." Ernie leaned closer. "You have to trust me."

David frowned at Westlock. "Let's cut a deal. We'll tell you how to get rid of the Europans and the Titans, and you let us go."

"How are you going to do that?" Westlock asked.

"We have a copy of a computer virus that disables Europans. I'll show you." He turned to Romeo and shouted. "Romeo, come over here."

"What are you doing?" Mickey asked David.

"Dude, you have to trust me," David replied.

Mickey frowned. "Trust? Sounds like a broken record around here."

Romeo ambled toward them followed by a squad of soldiers

being careful not to get too close to him.

"Yes, Master David?" Romeo said.

David took an electronic copy of the hieroglyphics they found in the Europan pyramid from his pocket. He extended it towards Romeo. "Look at this file and tell me what you see."

Romeo accessed the data, and within seconds, his screen changed to a field of blue with a central black square.

David walked around him. "Romeo?"

Romeo didn't reply.

David poked him with his hand. "Romeo, can you hear me?"

Romeo remained frozen.

David handed the data storage device to Westlock. "We know how to get rid of the Titans too."

Westlock took the copy of the Titan computer virus from David and handed it to his adjutant. "I don't need your help," the general said. "I have a weapon that'll kill all you aliens. It's code-named KATU."

Vickie sneered. "Sounds like sushi."

Westlock smirked. "Poisonous sushi, little Miss. Mouth. One bite kills all you aliens."

They heard the blaring of a car horn and saw a car roaring down the road. The driver had his arm out the window, showing something that caused the soldiers guarding the road to lower their weapons and let him pass. The car screeched to a stop near the general's Humvee and Frankel jumped out showing his military ID. The soldiers around the general dropped the muzzles of their weapons.

Frankel saluted.

The general didn't return his salute. "Nice job back there, *private* Frankel."

Frankel glanced at Mickey. "Thank you, sir."

"What's KATU?" David asked.

Frankel answered. "It's a bioweapon designed to kill anyone with non-human DNA." He looked General Westlock in the eye.

"If you deploy it, innocent people are going to die."

The general's face reddened. "What's innocent about a bunch of aliens?"

"My kids have alien DNA, and so do I," Pam shouted. "Are you going to kill us too?"

Westlock opened his mouth to speak, but Ernie spoke first. "General, can you give us a moment? I'd like to talk to my friends."

"I won't say no to an ex-marine, but talk fast. I don't have a lot of time," Westlock growled. He walked away with his adjutant.

Ernie made his way to the statue and gestured for everyone to gather around.

Chapter Forty-Two

David spoke first, to Pam. "You knew about your alien DNA?"

Pam nodded. "Why are you surprised? I play with DNA all day long in the Menagerie. One of the first things I did was test mine. Part of me's not human."

Vickie bit her lip and looked at Pam. "Dick and I figured it out, too, a while ago, but we were afraid to say anything."

Mickey cleared his throat. "Ernie, if you've got a plan, let's hear it before the general uses his bioweapon."

Ernie took a sphere from his pocket. His orb swirled with clouds of white and yellow. He pointed at Mickey. "Hold out your hand, the silver one."

Mickey extended his silver hand and Ernie placed the sphere in it. Nothing happened. The white and yellow clouds and the intensity of the orb's light remained the same.

Ernie took it back. "Now try yours," he told David.

David took his sphere, still glowing with pink and white clouds, from his pocket and placed it in Mickey's silver hand. The orb burst with light, all the colors of the rainbow, and Mickey could feel it vibrating. At the same moment, Romeo reactivated with all his lights blinking.

"Juliet!" Romeo shouted.

"Don't worry," Ernie said. "She's fine, in fact, she's in there helping us."

Mickey's silver arm began to change color, starting at the tips of his fingers which changed from silver to brown, then to red, and finally to normal skin color.

"It's working!" Vickie exclaimed.

The sphere blinked faster and brighter, and the process of change accelerated. Normal coloration worked its way up Mickey's arm until all of it looked normal again. He flexed his hand, then his elbow and smiled.

Vickie touched it. "It feels warm."

Mickey nodded. "It's my old arm again." They embraced.

"This is all great," David began. He glanced at Mickey. "Don't get me wrong, I'm happy for you. But we still have that bioweapon to deal with. What are we going to do?"

"Hang on. I'm not done," Ernie said. He held up his own sphere. "Davie, bring your sphere close to mine."

David held his sphere toward Ernie. As the two orbs came close to each other, both burst with white light. The closer David got to Ernie, the brighter the light became. "Mine's vibrating again," David said, "and it feels like it's getting hotter."

"Don't stop!" Ernie shouted. "Touch them together."

David thrust his sphere against Ernie's. When the two orbs touched, everyone heard a loud shrieking sound, followed by a blinding burst of light. Both orbs fell to the ground. The sphere at Ernie's feet appeared black as coal. Ernie kicked it with his foot and it shattered. "Thought so," he muttered.

David picked up his sphere. It appeared the same as before, a ball of pink and white fluffy clouds. Romeo moved closer to it and the orb blinked three times. His rose-colored lights did the same.

General Westlock came running with a squad of soldiers. "What the hell's going on?"

Ernie faced him, grinning. "We have a plan to end this thing, General, and it's a doozie." He whispered something to Pam.

Her lips trembled. "Are you sure about that?"

Ernie nodded. "Trust me."

"Heard a lot of that lately," David muttered.

Mickey held up his normal-appearing arm. "Sure have."

The general walked to the fence and motioned for everyone to join him. "Take a look down there. The fat discs are landing again and picking up the rest of the Cult members, thousands of them. Doubt it's for a joy ride. Those people used to be our friends and neighbors. My weapon will make sure nobody else turns into zombies." He spun around. "Do you want more zombies?"

Ernie took the general aside and they began to argue. After several minutes of it, during which Ernie held up his hands, pleading for the general to calm down more than once, they returned to the group. The general spoke first. "I think your buddy's plan is flat out insane, but I have nothing to lose by letting you try. You have thirty minutes." He started walking away, followed by his soldiers. "Starting now," he called. "He said you want that crazy reporter too." He waved his hand. "Take her and good riddance."

"Thirty minutes to do what?" David asked.

"Here's how it goes down," Ernie began.

Melanie Dilmore and her cameraman ran to join them.

* * *

Melanie Dilman faced the camera without her signature smile. She cleared her throat and gave the sign to begin filming. "This reporter has been informed that the battle with the aliens is not going well." She took a deep breath. "In fact, it's worse than we thought. There are two species of aliens, not one. In a last-ditch effort to save the world," she paused to wipe a tear from her eye, "we are requesting a conference with the aliens to try to make peace." She looked to the side and nodded. "Someone we all know and love, Pamela from Europa, has a message for the aliens." Melanie looked up at the sky. "Please listen."

Pam stepped in front of the camera, holding up David's sphere. She began to speak in slow, measured tones. "Officer Stevens, or whatever your name really is. I know you're listening to this. We offer you a trade." Mickey moved in front of the camera, held up both of his arms, then moved aside leaving Pam center stage again. She continued speaking. "Take me and the sphere that controlled Mickey's nannites, the same nannites I have in my body, and leave Earth."

"No!" David screamed.

Melanie gave the cut sign and the broadcast ended.

David ran to Pam, followed by the kids, both of them crying. "Have you lost your mind?" he exclaimed. Al and Bet clung to her legs, refusing to let go. Pam glanced at Ernie, then spoke to her family. "All of you have two very important things to do now, be brave, and trust me."

* * *

Stevens stroked his chin. "This is interesting. If we have that sphere and Pamela's blood, we can become immortal without turning into tin cans." He turned to his second in command. "Take us down to that park where the transmission came from."

"There's military down there. What if it's a trap?"

Stevens smirked. "What can they do to us? Throw rocks?"

* * *

Stevens' disc settled onto the Monument's lawn, scattering the general's troops and squashing one of the tanks. Fortunately, no one was inside. Stevens walked down the ramp toward Pam who was standing apart from everyone else. "I'll take you up on your offer." He gestured toward the disc's open door. "Shall we go?"

"Honey, please don't do this," David pleaded. "We'll find another way."

Pam looked into his eyes and kissed him. "There isn't another way. Trust me." She glanced at Ernie who nodded. "It'll be all right."

Pam followed Stevens up the disc's ramp and it lifted off.

Romeo tilted his head and watched them fly away with his tentacles around Al and Bet.

Chapter Forty-Three

Stevens put the disc into a hover in the stratosphere. "I have something to show you," he told Pam. He pressed a blinking light on the disc's wall. When a portion of it slid away, Stevens walked past her and kicked the inert form of a Europan. He pointed at the unit's designation plate in the middle of its chest. It read Unit One.

"I win," Stevens said with a self-satisfied grin. He held out his hand. "Now give me the sphere."

Pam held up the orb, still blinking with pink and white light. "Do you know what it is?" she asked.

"A repository of information," Stevens replied. "Nothing complicated about that."

"That's right," Pam said. "It contain all kinds of information. Watch." The sphere sent a beam of light to the viewscreen.

"What's that thing doing?"

"Giving you information," Pam replied. "That's what you want, isn't it?"

Double helixes flowed across the viewscreen, twisting and turning as they passed. Beneath the undulating snakes of nucleic acids, base pair combinations appeared in columns of chemical symbols.

"Nucleic acids, so what?" Stevens scoffed.

"Do you know what my hobby is?" Pam asked.

"Couldn't care less."

"I'm a geneticist, self-taught, but a damned good one."

Stevens yawned. "I make paper airplanes, but I wouldn't want to fly in one of them."

Pam pointed at the viewscreen. "Insert those genes in your DNA and they expand the volume of your brain. That's what you really need, not fresh organs."

Stevens smirked. "More brain volume? Are you insulting my

intelligence? You're an amoeba compared to me."

Pam replied, "Maybe, but my brain has enough storage capacity. Yours doesn't."

Stevens bristled. "That's ridiculous."

"You've kept your bodies alive longer than they're designed for. Your cousins didn't understand it either. Immortality is its own tyranny."

"How poetic."

"You've accumulated too many memories, had too many thoughts. Your brain can't keep up."

Stevens frowned and rubbed the back of his neck. "I don't know what you're talking about."

"You came here to harvest our organs and live even longer." Pam shook her head. "Bad idea."

"Really?" Stevens sneered. "With the nannites in your blood and your husband's sphere to control them, we'll be almost immortal."

Pam shook her head. "You still don't get it." She moved closer, challenging him. "Been having trouble remembering things?"

"I don't know what you're talking about."

"Who was Tocho?" Pam asked.

Stevens blinked. "Never heard of him."

"He was Ahotei's friend. Who was the High Chamberlain?"

Stevens licked his lips. "Who?"

"The Sect?"

Stevens took a step back. "The what?"

Pam pointed at him. "What's your real name?"

Stevens stared back. "It's …"

Pam folded her arms. "Don't know, do you?"

Steven's face reddened. "I've heard enough of this dribble." He suspended Pam in a neuroleptic field and jammed a needle into a vein in her arm. When he'd filled a large syringe with her blood, he took the sphere from Pam's hand and held it in front of her face. "You and the rest of your little band are dead meat." He returned to the disc's command console and spoke to his second in command. "Take us down so I can dump the garbage."

* * *

Stevens' disc slowed to a hover ten meters above the clearing. A door opened in its side and Stevens looked out. "Thanks for the nannites and the sphere," he called out. He held up the orb and it blinked three times.

"No!" Romeo ran towards the disc and jumped, but not high enough to reach it.

"Catch!" Stevens shouted. He threw a lever near the door and a female body fell to the ground, followed by a Europan.

David started running. "Pam!"

Vickie caught up with him and they dropped to their knees next to Pam's unconscious body. Romeo glided to a stop behind them and scanned Pam from head to toe. "She is alive, but has suffered multiple skeletal fractures."

David screamed at Steven's smiling face in the disc's doorway. "You bastard! I'm coming for you!"

Mickey, Dick, and Ernie gathered around the body of Unit One. Dick knelt beside One and poked at his silver skin. It dimpled but didn't bounce back. He got to his feet. "I think he's dead."

"It's not over, guys," Ernie said.

Stevens' voice boomed down to them. "Have to go now. Oh wait, I have one more thing to do. I forgot to kill everybody. AMF!"

"What does AMF stand for?" Mickey asked.

"It means, Adios Mother F … You know the rest," Dick said.

Mickey and David looked up at Stevens and raised their middle fingers.

Hiding in the bushes above the clearing, Westlock spoke into his helmet microphone. "Are the KATU canisters loaded?"

Rocket Squad One sent one click, and Squad Two sent two clicks.

"Excellent," Westlock said. "We'll never have a better shot at him than this. Prepare to fire."

Ernie tapped Mickey's shoulder and pointed up into the sky.

Mickey ignored him and held out his hand to David. "Dude, it looks like this is it. Sure been one whale of a ride."

Ernie tapped Mickey on the shoulder again, this time harder. Still, Mickey ignored him.

David shook Mickey's hand. "All over the damn solar system, Dude."

Ernie jumped between them and pointed at the sky. "Look!"

They looked up. "Another disc, so what?" Mickey said.

David shielded his eyes from the sun. "Is it Europan or Titan? I can't tell."

"Neither," Ernie replied.

Mickey glanced at him. "What do you mean, neither?"

Ernie grinned. "Keep watching."

A sleek, golden disc glinting in the afternoon sun came toward them.

Stevens' voice boomed down to them. "Any last words?"

In the shadow of Steven's disc, with Pam at her feet, Vickie pulled Al and Bet close. Dick joined her. "Mickey's right," he said. "It's been one helluva ride."

Vickie sighed. "Yeah."

Romeo stood behind them with his head down and his lights flashing pink and white.

Ernie ran to the center of the Monument's lawn and looked up waving his arms. "Nobody's dying today," he shouted. He pointed behind him at the golden disc dropping into a hover.

Stevens spoke to his second in command. "Is that one of theirs, a new model we don't know about?"

"Don't know whose it is," his second in command replied.

Stevens' amplified voice echoed over the Monument grounds.

"Haven't decided yet how to kill you … lots of options, you know … standby."

The golden disc settled onto the lawn and a portal formed. When it opened, a female humanoid dressed in gold stood in the doorway holding a sphere burning with golden light.

"Fire!" Westlock shouted. Two missiles loaded with KATU virus shot from opposite sides of the clearing, one toward each disc.

Frankel saw them and shouted. "No!"

Before the missiles could impact, the golden disc sent two beams of ruby-red energy to intercept them and the missiles disappeared.

Westlock threw down his helmet and kicked it.

The woman clad in gold descended the disc's platform with graceful strides.

Stevens shouted, "Get us out of here!" His second in command jammed the disc's power controls to the maximum and the band of energy around the disc's waist erupted with dazzling light. As the disc started upward, Stevens leaned out the disc's door and yelled, "See you!" The woman in gold glanced at him and flicked her hand. Fifty meters above the ground, the energy band around Stevens' disc flickered, the disc wobbled, and then it slowed.

"What's happening?" Stevens shouted.

His second in command stabbed at the controls. "I don't know!"

The disc lost power and dropped to the ground sending dirt and debris exploding toward everyone in the clearing with enough force to rip them apart, but the earthen missiles stopped in mid-air and dropped to the ground.

Ernie put his hands in his pockets and grinned. "Didn't I tell everybody to trust me?"

The woman in gold walked to Pam and knelt beside her. She spoke softly so only Pam could hear. "Always remember … it was love that brought me back to this place, not a golden disc." Pam opened her tear-filled eyes and tried to speak. The woman in gold placed her fingers over Pam's lips and passed her sphere over Pam's body. Pam's legs began to twitch. The woman in gold pulled away the sphere and stood. Pam smiled and rose to her feet. Vickie ran to her.

The woman in gold left them and walked to the inert form of Unit One. General Westlock and several of his soldiers dropped their weapons and moved closer to watch. Melanie Dilman, with her hair in disarray, stood behind them hugging her cameraman with tears ruining her makeup.

The woman in gold touched the center of Unit One's flatscreen head with her sphere. He shuddered, and then his screen lit with soft white light. She smiled at him. "Wake up Grandfather. I've come to take you home."

Epilogue

Unit One raised his head. His screen fluttered and then brightened. "Ruha?"

"Yes, Grandfather. It's time to go home and leave these good people to continue on their evolutionary journey." She turned and sent a telepathic message to Al and Bet. The twins joined hands and waved back.

One settled back onto the ground and turned his head away from her. "I'm not your grandfather anymore. I'm Unit One. Leave me."

Ruha glanced at her disc and a second humanoid dressed in gold, a male, left the disc and walked toward them. He stopped at One's feet. "You look like shit, old friend."

One's face burst with light. "Tocho?"

"It's me. Now get your ass off the ground."

One's lights fluttered to blue. "Let me die."

"Someday, Ahotei, but not now."

"I've done terrible things. I took your memories …"

Tocho smiled at him. "To spare us the pain of remembering what we lost."

Stevens ran toward them covered with dirt. One saw him and his face changed to a field of angry red lights. One struggled to his feet and amplified his voice. "You abandoned your own people and trapped us in these machines!"

Stevens pointed his shaking finger at One. "You never stopped hunting us! We've been outcasts for eons!"

Pam got between them with her arms outstretched. "Stop it, both of you!" She faced One. "Stop blaming him for things his ancestors did thousands of years ago, things he can't even remember." One's lights dimmed to a soft brown. Pam turned to Stevens. "And you … you have no right to steal other people's bodies to keep yourselves alive." Stevens mumbled something and looked away.

Ruha started back toward the golden disc. "It is done."

The din of battle coming to them from the city below ceased, replaced by the gentle sound of the wind flowing past the trees. One of the soldiers near the fence shouted. "All the discs are landing. The shooting's stopped."

Frankel ran to the fence and used his magnifying sunglasses to watch a Titan factory disc touch down in Pershing Square. "That's the disc that has Emma!" He ran back to his car and peeled rubber up the road.

Tocho took one of One's tentacles and started leading him toward the golden disc. "You need new clothes, old man. Anything but silver."

Ruha waited for Tocho and her grandfather at the top of the ramp, and then the three of them disappeared inside.

"Romeo," Ernie shouted. He held up David's sphere, blinking rapidly with pink and white light and gestured toward the golden disc.

Romeo ran to Ernie, cradled the sphere in one of his tentacles, and sprinted with his lights blazing to the base of the golden disc's ramp. "Please!" he shouted.

Ruha reappeared. Romeo bowed his head and held out the blinking sphere. "Help her."

Ruha smiled and Romeo bounded up the ramp.

* * *

The military vehicles turned around and moved up the hill, leaving large ruts in the Monument's manicured lawns. As it spun around, one of the tanks brushed against the statue of the four teenagers who took a ride on a flying saucer to Europa sending the statue crashing on its side. Al sat talking with Brie, holding hands on the lawn. Bet had Josh in a headlock, making out with him behind the largest tree and occasionally swatting away his roving hand. Micetro dozed on the lawn next to her, snoring contently, and near the fence overlooking the city, Dick talked with Ernie.

Mickey stood with Vickie near the fallen statue with his arm around her waist. Pam and David joined them, enveloping the four of them in a golden aura.

"What happens now?" Mickey asked.

Vickie poked him in the side. "We get married."

Mickey rubbed his ribs. "Yes dear."

Vickie smirked. "Get used to it."

David rolled his eyes. "Wait, it gets worse."

Pam poked David in the ribs.

"What's everybody doing after the wedding?" Mickey asked.

"Doesn't look like we're going back to Europa any time soon," Pam said.

David grinned. "Works for me."

Ernie and Dick joined them.

Mickey pointed at Ernie. "You've got a lot of explaining to do."

"Well," Ernie began. "It's kind of complicated."

David frowned. "Start talking."

Ernie pointed over David's shoulder. "Look!"

"You have to do better than that," Mickey said.

"No look!" Ernie said more excitedly.

They turned as one and saw two humanoids, a young male and a female, standing at the top of the ramp to the golden disc, holding hands. The female wore a gown of pink, and the male a suit of white. She held up a sphere with a soft mellow glow, and then they kissed.

LODESTONE
BOOKS

YOUNG ADULT FICTION

Lodestone Books is a new imprint, which offers a broad spectrum of subjects in YA/NA literature. Compelling reading, the Teen/Young/New Adult reader is sure to find something edgy, enticing and innovative. From dystopian societies, through a whole range of fantasy, horror, science fiction and paranormal fiction, all the way to the other end of the sphere, historical drama, steam-punk adventure, and everything in between (including crime, coming of age and contemporary romance). Whatever your preference you will discover it here.

If you have enjoyed this book, why not tell other readers by posting a review on your preferred book site. Recent bestsellers from Lodestone Books are:

AlphaNumeric

Nicolas Forzy

When dyslexic teenager Stu accidentally transports himself into a world populated by living numbers and letters, his arrival triggers a prophecy that pulls two rival communities into war.

Paperback: 978-1-78279-506-3 ebook: 978-1-78279-505-6

Time Sphere

A timepathway book

M.C. Morison

When a teenage priestess in Ancient Egypt connects with a schoolboy on a visit to the British Museum, they each come under threat as they search for Time's Key.

Paperback: 978-1-78279-330-4 ebook: 978-1-78279-329-8

Bird Without Wings

FAEBLES

Cally Pepper

Sixteen-year-old Scarlett has had more than her fair share of problems, but nothing prepares her for the day she discovers she's growing wings…

Paperback: 978-1-78099-902-9 ebook: 978-1-78099-901-2

Briar Blackwood's Grimmest of Fairytales

Timothy Roderick

After discovering she is the fabled Sleeping Beauty, a brooding goth-girl races against time to undo her deadly fate.

Paperback: 978-1-78279-922-1 ebook: 978-1-78279-923-8

Escape from the Past

The Duke's Wrath

Annette Oppenlander

Trying out an experimental computer game, a fifteen-year-old boy unwittingly time-travels to medieval Germany where he must not only survive but figure out a way home.

Paperback: 978-1-84694-973-9 ebook: 978-1-78535-002-3

Holding On and Letting Go

K.A. Coleman

When her little brother died, Emerson's life came crashing down around her. Now she's back home and her friends want to help, but can Emerson fight to re-enter the world she abandoned?

Paperback: 978-1-78279-577-3 ebook: 978-1-78279-576-6

Midnight Meanders

Annika Jensen

As William journeys through his own mind, revelations are made, relationships are broken and restored, and a faith that once seemed extinct is renewed.

Paperback: 978-1-78279-412-7 ebook: 978-1-78279-411-0

Reggie & Me

The First Book in the Dani Moore Trilogy

Marie Yates

The first book in the Dani Moore Trilogy, *Reggie & Me* explores a teenager's search for normalcy in the aftermath of rape.

Paperback: 978-1-78279-723-4 ebook: 978-1-78279-722-7

Unconditional

Kelly Lawrence

She's in love with a boy from the wrong side of town...

Paperback: 978-1-78279-394-6 ebook: 978-1-78279-393-9

Readers of ebooks can buy or view any of these bestsellers by clicking on the live link in the title. Most titles are published in paperback and as an ebook. Paperbacks are available in traditional bookshops. Both print and ebook formats are available online.